SIGHING WOMAN TEA

SIGHING WOMAN TEA

Mark Daniel Seiler

To order additional copies of this book, contact:
Xlibris LLC
1-888-795-4274
www.Xlibris.com
Orders@Xlibris.com
552723

Contents

PREFACE

The names of people and places have been changed to preserve the privacy and way of life of the individuals depicted. In the interest of clarity, several individuals are represented as a single composite character.

Two important things happened while writing this book. Much of what started out as fiction, became true in my life. And while that was going on, forgiveness seeped in and surprised me."

I want to thank Uncle H. for tricking me into a looking through spanking new eyes. Thank you Auntie E. for encouraging me to write down the stories of our island.

NORTH

In the dream I'm nine years old. I climb into an old, rusty car that is in the middle of a goat pasture. This is odd because where I grew up we didn't have cars, not even abandoned ones.

No key. So I take out my new Swiss Army knife and look for the lock pick. It's next to the baby scissors. I put it in the ignition and turn. A weak light flickers in the dash, and the gas gauge bumps up. I reach with my right toe and press the starter pedal on the floorboard, while my left foot pumps the accelerator. She coughs. I pull the manual choke and fire her up. I drive around the bumpy field chasing goats.

Still in the dream:

I wake up in the back seat. It's dark and the driver is wearing a black fedora. I can't see the face of the man in the back seat with me. There's a young woman in the front passengers side. She looks oddly familiar. I see lights up ahead and wipe the window with my sleeve.

The driver turns around. "Put your belt on."

I can't find one.

Blue lights are flashing. A cop is slowing traffic. I don't recognize his uniform. The street signs are in odd shapes, with words in an Asian script I've never seen before.

We drive for a couple more hours. No one says a word. Then we head down a steep driveway, branches scraping the windows. We slow as we round a hairpin turn and I see the ocean lit by a piece of the moon. We stop in front of an old stone mansion. A butler opens a tall entry door and we follow him inside.

We're early for the meeting.

Figas woke up on the bus heading south, as the driver announced the next stop, Guangzhou. The only Chinese he could remember was *wo bu mingbai*, "I don't understand." And *xiexei* and *shishi*. One meant thank you, the other to take a leak. He wasn't sure which was which, so he mostly smiled and nodded. By his calculations, they would arrive in Guangzhou just before sunrise. He switched on the overhead light and got out his notepad. He always struggled when it came to remembering and writing down a dream. Dreams fit, but they don't fit, he thought.

Climbing inside that rusty old car could mean going back to the old ways. That made sense. The secret meeting at the old mansion could be meeting Christopher Elant in France. Who was the woman in the front seat? "Cedar," he thought. "She'd be my age now." He reached in his pocket for the Swiss Army knife. Uncle Sun had given it to him on his ninth birthday. He couldn't remember anything before that day. "I was born in the bottom of that ravine," he thought.

The Chinese woman sitting in the aisle seat woke up and gave him a stare. She pointed out the window. "Guangzhou." They were entering the outskirts of the port town.

Figas made a small bow. "Shishi."

The woman smiled and pointed to the back of the bus.

THE LADY SLIPPER

Drink your tea slowly and reverently, as if it is the axis on which the world earth revolves—slowly, evenly, without rushing toward the future.
—Thich Nat Hahn

"Who could-a-figa'?" the captain called out in a singsong island accent.

Figas bounced up the thin gangplank toward Captain Martin, who was dressed in a spotless black sweater with tiny buttons and a mandarin collar. Both men made a small bow with their eyes.

"Permission to come aboard, captain?"

"Granted." Captain Martin gave a chuckle at the formality. "The first and I'll wager not the last. Welcome aboard."

"You're expecting me?" He put his hand out, but the captain embraced him. Figas was surprised how solid the old man felt under the wool.

Martin stepped back. "This trip or the next. You dogleggers always come back."

"Like a bad penny." Figas coughed to clear the emotion in his throat.

"The descendant of the great sailor himself, Thomas Burke." The captain gave the young man a long look. Figas was named after the legendary discoverer of Green Island.

"Shoes too big to fill," Figas said automatically.

On an island famous for its heroes and storytellers, Figas was a different breed. His friends piled on him for living in the Land of

13

Figures. "Hey, Figures!" quickly became "Hey, Figas!" He never denied that mathematics was his preferred realm, void of messy emotion and human drama. A sanctuary. "Nice to be aboard the *Lady Slipper* again," he said simply.

Figas followed the captain astern, remembering the hollow sound of his feet on the metal deck. The *Lady* may have been a fine ship in her day, but she looked a bit worse for wear. As he ducked under the rusty hatchway, the sleepy quiet of topside quickly turned to well-lit industry below. Men shouted at one another as the smell of breakfast sausage collided with diesel. The two made their way to the captain's quarters.

Captain Martin beamed at the tray of tea his steward immediately brought forth. "I'm afraid we've no tea chest to open and hear the Sigh," he said. "We just keep her in this bag." He smiled and pulled a bag from his desk drawer. The blue plastic was stiff and loud as he reached in and pinched a handful of tea, then sprinkled it into the teapot. The powerful fragrance of Sighing Woman Tea transported Figas across the world to his Parisian hotel of a month ago.

A small white envelope containing an invitation on thick cotton paper was waiting for him when he returned to his room at the Hotel Regina. He walked out on the small balcony and examined the embossed seal, which gave the flowing handwriting a three-dimensional feel.

"Monsieur Christopher Elant requests the pleasure of your company for tea. A driver will be waiting in front of your hotel tomorrow at 7:00 a.m."

His flight wasn't until the following evening, so he awoke before dawn, showered, and put on the same dark suit he had worn at the International Conference on Applied Mathematics and Numerical Analysis, where he had received an award. He felt grateful for the grant that had changed his life, paying for his studies over the past twelve years and allowing him to develop his groundbreaking prediction theory. And grateful for the many entrepreneurial opportunities now knocking on his door, though he had no idea yet which to choose.

A black limousine was waiting when he stepped out of the hotel. The doorman opened the limo door and offered him a pleasant day. Figas had never been in a vehicle so smooth and silent. He sat back and floated through the city, his curiosity lulled to sleep by the comfort of the ride. A short hour later they pulled down a narrow lane and stopped beside a small garden gate. The chauffeur sat at the wheel, smoking a yellow Gitane. All Figas could see were his sunglasses peering through the rearview mirror from under his cap. He hadn't spoken the entire trip and appeared unwilling to break his silence now. Figas signaled for him to roll down the dividing glass.

"Ou sommes-nous, s'il vous plaît?" Figas struggled with even basic French. "Can you tell me where we are, please? Hello?"

The driver shrugged and blew his cigarette smoke out, as only a disgusted Frenchman can do.

Conceding, Figas got out of the limo and tried the heavy cast-iron gate. It gave a long, satisfying squeak.

Inside, the sun was just beginning to challenge the dew on a thousand fragrant petals as Figas searched for a residence in the thick greenery. Crisp gravel led him beneath dozens of arbors of yellow and white roses, infusing the cool air with a dry sweetness. Unseen birds celebrated and bees hummed ominously. He turned, expecting a swarm, but found each little creature tempted by the pollen of a different blossom. His breath caught when he recognized the reflection in the water of a sleepy pond. Deep blue wisteria covered a Japanese wooden bridge.

He walked to the center of the bridge and squeezed his eyes half closed. Tall canvases, newly stretched and gessoed, seemed to merge with the images of floating water lilies and mustard-colored willow branches. Fat multicolored koi glided through slow-motion pigments. He had recently visited the Corcoran Gallery in Washington, D.C., where he wandered into the wing that housed Monet's giant water lilies. Now he was there again. He leaned over the bridge railing and laughed. One thing was sure: he was not a water lily. Whenever he entered water, he sank like a stone.

Thick, living brushstrokes revealed a red-tiled pavilion beyond the willow branches. As Figas neared, the gravel announced his approach.

A well-dressed man greeted him. Every detail of the man's appearance was flawless, from his hair to his perfect white teeth.

The rough features of his face were softened by a childlike glow in his cheeks. He held himself like a dancer-turned gentleman.

"Bonjour. Bienvenue."

"Bonjour, Monsieur," Figas replied.

"Je suis Christopher Elant."

"Je m'appelle Thomas Burke." Figas shook the man's hand.

"Enchanté. Please sit."

Figas was relieved to hear English.

"So what do you think of Giverny, Thomas? Lovely?"

"It is everything," Figas stammered, "it's everything Monet led us to believe, and more. C'est merveilleux."

"I must admit"—Elant gestured to the surroundings—"I prefer the paintings. Yet, one does feel lucky to be in such a place." They both laughed. It helped ease the tension in Figas's chest.

A small man with East Indian features set a tray with a tea on the marble table.

"This is my assistant, Mr. Black. He is also very good with figures. Mr. Black, how many cups of coffee are enjoyed across the globe every day?"

"A little over two billion, sir."

"And how many cups of tea each day?"

"Nearly three times as many, around six billion cups a day."

Elant poured and watched Figas's reaction with great enjoyment as the aroma reached him. This was no ordinary tea.

Figas brought the cup to his lips. The tea was hot and perfect. Silent hinges opened the sky. Butter-colored light filtered through the canopy as a saffron bird landed on a nearby branch and regarded him. Figas squeezed his eyelids, again feeling himself sink into the masterpiece. He allowed that the tea might be coloring his perceptions. Tea from his island home was known to have psychoactive properties. High levels of theanine in Sighing Woman Tea were well documented to enhance cognitive abilities. The brain emitted alpha waves, as if in a state of deep meditation. The observer and the observed melded together. Time kaleidoscoped. He playfully held up his left hand to the light and watched the shadows dance across his forearm.

Amidst this carefree joy, he stood alone in an unknown intersection, the site of a pending massacre, a passageway where heavy unseen objects pass uncomfortably near. Deep murky water pitched with no direction, or proof of land. He chose the direction of Mr. Christopher Elant. "You have very good taste in tea."

"Thank you, indeed. Sighing Woman Tea is reputed to be the finest in the world. The big teahouses classify it as FTGFOP. Far Too Good For Ordinary People."

"I've heard that." Figas involuntarily joined the gentleman's quiet laugh. "Mr. Elant, I'd very much like to know why you invited me this morning?" Figas stopped there, but easily could have asked, "Where are all the people? This must be a very busy public park on most days."

Elant set his cup gently on its saucer. A breeze stirred the vines behind him. The pattern in the gazebo's cast-iron webbing mimicked the patterns of the leaves. "I work for the Lance McCandish Foundation. I'm a senior director responsible for overseeing the majority of our endowments. We operate in thirty-seven countries, supporting the arts and sciences."

The director kept talking, but he didn't address the question. So Figas's mind wandered down its own track. He wondered how much Elant knew of his life. When he had finally published his prediction theory, his name appeared below that of the department chair. This seemed perplexing to Figas, who didn't remember Professor Albrecht contributing in any way. On the contrary, the professor had his graduate students do the bulk of his teaching, as well as publishing. During the award ceremony, Albrecht had thanked Figas for his "workmanlike attitude."

Elant paused, and Figas realized it was evident to the director that his attention had wandered. Instinctively, he chose a direct approach. "Does my being here have anything to do with my work at university?"

"I can safely say no, Thomas, though of course we've taken great notice of your many achievements with Professor Albrecht. And may I add, congratulations for the award you both received this weekend. A Nobel Laureate friend told me your prediction theory is changing everything from Hedge Funds to the Big Bang."

"That's a bit of an exaggeration." Figas blushed. It was true NOAA had upgraded its tsunami early warning system, thanks in part to his causation equations. But for every success there had been huge blunders. "Please go on. You were explaining . . ."

"What was the title of your latest paper? *Dependent Origination?*"

"*Dependent Origination and Outcomes.* It's a mathematical interpretation of early Buddhist thought, Nagarjuna's observations of nature. Causes and conditions make up all phenomena."

"Fascinating, Thomas. As you aware, we're living in a time of mass extinctions, cultural as well as biological."

Figas thought of the big five mass extinction events. "We have ringside seats to the sixth," he wanted to say.

"Every tiny corner of the globe is being funneled through the same modern combine." Catching himself on the brink of emotion, the director added more honey to his smooth voice. "A great deal of diversity is being lost in the struggle to become, shall we say, better off."

"I agree. It's no secret the world's getting smaller." Figas swirled the remaining tea in his cup, then stared as the tea leaves settled in the middle. Fortunately Einstein had solved the tea leaf paradox. But what was the director getting at?

Elant tried to regain the young man's attention. "Thomas, have you heard of the Sensation of Tea auction?"

"Can't say I have."

"A rare box of narcissus oolong was recently auctioned for one million Hong Kong dollars, which is roughly 129,000 US dollars. A small, unopened tea chest of Sighing Woman Tea went for 250,000 US dollars. Sighing Woman Tea has become iconic. The quality of the tea is being compared to that of a Château Pétrus."

"That's ridiculous. Is this a joke?" Figas was unable to suppress a laugh. "Shit." He took a couple of deep breaths and tried to sort through the probabilities. The tea leaves were staring up at him. "I haven't been there since I was a kid. Is everyone driving Beamers?"

"Thomas, you of all people must understand what this means. An ounce of Sighing Woman Tea is worth more than gold. Think about it. When oil or a mineral deposit is found in a village, what happens? We've witnessed it over and over again. The multinationals swoop in and take control. Villagers are either put to work or forcibly removed. Those who stand up against the corporations are labeled terrorists. They're hunted and killed."

"Over tea? Don't you think you're being a little dramatic?" Figas wanted to downplay the situation, but it was hard to deny the implications.

"The cultural identity of Viridis is still very much intact. Thomas, I'd be curious if you could name another place in the world making such a claim?"

Viridis. To hear the spiritual name spoken aloud disturbed him. "Do you mean Green Island?"

"Of course."

"You've got my attention, but I'm not sure what you think I can do about it?"

"Green Islanders are independent and stubborn. Not to mention secretive."

"Tell me something I don't know."

"Their fierce independence leaves them vulnerable to the tea cartels. Thomas, we believe they'd listen to you. I want to be clear, your island home is in danger of losing not only its cultural uniqueness, but also its sovereignty."

The door of the sky, opened so gently earlier, shut on Figas's head. "Are you saying history will repeat itself?"

"Yes."

"Mr. Elant, the golden age of tea and spices ended a long time ago."

"It's back."

"You expect me to believe a Dutch ship is once again going to sail into Salm Bay and hold the island ransom?"

"The Dutch East India Company is thankfully no more, but make no mistake, the multinationals today are no less ruthless than the old VOC. Thomas, believe me, if I knew what was going to happen, I'd tell you. You're the prediction expert. You tell me."

A crackly voice through the ship's intercom ordered the first engineer to report to the bridge.

"What's that, captain?" Figas looked down at his empty teacup and settled back into the present.

"The *Lady* and the Woman together again, for the first time." The captain gestured to his ship and the teapot.

"Indeed." Figas understood the captain's little play on words. It did feel good to be back aboard the *Lady*, enjoying a spot of Sighing Woman Tea. He tried to keep his emotions in check. He had no wish to embarrass himself in front of the captain.

The steward tapped on the door twice and entered.

"Mr. Wood will show you to your berth and explain your duties while onboard."

Mathanias Wood was first mate and captain's steward. He was a lean, middle-aged man, with thick muttonchops that did little to help his weak chin. Barefoot, he all but hopped along, touching only his toes to the metal deck. Figas imagined the first mate playing a pirate in Auntie Lan's Community Theater.

"Call me Wood." The first mate had the sour breath of an old milk carton. They came to the end of the starboard passageway. The small, dimly lit cabin was wedged in the middle of the ship. There was no porthole. A roughly made wooden chest was tucked under a single hammock.

"Not enough room to change your mind," Figas thought as he set his leather case down, wondering how two people could sleep there. He soon learned. Not at the same time.

"Mr. Wood, what does T.S. stand for?"

"Twin screws. She's a coaster, so she wallies a bit."

"I'm not following you, Mr. Wood."

"Wood, just Wood." The *Lady*, he explained, had twin screws, or two propellers. She was built for shallow water, so she rolled side-to-side, or wallied.

Working aboard the *Lady* for two weeks before their departure, crawling around in tight places where his long, skinny arms could reach, Figas came to understand some of her obvious traits, and also a few of her secrets. M.V. stood for motor vessel; in her case, a diesel. She flew the flag of Sri Lanka as her F.O.C., or flag of convenience. She was a "geared little coaster," built in Germany in 1938. Her outside hull was dark blue, with a thin red stripe at her loaded waterline. The berth Figas shared was aft, just behind the engine room, so he fell asleep to a choir of rumblings, hammerings and shrill moans.

Figas was shaken awake by the first mate at 4:00 a.m. He was to report to the engine room to help First Engineer Rebus replace a leaky gasket. Immediately! He found Rebus covered with a thin coat of grease and tattoos, giving his skin a dark complexion, despite a complete lack of sun. Ink flames enveloped his back and shoulders, and covered his shaved head. The man was burning in Hades right before Figas's eyes.

The big man turned from his work and regarded the young man with a wry smile. "The captain's little pet has arrived," Rebus informed his lover. The idling diesel answered in her secret language. He wiped the grease from his hands and wadded the rag in his back pocket. "Welcome to my hellhole."

The sweat rolled down Figas's forehead and burned his eyes.

"Can you handle a wrench?"

Figas shook his head, doing his best to not feel terrified.

"Didn't think so." He inspected the scrawny kid. "You better tuck in that baggy shirt, or the missus will grab and squeeze you to death on your first date." The stub of the first engineer's index finger pointed to the many moving parts to avoid. "Once we break her down, we'll be on battery only. If we don't finish quick, you'll have more than the missus and me to worry about." The hot laugh of Rebus did little to harden Figas's spine.

Seven hours later, the first mate climbed down the ladder and found Figas wedged under the starboard intake manifold.

"Troublewood! To what do we owe the pleasure?" Rebus was never happy with interruptions.

"Get cleaned up, Figas. The captain's invited you to his cabin for dinner," Wood instructed.

"A fine romper." Rebus sneered. "We're not finished here. You want to tell Himself that there's not enough juice left in the batteries to fire up the missus?"

"You can piss me about all you want, Rebus, but if in an hour the lad's not dining with the captain, you'll be explaining all this to Himself."

Figas craned his neck, but all he could see was Wood's bare feet going up the ladder. A stream of inventive curses bellowed from the man of flames. Figas tried to keep from laughing as he threaded the last bolt with his fingertips. Rebus handed him a greasy spanner, while carrying on with his colorful litany.

Aside from a small glass of port, the captain's food proved to be the same as that in the ship's galley. Neither the captain nor Figas spoke as they polished off their rations.

The first few sips of port loosened Figas's tongue. "What's in the hold, captain?"

"The big three: sugar, kerosene, and toilet paper."

"You trade that for the tea?"

"Ha ha! Good one, Figas."

"Why'd you call me a doglegger, captain?"

"You should know, your Green Island's not on the way to, or from, anywhere."

"That's a funny way of putting it."

"Have you heard of Point Nemo, or the Pole of Inaccessibility?"

"Never."

"Your little Island sits alone in the middle of the water hemisphere. Here, I'll show you." The captain took his orange chopstick and spun his plate on top of it. Before Figas could be amazed, a second plate was up and spinning. "You are Green Island there. I'm the *Lady* here, sailing toward you, against the churning current, our spinning plates."

Wood came in with biscuits and tea just as the captain lost control. The first plate wobbled and hit the oak, chipping an edge. The cranky steward grabbed the second plate as it began to teeter, and gave the captain an acidic stare. Wood quickly cleared the table, mumbling under his breath while he poured the tea.

Captain Martin continued. "It's a bit like in the early days of the volta."

"The volta?"

"The volta do mar was one of the greatest military secrets of its day. It never appeared on a ship's chart, but it was a source of power and wealth beyond imagining. The early Portuguese navigators discovered they must first sail in the opposite direction if they were to ride the southern trade winds around the Cape of Africa. The ocean's gyres spin like our plates. Hug the coast and take no risk, and the wind and currents will dash you against the rocks to your death!" The captain dunked his hardtack biscuit in his tea, drowning it enough to chew.

Figas tried to break off a piece of sheet iron, as the crew called it, before dunking it. "So to reach Green Island, you must first sail away from her?" Figas was starting to get the dogleg reference now.

"In essence. We feel for the seam where the ocean currents meet, where the thousand plates churn and no one way prevails. Do you understand?"

"I'm beginning to, captain."

"Run the wrong direction on a spinning plate." The captain's fingers scurried. "What happens?"

"You stand still?"

"Just so."

Figas felt his shoulders relax and lower. For a moment he was right where he should be. Going back was going forward. He had good reason to trust the captain. Evidently the old sailor could read his personal geography as easily as his ship's chart. Traveling in the opposite direction of where he wanted to go. Hugging the coast. What else had he been doing his whole life?

Port Salm

Soft yielding minds to water glide away, and
sip, with nymphs, their elemental tea.
—Alexander Pope

The *Lady Slipper* dropped anchor just inside the port an hour before dawn. Port Salm, Green Island, was more of a shallow landing than a protected harbor. It provided a decent anchorage in calm seas, but all freight had to be loaded onto flat-bottom boats to reach the pier. The captain's voice through the raspy intercom called Figas topside.

As Figas climbed the ladder, his eyes adjusted to the morning light. The harbor was completely filled with small boats and canoes. When the islanders caught sight of Figas, a thunderous roar came off the water. Flowers and paper lanterns filled in the space between the small crafts.

Aunties stood up holding cardboard signs with math equations on them:

$$\rho_{X,Y} = \mathrm{corr}(X,Y) = \frac{\mathrm{cov}(X,Y)}{\sigma_X \sigma_Y} = \frac{E[(X - \mu_X)(Y - \mu_Y)]}{\sigma_X \sigma_Y},$$

An old white sheet hung from the mast of a sailing canoe with painted letters, "Figas is back. *Dam it!*" Another sign read, "How much this pencil weigh?" A bunch of pencils were glued into a makeshift dam under the painted letters.

Figas stood there, shocked, tears running down his face, unable to process what was happening, coughing, crying and laughing all at once. Captain Martin radioed ahead, and as planned, feathered the *Lady* into the harbor just before first light. It was Sunday, the morning after Zhu Yong Jiē, the Wait of Courage festival.

Figas had been away nearly half his life. Now he studied the green hillsides for change. None were immediately apparent. The rising sun shone just below a dark cloud, casting an orange and yellow light on Salm Bay, giving it an unreal quality. Honey-colored light pierced the layer of palms and backlit the ironwood trees that ringed the cove. Smoke from several large bonfires hung over the water. Not a single person remained onshore. All those who were physically able took part in the festival by spending the night on anything that would float. Figas recognized many of the faces, but was too overwhelmed to recall their names. Luckily, it was polite to call anyone older Auntie or Uncle. "That makes it a little easier," he reminded himself.

Figas stood by the rail speechless. Unsure of what to do, he clapped his hands, applauding them all for giving him such a warm welcome home. They answered with a sustained roar. He'd convinced himself that he didn't matter in the world. Why would anyone care if he stayed or left? He had always been good at inventing things, some of value. Other products of his imagination were negative integers. When it came to the emotional realm, a myriad of abstractions took the place of real memories.

He had never been caught in such a massive misinvention. How could he have forgotten his love for his home? How could he have forgotten that he was loved? The scariest things were the things most dear.

The young lady who had been chosen to be the daughter of the island climbed the rigging near the bow of the ship and balanced herself on the narrow handrail. Woods and Rebus grabbed Figas and tossed him like a sack of rice overboard. The crew let out a cheer, proud to deliver their cargo with such style and panache.

When Figas hit the water, he sank like a stone. Something grabbed hold of his ankle and pulled him deeper. His eardrums pounded, unable to adjust to the depth. He held his fingers to his nose and blew to equalize the pressure. He opened his eyes and kicked his feet.

The young woman on the rail made a perfect dive from the bow and shot through the water right past Figas. She swam up from below, smiling. She tilted her head, gesturing for him to relax. She held his hand, and he felt light as cork. As a boy, he had struggled to find a scientific reason why he didn't float. He posited that it was his lack of body fat. His best friend, Cedar, had teased him, "If that were true, Figas, your fat head would float like a beach ball."

When they reached the surface, a chorus of cheers burst over them like breaking surf. Captain Martin stood on the bridge with his arms crossed, most pleased. "A small rock holds back a great wave."

The two were whisked onboard the ship on the shoulders of two big islanders.

"Look! What has the daughter of the island brought up from the depths this year?" Captain Martin yelled over the crowd.

"Ooooh!" the crowd teased. This year's Zhu Yong Jiē was proving most auspicious.

The young girl stood on the rail and made another perfect dive, leaving no splash.

Figas awkwardly balanced on the rail and jumped feetfirst, getting water up his nose. He was plucked out and paddled to shore, where he was mobbed.

HOME

Ferryman, for tea, scoop up those reflections of cherry blossoms.
—Sakai Hōitsu

After being squeezed and kissed by every Green Islander on the south shore, Figas was pried from the last few aunties pawing him by Uncle Sun, his mother's brother. Together, they climbed the familiar steps of the thumb-shaped ridge to the soft swinging bridge that connected Salm Bay to the high tea terrace country, which the locals called Upwise. Figas counted the familiar cracks in the stone steps, his feet naturally avoiding them. When they reached the top of the rise, he stopped to take in the magnificent old swinging bridge. Near its curved belly hung the little teahouse, where the bridgeman lived. The fragile structure was held in place by two massive cables that ran beneath the floating planks. Light filtered through the delicately carved lattice walls. Old man Teagate bowed low as they passed by his little teahouse suspended in the middle of the bridge. Figas bowed to the ever-present guardian between the two worlds of Salm Bay and old Viridis. The old man had a partially finished tea chest in his wrinkled hand and a carving knife in the other. The curved lid of the tea chest mirrored the shape of his tiny domicile. To Figas, he looked like the same old man he had known as a child. They said old man Teagate could recognize who was crossing his bridge after just two steps on his woven web. Green Islanders believed evil was afraid to set foot on his bridge, knowing it had no hope of reaching the other side.

To Figas, the island had always been both big and small. As the crow flies, she was scarcely fifty miles at her waist, but that hardly accounted for the many deep ravines that radiated around her. Rolled out flat, she was vast. The deep green pastures east of Salm Bay could easily support horses, though horses would never manage the steep steps of the Thumb, or hope to cross the many delicate rope bridges. The sea dominated the lowlands; fishermen with their small boats and canoes, and the stocky wharfies of the docks. Teachers, missionaries, and small-business owners mixed with the odd fish of Salm Bay.

The island was both old and new. Half the houses had electricity and modern conveniences, while the other half used oil lamps, outdoor wells, and woodstoves. Family came first, rivaled only by the growing and drinking of tea. Education was also held in great esteem. Like Figas, many of the young traveled abroad for schooling. No one seemed rich, but Figas didn't recall any family going without. No two mango or avocado trees agreed on the seasons. When the fruit was ripe, it came on like the rains. Family fruit stands dotted the front entrances of most residences. Inside the screened-in little bastions, one found baskets filled with everything from cucumbers to tropical flowers—whatever grew in your yard and was ripe. One could leave money in the box or exchange a bag of purple sweet potatoes for one of green papayas. Figas watched an auntie leaving gigantic zucchinis she had neglected to pick in time for trade at her neighbor's stand, clearly a transgression of the code.

"At least the honor system is still intact," Figas joked to his uncle as they witnessed the exchange. The gleam in Auntie Hiruko's eyes told them it was payback.

Upwise had remained old Viridis. Tea terraces of every shape and size fit between rock walls and dark shelterbelts. Broad mountain ridges were covered with giant monkeypod trees, shading the effervescent tea plants. The dozens of microclimates tucked into her folds supported their own unique wealth of species. Desert plants dominated the hot and dry West side, while succulent flowering plants flourished on the wet East side. The path meandered up a grassy ridge before weaving between giant boulders. When they had cleared the big rocks, Figas turned around to admire the vast blue ocean behind them. Small white caps mixed with cotton and silk clouds.

"Is that Stony Point?" Figas pointed to the near cliffs.

"Yes. The blue cliffs where Zoraida leaped centuries ago." The old place became fresh and new again in Uncle's mind.

Figas led the way across a rolling green tea terrace. Suddenly a little dog gave two piercing barks as it ran to greet them.

"Is this your dog, Uncle?"

"This is Ciao. She's just explaining I belong to her. Ciao, this is Figas. He's coming to live with us."

"Nice to meet you, Ciao."

"Nephew, the place in back is all ready for you." Uncle made it sound like he and Ciao would be hurt if Figas even thought of living anywhere else.

Uncle Sun was one of Figas's favorite relatives, though he'd never known his first name. Figas stood and admired Uncle's little place in the middle of the tea. A blue tarp was draped over the back roof, tied down with round rocks, the way a fisherman would weigh his nets.

"Look, you have your own way in and out," Uncle explained as he gave the grand tour. "With your own walled garden and a good view of the sky." A small orchard of fig and orange trees sat between the small cottage and the main house.

"What a little paradise you've created, Uncle."

"Funny you should say it that way, nephew. Pairidaeza is the old Persian word for walled garden. From it comes our word paradise."

"Nice."

Figas looked around his room feeling very lucky. It was small and sparsely furnished, but the scale was pleasing. Compared to bunking with Wood on the *Lady*, the little room was palatial, and much better smelling. He recognized the beat-up guitar case in the corner.

"Easy to sweep," Uncle explained. "Nothing to move out of the way."

"I love it. Thank you so much for inviting me to stay."

"Don't sound so surprised. I could use a hand around here."

"You got it."

Figas was keen to help out, but he didn't think of himself as exactly handy. He soon learned that Uncle didn't have a jacket—the metal water sleeve that fit inside a woodstove. The jacket provided enough hot water for a brief shower. Uncle was old school. He did have a couple of electric lights, but he bathed the traditional way, singing the "Seven Ladle Song" as he ladled the cold water over him.

After Figas's traditional bathing experience that evening, he asked many questions about the jacket. He knew for what he would be saving his money.

The following morning, Figas found Uncle up on the roof. He had rolled the blue tarp neatly to edge and was working on the slate ridge caps. The mortar securing them had long since crumbled. He clipped the copper wires that held the slates in place and began stacking them on the chimney to be reset later.

Ciao announced Figas's new boss as Mr. Hu emerged from the tea field. Figas had been hastily introduced to this cantankerous old man during the festivities the previous day. He wasn't quite sure what his new job entailed, only that he would be helping with the accounting process in the main tea offices.

The tea boss shouted up to Uncle, but the strong breeze rustling through the leaves made it impossible for them to hear one another. So Hu waved Uncle down.

The spry old gentleman clung to the roof slates, careful not to step in the vulnerable center and crack a tile, then climbed down the ladder.

"What's so important?" he asked.

"Do you want to have tea?"

Uncle motioned for Hu to climb the ladder, then pointed where to step to avoid damaging a slate. When both had made it to the ridge, Uncle turned to his contemporary.

"No."

"No what?" asked Hu.

"No, I don't want tea."

"Turtles and eggs!" Hu spat out the Chinese equivalent of son of a bitch. He climbed back down, stepping where he liked, and stormed off.

"What did you say to him?" Figas yelled up at Uncle.

"What?" Uncle waved for him to come up. "Can't hear you."

Emma and Fioré

While her lips talked culture, her heart
was planning to invite him to tea.
—E. M. Forster

Uncle Sun, the person in charge of visitors' visas, considered the request of the two newcomers. Michael Fioré and Emma Carroll had sailed on different vessels, but arrived during the same week. Uncle Sun was comfortable with the coincidence, as long as they ended up being who they said they were. Unfortunately, too often innocent tourists arrived only to go traipsing about in hopes of discovering the secret of the Sigh. Such tourists were fine in Salm Bay, but it was altogether a different matter to have them wandering about Upwise.

Emma Carroll's story seemed a bit simple to be true. Fioré, on the other hand, was one in a long string of documentary film directors. Why had he traveled all this way after being denied permission to film? Uncle decided to trust his intuition. These two new arrivals needed to undergo a test if they were to receive visitors' visas, not just temporary thirty-day visas. If they wanted to cross Teagate's bridge, they would need to pay a visit to harbormaster Grimmes and go through the formalities.

Dutch Moreno, the boss of the wharf, watched the tall, slender figure of Emma pause to take in the graceful habit of a Poinciana tree in full blossom. He had an unobstructed view of the Port of Entry office from his second story perch. The white office building sat just across the street from his pier. Salvaged portholes were dressed with sun-rotted rope. The structure had the look and feel of a rickety old vessel.

To Emma, the place seemed to almost sway in the stiff breeze coming off the bay. She stepped lightly onto the squeaky entryway and opened the old glass door. She was invariably early for an appointment. When her eyes adjusted, she was disappointed to see the condescending, overdressed Italian man she'd had the misfortune of meeting earlier in the week. She noticed him the first day she arrived, crowning the bill of his Yankee cap, looking as if his mother had dressed him. In her experience, when an Italian man heard the word *no,* he regarded it as foreplay.

She set her small handbag on the worn glass counter and looked in vain for a bell to ring. It seemed far too quiet for anyone to be about, so she took her chances and called out in a clear high voice.

Ten minutes later, an elderly gentleman opened the back office door. He moved in slow motion, smiling broadly when he was close enough to make out her features. He wore what Emma thought was a captain's hat, complemented by a light-colored suit and soft canvas shoes. Harbormaster Grimmes had been the welcoming face of Green Island for going on fifty years. He'd never been quick, even in his youth. This Tuesday morning found him traveling at a methodically prudent pace.

He asked Emma for her passport, and she turned it over. "These things take time," he muttered. "What? Oh yes. Thank you. And you, as well."

Emma had no idea what the old man was talking about. "My god," she thought, "I'm going to be stuck here with this pompous idiot director." She looked over at him, toying with his Rolex.

"And how are we today?" Fioré stood up with a small flourish.

Emma ignored him and looked for a magazine to read. She hated that kind of statement. *How are we today?* How many people was she, anyway?

Fioré made a polite comment to do with the weather. Neither of them had any reason to believe anyone was listening in on their conversation.

Emma felt the man's eyes on her legs. It made her uncomfortable, to say the least.

"I get this all the time," he began in earnest. "People see your movies and when they meet you, they become a little shy. I assure you, I'm very shy myself." He studied the gold in her saffron hair, which lay against her tan neck and shoulders.

Emma leafed through the old magazine, without looking up.

Two hours later, the harbormaster made his way slowly from his office to the glass counter. "Be here tomorrow at nine. I'll have the rest of your paperwork to fill out. Please feel free to enjoy Salm Bay and its environs. You may climb the Thumb, but don't cross the swinging bridge please. What's that now? Yes, tomorrow! Be on time, and bring your dasturi. Thank you and goodbye. I have to close for elevenses."

Emma didn't know if she could bear much more. How long would this take? And what was a dasturi, some kind of bribe or fee?

The next morning was much the same. Emma brought her own reading to help pass the time. She wore long jeans, sunglasses, and a wide-brimmed hat. Fioré kept up his polite banter, knowing he would wear her down, given time.

When Emma could no longer endure his stupid comments, she went on the offensive. "You're the guy with a chic loft in New York, with a white carpet and chairs made of cow horns." Emma stared at him. "I'm right? I thought so."

Fioré returned her gaze with good-natured calm. Her attitude reminded him of a young Kate Hepburn. "I assure you, I'm not gay."

"Exactly!" She stood up. "Everything out of your mouth." She couldn't believe it. She threw up her hands as if to say, "Thank you, Your Honor," and sat back down, resting her case.

He smiled in amusement. "Is it really so bad to be manly? Or worse, to be confident?"

"On both counts, I'm sure you'll never know," she added drily. "Tell me. Did Socrates say, 'Know thyself' or 'Fall deeply in love with thyself'?" She swung an imaginary mic in his direction. "Back to you."

"Socrates, I believe, *was* a homosexual," he countered.

She snorted involuntarily. This little waiting room was getting the better of her. "Of course, you could never take orders from someone who isn't a man's man."

Fioré reached down to wipe a smudge from his Giorgio Brutini boot. "It would save us both a great deal of time if you would simply share what you find so objectionable about me."

"One can only hope we don't have *that* kind of time." She stared at his ridiculous boots. "What was it with people and their footwear?" she wondered. In fact, her mother had explained it to her at an early age: it's all about des chaussures. First you decide what heels you're going to wear, then you pick your outfit. It isn't enough to have high cheekbones. You must wear the highest heels you can walk in to ensure your butt cheeks are high as well. Of course, she discarded that sort of wisdom when she moved from France to America to attend Middlebury College and spent her weekends hiking the Green Mountains. She opened her book again and tried to concentrate.

Fioré laughed quietly to himself. It was like trying to spread a pat of iced butter on fresh ciabatta. He would enjoy le dernier mot. He wanted to say, "Aren't you tired of being disappointed?" but a direct approach would never work with a woman like Emma. It was best to stay as formal as possible. He had to be firm, or he had to wait. He would find a way to decant her secrets. Licking his finger, he took another shot at the boot smudge. Her blonde hair brushing over her dark shoulders was more than pleasing.

"Occhio scuro e cappello biondo é il piu bello del mondo," he said to himself: dark eyes and blonde hair are the most beautiful in the world. She wore no makeup or jewelry, so doubted she'd dyed her hair. He was disappointed in her drab sandals. What was she trying to say in those flat heels?

He remembered taking great notice when she came ashore from the *Angel's Trumpet*. Her movement had been easy and flowing like a sarabande, her funny little handbag over her shoulder. At first he could see only her bare wrist, forearm, and shoulder. Then her full lips, eyes, and nose emerged from under the rim of her hat. He wondered how her dress could be off the rack, the way it followed her curves so effortlessly. Her features were classic, perhaps even beautiful. When she had passed an old woman selling fruit, she smiled and said hello. The moment her features became animated, Fioré felt a slow motion jolt.

Across the small waiting room, she was well behind her defenses. He wished he found her ugly, odd, or even boring. It would make everything much simpler. She bit at her lower lip when she turned the page. She must have good eyes to read with shades. He turned his attention to her book: *Sulwan al-Muta*, by Ibn Zafar al-Siqilli.

"I prefer Machiavelli. If you want to go down that road, I say go all the way."

"You would." She dismissed him automatically, but wondered how he could possibly know who Ibn Zafar was. She pulled down her Ray-Bans.

"You don't have to push out your breath like that," he said mildly. "I believe it was Voltaire who first recognized the contributions Arabic culture brought to medieval Europe."

"For instance?" She couldn't believe what she was hearing. A book and its cover?

"I don't know . . . say, Averroes and even Alhazen. One just needs to look at the many Greek texts that were translated into Arabic and then later into Latin." He knew better than to use any more rope, lest he hang himself. The ensuing silence seemed to call his bluff. He decided to stay the course.

"All right, I'll say it." She paused, then closed her book. "I'm surprised, a little impressed even."

"Impressed? Now I'm surprised." He managed to get a little laugh from her.

"So, how much do you know about medieval Arab scholars?" Emma smiled in curiosity.

"I don't know, enough to, say, make small talk over dinner?"

Uncle came in the side door for elevens. Grimmes made tea in his back office on a hot plate.

"So, Captain Grimmes, do you think they may have known each other before this week?" Uncle asked.

"I can safely say no."

"He is a film director, I understand. What do you make of her, captain?"

"She keeps company with the seraphim."

DOMICILE

Love and scandal are the best sweeteners of tea.
—Henry Fielding

Lantern Street emerged from the wooden pier and ran to higher ground, straight through the heart of downtown Salm Bay. The storefronts were a mixture of stone and painted wood. Rusty tin and canvas awnings hopscotched the street with a magpie rhyme. Monkeypod trees filled the gaps between businesses. In the center of old town was the mother tree, whose generous arms nestled and shaded the town's plaza.

As Fioré walked along the sunny side of the street, the faded lettering on a plate glass door caught his interest. Irony Cleaners. His clothes could use dry cleaning. A bell attached to the door announced his business as he stepped inside.

An Asian woman who appeared to be in her late seventies pushed through a beaded curtain and showed him a yellow and gold smile. "Yes?"

"Hello, I would like some clothes dry-cleaned."

"Yes. Hand wash."

"I would like dry cleaning please."

"Yes."

Fioré wondered if she understood. "Do you provide dry cleaning?"

"Local dry cleaning."

Fioré had a hunch that meant hand wash. It would probably shrink his clothes, but what choice was there? "Okay, I'll bring them tomorrow."

"Where you stay?"

He was surprised she had more words in English. He pointed toward the end of town to the small hotel.

"Not so nice place. I have clean room. Follow me.

Emma knocked gently on the door above Irony Cleaners, hoping she had found the right place.

"Come in. My hands are full at the moment."

She entered from the dark back steps to find Fioré, in a finely made muslin shirt with a tiny top button, pumping a kerosene stove. When the burner was blazing, he threw a handful of fresh ingredients into a heated saucepan.

Two tall candles gave the room a warm feeling. White linen hid what she suspected was an old, scratched tabletop. The table was slightly off kilter, with one candle leaning toward magnetic north, the other to the back forty. It made her smile.

"What smells so wonderful?"

"Hold on, I'll be with you in a second."

Emma unwrapped her thin aqua blue shawl and draped it over a chair. She wore close-toed sandals and pink capri pants. Her sheer white blouse benefited from rose glacé flowers around the neckline. Her hair was balanced neatly on her head, in the style of an early Gibson Girl. She set her clutch down on the little table and let out a sigh. "What a hectic day!"

He washed his hands before pouring her a glass of '85 Gaga Barbaresco. He'd traveled with two cases of a reliable red and twelve bottles of his favorite. He ended the pour with a slight twist, like a waiter hoping for a generous tip. He held up his glass and swirled. "Nice legs." He observed the thick wine clinging to the sides of the crystal, but then remembered he needed to be careful with his language around Emma. "Scusami, Emma. The cook needs to pay some attention to the meal." They clicked glasses and each took a small sip. "Please, make yourself at home."

Emma let the wine open in her mouth; the fine finish danced around her throat on the way down. "That's a nice bottle of two-buck chuck. Fantastico!" Emma had been roughing it since she got to the island.

"Grazie."

As Fioré stirred the fusilli doppia into the boiling water, he reminded the angels of his better nature to be on high alert. He was cooking for a lady, after all.

Emma strolled around the room, poking at its meager contents. They had both been on the island for just over a week, but he was living in relative style, while the stone boathouse she was staying in was dark and dank. On a makeshift shelf were an iPad and a worn paperback copy of *Finnegan's Wake*.

"La cena è pronta," he announced. "It's ready."

"That was fast."

"Oh!" Fioré turned around, feigning upset. "The three words an Italian man never wants to hear."

Emma let the double entendre die on its own.

They sat on the two rickety chairs. The table wobbled when Emma took her folded napkin, making the candles dance. She did her best to mask a giggle. They were quiet for a moment, looking at their plates. She thought he might say grace. But Fioré held up his fork, and she did the same. They clinked them together and dug in.

"This really is marvelous," she said, her teeth struggling with a hunk of sticky noodles. "How did you make such delicious pasta in ten minutes?"

"To be fair, hunger is the best sauce. I use simple ingredients— the best Roma tomatoes, my favorite olive oil, fresh garlic, and the finest semolina pasta. This dish is called puttanesca."

"As in?" Emma made a face.

"As in the Italian puttana, you know, a working girl. A quick meal between clients." Fioré stopped talking and took a bite. The conversation wasn't going as planned.

"You've got a real knack, Fioré. You really do." Emma shook her head in a way that said the evening was over before it had started.

"Come on, Emma." He gave her his best smile. "Remember, we were going to discuss the Rinascita, the Renaissance." He held up his glass. "Prosit!"

"Cin cin." She smiled, trying to turn over a new leaf.

"That's a nice little bag you have." He reached over to touch the clutch, still on the edge of the table, then pulled back when he saw her expression. "What's the matter?"

"Fioré. You really don't have manners that would make a grandmother proud."

"You think I'm not polite?" he said rhetorically. "At least I didn't try to peek inside." He eyed the little bag. It was right out of the forties, not a reproduction. The thin leather straps looked to have been added later.

"It was my mother's." She could tell he wasn't going to leave it alone. "My father gave it to me when I was little. It smelled like my mother. Clutch and I, we go way back."

"Nice to meet you, Clutch." He pushed his chair back to stand up, as one might when meeting a lady. But the look on Emma's face changed his mind. In an instant, he put it together: she had lost her mother when she was a child. He took a sip of wine.

"So, Emma," he said after a long pause, "history is your passion?"

"Yes. I love it." She perked up.

"Italian history?"

"Medieval Sicilian, if you must know."

"I must. Frederick or further back to the Norman kings?"

Emma looked startled. She wondered if Fioré had managed to study up in the few days since they'd met. "The Norman kings, specifically the brief but important reign of Roger II."

"Why the Dark Ages? I mean, a pretty bleak period, wasn't it?"

"To be clear, we're talking about the twelfth century." She knew people often confused the Dark Ages with the Middle Ages. "Bleak in some ways, I'll give you that. But don't you think when the world repeats the same behavior over and over, it might be a good idea to take a closer look?"

"What do you mean?"

"Holy wars in the Middle East. Plague. The end of the world. Have you read any good dystopian screen plays lately?" She took a sip of wine to let her point sink in. "We're taught in school that the Roman Empire fell. Then the world lay fallow for almost a thousand years. And then voilà, it's the Renaissance."

"You sound like someone with an axe to grind."

"You asked me what I'm passionate about. Should I go on and on about my favorite shade of mascara?"

He refilled their glasses. He hadn't expected to meet a woman like this in the middle of nowhere. "I can tell you what I do find fascinating about medieval Muslims."

"What's that?"

"Their love of wine." He held up his glass and took a big sip. He'd always wondered why during the golden age of Islam, piety had been observed differently. Consuming alcohol was hardly forbidden.

"'The grape that can with logic absolute the two-and-seventy jarring sects confute: The subtle alchemist that in a trice life's leaden metal into gold transmute.'" Emma quoted Omar Khayyam.

"Drink before the tavern closes." It was the only line of the poem he could remember. He emptied his glass. She was such a serious girl. What had he said now? "Look," he said, leaning over the table so she could see the sincerity in his eyes, "I meant no offence. I'm interested in what did you call them? . . . those fallow fields. What do you find so fascinating about medieval Europe?"

She set her glass down, untouched, as she met his gaze. "Do children learn in school that al-Idrisi already knew in the twelfth century that the world was round, that he made a globe in pure silver and another sphere of the stars? Do we learn that people of all races and faiths—Muslims, Christians, and Jews—lived and worked together successfully a thousand years ago? Roger's court in Sicily included the greatest thinkers of the age. It's now accepted that Roger laid the foundation for what was to follow in Northern Italy. The Renaissance. The institution of the Pope outlasted him, yes, but at what cost?" She picked up her full glass. It was hard to tell if Fioré was really following or just indulging her. Maddening, really. She drained most of the glass, then spoke with all the passion she could muster: "It's as if history remembers every bad thing that ever happened, but forgets about all the good! We're taught to memorize the date of 1066, when William invaded England. The more interesting date is 1061, when Roger d'Hautville crossed the Straight of Messina with only two hundred and seventy Norman knights and conquered Muslim Sicily."

"Why's that important?"

"I said interesting, not important."

"Go on."

"The same Norman knights who planned the amphibious assault of Sicily took what they learned and five years later used it to conquer England."

"Okay, that's interesting. But it was a long time ago, Emma." His second glass of wine had his mouth slightly ahead of his thoughts. "I'm not sure what it has to do with the world today. I guess I'm more interested in what's happening in the world right now."

"Okay, Fioré. Don't you think that a thousand years from your interesting present, they'll look back on us as a work in progress?"

"Probably."

"I'll be honest. Deep down in our cultural fabric, we're not so removed from medieval times. And I don't just mean the Taliban or al Qaeda. At the same time, the moments of real illumination have escaped us. They've been replaced by farcical stories, bad renditions of actual historical events, accompanied by grievously poor translations of the sacred texts. A beautiful, poetic language has been turned into concretized dogma."

"You're getting a bit deep, Emma." He poured the remaining wine into her almost empty glass, leaving the sediments in the bottom of the bottle. He looked at the soft skin around her neck and shoulders, keeping his eyes level. He wanted her. He told himself she was undressing in her own way, revealing herself. He could see her playing the leading lady in a historic drama. He colored in the storyboards. Anna Komnena. "So, are you saying that way back when we made a left turn?"

"A left turn? I'm saying we veered into the oncoming lane. We went from loving God to killing for God without even noticing. In the West, we're convinced we possess all the great scientific knowledge. Who knows, maybe it's true. Let's hope we also have another awakening left in us. We better have."

Fioré raised his glass. "To an awakening!"

"To an awakening." She had no problem drinking to that. Why not tell him? She stole a look at him while he savored his remaining wine. She set her glass down, hoping he wouldn't open another bottle. If he did, that would tell her all she needed to know about his intentions. Could she trust him enough to tell him the real reason she had come to Green Island? Where the East met the West was never simple.

"Look, Emma, I hope you understand I meant no disrespect. I was just hoping you could bring it all into the present tense a bit. That's all. Peace?"

"Sure, Fioré. Peace." The moment seemed to have moved on. Instead of disclosing more, she turned the focus on him. "Tell me what's going on with your film project? When will you begin shooting?"

"One thing I have learned is that visiting Green Island is something you do on her terms. It's not easy getting into a party you haven't been invited to, but people here take that to another level. I've brought a small GoPro camera to study site locations and check lighting during different times of day. The rest of my equipment is waiting with my crew in Canton, ready to catch the next available boat. That is, as soon as I make my way through the local bureaucracy. It's ridiculous."

"Tell me about it."

"I'm starting to wonder if the dasturi Captain Grimmes mentioned is in reality a bribe." He explained that he couldn't quite make out the local officials. Were they just being coy? He didn't want to offend them by offering a large payment too soon. "Delicate matters," he concluded, "sometimes take time."

A Collection of Habits

The price for this tea is anything from a hundred in gold to a half sen. If you want to drink free, that's all right too. I'm only sorry I can't let you have it for less.
—Baisoa

The night-blooming jasmine that wrapped around the front porch dropped its fragrant flowers on the low table where Uncle Sun sat reading. In the heat of the late morning, the dried petals curled into the shapes of brown spiders and were known to give first-time visitors a fright.

Hu was no stranger to morning tea. He emerged from the tea field, Ciao barking happily at his heels, contesting his every step.

"As the oldest and wisest, I'm entitled to the first word and the last. Not you, you scruffy little mutt!" Hu was convinced the dog could read his thoughts.

Uncle looked up from his book and smiled. Hu's pinched face was priceless. The crabby guest took his customary seat across the table and regarded the text written in Chinese characters. He quickly recognized one of the four classic novels of China.

"The immature shouldn't read *Water Margin*."

This was said with such dryness that Uncle howled in delight. The story of a hundred and eight bandits, thought to inspire revolution in the young, had in fact been banned by the emperor.

Inside the kitchen, Figas was stuffing more kindling into the stove. He could hear the two on the sun porch arguing, or as Uncle put it, "having morning tea." Figas leaned over the sink, closer to the open window so he could hear better. Uncle had recently explained how Hu's teaism differed in more than a few respects from his own.

The water reached a rolling boil, and Figas brought out the tea tray. The two gentlemen had all the outward appearances of being settled. Figas bowed, then carefully folded a white towel and ritually wiped the rim of their tea bowls, symbolically cleansing them. He quietly poured and bowed again.

Uncle tapped the low table with three fingers to show respect.

Figas glowed with deep satisfaction, appreciating the tradition. In Southern China during the Qing Dynasty, Emperor Qianlong would travel the countryside in disguise so he could glean insight into the lives of his subjects. He frequented a certain small teahouse. To preserve his anonymity he would pour the tea for his retinue. His men were deeply ashamed, but were unable to bow, lest they give away their emperor's identity. One member of the entourage devised a clever solution: he would gently tap three fingers on the table. One finger represented his bowed head, the other two his prostrated arms.

"They're just weeds and rocks." Hu pointed down the hill to the tangle of wild trees and renewed his case for removal of the shelterbelts dividing the tea terraces.

"Sweet tea! Inside your head is the thicket. You're blood relations. If it helps you, think of the old wolds as nature's little pyramid scheme. A hedge fund." Uncle never tired of puns, especially if they pointed out Hu's love of money.

"It's simple math, Sun. Let me break it down for you: more area planted, more tea plants, more tea." Hu sipped and gloated, like a fat mosquito too full to fly.

"As I've explained, Hu, most of those are neem trees. They're a natural insecticide, slowing the reproductive cycle of insects. Let me break it down for you: more neem, less bugs, more tea."

"You'd run after one dead leaf to hold over your head for shade." Hu chuckled, taking a moment to revel in his own wit. He was burying his opponent with such ease.

"Sweet tea! Have any leafs fallen? That crinkling sound between your ears is just another deciduous gray layer dropping off."

Hu blinked in an exaggerated fashion.

"Ha! There's your octogenarian eye roll."

"Nonsense." Hu pushed out his breath and blinked again.

Uncle thought of his old companion not so much as a person, but as a collection of bad habits haphazardly pasted together. Hu's competence was overshadowed only by his ridiculous overconfidence. His bitterness was enhanced by the fact that he'd never once been elected to the council. "You would turn the whole island into nothing but tea, shoo every last bird and animal into the sea yelling, '*swim!*'"

"Forgive me for not sharing your youthful love of the obvious. There are too many thickets, filled with rats and pests." It was well known Hu hated birds. He stuck his tongue out and smiled, showing his gold teeth. He had a weakness for sugar cakes.

Figas craned his neck out the open window. You'd think Napoleon had just outflanked the Duke of Wellington.

"What kind of human being doesn't love birds?" Uncle blew on his tea. "Birds, by the way, feast on tea mosquitoes before they bite the new tea leaves."

"Birds live in trees. Big trees cover the island."

"Birds make their nests in thickets, where they feel safe. Don't you ever go outside, Hu? Or is it unpleasant to count money in the fresh air?" Uncle sipped.

"When I *do* go outside, it's the twenty-first century. Silly youth sitting on his porch reading *Water Margin*. You need to wake up, Sun. It's the modern age! The tea is hot!" Hu sipped. It was true that Uncle was three weeks younger than Hu—a fact that needed frequent reminders.

"Your god is not an outdoor god?" Uncle asked.

"Yíwàng de ba!" Hu cursed and stormed off, as was his habit.

Figas sneezed, his head still out the window.

"Yi bai sui. The Chinese say, may you live to be a hundred." Uncle gestured for Figas to join him. "Bring your cup, we mustn't waste good tea."

Figas sat down and looked in the direction where Hu could still be heard swearing to himself. "Is Uncle Hu in charge of the tea?"

"Hu's in charge of selling the tea at market. He has an MBA from Columbia. Over the years, he developed close relationships with all the big tea auctions in the world—Guwahati, Pu-erh, and Xihu Longjing. It may surprise you, but Hu is a well-traveled, formidable international businessman."

Figas shrugged, as if to say he wasn't at all surprised. But how to mobilize Uncle Sun? "Hu calls you a retrophile," he said, fishing around, trying to get a rise out of his uncle. "I heard him say you're good at being in the present as long as it resembles the past."

"Hah! Call me a retrophile. Any day!"

"Actually, I think he called you a retrophiliac."

"Even better." Uncle sipped with appreciation, his eyes half closed.

Frustrated, Figas decided to try a more direct, serious approach. He cleared his throat and waited for his uncle to open his eyes. "So," he said, when he felt he had the floor, "have you spoken to Uncle Hu about Christopher Elant's warning?"

"What warning?"

"You remember, Uncle, about the big tea cartels being interested in Viridis."

"If you're concerned, talk to Hu yourself."

"That would be difficult."

"You mean you're chicken?"

"Basically."

Uncle proceeded to explain that unlike coffee or cocoa, there was no international market price for tea. There were simply too many types and qualities of tea grown around the world. Hu sold their tea directly through the three big auction houses, so it was generally at the top of the leader board in terms of price. "As you know," he said, "we sell no loose tea, but a blend packed inside our special tea chest. It is very unlikely Sighing Woman Tea will ever be duplicated. Hu may be a pain in the backside, but he knows his trade. Never play fan-tan with him, or he will take all your money."

Figas frowned. He had been counting on Uncle to be onboard with his mission. "Did Uncle Hu mention that a tea chest that used to go for a hundred U.S. dollars now sells at auction for 250,000? Our tea has become world famous, an obsession. Rich clients are paying for a once-in-a-lifetime experience. They're booking private rooms in the most prestigious teahouses, from Beijing to San Francisco, all in hopes of hearing the Sigh. Gold leaf on chocolate cake is passé. We're talking big bucks, Uncle."

"I understand, nephew. Worshipping the fatted calf is hardly new. But since you mention it, that would explain Hu's improved disposition." Uncle grinned in the direction of Hu's house. He cupped his hand behind his ear to see if he could still hear cursing.

"Do you get it? Really? Big money brings big wheeler-dealers."

Uncle stood up and pumped out his chest, doing his best impersonation of a big wheeler-dealer. "You know, we're not unlike the Swiss around here, guarding their chocolate. The bridges and tunnels along their border are rigged with explosives to protect against invaders. We have old man Teagate." As he deflated his chest, he couldn't help but notice the irritation in Figas's eyes. He put his hand on this nephew's shoulder. "All right, young master Burke, you're invited to come to the next council."

"Thanks, I'm planning on it."

"A couple of meetings should cure what ails you. We've more to fear from the erratic rains than from evil tea consortiums."

Figas drained his cup and stood up. "You know, maybe Hu's right. You are a retrophile. That explains why you don't understand any kind of change."

Uncle's eyes narrowed in appreciation. He made a small bow. "You're coming up nicely, nephew. In two or three years, you will be a formidable companion for tea."

Figas Visits Auntie

Find yourself a cup; the teapot is behind you.
Now tell me about hundreds of things.
—Saki

As a footie messenger rushed past on the narrow path, her oiled leather bag thumped Figas's shoulder. The speedy messenger took no notice. Figas wanted to ask her if he was on the right track, but footies never lingered. He stretched out his stride, heading for some shade. The hard basalt layer—which the locals called pork belly and streak o' lean, streak o' fat—ran gray and white up the canyon wall, reflecting the fierce midday sun like an anvil. His shirt was soaked through, and his water bottle nearly empty.

He looked up the slope at a scattering of red poppies mixed with grass. A lone magpie flew, bobbing up and down with each beat of its wings.

Earlier that morning, he had opened his eyes to the intense color of dawn hammering the mountain outside his bedroom window into copper.

Uncle was sweeping the threshold when Figas came in.

It hurt Figas's back to watch Uncle use that short ratty broom. "Why don't you get a decent broom?"

The old man looked confused. "This one's still good."

"Yeah, right. I'm going to visit Auntie Lan today."

"Better pack a lunch. It's a long way over there." Uncle picked a small handful of broken bristles off the floor. "Give her my best."

"Why don't you come along? You can tell her yourself."

"Can't today. Have to pull a tooth."

"What tooth?"

"Any tooth."

"Very funny." Figas thought for a moment. "I'm not sure you should try to pull it yourself, Uncle. You better see a specialist."

"What sort of specialist?"

"A coinci-dentist!"

"Ah, very good. Yes, very good, Figas." Uncle squinted in amusement. He enjoyed seeing his nephew shed some of his heaviness.

"So, what's your problem with Auntie Lan?"

"Huh?" Uncle turned the short broom around and explained to the remaining thatch. "Every day we wake up and say, 'How is this life even possible? It's a miracle!' Yet accompanying the wonderful mystery of the possible is the impossible, including its incarnate form." He turned to Figas. "You call that form Auntie Lan!"

"What are you saying, Uncle?"

"I'm saying the woman is impossible."

"I remember her as being a little stubborn."

"Stubborn? Stubborn allows for the possibility of another point of view to be stubbornly against. Stubborn is a warm breeze in a Siberian spring."

On the far side of the tea field, the cracked yellow path settled against a clear stream. Pointy tipped reeds lined both banks. Red twigged branches leaned out like nimble dancers, and clouds of white flies hovered over creases of light and jostled their way through the dark leaves. Beside a smooth river rock, the yellow-green eyes of a big bullfrog watched Figas dip his feet into his private pool. The delicious, cool water reminded him of his lunch. He pulled it out of his satchel and ate until the afternoon heat once again felt welcome. He set off, carrying his sandals, his bare feet feeling their way over the moss-covered stones.

He abandoned the main trail and headed down a shaded draw. He had put off this visit to Auntie Lan for as long as possible. He opened a familiar sagging gate and looked in both directions for the old goose that would chase him around the yard. The moment his foot found the wooden step, Auntie opened the screen door.

"Well, finally!" She seemed the same, her hair still bothering her face, though it had all gone to gray. She wiped her hands on her old dress. "Come in, Thomas. Don't gawk at Auntie."

Figas set his sandals on the porch and stepped inside. The pungent mix of spices that greeted him suggested Auntie had spent the morning cooking for him. "How did you know I was coming to see you today?"

"A footie dropped by this morning and told me you were puffing up the canyon." She almost smothered him with a hug, then stood back to examine her guest. "What a slender young leek! Who could-a-figa? So handsome, and you have your father's eyes, Thomas." She gave herself a moment to remember her younger brother. "Come and sit down. You must be famished."

It was so hot inside Figas wished he could take off his shirt. Several large pots with mismatched lids were gurgling over and hissing on the cast-iron cooktop. Auntie peeked into the oven and adjusted the flue then set a small plate of sliced fried yams with an oozy green relish in front of him to start things off.

Figas dipped a yam and took a taste. "Minty and refreshing, Auntie."

"So what are you doing now that you're home?" Her back was to Figas as she labored over the stove, but he could feel her voice steeped in the dramatic.

"I don't know." It was the truth. Despite his theories, he had no ability to predict the course of his own life.

"You don't know?" she puffed, setting a chipped enameled lid down none too softly on a large kettle of sabzi. She wiped her right hand on her dress, while keeping the wooden spoon going with her left. Then she turned and squared herself to the table. "Tell us what you're not doing then!" She rolled her free hand, "Come, get the ball rolling!"

"I'm working in the tea, helping Mr. Hu create a more efficient accounting process for the harvesting and tracking."

"Oh," she said, clearly disappointed.

For the next two hours Figas ate the best he could, cursing his uncle for packing such a big lunch. When he had worked his way through four courses, the main dish of sumac-spiced fish was brought forth from the depths of the oven. All through the meal, he kept any trace of a smirk from his face as Auntie burst into flight, like a startled pheasant that once airborne glided straight to its destination. In this case, that destination was his future.

"You finished your degree?" she queried, not waiting for a reply. "You should use it. In fact," she said as sweetly as her voice would allow, adding a few seconds of silence for dramatic effect, "I always thought Thomas Burke should become a teacher."

Between mouthfuls, he described his academic experience. He had spent almost no time in a regular classroom, having designed his graduate work himself. He had no idea how to teach a class of students, and more importantly, no inclination to do so. The award he just received guaranteed a fat paycheck was out there waiting for him when he was ready. He formed his lips into the shape of a smile, and thumped his index finger on his painfully tight stomach. "The high pitch of a ripe Crenshaw," he said to himself and scratched the rind.

His explanation seemed to fall on deaf ears. Auntie continued to ladle out her vision of his future. "These fledglings need guidance," she muttered to herself. "Thinner than a raffle turkey, with half the sense."

Ciao's patented two barks stole Uncle's attention from his book. "Did she make her Sagittarian stew?" he called out.

"I believe so."

"And bake a pie?"

Figas hobbled onto the porch and slumped down. "Oye. She baked pies. Three of them. I managed reasonably well until the third."

"Managed what?" Uncle asked between giggles.

"Managed not to tell her about the big lunch you packed me. At least not until that last berry pie."

"Sweet tea and vinegar! You would do this to me, your own flesh and blood?" Uncle looked over at Figas, who was smiling. "You teasing me?"

"I don't know. Ask Auntie."

"Ask her?" Uncle shook his head. "Tell me, please: did you at least eat some of that last pie? Or do I have to wedge a chair under the door handle before I go to sleep tonight?"

"As you're always saying, Uncle: the universe is an exciting little place."

THE ORIGINAL CROSS

The Original, born before the green fire was lit. When compassion was a sleepy child.
—Master P'O

Emma instinctively bowed under the low doorway. The elderly woman, Es-sahra, noticed her passing in the waning evening light and invited her in for tea.

When Emma's eyes adjusted, she took in the dimly lit room. It was modestly furnished, with a bed in the far corner, opposite a small round table and two chairs. A brass hedgehog teapot gently whistled on top of a small masonry woodstove. Emma admired a collector's plate that hung on the far wall, depicting the mountains and craters of the moon in vivid detail. It seemed to cast a silver glow. A round object on a wooden mantle near the room's only window drew her close.

"May I?" she asked before picking up the milky-colored sphere. She held it to the light. It felt like polished bone, but it was semi-translucent. "What is this, Auntie?"

"It's an old tree seed, my dear. A numen. We call it an Original cross."

"I'm sure I've never seen this tree."

"Neither have I." The older woman laughed. "Would you care for a chocolate with your tea?" She set a bowl of foil-wrapped chocolate kisses on the table.

"No, thank you." Emma had heard of a numen. She guessed it was a kind of sacred object. She realized she wasn't being polite, but she was unable to set the orb back on the mantle. It was like a large glass marble, only very light and somehow alive. She held it up to the window and examined the tiny black veins intersecting within the sphere.

"How can all these lines intersect, yet be so slender where they meet?"

"You're very quick to the heart for a young person."

"I'm not sure how this is even possible."

"Everything in our entire life happens at the same moment, yet we don't find this mysterious." Auntie poured tea.

Emma carefully set the object on the mantle. "What did you just say?"

Es-sahra sat down at the table and gestured for Emma to join her.

"Original cross?" Emma asked as she sat down. "That's an interesting name for a tree seed."

The old woman regarded her guest before speaking. "For many early cultures, the cross was a sacred symbol. The Celtic solar cross for instance, and the Egyptian ankh."

"The crux ansata, the key of life." Emma chimed in.

"Yes, very good, Emma. We have many stories devoted to the early cross. As a people, we love to imagine what it was like thousands of years ago when our ancestors communicated, before spoken language, gesturing with their hands or using a stick to scratch a narrative in the sand as they sat around a fire. Not so unlike you and me here this evening." Es-sahra's gentle laugh complemented her easy smile and clear dark eyes.

Emma liked the idea of a narrative before there were words. "Go on, Auntie, please."

"We imagine a line scratched in the sand, a path traveled, a stranger met. This new companion draws her journey with a walking stick, across the desert. Our lines join or cross one another. One thing meets another. What is more elemental, or essential, in this world?"

They sipped their tea in silence.

"Auntie, where does the ancient cross in your story meet the Christian cross, if I may ask?"

"Of course you can; you're kind to even listen to an old woman. Green Islanders have a strong connection to early Christian traditions. We regard Christ on the cross as a powerful symbol."

"Please keep scratching that line in the sand. I'm still a little lost in the desert."

"Very well. Two intersecting lines mean a myriad of different things to different people. To a Green Islander, it would seem the world regards one line as something, and the other line as something different. One thing against another different thing."

Emma tried to make the connection. "Are you saying it's like yin and yang?"

"The yin and yang symbol, you remember, is not fixed, but is always in motion, always turning. Each half contains a portion of the other at its heart. This smaller portion spins as well, continually seeking balance."

"So you're saying Christ on the cross wasn't a sacrifice?" Emma sighed, more lost than ever.

Es-sahra laughed and took a small sip. "A great sacrifice, indeed."

"Auntie, don't worry, you won't offend me by sharing your stories of the island. I love hearing them, honestly."

The old woman leaned over and whispered softly in Emma's ear. "Christ is the prisoner of opposites. For us, he has been brutally nailed to one thing against another for eternity." She sipped her tea.

They sat in the quiet while the light of the evening faded further.

"And the Original cross, Auntie, what does it represent?"

Es-sahra reached over and placed the sacred object in the young woman's hands. "Look at all those intersecting lines crossing in the center, traveling outward in the opposite direction to infinity. Where do you think we are?"

"At the center?"

"I agree, in the center in this very moment, sustaining the contradictions of life as best as we're able. Journeying outward and inward as far as our courage allows."

The following morning, Emma volunteered at the Island School. During morning break under the big monkeypod tree, she asked the children about the Original. They had wildly different descriptions.

"Is it a he or a she?" Emma had her notepad ready.

The kids busted out laughing. A ten-year-old girl named Na'ila struck a serious tone. "The Original is not an it or a he or a she."

"What does that leave?" Emma asked.

More howls ensued and the crowd grew.

Na'ila remained patient. "The Original is a Thou."

"Soft as rain," her younger friend, Tsani, offered.

"Clear as a calm sea," said a boy, holding his hands like a pair of binoculars to help him see into the water.

"The Original's shadow is a rainbow," another small girl said as a matter of fact.

"Have any of you seen him? I mean, Thee?"

Emma was bringing down the house. Mrs. Morris walked over and listened in before breaking up the party. "All right, everyone. It's time for our afternoon lesson."

That evening, Emma knocked at Es-sahra's door.

The frail woman welcomed her with a comforting smile. She lit an oil lamp and adjusted the wick. The flame billowed against the chimney glass, blackening it. So she dialed down the flame and blew it out. She removed the hot chimney, holding it near its base so as not to burn her fingers. Emma studied the lines in the old woman's face as her thin fingers carefully trimmed the edges of the wick with tiny scissors. When the lamp was relit, the flame was a perfect arc, illuminating the small room. They settled into a nice pot of tea.

"Would you like a chocolate? Oh, that's right, you don't care for them."

"I love chocolate, Auntie. I'm just trying to cut back."

Auntie wiped the lampblack from her fingers with a tea towel. She opened an old biscuit tin and took out a crumbling cinnamon cake. She set the pieces on a small plate for them to share. The aroma of tea and cinnamon chased away the kerosene smell.

"These are not too sweet," Es-sahra promised. She could tell by Emma's mannerisms that she was brimming with questions. "There's a long-standing jest," the old woman began, her eyes full of mirth. "God is the—how do you call it?" She looked up at the rafters, frustrated not to be able to recall the word. "It's the goat's intestine. They use it to stuff the meat scraps they take from the bones and grind up with spices."

"Sausage?"

"Yes, but not sausage, the casing of the sausage. We take the world into ourselves, grind it up, add our own experiences like spice. We squeeze infinity into a familiar shape that we can recognize."

Emma smiled at the image of God as a sausage skin. "Auntie, when I asked the children at school today about the Original, they had these interesting poetic descriptions. Why is that?"

"When we're young, it's easier to envision meaning through objects. As we grow older, we often find the need to look beyond form. Young people get caught in what things look like and begin to think that's what they are. Older people find it a little easier to speak of invisible things. Wouldn't you agree?"

"I would."

"How is your tea?"

"Soft as rain."

Everything Is a Chord

Come, ye tea-thirsty restless ones, the kettle
boils, bubbles and sings musically.
—Rabindranath Tagore

"Chord? Everything is a chord. No notes or sounds are possible without other notes and sounds," Uncle Sun explained to his nephew.

The rain was clattering on the roof. The two little windows in Uncle's study were steamed up, wicking moisture onto the sills. Figas pulled on the chain hanging above his head. The bare bulb illuminated the small room. Uncle made a face.

"It's dark in here, Uncle! And your quarter notes look like chicken scratch."

"It's not that."

"What then? You're too cheap to pay for electricity?"

"It's the sound."

Figas couldn't believe it. He pulled the chain, waited a moment, and pulled the light on again. The filament gave off the faintest high-pitched hum. He tugged the chain off. "Okay, I'm not going to argue with 'everything's a chord' or that 'the bulb is singing flat,' but you have to admit you're playing that mordent like a trill!" Figas pointed to the first measure of the handwritten score of his favorite sarabande, from the *French Suite*. Originally for piano, Uncle had scratched out an arrangement for viola and guitar. So they might, as he put it, "take a hack at it."

"Okay, Segovia." Uncle tried to be conciliatory. "We mustn't get carried away. It is Bach, after all."

"The consummate romantic," Figas joked. But he meant it. When Uncle played Bach, it sounded akin to a Puccini aria. Played the usual stiff-fingered way, baroque music sounded rigid. The sound coming from Uncle's viola was living, breathing, and unearthly.

When they finished the piece, it was dark in the room. Figas gently set his guitar against the wall and relit the lamp. "Can I ask you a personal question?"

Uncle didn't glance up from wiping his viola strings.

"Is it true that you studied at Tanglewood?"

"Ah, yes." He laid the viola on his knee. "It was the summer of 1959. I was in my second year at Cornell, studying composition. My professor had entered a piece I'd written on my behalf, and lo and behold, I was invited to the Berkshire Music Center, as it was called then."

"What style of music was it?"

"My composition was entitled *Tathata*. The Buddhist notion of the ultimate nature of all things expressed in phenomena but not expressible in language. You get the idea—lots of beeps and honks!"

Figas nodded with amusement.

"In those days, I lived mostly in my head. A red-headed kid with Coke bottle glasses. I can tell you I was quite taken back by the whole experience. I've always been a surer hand at arranging than at writing, so I was surprised my little piece garnered any attention. On the second day of camp, I was informed that the orchestra would perform my composition. During the first rehearsal, I sat at the back of the big tent and plunked along on my viola, working on a harmony I was hearing in my head. The guest conductor, Dr. Furtenhauser, a stern old German, took exception to my efforts, calling back to me, 'You in the back! The composer deserves more respect than you're showing. Don't you agree?' Furtenhauser pointed to the exit. I gathered up my viola, not even bothering to fasten the case, and left."

"What do you mean, you left?" Figas tried to suppress a laugh.

"I caught the bus back to Ithaca."

"You didn't stay to hear your piece played?"

"No."

"Have you ever heard it played?"

"No."

Figas busied himself tuning the B string on his guitar and waited for the awkward moment to pass.

Uncle loosened his bow. After a few minutes he continued: "I told myself I didn't want to hear my music conducted by this dictatorial fellow. The truth is my feelings were hurt. Perhaps I was just embarrassed by the room full of great players and this master conductor from the old country, and didn't feel I deserved the attention. To this day, I'm not altogether certain."

"Didn't they know it was you who had written the piece?"

"I was a shy kid and hadn't stepped up to introduce myself. It was my big moment—not just for me but for the pride of Green Island. To say I wilted would be an understatement."

"Sounds like you took a bit of a fall." Figas hoped Uncle didn't resent his prying.

Uncle giggled, breaking the tension. "Caduto dalle nuvole. But they do say it's not the fall that kills you."

"So now that you're old and wise, what would you do in that situation?"

"I would let out a big laugh. Because it really was very funny. 'You in the back! The composer deserves more respect than you're showing.' Ha-ha!" Uncle doubled over.

"And then?" Figas goaded.

"And then? Ask directions to the bus station."

The Cookie Stash

Never trust a man who, when left alone in a
room with a tea cozy, doesn't try it on.
—Billy Connolly

Uncle Sun watched Emma approach from a distance, amused. She appeared to be walking against a gale force wind. The intense angle was cartoon like. "A very driven personality," he thought.

Emma was pleased to find her visitor visa waiting at the Council of Visitors office. She took the opportunity to request access to the island's historical records. Diya Montri dug through various file cabinets and pulled out a copy of each required request form.

"How can such an out-of-the-way place have so much red tape?" Emma wondered.

Diya patiently explained how to fill out each form, then excused herself. Emma was welcome to stay and complete the forms, if she wished.

The moment Diya had left, Emma's eyes scoured the office. Three large unlocked file cabinets seemed to beckon her with the sweet modulations of a siren's call. A powerful temptation grew as she felt drawn toward the contents of each. "Serenum scopuli," she whispered to herself. It was all she could do to remain seated in her chair. What were the names of those islands? Peisinoe, and Thelxiepeia? She picked up the small tea chest on Diya's desk and looked closely at the delicate red wax seal. She could clearly make out the familiar imprint.

"What do you have to say for yourself?" She had hold of the little culprit responsible for bringing her all the way across the world. She wanted badly to ask Diya or Es-sahra about the map, but couldn't take the chance. Not yet. She set the tea chest down and sat on her hands until Diya returned.

"Have you completed the forms?" Diya asked, taking her seat behind the desk.

"No. May I take them with me?"

"Of course."

After Emma left, Uncle came in by the side door. Diya gave him the broad strokes.

"So she didn't open a single drawer, not even this one?" Uncle asked.

Diya could read the tea leaves. She opened the bottom drawer where she kept her cookies and offered Uncle a pistachio crunch. "Did you come by just to hit my stash, or is there something else?"

He scratched his rib through a hole in his worn cashmere. "Tell me everything she did after you left your office. Please."

"Well. She talked to herself awhile."

"What did she say?

"Saranam scoopley, and something about paysino."

"Serenum scopuli perhaps?"

"Yes, I think that was it."

"Your three big cabinets here." Uncle paused in thought. "The three mythical islands of the Sirens. Please, what did she do next?"

"She picked up the tea chest, and then put on her glasses. She looked at the wax seal for a long time. Then she said, 'What do you have to say for yourself'?"

"Can you remember anything else?"

"She sat on her hands and fidgeted, so I decided to come back in."

"Thanks, Diya. Good job. Now I have to run."

"That's too bad."

Uncle ignored her sarcasm. "Is Vaughn still in his office?"

"I don't know, but please don't let him see that cookie."

Vaughn Chan was typing in front of his old computer monitor. He had graduated from Harvard Law ten years prior, and so was called Harvard upon his return. Which quickly became Hava, and because of his salty disposition, later Hava Bitch. He was in charge of international relations, and was the official spokesperson for Green Island. Most importantly, he was also the island's best techie. Diya like to say computers had been invented so Hava would have something to do with his life. He had the irritating habit of always having to be right. If you doubted his version of the facts, he would blurt out, "Goo', foo'!" Meaning "Google it, you fool."

"Did Diya give you that cookie?" Vaughn asked without looking up.

"She always plies me with treats when I stop by," Uncle complained.

"That little . . . !" Vaughn was clearly chapped, punching at the keyboard while Uncle crunched. "To what do I owe the privilege?" Vaughn inquired less than enthusiastically. He knew better than to act too willing when it came to Uncle's little favors. His computer had been acting up all morning. It was time to perform a little percussive maintenance if the colored wheel didn't stop spinning.

Uncle admired Hava's creative use of duct tape to hold the monitor at its proper angle. "Hava, I need you to do an Internet search regarding our lovely guest, Miss Carroll."

Quicker, Easier, and More Convenient

You can never get a cup of tea large enough
or a book long enough to suit me.
—C. S. Lewis

Emma decided to continue volunteering at the Island School while the rest of her paperwork made its way through the system at a snail's pace. She watched some of the children playing the game of Pepper during break.

Young Na'ila explained the rules to her. "It's stick ball. If you catch the ball at the front of the line, you get to pitch to the batter. If you drop the ball, you go to the back of the line. If the batter misses, it's a strike out. The pitcher becomes the new batter."

"I think I understand. Thank you, Na'ila." Emma watched a few rotations before looking for Mrs. Morris.

Inside the carved ironwood doors of the school, at either side of the entrance, wooden shelves were filled with an odd assortment of clay Buddhas. The statues looked as if they had just come out of the kiln. Some reminded Emma of the first clay cup she made in school, others looked like monks in a monastery had made them, delicate and perfect. Many were comical. A tall Buddha stood high above the rest, a fat body and long neck, with the head of a coifed poodle. The little nameplate read *Boodle*.

Mrs. Morris finished organizing her lesson and greeted Emma. "We're doing a semester on world religions. What do you think of the statues?"

"Really fantastic!"

"Originally Buddhism was symbolized by the Wheel of Dharma. No statues depicted the Buddha until after the Greeks invaded northern India, bringing the tradition of carving deities into stone."

"Alexander the Great crossed the Jhelum River in the Punjab in fourth century BC."

"I forgot you said you were a history major. Yes, the Five Rivers region."

"I really like this one. What is this? A fire extinguisher on his— or *her*—back?"

"That's one of my favorites, as well. Fletcher Kim's work. She's in her tenth year. An exceptional student." Mrs. Morris pointed to a round-faced girl with straight black hair playing Pepper. "I'm recommending Fletcher attend art school abroad next year. Although her Buddha is modern, she shows historic understanding of her subject."

Mrs. Morris picked up the Buddha and handed it to Emma for closer inspection. The bright glaze was silky smooth. Emma could almost read the tiny warning label on the red canister.

"The female Buddha is called Tara. I believe our young artist is making a visual statement about the meaning of the Sanskrit word *nirvana*."

"The state of divine consciousness the Buddha achieved upon enlightenment."

"Exactly. It's interesting that the literal translation of nirvana is to extinguish, to blow out the fires of greed, hatred, and delusion. Our modern Tara is using technology to achieve a quicker, easier, and more convenient result."

Emma laughed quietly to herself as the children made their way to their seats after morning break. She noticed young Tsani with a small handbag sporting three pearls. "That's a smart-looking bag you have."

"Thanks." Tsani was proud of her stylish bag.

Emma showed off Clutch.

Tsani's smile beamed her approval.

"You may ring the bell, Miss Carroll."

Emma took up the wooden mallet and struck the big metal bowl. It resounded through the one-room schoolhouse, cleansing the air and settling the students.

A Leap

I am in no way interested in immortality,
but only in the taste of tea.
—Lu T'ung

Figas set the heavy bags down on the twentieth step of the Thumb and rested. Uncle's grueling list of errands had had him running around town the entire day, and now it was getting dark fast. By the time he made it through the boulders at Stony Point, it was pitch-black. Figas was glad his feet knew the way home. He enjoyed sneaking up on Ciao whenever he came home late, so he walked as quietly as possible. Even so, she always heard him coming.

"Sweet tea!"

His foot struck something lying across the path. Next thing he knew, he was on his arse, groceries strewn in all directions. He caught his breath and rolled over, raising himself on one elbow, and squinted to make out what was lying on the path. He crawled over and touched the little dog. Her fur was wet and sticky.

"Ciao!"

He could feel her breathing, but couldn't rouse her. "Get up, girl," he coaxed. "What's the matter?"

He was about to lift her into his arms when he heard a faint tap coming from farther up the trail. He looked up in time to see a red flash. Seconds later, another tap, this one closer. A red streak zinged across the rock beside him, followed by a dull thump and a puff of dust.

Something was very wrong! Figas jumped up in disbelief. A red light flashed over his left shoulder. He dodged behind a boulder as another streamed over his head.

"Frickin' silencers! Are you kidding me?"

There was nothing he could do for Ciao now. Scrambling over the groceries and back onto the trail, he did the only thing he knew: follow his instincts. Figas's life had been a slow-motion emergency for years, with sirens wailing just below the range of human hearing. Running for his life didn't seem unnatural.

He could hear men shouting behind him. A red beam caught him in the eye, making it more even more difficult to see in the dark. He was surrounded.

Is this what Elant had warned him about? What had he said? Ruthless. The multinationals were as ruthless as the old VOC.

If this was the case, there was no time to formulate a plan. Sometimes the old ways were the best. As much as he hated it, he had only one alternative.

He ran for all he was worth downhill.

He could barely make out the rim of the cliff in the dark as he timed his leap. Hopefully it was high tide. His left foot was on earth, and then there was only air. He tumbled forward three times, floating like a speck of feather down.

Sound disappeared. He felt the softness of Cedar's hair and pressed her head against his shoulder. He could feel her heart beating. Some part of his brain computed the arc of his descent.

His knees slammed into his chin when he hit the water. The pressure in his ears as he sank was almost unbearable. It was the dogleg Captain Martin had spoken about. The volta do mar. The trajectory of his life traveling away from the world. His chest convulsed. He did his best to stifle the reflexes in his diaphragm.

"I'll do better. I'll make a contribution," he promised.

Then suddenly he felt the soft touch of a child's hand and grew light as sun-baked cork. When he reached the surface, a wave broke over him and slammed into the sea cliff a few feet away. He gulped air and kicked away from the crashing breakers.

"I have to raise the alarm!" he thought, swimming as hard as he could, keeping the dark cliffs well to his left. If he could find a buoy with a bell, he would ring it. If that didn't work, he would swim far enough north to safely come ashore and make his way to town.

Ahead of him, a small light was bobbing in the waves. He rubbed the salt from his eyes as he drew closer. An elegant wooden canoe was moored to a faded orange buoy. A shoji lantern was poised in the middle of the empty boat, throwing its faint light onto the waves.

He ducked under the outrigger and lifted himself into the canoe. It was in pristine shape, as if someone had been there within the hour. His eye fell on a small green basket tucked under the woven-mesh seat. As he caught his breath, he tried to work out what was happening. Clearly, someone had set him up.

"This must be a prank!" he muttered, his mind racing through all the probabilities. From the first day he had arrived back home, he had droned on about impending doom. His own paranoia had washed him over the cliff. But why? Was it a rite of passage? He wanted to be mad, but like it or not, he had to hand it to Uncle and his posse.

He pulled the basket from underneath the seat and untied the lid. Inside was a black ceramic tea bowl. It was light for its size and appeared to have been molded by hand. He held it close to the lantern. Hundreds of careful repairs had been done over the centuries. As he stared intently at it, he lost his equilibrium and had to brace himself against the gunnel of the canoe. This black bowl was straight out of the stories of the ancestors, the history of the island he had learned in school.

"The bowl of memory!" The sound of the words gave him gooseflesh.

Quickly he put the living artifact back into the basket and snuffed out the lantern, then untied the canoe and began to paddle north. He knew exactly what he had to do now.

In less than an hour, he reached the small beach on the backside of the Thumb. He jumped into the shallow water and eased the craft through the shore break, dragging it well past the tide line. Cradling the basket in his arm, he climbed the steep backside of the Thumb for the first time. He recalled the story of the Original's flexible hands. How crazy was it that he was climbing the backside of the Thumb? And in the dark, no less. Upwise was the palm of her hand; the ridges separated by steep ravines, her many fingers.

He'd crossed over the swinging bridge only a few hours ago, but that seemed an eternity.

He wondered if Teagate would notice he was coming again from the same direction. He decided the old man would not let on, even though he was clearly soaked to the bone.

The Bowl of Memory

*Who would then deny that when I am sipping tea in
my tearoom I am swallowing the whole universe with
it and that this very moment of my lifting the bowl to
my lips is eternity itself transcending time and space?*
—D. T. Suzuki

When Figas crested the rise, shoji lanterns lit the bridge before
him like Spring Festival. He ran across the swaying span in his
squeaky, wet sandals. The lanterns moved like the undulating scales
of a serpent, rising and falling. He recalled a song he'd learned as a
boy: "The river holds still, the bridge begins to flow."

To his astonishment, old man Teagate was nowhere to be found.

Figas's heart pounded in his ears. What day was this? What
holiday? Day or night, it wasn't possible for the gatekeeper not to be
on his bridge. "Hello!" he called out. When there was no answer, he
crossed the bridge.

Following his instincts, Figas climbed northeast to the center
of the island. When he reached his destination, he found another
lit shoji lantern. An unopened tea chest sat on a tea towel beside a
teapot and an old ivory tea bowl. The white bowl resembled the one
in his basket. He picked it up; it felt as though a child had made it.
It was far from symmetrical. He took the black bowl from his basket
and set it beside its sibling.

He walked to the dark tree line and listened for the slightest
sound before gathering twigs and dry grass for a fire. He carefully
arranged them between three blackened stones. He could make tea

71

in his sleep—not that he was tired, far from it. He felt energized and strangely calm.

Setting the full iron teapot on the raised rocks, he lit a twig from the candle in the lantern. It surprised him how, with such focus, everyday movements became ritual. The fire smoked and popped. Shadows danced and darted about the holiest place on Viridis. As he stared into the flames, he remembered the Latin word for hearth was *focus*.

When the water was hot, Figas broke the red wax seal and opened the chest. The sound of Lijuan's sigh echoed in the quiet. He ritually folded the tea towel and cleansed the rim of the black tea bowl and poured it three-quarters full. He listened to the dry tea infusing with the boiling water. He stood up and placed the tea bowl a few paces away on a flat rock, just as master P'O had done a thousand years before.

He sat again and overpoured the other bowl. Then he lifted the boiling hot ivory bowl with the back of his fingers, carefully spilling three drops into the gravel as an offering to the ancestors. He held the cup above his head, conjuring the spirits of master P'O and the Original, holding the sacred pose known as *open dimension*. The burning hot bowl branded the skin on the back of his hand.

Figas took a small sip. Soft shapes came into crisp focus, but without order, then retreated back from where they'd come. He let his thoughts go without attempting to follow. Time ceased to be a unit of measure, but a dimension he shared. He watched, comfortably at rest in the place before intention.

A bird sang a prophecy to the eastern rim of the sky. Milky light washed away the stars, leaving only Venus and bright Jupiter in the East. More voices joined in, until the dark break of trees emanated a chorus of hallelujah, exalting the marriage of the night to the day. The illuminated wings of tiny insects merged with those of white egrets flying high overhead.

When Figas became aware of his surroundings, the sounds of his eyelids opening and closing were Taiko drums, his breath a roar.

He stretched his numb legs and retrieved the dark tea bowl from the flat rock.

It was empty.

The hairs on the back of his neck tingled. He felt the rock underneath for dampness. It was dry. The old cup could have leaked. He let go of the urge to test his theory.

He packed both tea bowls into the woven basket with the tea towel between them. He left the tea chest on the flat rock.

During his trek home, every person he encountered bowed to let him pass. He felt strange. There was no space between himself, the people he met, or the path under his feet.

"There is no *between*," he said to himself and laughed. "At least not today."

He had crossed over an invisible threshold. "I can't get away, because there is no *away*." His mind turned everything into a liminal farce. Separation, in a believable sense, no longer held meaning. He knew he couldn't explain or ever retrace his steps. Master P'O was a trickster. Yes, he was.

Ciao barked once and then hesitated before making a long, happy growl.

"Come here, girl! So you're all right!"

He shifted the green basket and picked the little dog up, then carried her to the house. She licked his face. Two air rifles leaned against the garden shed. Cheap laser pointers were duct-taped to their sights. Figas fit the last pieces of the ruse together.

Uncle swept the threshold, ignoring him. Doing his best to keep a straight face.

"I could have jumped off Stony Point and died!" Figas tried to sound as indignant as possible.

"Your rite."

The pun was too much for Figas. They both cracked up.

Uncle laughed so hard, tears came to his eyes. He put down his broom and took the basket from Figas. "You sit, nephew. I'll bring tea."

He went into the kitchen and set the two sacred tea bowls on the table. "Crazy youth!" he called out the window. He put the kettle on and washed his tears away in the basin. He was humbled by his nephew's passion. The boy really had gone for broke. He was bursting with pride, but didn't want his emotions to cloud the boy's achievement. After a few minutes, he came out with their usual tea tray.

"You going to drink tea with that mutt in your lap?"

Figas hugged the dog, ignoring his tea. "What happened to Ciao? Did you drug her?"

"Seems fine to me." Uncle took his cup and sipped, hiding his mouth.

"Seriously?"

"Maybe something she ate."

"Are you really going to play it like this? I saw the air rifles by the shed. You must have had help." Until he'd found the canoe tied to the buoy, Figas had been sure the island was invaded. Now he just wanted the truth. "Is it a secret society?"

"Who could-a-figa?" Uncle kept any trace of a smile from his face.

"Enough false cadences, Uncle. Tell me who's in your gang?"

"Nephew, what an imagination you have! Secret societies? Secret passageways? Maybe a magic train that whistles 'woo-woo'!" He could see his nephew was not amused. "What was I saying? Hmm, lost my train of thought."

"Not funny."

He set Ciao on the porch and picked up his tea. He watched her scratch, reaching for that hard-to-get spot in the middle of her back.

Uncle broke the silence. "Where were you last night?" He could see the backside of the young man's fingers were red and swollen.

It was not a big surprise that Uncle wasn't going to come clean. What surprised Figas most was that he didn't care. It was said Master P'O would neither refute nor deny when asked a direct question. Uncle had studied well. "After my little swim, I went to the shrine of P'O. I sat and made tea."

"Is that all?"

Figas took a sip and held his teacup before setting it down. "Just before dawn, I felt like I was climbing a hill spiraling up, around and around. By a beautiful accident, I was already at the center, walking in the opposite direction, my fingertips following a Fibonacci curve that wound outward. I remembered being two years old. I remember my mother's face. I'd forgotten what she looked like. I remembered Cedar. It felt . . . It feels like she's with me."

It was clear Figas was not pretending, nor imagining. There was no intermediary, only tea mind. Uncle was reminded of the great tea masters of the past who were capable of perceiving the world whole. "'If you happen upon yourself, remember what you look like.' Master P'O said that."

Figas nodded. "I never knew stillness was dynamic."

"I need to wash some rice for dinner." Uncle went back into the kitchen and poured fresh water to wash his face. "Crazy youth."

FULL MOON

If there are no spots on a sugar cube then
I've just put a dice in my tea.
—Robert Rankin

The overenergetic Winston was the spring festival's organizer. He was keen to atone for the debacle last year, when he had the idea of James Joyce Day. "Who doesn't love Sunny Jim?" Winston wondered aloud, remembering what a portrait of a disaster it had been. This year would be different.

This year, he began preparations well in advance and signed up twenty volunteers to create a giant papier-mâché full moon. Winston's active imagination and whimsical vision equaled his unceasing ability to get people to say yes when they really meant no. His creative powers were approached only by his crankiness. Everyone loved Winston, and they trusted that everything would work out fine in the end. However, the volunteers, including Father Murray, didn't relish the certainty that their lives wouldn't be their own until the event was over.

The young priest rolled up his sleeves and was soon elbow deep in sticky rice flour and water. He carefully dipped strips of newspaper and applied them over the giant weather balloon Winston had ordered especially for this purpose.

"Vicar, give me a hand!" Zeno, foreman of the tea-picking crew, called out from the dark side of the moon. "Please!" He sounded desperate.

The priest had grown accustomed to being called the vicar. He didn't love it, but he didn't have a great deal of choice in the matter. The more he showed his ire, the more the locals poured it on. He orbited counterclockwise. "Zeno, there's a benga fly on your forehead!"

"Nice try." Zeno knew better than to swat at an imaginary fly, just as the vicar knew better than to get closer to him when his hands were covered in goop.

The young Muslim cleric Ali bin Abu was under a tree by himself, working on a papier-mâché goat. Winston had told him repeatedly that it needed to be a cow, but the Prophet Muhammad had not milked cows. Everyone knew the Prophet took pride in milking his goats. If an animal was indeed going to jump over the moon, it was going to be a goat.

Winston made his rounds, checking on the progress of his team. "It looks like a goat," he said, disappointed.

"That is because it is a goat."

"The cow jumps over the moon." Winston was about to blow a gasket.

"That is ridiculous, if you think about it," the young cleric patiently explained. "Cows don't jump; however, goats have an amazing ability to leap."

"Fine, Ali." Winston threw up his hands. "But I have to tell you—it looks like a piñata!" As he stormed off, he saw Rabbi Morton helping Reverend Betty with her tall silver headdress. He decided to wait behind the wagon float and eavesdrop.

"I would say you are more of a dish," Rabbi Morton suggested.

"God protect you, Morty, if you argue with Winston. He's already going to have a cow over the goat. Besides, what are you saying—that I'm not thin enough to be a spoon?"

"Never."

She was satisfied with his answer. "Have you heard the young girl playing the violin? She's wonderful. Don't worry, nobody is even going to notice the two of us."

"I only volunteered for this because I get to run away with you at the end of the parade."

"Oh, that's so sweet," Betty spooned.

Father Barrett—known as The Italian—approached the parade preparations with a look of half disappointment, half contempt. "If only they'd put a fraction of this energy into saving their souls," he muttered. He saw that Father Murray had a strip of newspaper glued to the back of his black cassock and didn't know it. He wasn't convinced the young man had what it took to be a priest. He hadn't met a young person with any backbone for longer than he cared to remember.

The Italian's moniker was brought to life by his overfondness of form, which Green Islanders found humorous in a spiritual professional. Why did it matter what things looked like, when your business was purported to be with one's soul? It was generally understood that Father Barrett had a heart of paste.

"Out! Kissing the statues, your eminence?" Uncle shouted from behind Father Barrett.

The old priest involuntarily jumped, as if butted by a goat.

Father Murray hid behind the moon, unable to hide his reaction.

Uncle laughed conspicuously.

"Adhibenda est in jocando moderatio," Father Barrett said stiffly. He was tired of Uncle's sense of humor. "One should have moderation in humor."

Uncle was already on his way to admire the full moon. "What was that, your grace?" He cupped his ear and feigned hard of hearing. "Did you say you're a stranger to humor?" Uncle believed the divine was inherent in all things, hidden in the most unlikely of places. So it followed that the divine would be especially inherent in Father Barrett. The fact that the old priest was completely unaware of this made it all the more precious.

Father Barrett reached for composure. His face and neck turned bright red, as if he were choking on a fishbone from Friday's supper.

Many locals were so fond of this shade of crimson against his clerical white collar that they didn't want to miss an opportunity to view it. They went to Mass and stood up during the first reading to ask questions, which provided the desired effect. The most egregious occasion occurred when, against his better judgment, he allowed Zeno and Viggo to do a reading during Christmas Mass. The two youths approached the holy altar with the proper solemnity, and then without any warning, burst into a rap, alternating verses between them.

Viggo turned his face away from the crowd, vogueing like a flamboyant fashion model, while Zeno hit the bridge.

"The postman's name was Yahweh."

"The milkman's name was Zeus."

"Didn't seem to matter what Joseph did . . ."

"Mary was on the loose."

"Don't care what you do with your hot dog."

"Don't care what you do with your roll."

"When you're tellin' stories of the prophets . . ."

"Try and use a little self-control."

"Cha!"

Father Barrett leaped to his feet, adding genius timing to the routine. The congregation erupted into a spontaneous hallelujah. The priest thanked the boys and smiled. Boos followed when the congregation realized Father Barrett intended to halt the performance.

Zeno's surprising baritone matched the rhythm of the dance. Viggo answered in a high falsetto. They completed their choreography, all the way out the side exit. The roof came off.

"Thank you, f-funky Jesus."

"Thank you, thank you."

"Tha-tha-thank you, fa-funky Jesus."

"Tha-thank you, thank you."

After the service, Father Barrett admonished them in private for their lack of morals.

"It was a joke, father." Zeno didn't understand the problem.

"Never disrespect the Virgin Mary. You should be ashamed," he explained.

"Oh, we are Father, believe me."

"Va bene, scusi Monsignor." Uncle interrupted Father Barrett's private Inquisition. "You must forgive Winston and his overzealous vision. Sometimes he gets carried away and creates grand theater he doesn't fully understand. A bit like church in that respect." Uncle's amusements were cut short as he saw his karma speeding toward him. As much as he wanted to hide behind the Italian's black robes, he bravely stood his ground.

"So, there he is. Walking proof that being petty pays off." Auntie Lan completely ignored Father Barrett as she zeroed in on her mark.

"Am I somehow supposed to know what you're talking about?" Uncle said calmly, raising his arms in a gesture of surrender.

"Sending the boy to me with a packed lunch!"

"He told you such a thing?" Uncle was outraged.

"He didn't have to. I'm not dim. I could smell what you call food on his breath before he came through my door. Really, Red! You can be such a child." She dismissed him and walked on.

He hated his childhood nickname. He did his best not to let it show, but she always managed to get under his skin. He had to give her that much: she really was a great teacher.

RARIORA

*Water is the mother of tea, a teapot its
father, and fire the teacher.*
—Chinese proverb

Emma was unaware of the comical figure she struck as she passed two local women. She was tilting so far forward, making a beeline to the library, that the younger of the two yelled in her wake, "Careful the face don't make brake!"

The older woman playfully hit the younger. "Can't you see? She's walking straight into the earth to see her people down there." They stumbled over in laughter.

When she reached a large cemetery that rolled undisturbed down the green hillside, Emma paused. She climbed onto a large rock to catch her breath. Tufts of silver fescue piled itself around the naturally shaped headstones. Moss and lichen covered them. Emma recognized the calm figure of Jizo, who watched over the souls of children when they departed this world early. She was tempted to linger, but it had taken almost two weeks, and a mountain of paperwork, to get access to the island's historical materials. They were archived in the main library, one of the oldest buildings on the island. "First things first," she told herself.

Emma walked briskly past a small white church that had the intimate proportions of a chapel. Halfway down a line of cypress trees, an Asian-inspired roofline merged effortlessly with the windswept landscape. She paused to take in the moss-covered roof.

Newer, repaired tiles mixed with the darker, weathered slates. The curved mosaic of the roof reminded her of traveling through Israel in an air-conditioned bus. On the left side were tall antennae atop skyscrapers, doubtless early warning systems. On the right, she could see caves where people still lived. It was a puzzle in the making for archeologists who would excavate in a millennium. Were they living in the Stone Age or the Nuclear Age?

She realized how much energy it took to sustain the opposites that Es-sahra so eloquently described. Everywhere she went on the island, she experienced the tension between old and new, simple and complex, highly educated and rural poor. It challenged her rational view. The easiest thing to do was to say it was all "rather quaint." How could an isolated culture also be a nexus? Peripheral cultures assimilated knowledge over time from the outside. Here, it seemed, the seeds were brought and left to grow undisturbed. She was here to observe and learn, yet as carefully as she moved, a contaminated amalgamation swirled around her.

She walked under the outstretched eaves of the old library and felt the thick limestone walls. Centuries ago, the settlers had ground coral and brushed on the whitewash paste with a coarse broom. She felt her heart beat under her breath. She was all too aware of her addiction to *rariora*, rare books. In a state of full arousal, she pulled open the thick library door.

The musty odor of old manuscripts filled Emma's nostrils. Stacks of papers were tucked beside volumes of every size. Brimming shelves from floor to ceiling held moldy leather tomes. Sutras written on palm leaves were displayed in a sealed glass cases. Large clay pots alternated with labeled cardboard boxes. Emma stood frozen, her mouth half open.

Miss Anjou, the old librarian, looked up from her desk with her good eye. Her welcoming smile went unnoticed until the two teenage girls giggling in the corner snapped Emma out of her reverie.

"Hello, my name is Emma Carroll. Miss Montri sent me. Here's my paperwork." Emma opened Clutch and unfolded the stamped permits.

"I know. I'm Mrs. Anjou. How may I help you, Miss Carroll?"

Emma paused, unsure of where to begin.

"Are you looking for something in particular?"

Auntie Anjou seemed to have fallen from the heavens. If Emma couldn't trust this sweet librarian, whom could she trust? "Please call me Emma. I'm not sure where to begin. Perhaps you could show me the earliest materials you have."

Auntie Anjou led Emma to a small back room with a round ironwood table. "Make yourself comfortable. I'll bring a couple of items I think you'll find interesting."

Emma sat down and pulled some burrs from her socks. The sticky seeds reminded her of the mobility of ideas in the ancient world. Maybe one of these little hitchhikers had traveled with her from Sicily. Who knew what kind of damage one could wreak on the island if it were to take root?

Auntie Anjou returned with two leather-bound volumes on a metal cart. Wearing soft white gloves, she placed the largest manuscript on the table and opened its worn cover. Emma reached inside Clutch and pulled out her own white gloves. The little bag had just enough room for a small pencil (pens not being allowed near old books), a baby-size hairbrush, a drugstore pair of 3x glasses, and a dual-powered square magnifying glass. The old librarian watched as Emma carefully examined the bookplate on the inside cover. *Ex libris viridi.* Beside the Latin was a red woodblock stamp of Chinese characters. Emma knew the chop was a signature.

"Do you know this character, Auntie?"

"It indicates a bird in a nest. A bird returns to its nest when the sun sets in the West."

"Of course. The hanzi for the direction West." She pulled out her magnifying glass to confirm it was cinnabar paste, not red ink. "And this next character?"

"It combines the radical *plant* with the character *change* to indicate a flower, or blossom."

"Western Blossom. What a beautiful name." In China, Japan, and most Asian countries, Emma knew, a young person had a seal carved for his or her name, to be used in lieu of a signature. On the lower left of the inside cover, a finer blue stamp depicted a shield in combination with an Original cross.

She studied the first few pages, while the old librarian patiently turned the delicate sheets. The vellum had lost its natural oils over the years becoming brittle and powder dry.

"I see you've been around old books," Auntie Anjou said after a short while. "When you're ready, go ahead and turn the next sheet yourself."

"Thank you. I'll be careful."

Auntie watched the young woman closely, carrying out her own research. The old librarian had never seen anyone with such a delicate touch or a better technique for handling old vellum.

"What do you call these little scribbles here on the edges?" Auntie Anjou feigned forgetfulness. Sometimes a researcher had to be sly.

"*Marginalia.* It's often an important key of discovery. Once when I was . . ." Emma caught herself. It was better to stay under the radar. ". . . at our library in Vermont, I found a little note in the margin. Anyway . . ."

"Of course, dear." Auntie Anjou left for a few moments, then returned with a small light.

"An ultraviolet lamp. You read my mind, Auntie."

The older woman turned off the overhead light. The faded ink jumped off the page.

"Do you know what this old text is, Auntie?"

"It's an early book of medicinal plants."

"In several languages." Emma recognized the more obvious scripts.

"Six altogether: Syriac, Greek, Persian, Hindi, Latin, and Berber."

"I believe this is a lacunose copy of a famous work by the medieval scholar al-Idrisi. He is known for his early maps, which often included the flora of the region. He was the greatest geographer of his time. This looks like his *Kitab al-Jami-li-Sifat Ashtat al-Nabatat.*"

"Famous indeed," the old librarian giggled. "It seems to have traveled all the way to Vermont."

Emma's face turned red. She'd been caught in a fib. But she couldn't hide her enthusiasm.

"Auntie, do you have any materials referencing the maritime silk road?"

"I believe that would be a promising approach. Let me see what I can dig up."

"Marco Polo and the overland routes to China get all the attention, but the vast majority of the goods traveled by sea.

"Really?" Auntie Anjou smiled.

WEST MEETS EAST
ANCESTORS

*Steam rises from a cup of tea and we are
wrapped in history, inhaling ancient times
and lands, comfort of ages in our hands.*
—Faith Greenbowl

"What treasures, my lord, do you expect to find in the holy land?"
Having just peeked over a small rise, the sun was on Mason as he
spoke. Pink shards of light illuminated their horses' breath.

"My dear Mason . . ." Thomas Burke chuckled in amusement.
Yet it was a serious question. He doubted what lay ahead would be
pleasant. The farther south they rode to Antioch, the warmer the
days and the cooler the nights.

A man of few words, Mason didn't wait for an answer. He kicked
at the remaining coals from the last evening's fire. He shook out
his blanket and wrapped the patched pot they used to boiled water
and cook soup, and stuffed it into his saddlebag. The rest of the
encampment slowly began to stir. A small band of Norman knights,
crusaders on their way to Jerusalem.

Burke pondered Mason's question while cinching the billet strap
of his saddle with a quick pull before his horse could suck in more air.
His brindled steed, Aristotle, turned his head, acknowledging their
morning game. "My good Mason," he said finally, "what stories have
you been reading? That is the bigger question. By treasures, do you

mean the grail or a lamp with a maji inside?" Burke wondered how long his large companion had kept his question salted away.

Burke swung effortlessly onto Aristotle's back. A graceful middle-aged knight, he had lived most of his mornings like this: sleeping cold on the ground, no breakfast fire, straight into the saddle to warm his limbs. It wasn't his hearth he missed or his modest lands in the Saire Valley, but his collection of books. He always managed to pack a favorite or two; this time he had a work by Pierre Abélard, a man of God who fell in love with Héloïse, and whose pursuit of reason found him few friends. Abélard's summi boni philosophy had piqued Burke's curiosity. "By doubting we come to enquiry, and through enquiry we perceive truth." Abélard's words bore a striking resemblance to Burke's own questions of faith.

"Or do you mean goblets with giant green jewels? Or perhaps tents filled with beautiful maidens, their young faces modestly veiled . . ." Burke continued to add treasure upon treasure. He could see his humor was wasted on Mason. A giant of a man who would rather walk than ride, luckily for his percheron pony, Edda. And walk, gentle Mason could, all through the heat of the day. Walk and think.

"All right, come now." Burke tried to pry more out of his squire. "What mean you by treasure, my good fellow?"

"I couldn't say, my lord."

They went ahead of their companions, a band of two dozen men of arms, for most of whom they felt little regard. Their leader, Gifford of Meulan, was an honorable man in Burke's estimation. The other lords were a different kettle of fish. Two days prior, Lord Ramos had given Burke the Lie—an insult worthy of a challenge.

"Is Lord Burke ashamed to be a soldier of Christ?" Ramos had taunted. It was true Burke wore his regular riding gear, without the red cross of a crusader or the usual penoncel.

"I wear my devotion where it belongs," Burke calmly replied. "In my breast."

This brought forth a few random chuckles, which stung Ramos, causing his eyes to narrow in hate.

Burke would try to steer clear of trouble for a few weeks, at which time they were to meet a large gathering of pilgrims journeying to Outremer, the holy land beyond the sea.

By the time the sun had warmed their hands, Burke felt he understood what his quiet squire was asking. "Is it that you mean to know why we march to Jerusalem?" Burke looked down to his giant friend walking beside his horse.

When the new Pope of Rome, Urban II, declared, "Deus la volt!" the call went out to all able-bodied Christians: it was the will of God that they take back the land of their Savior from the heathen Saracen, the Seljuk Turks. With help from the influential Bernard of Clairvaux, Pope Urban rallied all of Europe to his holy war. It was said farms lay empty from Normandy to Flanders, and all across Germany. Plenary indulgences were granted to the hundreds of thousands of knights who took up the cross to become knights of Christ. Their worldly sins were forgiven as they drew upon the treasury of merit accumulated by Christ's meritorious sacrifice on the cross. Jerusalem had been secured years before, but the road through Antioch was far from safe for any traveler.

"If we knew why, Mason, would we need to go?" Not that Burke had any wish to stay in one place. Though he owned fertile bottomland, he had never enjoyed the working of it. "If I must own a reason, I would say to see where it all began. With each day's ride, the closer we will come to where the world was made, and so in turn be unmade."

His squire looked puzzled.

"New places, Mason. Strange places filled with strange people and new ways, other ways."

"Other ways, my lord?"

"Yes, other ways. To this old fool, new ways are a bit like a treasure. Who knows, perhaps we'll meet the twelfth imam." Burke couldn't help but laugh at his own humor, knowing he'd never be able to explain the complexity of the world beyond the sea. "Good Squire, have I ever told you the tale of al-Mahdi?"

"No, my lord." Something in Mason's voice told Burke that this was not what the big man had on his mind.

"Have you ever killed a man?" Burke knew the answer, but felt he might have hit upon the source of his friend's distress.

Mason shook his head and stood still. "If Christ teaches us peace, why is it we march to war?"

"My dear friend, you've given voice to what we're all asking in our hearts." Burke was often surprised by the agility of the younger man's mind. "A soldier who stops asking that question cannot rightly call himself a man. Yet the Pope's champion, Father Bernard, has promised us that killing a heathen is not murder or homicide, but merely destroying evil. Malacide. Killing is therefore not only permitted, it is justified. Furthermore, our lifetime of sins and the blood on our hands will be washed away. We'll spend eternity in heaven. Don't you believe the words of our Pope and Father Bernard?"

Mason could sense in his lord's voice that he himself neither believed nor respected either of these great men, though to say so aloud would be folly. This led Mason into ever deeper water.

"Rest easy, dear Mason. Don't trouble yourself any further. When it is time to fight, you'll know in your heart what you must do. If you are looking to apply Aristotle's gift of reason, I would say that the world has never been a logical place. I'll wager, by the time the sun sets in the West, this much will remain unchanged."

Mason grunted in a way that put the matter to rest. He could not understand how killing someone, even a Saracen, would place him closer to heaven.

Heathens

A true warrior, like tea, shows his strength in hot water.
—Chinese proverb

Near the reeds of the far river bank, a merganser dipped beneath the surface. Burke watched the surface of the water, guessing where and when she might come up.

Mason rubbed a salve of comfrey on the sore hocks of Aristotle's back legs, where the hot, dry desert had caused sallenders, a lesion of blistered skin, to form.

A predawn attack on their encampment had left their leader, Gifford of Meulan, dead. He had been tending the horses when he called out, "Qui vive!" Six Saracen knights rode down on him and the sleeping encampment. With only his sword, Gifford killed the first knight and cut down the horse of the second. The battle had been brief, leaving three of their company dead, and all six of their attackers.

They dug the deepest grave for Lord Gifford. When their prayers ended, the men-at-arms wanted to know why half a dozen men would attack when outnumbered five to one.

"Only cowards attack men while they sleep." Lord Ramos was always quick to judgment.

Despite their grunts of approval, the men were clearly unsettled. A bitter anguish mingled with bewilderment and grief.

Burke said softly, "Best get used to it." He helped Mason bury the Infidel knights, laying their curved swords across their chests.

The company mounted and continued eastward. Just over the first rise, they came on an encampment. A group of women were folding stripped tents and loading camels. It took the knights only a few moments to realize to whom these women belonged.

Sensing what was about to occur, Burke broke down the hill, Mason and Edda in tow. Then Burke turned Aristotle uphill and faced the company.

"Lords!" he called back to them, "I beg you to listen for a moment!"

"Stand aside, fool!" Lord Ramos demanded. "Would you deny us? This is the camp of the men whom attacked us!"

"I see no men, only defenseless women. And one young boy. Leave them. Take the high road, I pray thee!" Burke knew the best the women could hope for was a quick death.

"I think you mean *heathens?*" Lord Ramos knew what he saw.

Lord Bayeux, Fitz Rou, and the rotund Lord Malet spurred their horses forward, joining Ramos.

Burke turned to Mason and with his eyes gestured for his companion to get on his horse.

Mason shook his head.

"Mason, please remind the gentlemen of the code to which we are all sworn."

The big squire let go of the reins of his horse and stepped closer. For most, it was the first time they had heard the large man speak. His voice boomed across the hillside. "To fear God and maintain the Christian religion."

This sent a roar through the impatient knights, exciting the horses.

"To protect the weak and defenseless." Mason's voice rose over the stamping hoofs. "To live for honor and glory, to fight for the general welfare of all, to respect the honor of women and to refuse no challenge from an equal!"

"Well said, Mason." Burke was proud.

The Spaniard Montero rode forward on his dappled gray with a look of disbelief. "Come now, Burke, do you intend to throw your life away for these faithless heathens?" Montero smiled at the absurdity.

Burke looked toward the women, now huddled together. "Faithless? I think not. Another faith, I'll grant you that."

"I haven't traveled this far to do battle with my kinsmen. I'm for Jerusalem. Those with God-given sense will quit this place." The Spaniard and his three squires rode East.

Ramos broke the silence. "Your allegiances become clear at last, Burke!" he spat. "Go back to your books!"

This caused a derisive laugh from the company. Most found Burke too mild for their taste. They had joked among themselves that the delicate lord had to squat when relieving himself. It was an insult to be challenged by such a dandy.

Burke patted Aristotle's neck. "I promise to quit my books if you will promise to quit your mother's bed."

This provoked sneers and laughter from the company. Ramos grabbed a lance from his squire, and leaned forward for the charge. Burke drew his sword, then quickly nudged his horse to the left. The tip of the lance cut through the air like a whip, passing a few inches from Burke's face. He kicked Aristotle into action, racing up behind Ramos. With the flat of his sword he slapped Ramos on the back of his helm. The big knight careened off his horse and lay still.

Mason ran up quickly and grabbed the lance, tossing it to Burke as he rode by.

"The horse, Mason!"

The big man turned light on his feet and gathered the reins of the black charger.

"Get the horses to the boy there and defend yourself, Mason!"

Fitz Rou raised his lance; his charger reached a gallop in one lunge. Burke knew without a shield he was easy prey. At the last moment, he hurled his lance at Fitz Rou and slid off his saddle to the opposite side of Aristotle, ducking the lightning thrust.

Fitz Rou, sure of his mark, paid no heed of the flying lance. It caught the chainmail around his neck, violently snapping his head to the side. He crumbled to the ground, writhing in agony.

Once the Saracen boy understood what was happening, he ran toward the fighting. He grabbed both reins from Mason and leaped on Edda's back, then raced down the hill with Ramos' black stallion in tow. Burke watched as four women rode across the sand to safety. He turned and spurred Aristotle back up the hill.

Lord Bayeux raced toward Mason. The big man on foot drew his long sword. To the mounted knight, Mason looked like a fat pumpkin, the kind he skewered in practice. He bore down on his prey like a falcon, his razor-sharp talon a second away from tasting flesh. Mason caught the tip of Bayeux's lance with his sword and directed it into the ground. The wooden shaft shattered, catapulting the knight into the air. Mason came on him, slamming the pummel of his sword against the fallen man's temple.

Burke let out a sigh of relief.

Mason gathered the dragging reins of Bayeux's horse. Lord Malet aimed his crossbow and sent a quarrel through the big man's back. Mason dropped on his side.

Burke let out a cry and charged straight into the knights, scattering them like a cloud of black hornets. His sword tore through Malet's chainmail, killing him instantly. Burke fought into the clear, but Aristotle's front leg was shattered. As they tumbled forward, Burke managed to roll free and get to his feet.

The knights were confused, wanting to fight Burke one at a time. Unable to withstand the temptation, two young squires rode straight for him.

Mason rolled on his back, pushing the short arrow through the front of his left shoulder. He grabbed the sharp tip and pulled it through. He swooned, but managed to stumble uphill toward his master.

Burke heard the charging hoofs; he wheeled around, gauging which of his attackers would reach him first.

Mason picked up a rock and hurled it toward the head of the closest stallion.

Burke heard a hollow crack and watched the first mount careen to his left, crushing the young squire's leg. He managed a pass at his other opponent. On the third pass, Burke feigned exhaustion, dropping his sword.

The youthful damoiseau came in close, eager to finish his enemy with a single stroke. Burke lunged, misura stretta, surprising his opponent. He was running for his life before the young man fell from his horse.

Half the remaining knights set upon Burke, the rest held their horses in check and watched.

Malet burst down the hill toward the camp of women.

The Saracen boy leaped on the back of Bayeux's horse. Waving a scimitar, he let out a yelp and rode uphill to meet the knight.

Mason bashed his way through the knights bunched up around Burke, pulling them from their mounts violently to the ground, frantically trying to reach Burke before it was too late.

Burke's right shoulder was cleaved open. The blood running down his arm caused his sword to go slippery in his hands. His left hand rested the sword on the ground between thrusts, giving open invitation. He wasn't able to raise his right arm to wipe the burning sweat from his eyes. His attackers scattered and jostled around him like black carrion crows, squawking and waiting.

Pain shot through his back when Burke tried to turn his head. The black and white sides of the pavilion billowed lazily in yellow light. He thought the sun was rising, but he couldn't tell hot from cold. Perhaps it was evening. The fingers of his left hand felt the impossible smoothness of the sarcenet silk wrapped around him. He was gasping for breath in an attempt to place himself.

"Mason!" His throat burned like salt sand in a wound. "Mason!" he rasped.

Two young women rushed into the tent, their features covered. They held him down. Burke fought to get to his feet. A tall woman entered. With a fierceness he wasn't able to match, she commanded him to stop. A crescent moon pendant hung from a fine chain around her neck. She put her hand against her cheek, like a child sleeping. "Nehm!"

He stared into her eyes and screamed, "Mason!" This sent his whole body into a spasm. He passed out.

When Burke awoke he was firmly swaddled in Arabian silk, unable to move.

Mason had been far too heavy for the women to carry. They pitched a tent around where he fell. He had lost a lot of blood, but his wounds were beginning to close. The women nursed him, squeezing drops of water from a silken cloth. The cool liquid ran between his split lips, down his parched throat.

The women tried to explain to each of the strange men that the other lived. The tall woman with a commanding voice rolled up the side of the tent so Burke could see where Mason lay.

He laughed to see his big friend being spoiled by two nurses. Knowing that Mason still lived was better than any medicine.

The crescent moon pendant tumbled out from the woman's décolletage. Burke looked her in the eyes and thanked her. "Shukran."

"Hisan!" Young Ma'mar galloped with his fingers, enthusiastically acting out the entire story once again. His audience had grown over the weeks as they neared the port city. "My father, al-Ghalib, was killed in battle. But the Infidels fought bravely, ten to one, saving my mother and my father's younger wives. Now we travel to my uncle in Sicily. He will decide our fate. I've asked my mother to release me to serve the Infidels and repay our debt. She says my uncle must decide. My uncle will not want my mother; she is too old and doesn't listen." Ma'mar talked nonstop for an hour, his servant, Musa, leaning over occasionally to fill them in on details they didn't understand.

Mason's eyebrows remained high, unable to grasp how long the boy could go on.

Burke was not so patient. "Mason," he grumbled, "Perhaps we should make quick work of this long-winded fellow!"

Musa wheeled around in disbelief. He appeared ready to strike.

"Calm yourself, Musa. I was merely jesting. You must know how much we appreciate everything we're learning."

"Allāhu Akbar!" Musa shook his head as if recovering from a scare. "Just now, Prince Ma'mar said—"

"Prince?" both men said at once.

"Yes, prince. Did you understand what he said about his mother? She was speaking about you."

The men shook their heads.

"His mother asked Allah, 'How can a man be so excellent with a sword, without knowing which end he is holding?'"

Burke wondered how much of the lady's speech had escaped him. Outside the tent she was like a baby lamb, but inside she ruled with an iron fist.

"I will go with you," Ma'mar said to Burke that evening. "No matter what my uncle decides, a xebec waits for us in Anttalia. You can't stay here. You would both be murdered in your sleep by week's end."

Burke knew the boy was right. They would never be safe anywhere again.

"What is a xebec, my lord?" Mason asked.

"A small and fast sailing ship. We should reach the port city of Anttalia in a few days." Burke explained how the Byzantine emperor, Komnenos, had lost control of the coast three years earlier to Zengi, the feared leader of the Selijuq Turks. The rumors of Zengi attacking Constantinople were becoming more and more believable.

Wearing the long robes of a Muslim trader, Burke and Mason hid their unshaven faces under a keffiyeh. Musa bartered away their horses, keeping only a single camel packed with necessities. He led the two men through the narrow streets of Anttalia into the busy bazaar. The women followed a respectable distance behind.

The xebec was fully loaded, awaiting them beside the bustling pier. Musa greeted the captain and handed him a small bag of gold. When the arrangements had been completed, he waved the company aboard. The women hurried, wanting to be out of sight as quickly as possible.

Burke noticed Mason was hesitant to cross the short gangplank.

"What is it, Mason?"

"My lord, I care not for boats."

"Can you swim?"

"I don't know. You?"

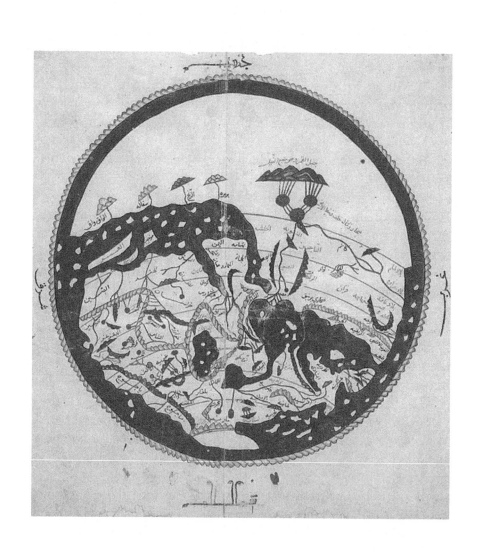

A Hunger for
the Classics

A man without tea in him is incapable of
understanding truth and beauty.
—Okakura Kakuzo

Emma once again forgot to eat breakfast or pack any food for lunch. When she got to the library, all the best tables near window were filled with students cramming for exams. She waved to some older students she was mentoring, and then sat down at a small table in the corner and pulled some documents out of her backpack. Among them was a copy of al-Idrisi's Tabula Rogeriana. Her father had given her this colorful map when she was a child. Al-Idrisi was an important member of King Roger II's court. She compared the map to another document with the sketch of the wax imprint made by the signet ring used to seal the tea chests. The imprint had the same cartographic image. She was getting close. Now she just needed proof.

The morning flew by as Emma read stories about the island's heroes and heroines. Many of these legends took on mythological motifs of their own. It would take time to connect all the threads. She could hear her father's words: "Emma, your argument lacks philological analysis, archeological grounding, and historical context."

That would not deter her. But she did acknowledge the problem. What she really needed to know was whether the ring itself had survived. If it existed, and she could ground it in the historic context of the Song Dynasty, she could publish her findings.

By late afternoon Emma felt she had gone as far as she could in a day. She stuffed her papers back in her pack, slung it and Clutch over her shoulder, and approached the information desk. "Auntie Anjou," she said, "thank you for helping me sort through your wonderful collection. I'm wondering if tomorrow you could show me any remaining materials on the ring of passage?"

"I may be able to dig up some additional references, but I think you've already been through all the relevant material. I assume you've examined the ring itself."

"Excuse me, Auntie? How would I do that?"

If Auntie was surprised, she didn't let on. "It's on permanent display in the shine atop Castorp Hill." She drew a quick map on a scrap of paper. "Lijuan, the Mother of Viridis, is interned there. It's a round building that sits all by itself. You can't miss it. I think you'll appreciate the early Arabic arch. The only window looks down on the old quarter of Salm Bay."

Emma offered to help Auntie reshelve the volumes she had used, but Auntie could see she was practically dancing on her toes, eager to get to the shrine before sunset. "Don't you worry, I will quickly sort this out," Auntie said with a smile. "Off you go."

Emma was lightheaded from not eating all day. She blazed through town and bounded up the steps of the Thumb. Halfway up, she shaded her eyes against the sun, now low in the sky, and looked across the ravine. She caught a glimpse of white through the trees near the top of the opposite ridge. The Shrine of Lijuan. She charged across Teagate's bridge like a newborn colt. Leaning forward in her single-minded purpose, she was oblivious to the herd of goats that trailed in her wake, snatching nibbles from the loose beadwork on Clutch's underbelly.

The herd followed as she opened the gate to the shrine and entered the well-kept grounds that surrounded the circular shrine. The limestone paste near its foundation had crumbled over time, exposing tightly fitted stones. She had never seen a building like it. The arches reminded her of a block print of the Timurid Gardens of Persia. The floor was a mosaic of black and white pebbles set carefully on edge, creating an inward spiral. A shaft of golden light shone through a leaded window, illuminating the chamber. In the center was a round table. On it a tiny object glittered.

Hooves clacked across the dimpled floor, echoing into the high arches. As Emma watched in horror, a white nanny reached with outstretched lips, nibbled at the object, then quickly swallowed.

"No!" Emma screamed, startling the goats. They bolted for the door, knocking her over. Clutch slid off her shoulder as she landed against the stone floor. Encumbered by the heavy pack still strapped on her back, she crawled forward in a vain attempt to catch the white goat.

"Stop!" she screamed.

But it was too late. The goats were gone. As she pulled herself together, she remembered Es-sahra. She would know what to do.

Half an hour later, Emma pounded on Es-sahra's door. "Auntie! Auntie!"

"Child, what's happened?" The old woman frowned as she squinted into the light. "Come in and sit down."

"There isn't time. We have to hurry!"

"Is someone hurt?"

"Yes! I mean no! We have to get to the temple. Please, Auntie!"

"The temple? Child, come in and tell Auntie what has happened."

The old woman's firm tone helped Emma calm down. She stepped into the dimly lit room and sat at the table. "I went to the Shrine of Lijuan," she began, "to see her ring."

"Her ring?"

"Yes, and a herd of wild goats broke in . . ."

"Goats?"

"Yes, a white goat . . ."

"All right, listen to me. Everything will be fine. Sit here and be still. I'll be back in a few minutes."

Es-sahra went outside and struck the bell hanging from the corner eave with a wooden mallet. She repeated her pattern slowly three times. When she turned around, Uncle Sun was standing by her front gate.

"You!" She let a puff of air in disgust. "You should be ashamed of yourself!" she whispered in a shout.

"Calm yourself. There's no need for all this. I've merely arranged to have tea with you and your young friend."

"Do you know how upset the poor girl is?"

"Good, then perhaps we'll enjoy a little sweet truth with our tea."

SICILY

*The best quality tea must have creases like the leathern
boot of Tartar horsemen, curl like the dewlap of a
mighty bullock, unfold like a mist rising out of a
ravine, gleam like a lake touched by a zephyr, and be
wet and soft like a fine earth newly swept by rain.*
—Lu Yu

A harbor pilot boarded the xebec and eased her gently into
the crowded port of Cefalú. Mason and Ma'mar leaned over the
curved leeward rail and stared into the turquoise water as the ship
glided slowly to her moorings. News of their arrival had traveled
quickly. A ship of war had met them the night before, off the coast
of Marsala. They had sailed the longer southern route to avoid the
treacherous Strait of Messina, the ancient Charybdis of Jason and
Odysseus.

The ammirratus ammiratorum, George of Antioch, had sent the
naval escort. Prince Ma'mar's uncle, bin Omar al-Fajri, was a kaid,
a high Palatine official, so it was only fitting they should receive an
official welcome.

Burke watched Mason's eyes grow in size as they entered the
harbor. Prince Ma'mar joined them by the rail and explained that
only Cordoba, the capital of Moorish Iberia, rivaled al-Madina in
size and wealth.

Mason could not imagine a larger place; it went on for as far as
the eye could see.

"Have you been to Sicily before, Prince?" Burke asked.

"As a child. My uncle lives in the upper city, just inside the east gate. The people call it the Kalsa."

A royal invitation soon reached the captain. He was ordered to deliver the widow of al-Ghalib; her son, the prince; and the Norman knight to the city gates in two hours time. An honorary escort would ensure safe passage to the Zisa, King Roger II's palace.

"Captain, may my squire accompany me?"

"Certainly to the gates of the Zisa. Beyond that I cannot say. What I do know is that the king's invitation is a command."

Two hours came and went, and the widow failed to appear on deck. The captain was in a rage. He knew his very life depended on delivering his charges. He knocked on the cabin door and implored the lady to hurry.

A short while later, the widow emerged in a black burqa. In his spotless black jerkin, Ma'mar looked every bit a prince. Burke and Mason wore borrowed tunics.

Fearing his head on a spike, the captain ordered his crew to pull for shore double-time.

The royal guards waiting at the city portal were all a head taller than Burke and wore their hair long over their shoulders. As the party moved toward the palace, two knights took the lead, wielding short spears to clear the way. Mason was amazed by the variety of people they passed. Men with long beards smoked hookahs and watched them from under open arches. Every window seemed filled with onlookers. The narrow lanes were chock-full of citizens vying for a glimpse of the famous strangers. Just inside the high walls they passed a mosque with a blue dome.

They halted at the entrance to the Zisa. A court eunuch appeared from behind an embroidered curtain and ushered them into the outer courtyard. There, a royal official addressed them in no uncertain terms, instructing them on etiquette and court protocol. The widow al-Ghalib and the prince were to have an audience with the king. Lord Burke would be called in due time. They were to keep their gaze toward the floor, to not speak unless directly addressed and to bow when others bowed.

"My squire will accompany me," Burke informed the official.

The eunuch made a quick gesture, snapping the guards to attention. "You are about to enter the court of King Roger II, by his royal invitation. Do you comprehend?"

The widow gave Burke a look that could have withered men to stone. She had not saved his life to watch him cast it away at the first opportunity.

Burke looked back at her and then to Mason, lifting an eyebrow. His meaning was clear: had not this lowly squire fought and killed to save her life?

The widow spoke to the court attendant, using the same voice Burke heard when they first met. The eunuch disappeared behind the curtain.

Burke was impressed that Ma'mar knew better than to speak. That could not have been easy for him.

After what seemed a small age, the eunuch returned and gestured for them all to follow him. He reminded them to keep their gaze lowered.

The palace's name derived from the Arabic *al-aziz*, meaning splendor. When they entered, they understood why.

"Hold your head up, Mason," Burke said for any to hear. "You're a man among men now, nothing more and nothing less."

Mason, having taken the words of the eunuch to heart, never raised his eyes higher than the ankles of the knight who preceded him. Only, after many twists and turns, when they finally stood before Roger the King, could he no longer resist temptation. In addition to the full court of lords, the lavish hall was packed with onlookers. One and all had come to see the Christian hero who had fought his own kinsmen to save the honor of al-Ghalib's five wives.

The king was smiling, perplexed as to why these famous strangers had no manners. Formal introductions were made, lasting longer than was comfortable for those not used to such things. Then Roger whispered to an attendant for the hall to be cleared. It wouldn't do for these foreigners do further harm to their social standing by displaying their lack of manners. Roger was almost in the humor to give the headstrong widow to this raven-haired knight.

Ma'mar and his mother remained silent, their gaze to the floor. Burke found the situation interesting, but he wasn't looking to curry favor. If he was to be paraded about and ogled, at least he could share the glory with his faithful squire. He looked into the king's eyes.

"Have you been in court before, Lord Burke?" the king asked.

"No, your majesty."

"One thought perhaps not."

The king made the new arrivals his personal guests of the palace. Burke and Mason were shown to luxurious chambers, a sharp contrast from sleeping on the ground.

The following morning, a handsome, well-traveled knight introduced himself. "I welcome you to our humble kingdom. I am Lord Berengar, at your service." The blue-eyed knight bowed low. "I trust you've been treated well."

"In truth, the king's invitation lacked a certain courtesy."

"How so, Lord Burke?"

"I'm not inclined to be paraded around like a piece of meat on a stick."

Berengar burst into laughter and slapped his new companion on the back. This new fellow had pluck. "Am I to know to what you refer?" He acted slow of cognition.

"To whit, Lord Berengar. Who were all those lining the streets upon our arrival?"

"News of your exploits reached al-Madina three weeks ago. In the present political climate, you're a godsend to Roger. He hasn't built an empire without knowing how to use what comes his way."

"Berengar, be plain. Of what possible use are we to your king?"

The knight explained that Roger had successfully supported Anacletus as Pope against the illegally elected Innocent. As a reward, Anacletus made Roger king on Christmas day. But the meddlesome Bernard of Clairvaux, Innocent's staunch supporter, used his influence to raise a coalition, calling Roger a half-heathen king. At the same time, Roger's brother-in-law, Ranulf, launched his own rebellion. Berengar threw up his hands. "For ten years we've fought in Apulia against that snake Ranulf."

"I heard Roger had Ranulf dug up after his death and thrown in a ditch."

"He deserved worse. After Anacletus's death, Innocent was made Pope. Now, once again, farms and villages are empty across Europe. With the help of his hack, Bernard, Innocent has convinced hundreds of thousands of simpleminded souls to free the Holy Land from the Muslim Turks, promising all their worldly sins will be washed away in blood of nonbelievers."

"You don't believe it within the Pope's power to grant indulgences?"

"Hah! I believe I'll burn in hell for the things I have done." He laughed. "I accept it as inevitable. But make no mistake: my king prefers the wisdom of Plato and Socrates to Bernard's false promises."

"King Roger is a well-read man?"

"I believe him to be at once a soldier, a skilled statesman, and a man of culture who prizes knowledge above all things. If you're curious, I'll arrange a visit to the royal library."

"If that will elucidate why your king is making a pawn of me."

"I promise, I've not forgotten your query." Berengar liked this newcomer well. "Rumor has it, Lord Burke, you have a love of books."

"If I didn't know better, Berengar, I would say the king sent you to bring me into the fold."

The following day, Burke and Berengar made their way to the royal library. Burke learned that Berengar was a member of the familia regis and was well paid as a loyal member of the king's military household.

Burke was curious. "May I ask you why you serve your king?"

"I came here as a youth, with nothing but a horse and saddle."

"And now you are a lord."

"Roger does not stint in his use of the treasury. I won't lie to you, Burke, the work suits me well."

"You enjoy fighting?"

"Compared with boot making, clearing land, or milking sheep? Then, yes. I ride out every few months and do a bit of this or that. Scoundrels abound everywhere, as you well know. I can honestly say I love my king, and he is fair by any measure. He could have run every heathen out of his kingdom years ago, but he makes room for everyone. You mention the people you saw in the streets. Have you ever seen Catholics, Jews, Muslims, Lombards, Black Berbers—shall I go on—all living and working together? Roger cares not which god you fear or which language you speak."

"Yesterday I witnessed your king speaking to my Muslim companions in their own tongue. I saw how they revered him. I'm not a complete fool, Berengar. I do have eyes in my head." Burke knew there was more to the situation than the king's man was willing to reveal. He also knew what would be required if he chose to stay. "I swore my fealty to Lord Gifford, who is now dead. I killed his successor, Duke Ramos, a few hours after we buried Gifford. In the blink of an eye, I found myself here, and if I'm not mistaken, used for political gain. If I'd known in my youth, that I would someday be fighting my own brethren, I would have stayed home and milked my goats."

The two stood in silence. "Look, Berengar, Ramos was no angel, but many of the men I've killed were but children." Burke trailed off, his voice started to give way.

Berengar caught Burke's shoulder and held it firmly as he looked into his eyes. "Speak no more of it. I, too, have had my fill of killing well-meaning youths."

In silence, the two proceeded to the library. They walked under graceful arches that held the cool morning air into the afternoon. A porter crossed the hot stone courtyard and met them by the front entrance. He led them down a mosaic-tiled corridor and through the doors of the library. Burke admired how leaded glass windows lit the massive chamber. Filled to its high ceilings were scrolls and books of every size and variety. Berengar introduced Burke to the curator, a small Jewish man in black robes. Ben Zoma guided them through the king's collections. Byzantine and classical Greek works filled an entire wing. Scribes dipped cut quills into pewter inkwells—so focused on their work, the newcomers went completely unnoticed. The sound of quills scratching parchment filled the near silence. The feeling of energy all about them reminded Burke of the preparations before battle.

On Burke's subsequent visit to the royal library, Berengar introduced him to the master cartographer al-Idrisi. Born in Ceuta, he had traveled throughout northern Africa and Europe, until Roger II had made him an offer he could not refuse.

That afternoon, al-Idrisi was interviewing a famous emir who had just returned from China. Many years before, the king had promoted Captain al-Waddu to emir for taking seventy galleys and attacking the Byzantines, then sacking Athens. He ravaged the Ionian coast as far south as Thebes, pillaging the silk factories there. In a brilliant move, al-Waddu brought the Jewish silk weavers back to Palermo, where they set up shop and began the Sicilian silk trade. The emir was now forming another expedition to China. The rich and influential merchant al-Isa-Mussa was trusting him to deliver a special Venetian murrine glass, unlike any other in existence, said to be worth twenty ships filled with silk.

The emir reasoned the safest way to travel with such a precious cargo would be to treat it as though it were of little value. He knew the greater the guard he placed around it, the more attention it would draw. The only hope to outnumber an army was to send an army. What he needed was a few good fighters, and none were fiercer than the Norman knights in Roger's pay.

Burke's eyes lit up as the emir talked of monsoon winds, incensed palms and exotic spices. Al-Idrisi soaked in every detail of the emir's description of the East, laughing with delight.

Later that evening, Burke approached Mason with his idea.

"New ways and new places, my lord?" Mason asked.

"Just so, my friend. Just so."

Mason understood that meant they could never return home. But much as he enjoyed Sicily, he doubted it would ever feel like home. After a long silence he answered. "Perhaps, my lord, we should learn to swim if we are to sail to the other side of the world."

"Ever the pragmatist, good Mason."

To select his crew, the emir used the ruse of a tournament. Blunt blades would be used in combat. To the winner would go a special ring. The king's silver ring would grant safe passage to the one who wore it.

Despite precautions, it wasn't uncommon for men to die during such combat. Pope Innocent had recently denounced the tournament and forbade Christian burial for those killed while taking part. Yet hundreds of the best fighting men arrived from all corners of the kingdom to answer the emir's call.

Burke watched the first few days of fighting, studying his opponents. He instructed Mason and pointed out the different fighting styles of each knight, his weaknesses, and how they might best be exploited. He advised his squire to be ready.

On the final day of the tournament, Burke entered the melee. This caused a small uproar with the competitors who had already won several contests. They brought their objections straight to Burke en masse.

The largest pushed Burke in the chest.

"As you wish, gentleman." Burke bowed and drew his sword. He was on all twelve of them before they could respond. Two swords quickly hit the stone pavers, by rule eliminating the contestants. Mason should have guessed his lord would not think it fair to fight them one at a time. The big squire reached into the fray and knocked two men's heads together, crumbling the knights to the ground. A third knight turned on Mason with a long knife.

Lord Berengar, who had been watching closely, jumped forth and placed his sword gently across the attacker's neck. "It isn't polite to challenge an unarmed man. Hand the gentleman your sword and apologize."

When the knight had handed Mason his sword, Berengar pommeled the side of the rude contestant's head. Mason used the sword to bash his way through three fighters until he was alongside Burke.

"Are you after the ring as well, Mason?" Burke bated his faithful friend.

This incensed the big man. He swatted a knight to the ground with the flat edge of his sword. Burke had made a clean touch on several of the knights, but they had kept fighting. The judges tried to intervene, but the emir held up his hand, curious about the outcome. When Burke's left forearm was laid open, he set to work dealing out his own real punishment. The two companions fought back to back. Berengar quietly took out a few challengers, without entering the main fray.

With each lunge, Burke made an attacker pay. Soon it was down to a reasonable five on two. Burke went on the offensive. Two more knights stepped away, until it was Burke and Mason against three of the king's royal guard. Burke slashed open an opponent's right forearm, causing him to drop his sword. The remaining fighters circled each other, as the growing crowd pressed in, cheering hysterically. Mason's opponent managed to stick him in his ribs, but Mason trapped his attacker' sword, breaking it off near the hilt. When his opponent reached for his knife, the big squire landed a blow. Berengar drew his sword and stood beside Mason. None among the fighters had been interested in challenging Berengar.

"Your fellow has rye in his wrist," Berengar boasted to Mason.

Burke and the last remaining fighter circled one another, exhausted, each studying the other's footwork, searching for a weakness.

"I like your German style very much," Burke complimented his opponent. The large blond knight moved like a cat.

"My father's influence," the young fellow volunteered, trying to catch his breath.

"He taught you well. What was his name?" Burke switched his sword to his left hand, gauging the strength of his grip.

"Ulrich of Luppia."

"Hans Ulrich?"

"Yes, did you know my father?" The German's rubicund complexion flushed a deeper red.

"Well enough to still be alive," Burke admitted.

The two men laughed and lowered their swords. Mason and Berengar came in close to make sure the contest was over.

"What's your name, son of Ulrich?"

"Hans."

"Of course. I'm Burke, and this is my squire, Mason."

The two knights embraced. Berengar gave Ulrich a long look before disappearing into the crowd.

The judge of the tournament invited the three men to stand on the platform. They held up their arms with effort, and were declared the winners. They were led through the cheering crowd to a nearby private chamber, where al-Isa-Musa awaited them.

BRIDGET

*There is no trouble so great or grave that cannot
be much diminished by a nice cup of tea.*
—Bernard-Paul Heroux

If Emma was surprised to see Uncle Sun join them, she didn't let on. Without touching her tea, she leaned forward in her chair, anxious to relate her story to Auntie Es-sahra. "As I was saying," she began, "the white goat snatched the ring—"

"Was it a nanny or a billy goat?" Uncle interrupted.

Emma glared at him. "Does it matter?"

"Of course it matters." Uncle refused to be any clearer. "These are finely trained animals," he muttered.

Emma was beside herself. The old immigration agent should stick to his visa business and stop meddling in matters he knew nothing about. She stood up and turned her back on Uncle. "Auntie, please! We must hurry if we're going to save the ring. We can drink tea later." She made for the door.

But Es-sahra didn't follow. She stood and opened the window to let some fresh air into the little room. While her attention was elsewhere, Uncle reached for a chocolate kiss. She wheeled around and swatted his hand away. "Emma, sit down. Trust me, talking is the most important thing we can do right now."

Emma stood in the doorway. She knew of no reason to distrust Auntie. "You must know," she said reluctantly, "that Lijuan's ring was given to Thomas Burke by King Roger II of Sicily. It is almost a thousand years old."

"Yes, we know, dear." Es-sahra was not enjoying being a part of this. "Tell us why the ring is so important to you."

"The ring is an important part of your history."

Uncle set down his cup. It was clear the young lady had no intention of revealing anything personal about herself. "Miss Carroll, why did you go to the temple today?"

"To see the ring. Obviously."

"Why?"

"You want to know my motivation?"

"Yes, yes, very good."

The two faced off in silence for a moment. Emma could see he was not about to back down. "All right, Dr. Sun. A friend sent me an article last January about your Sighing Woman Tea and the mystery of the Sigh. There was a close-up of a tea chest. I noticed the Tabula Rogeriana imprinted on the red wax seal. Having grown up with a copy of this map in my room, I had to come here and make the connection. I sold my car and bought a one-way ticket to Canton. I landed a job crewing on the *Angel's Trumpet*. I want to discover how the ring with al-Idrisi's forgotten map came to be on the other side of the world. You see," she said, warming to the subject in spite of herself, "there's a growing acceptance within academia that Roger's court of Arab scholars planted the seeds that blossomed into the Renaissance two centuries later. His kingdom was tolerant of every faith and race. He refused to take part in the madness of the crusades."

"History is fascinating," Uncle agreed. He was trying to be patient and let her follow the brush.

"The crusades robbed the Middle East, destroyed their universities, and collapsed their culture. The crusaders brought their knowledge back to Europe and claimed to have created it themselves. We live in a world today where many Muslims are unaware that the basis of modern medicine originated in the Middle East, along with algebra and the scientific method. Do you think the domes of Europe could have been built without the knowledge--"

"It's not that I don't appreciate the insights into your personal Weltanschauung, I do. But what does this have to do with you being on Green Island?" Uncle was finding it impossible to circumvent the young woman's defenses.

"I don't remember needing your approval to lead my life." Emma's voice was full of contempt.

"Indeed. I couldn't agree more. However, Miss Carroll, may I remind you that you're here on a visitor's visa," Uncle stated without emphasis as he pulled a copy of her paperwork from his shoulder bag. "I see you've written *tourist* on your application."

"So?"

Uncle took a minute. "So, you lied."

A sense of discomfort filled the small room. Emma noticed Es-sahra wouldn't meet her eye. Yet she felt as if she were seated under the old woman's microscope. What didn't these people know about her? Truly, the chances of getting the ring back seemed to be dwindling by the moment. Emma held back a sob. "Can I continue my research?" she pleaded. "Will you let me stay?"

"As the immigration agent, I'm the one who's asking the questions." Uncle made his voice growl. "The only reason we're here is that you told your friend Es-sahra what happened. If you'd done anything else, we wouldn't be having this conversation."

"It feels more like an interrogation than a conversation." Emma took a chocolate kiss from the bowl, unwrapped it, and popped it into her mouth. So much for cutting back on chocolate.

"Reveal the real reason you're here. Then maybe we can salvage trust." Uncle successfully reached for a chocolate. Es-sahra gave him a bitter stare.

Emma looked from one elder to the other. Both were waiting for her reply. "My father was African. He was born in Ceuta, Morocco."

Uncle found it curious she would say Morocco, not Spain. Was he about to catch her in more lies?

"Al-Idrisi was also born in Ceuta, and like my father had a great pride in being African. My father had a passion for cartography and published several influential papers on al-Idrisi. My mother was French. We lived in Lyon until I was ten. When my mother died, we moved to England. My father worked very hard, eventually earning a chair at St. Edmund Hall, Oxford. In his last year there, he published a controversial paper connecting medieval Norman knights to the Arab spice trade. He claimed Europeans reached China in the twelfth century, a hundred years before Marco Polo. As a result, my father was ridiculed by his peers and forced out of the college. He never fully recovered. His health failed that summer. What you have to understand is that Thomas Burke's ring, along with other evidence in your historical archives, supports my father's theory."

"How old were you when your father left Oxford?" Es-sahra asked.

"Thirteen. He taught me how to do research. It's what we did together. Now, Dr. Sun, please help me find that goat!" Emma dropped her head into her lap and sobbed like a baby.

"No need, my dear." Uncle reached into his pocket and took out a handkerchief and gave it to Emma. While she blew her nose, he dug into his shoulder bag and produced a small purple pouch. He untied the small string. "Hold out your hand, Emma."

The heavy silver ring bounced into her palm.

Her blurry eyes tried to focus. The ring's worn face was almost completely smooth. Only a hint of the original design remained. "My god!" Emma was incredulous. "Thomas Burke's ring?"

"We've used a copy signet ring to imprint the wax for generations," Uncle explained.

"But I don't understand. What did the goat eat?"

"Oh yes, a piece of chewing gum in a foil wrapper curled once around my finger." Uncle slipped the silver ring onto Emma's finger. "You can see Thomas Burke's hand must have been small."

Speechless, Emma stared at her finger.

"I do apologize," Uncle continued. "You've no idea how many people come here as tourists each year and search high and low for the secret of the tea, or some such nonsense. I won't go into all the trouble it's caused us. Suffice to say, we have suffered from our naïveté. Our little white nanny—your friend Bridget—has eaten her fair share of secrets." Uncle's giggle started to leak out. "We work hard to keep the old culture of Viridis alive and intact." He was starting to feel guilty for playing the heavy to such a smart young woman. "You, my dear, have been quite the challenge. I'm still not sure what to do with you."

"But you'll let me stay?"

"I don't see why not."

"So, you trust me then?"

"Do you trust me?" Uncle winked.

They finished their tea. "I'm sorry for all the fuss." Emma put the ring back in the purple bag, tied the string and handed it to Uncle.

"Thank you for sharing this with me, Dr. Sun. Thank you for tea, Auntie. I hope to see you again soon."

"You're always welcome." Es-sahra hugged her young friend and walked her out. She came back inside and gave Uncle a cold look.

Uncle had his face in his hands. He was exhausted. "I don't understand that girl."

"You're a lifelong bachelor?"

"Yes. So?"

"So you don't understand *any* woman." Es-sahra cleared the table, giving Uncle the clue it was time to leave.

"Thanks for the tea." He bowed, opened the door, and started for home.

Es-sahra called after him, "Why did you change your mind and show her the ring?"

"Who said I changed my mind?"

THE CRESCENT MOON

Although my neighbors are all barbarians and you, you are a
thousands miles away, there are always two cups on my table.
—Anonymous, Tang Dynasty

"You have all three acquitted yourselves well." Al-Isa-Musa
invited the competitors to sit. The emir joined them and went to work
laying out his proposition. They were invited to sail with him around
the world to China. Upon their return they would be rewarded with
fifty silver ducats and thirty gold taris.

"I'm sworn to guard the king, but I thank you for your offer."
Ulrich stood to leave.

"Please sit, Lord Ulrich. I have permission from the king." The
emir signaled to a squire, who brought in a small box. "Here is the
Ring of Passage. There was to be only one champion, but you've
forced my hand." He took the silver ring from the wooden box and
set it on the table. It was etched with al-Idrisi's terrestrial planisphere.

"Clearly Lord Burke is the winner," Hans Ulrich declared.

"Nonsense, Ulrich." Burke smiled.

The emir slid the large gold ring off his own finger and set it next
to the silver one. "This gold ring was given to me by Roger upon my
return from Thebes."

"Ring or no ring, I stay and guard my king," Ulrich repeated.

"Ulrich, son of Ulrich, here is my gold ring. Take it and serve
your king well." He bowed to let the young man know he respected
his decision.

Ulrich bid his farewell.

The emir turned to the dark-eyed Norman. "And you, Lord Burke, do you and your squire travel with me to China?"

"Ring or no ring."

"I have your word?"

Burke knelt before the emir and swore his fealty. The emir took Burke's left hand and slipped on the silver ring.

Preparations were quietly set in motion for their expedition. Al-Idrisi instructed Burke to take detailed notes of their voyage, especially the Pearl River Delta, once they reached China. They were to sail in two days' time on the early morning tide.

Ma'mar and Musa found Burke packing up the books he had collected with the help of Ben Zoma during his time in al-Madina.

"I have good news," Ma'mar said. "My uncle has released me into your service. I am to sail with you day after tomorrow, if you agree."

"Keep your voice down. Do not speak aloud of the emir's plans."

"The emir promised that if you agreed, I could accompany you." An awkward silence followed. "So, may I come, my lord?" Ma'mar dropped to one knee.

Burke watched the young man for some time before speaking.

"If the emir has granted permission, I could do no better than to have you and Mason as my companions. Stand up." Burke helped the prince to his feet. "And tell me, how is your mother?"

"She is well, my lord."

"And well taken care of?" Burke could tell from Ma'mar's face that the boy did not wish to answer.

"She is well, my lord," he repeated.

"Tell her I wish to see her this evening. Please arrange it."

Ma'mar returned just after the midnight bells of Matins.

"If you are ready, my mother will receive you at her residence."

Burke followed the boy through the maze of streets, past the southern gates of the palace and into the Kalsa. The boy halted in a narrow alley by a low doorway.

"Thank you, Ma'mar. It's late. Get some rest. I can find my way back."

"Yes, my lord."

Inside the small, sparsely furnished room, an oil lamp burned on a low table. Burke recognized the black and red silk cushions. He sat and leaned over to smell the camel rug.

The widow entered quietly, dressed in black, her hair modestly covered. Burke wondered if she were now poor, or if these few familiar belongings were what she valued most.

She sat keeping her eyes on the floor.

Where was the fierce woman Burke had met a month before? He had come to say goodbye and thank her for saving his life. But most of all, to ask her something he felt shame for not knowing.

"Masaa el kheel." He wished her good evening though it was now early morning, but he wanted to show her he had learned some small bit of Arabic since they'd last met.

She welcomed him.

And he asked how she was.

"I am well," she told him.

Clearly she wasn't. But he was in no position to challenge her. Instead, he asked the question he had come to ask her: "Maa 'ismik?"

She looked at the floor. "Na'ila."

He bowed deeply, then continued in French, thanking her for saving his life and that of his dearest friend, Mason. He promised he would take good care of her son. He trusted she understood his meaning. He stood and bid her farewell: "Ma'a as-salamah."

Na'ila looked down and wept, softly at first, then violently.

Burke hesitated, hating himself for coming, and even more for his inability to come to her aid. He tried to exchange the anguish he felt for thoughts or words. His right hand gripped the hilt of his sword. He slashed about in his mind at moving shadows. "Shukran, Na'ila."

"Wait." She removed the crescent moon pendant from her neck and placed it in his hand, touching him for a brief instant.

After sunrise, Burke questioned Ma'mar. Na'ila's husband, he learned, had died a martyr. By rights, his widow should have inherited his estate and been able to remarry in a few months. However, her reputation had suffered irreparable damage. She would receive nothing. When Burke inquired about the nature of her misdeeds, he received no adequate reply from the young man.

He went then to Lord Berengar and begged to learn about the nature of the lady's predicament. The knight explained that the widow had evidently spent time alone in her tent with a heathen. Burke was confused, until he realized who the heathen was.

Why had Na'ila and Ma'mar come back that day, after riding away to safety? He felt shame for never asking her. If she had left Mason and him to die, she would now be untarnished. Instead, she was forever between worlds.

Burke found Ma'mar and admonished him for not being forthcoming about his mother's situation.

The youth replied that women were in charge of the home. Outside the home was the world of men.

Just after the bell for Lauds, the hour of prayer between midnight and dawn, Burke and Mason headed for the ship. Dogs barked as they wove their way through the starlit streets. They found the emir striding across the deck, his hands on his hips, stepping over coiled lines. He was giving commands in an uncharacteristic soft voice.

The crew went about their work with practiced skill. In a short while, they quietly warped out of the harbor, as the silhouette of al-Madina quietly blended into the dark mass of land behind them.

Burke and Mason watched the coast fade into clouds on the horizon. The open water filled their hearts.

Ma'mar and Musa joined them. "We wish to know," the prince said, "what precious treasure we carry that we must sneak away in the middle of the night?"

"It is indeed a secret." Burke spoke in a tone that no man would mistake. "We have aboard a great lady and her four attendants. She is to be married to a wealthy raja in the East. It is our duty to protect her with our lives. You must swear to speak of this to no one. Our very lives depend upon your discretion. Do you swear?"

"Of course, we swear." They bowed on their knees.

Burke and the emir had invented the story out of necessity to conceal the value of their cargo. The seven wooden crates filled with Venetian murrine glass were said to be the dowry of the lady. Although pirates were always on his mind, the emir was most concerned with the desert crossing. He hoped their small caravan would blend with the multitudes traveling toward Mecca in the months leading to the Hajj.

Dawn found scarcely a cloud on the horizon and a favorable breeze. Five women in black emerged from their cabin below, needing fresh air. When recognition began to sweep over Ma'mar's face, Burke swiftly stepped to his side. His strong grip dug into the boy's shoulder as he whispered to remind him of his oath. Burke could see the anger in the boy's face, but managed to keep any hint of a smile from his own. He should have told the boy. He felt Ma'mar deserved the chance to say farewell to his mother, if only symbolically.

"Treat the ladies with respect. Lower your eyes!" He said to the boy in a harsh voice so the whole crew could hear. He then tapped Ma'mar on the shoulder and winked.

Burke had explained to the emir the nature of the debt he carried concerning the widow. The emir had been quick to turn the situation to their advantage. Over time the boy would come to understand.

TRAVELS

Each cup of tea represents an imaginary voyage.
—Catherine Douzel

They crossed the southern Mediterranean, with fair winds and calm seas, finally sighting Pharos, the lighthouse at Alexandria. Since it was just after midnight, they set anchor and waited till morning for the harbor pilot. The following afternoon, they docked beside a river barge. Before transferring their goods, the custom agent came aboard to inspect their cargo. The emir negotiated a fixed market price and paid in gold the levy tax for passing through this part of the caliphate.

Burke and Mason, once crusaders, found themselves joining a different set of holy pilgrims. Now, rather than fight their fellow man, they would battle the wind and sea. For Burke, it was a welcome change. Under the green banner of the caliphate of Fatimid, they sailed upriver to Cairo and then on to Aswan, where they joined the barley caravans bringing food to the holy cities. After two weeks of beating against a sweltering wind and a strengthening current, they traded the muddy Nile for the clean sands of the open desert. Burke rode on a Sabino stallion beside Musa and practiced his Arabic. Mason, on a white Arabian mare, was their rear guard as they moved ever farther from Jerusalem and closer to Mecca. The early morning attack and loss of Lord Gifford was still fresh in Mason's mind; he rode without speaking, frequently looking over his shoulder for signs of danger.

On the first evening of their desert camp, Burke admitted the heat was affecting his eyesight. He saw all manner of things in the waves of heat rising off the baking sand.

Mason broke his silence. "If one covered an egg with this sand it would be ready to eat the next morning."

The emir drank a small coffee and recited a poem to his companions, as he liked to do before they set out each day. In this one, Tarafa compared the slow movement of the litters that carried women across the desert to that of ships at sea.

Na'ila sat with the other women, hiding her distaste. She had never before traveled in a litter and would have preferred to ride on horseback. But the emir insisted. Every man's eyes were fixed on the curtains of the litter, trying to catch sight of the lovely creatures who inhabited the silk interior. The crates of priceless glass, packed tightly in straw, were carried by seven camels, and went completely unnoticed.

Despite the emir's concern of a desert raid, the company reached the tiny port of Ayhab on the Red Sea, without incident, on the twentieth day. Waiting in the small harbor was a well-fitted ship with a shallow keel, ready to carry them through the crystal-clear waters to Jeddah. A two-day sail brought them to the largest port of the Fatimid caliphate, which enjoyed diplomatic ties throughout the Indian Ocean, extending all the way to China.

Every day, thousands of pilgrims arrived on Jeddah's shores to fulfill the dream of every Muslim: to make the holy pilgrimage. The emir's crew transferred their cargo to his own ship, an open ocean vessel. He had entrusted his flagship to his first mate, Malik, three months before. In the cover of darkness, the women emerged from below the small ship, guarded by Burke and Mason, and safely boarded the flagship. The bow had a ferocious figurehead, not unlike what Burke had seen on Norman vessels of war.

It took three days of animated negotiations for the port master and the emir to settle the demurrage fee. It was rumored that the port master was a Maltese Christian who had converted late in life. The caliphate was known for its tolerance. Burke found it entertaining to watch the port master treat the emir like any other ornery ship's captain. The emir had the most splendid ship in port, so it followed he should pay a splendid fee.

For three wonderful mornings Burke made his way through the large bazaar in search of breakfast. His Arabic had improved enough to refuse the onslaught of merchants with subtlety and grace. Their main question was whether he was on his way or returning from holy Mecca? Burke soon learned it was easier to answer "on my way." No one would accept the idea that he might simply be passing through.

It was the last week in October, and the monsoon winds would soon be upon them. The emir's instincts served them well. After a two-day sail out of Jeddah, they caught the winds of the azyab monsoon, which swiftly carried them across the Indian Ocean. They reached the Malabar Coast by mid-December.

The emir stood on deck just before sunrise. This was his favorite hour, when he could sight land exactly where he knew it would be and guide his ship straight into port. He delighted in his connection to the stars, for they whispered in the truest of all languages.

Burke joined him, as the light grew brighter. He could scarcely believe it was winter; the days were thick and hot. The cool morning air was cherished. He had taken quickly to the art of navigation over the past month, learning all he could from the emir and Malik. He learned to use the kamal to take measurements using the position of the stars.

"Hold the end of the string in your teeth," the emir had instructed. "Position the lower edge of the card even with the horizon and in front of Polaris. Now count the knots, each a finger width apart. This will give you the issabah measurement."

"Our position north and south?" Burke was catching on.

"We'll make a sailor of you yet, Burke. When you've mastered the issabah, we will go on to find the azimuth. You must crawl before you can walk."

Burke thought he could grow used to more time spent at sea than on land. The endless waves brought a sense of peace he hadn't known before. Ma'mar, however, found life aboard ship too confining. His only solace lay in beating his large friend at chess. It was entertaining to watch Mason, with his giant hands, move the tiny pieces of the traveling set. Mason did his best not to become frustrated, but was too honest not to let his feelings show after a defeat.

It was Na'ila's habit to sit on deck in the early hours and enjoy the fresh air. The crew never looked at or addressed her directly. When they warped out of the port of Kulam Mali, no one spoke of why the women had stayed aboard. Most of the crew had sailed with the emir for years. They had faith in Allah and al-Waddu. They knew they were in the hands of a man who was intimate with all creation—the sea that held them, the winds that bore them and the heavens that went completely untouched by the other two.

"Enjoy your time in Kulam Mali," the emir said as the two men watch the sun rise over land, for the first time in months. "We will linger here until the cyclones of the azyab die down. If Allah is willing, we will leave by the next moon. We've reached the Spice Coast well ahead of my expectations. Now we rest, take on fresh water and sweet fruit. When the sea is ripe, we will continue our journey to Mulam Mali, and then around the southern tip of India to Kalah Bar. The harbormaster there is a great friend, though I'm afraid his hospitality is known to slow progress like a colony of barnacles on the hull. From Kalah Bar it is a relatively smooth sail to Canton."

THE PEARL RIVER DELTA

Tea began as medicine and grew into a beverage.
—Okakura Kakuso

The excitement was contagious as the ship glided into port. The carved figurehead on their bow and the arc of their sails announced their arrival. They had reached the other side of the world. Their cargo was intact, and the emir had not lost a single soul during the voyage. The fullness of the moment captured everyone aboard. Na'ila and the entire crew stood on deck and watched as they passed massive junks. All activity seemed to halt as their vessel quietly warped to her moorings.

Canton harbor was perfectly placed on the edge of the busy Pearl River Delta. It was the center of the southernmost province of China, and the farthest port of the maritime silk road.

The plump port master met the shore party on the pier, bowing low several times. Within the general pleasantries about the weather, the emir inquired about the prevailing winds. The port master assured him sailing conditions would be favorable for many more weeks, leaving plenty of time to conclude their business.

Recalling al-Idrisi's instructions, Burke planned an excursion upriver. After securing permission from the emir, he hired a guide, who in turn found passage aboard the river junk *Li Mei*. Burke purchased a robe of simple sturdy cloth to help him blend in, though his posture and way of moving betrayed him well in advance of his light skin and round eyes. His large nose seemed to be a point of amusement everywhere he went. Children followed him laughing, as though they had met a comedian.

Burke was not surprised to learn that holy pilgrimages also took place on the far side of the world. When he first told his guide he wished to head upriver, the fellow assumed he intended to visit the Temple of the Six Banyan Trees. Burke had to ask what might be the special attraction of that temple.

"The tea master of this temple," the guide explained, "is known to teach without the need of books."

Burke loved books, but a holy man without a Bible or Qu'ran—now, that was intriguing! "You must take me!" he exclaimed.

The guide admitted he had never met the tea master. "Most travelers only care to see the Buddha. But you can try your luck."

Having taken meticulous notes on their journey thus far, Burke determined to redouble his effort in recording every detail on the river trip to later share with al-Idrisi.

He nearly had to tie Mason to the mast to keep him from following. "You must stay and guard the porcelain until my return," he insisted.

"I care not for porcelain, my lord."

"I know. In truth, you must remain here so the impatient emir doesn't decide to sail without me. Guard the cargo and make sure the emir waits. I swear I will return in one week."

"Yes, my lord."

"I will give you good report of my journey. And, Mason, keep Ma'mar out of trouble."

"I will keep the emir from sailing. I will guard our cargo. But the boy?" Mason shook his head.

Master P'o

With melted snow I boil fragrant tea.
—Mencius

Burke rested at the summit and took a moment to look down on the mist clearing from the valley below. The outline of a six-story pagoda rose above the rest of the landscape. The dirt road was full of farmers on their way to work in the surrounding rice fields. The temple grew ever higher above the thickening forest.

A young monk named Shi-Lun greeted Burke and his guide at the temple gate with a bow. They quietly followed him over a high-arched bridge that overlooked a pond of colorful koi. The meandering path led them to the temple steps. The incense grew thick as they ascended the first level. A golden Buddha seated on a lotus greeted them. Shi-Lun kicked off his slippers with one fluid motion, gesturing for Burke to remove his boots before stepping foot into the temple. Fresh flowers adorned the altar. The monk bowed to the Buddha of everlasting light and then helped Burke to light a piece of incense and place it in a golden bowl.

Dozens of monks sat on the wooden floor chanting and striking bells.

Shi-Lun explained that Amida Buddha held his right hand up in a mudra that meant "Don't be afraid." His left hand turned downward in such a gesture that meant "May all your wishes come true."

Burke asked Shi-Lun what message this prophet brought. His question was met with a smile and a reply Burke didn't fully comprehend. "The Buddha is the one who woke up."

They climbed the winding steps of the graceful structure, which took them high above the canopy of majestic trees that stretched out beyond the temple grounds. They seemed to be looking down from the clouds. The six great banyan trees gave the impression of a vast forest, one tree moving into the next without distinction.

To Burke's surprised, Shi-Lun said he had never met the tea master. He had only been a monk at the temple for a few months, and was fully occupied cleaning the halls. He thought for a moment. "There is an old man who lives on the other side of the farthest great banyan." He pointed west. "Perhaps he can help you."

Burke thanked Shi-Lun and set off with his guide in search of the old man.

Burke couldn't believe his eyes as they wandered through the maze of giant trees. He never had imagined a single tree could grow as large as a castle. Just when he felt they were lost, an old peasant greeted them with a deep bow.

"Can you tell us where we might find the tea master?" Burke asked.

"Please come this way."

They stopped a short distance from a little ramshackle hut that sat under the hanging vines and thick roots.

"The master is busy preparing for his departure. You may not see him today."

Burke was disappointed. He had to return to the ship the following morning if he were to keep his promise. "May we see him tomorrow?"

"The master is leaving to the wilderness. We are saddened and pray he will stay." The peasant sat down on the ground, distraught but also curious. "May I ask why you seek our master?" He looked as if he had never seen a white man before.

"I've been a soldier. Killing is the only skill I possess. Now I've become a traveler, but . . ." He struggled to arrange his thoughts. "I've traveled far, but I've remained the same man. The truth is, I no longer wish to be a soldier, to fight. Kill or be killed." He had confessed to Mason many times during their journey that he would rather die by a lion's saber jaw than by cold honed steel.

"Why come to this place?" the peasant asked.

"Your master is a wise man. I wish to ask him if it is possible for a man to change how he lives in this world. If it is possible to become a man of peace."

"I see. Please rest here for the night. I will bring food and ask the master if he will see you before he leaves to the wilderness. You are most welcome here." The peasant gestured at the enormous tree surrounding them. "You are under a bodhi tree."

An hour passed and the peasant returned with an ivory-colored bowl of rice and a black bowl of steaming hot tea, both covered with large green leaves. The three men shared in silence. It slowly grew dark.

"The master instructed me to tell you," the peasant man said before he retired, "that if you sit all night and meditate in peace, he will see you in the morning. He says if you break your meditation for any reason, you will not succeed in your desire to become a man of peace."

Burke bowed and thanked the peasant, who bowed in return before disappearing into the trees. His guide was already fast asleep. Burke found a spot near a large root, where he could just see the light of the tea master's hut. A short column of ants made their way through the fallen bodhi leaves and over his folded knee. He summoned the strength from all his years of battle and tried to become still. He fought the urge to move, as well as all the urges that followed, one after another. He fought the urge to be angry. He had no wish to be defeated by himself.

The heat of the day lingered under the massive trees. The sweat rolled into his eyes and stung. The bow work of a thousand crickets throbbed in his skull. It became the longest night of his life.

Two hours before dawn, he heard a clash of steel and men's voices calling out.

His guide awoke and listened in the direction of the master's hut. "Imperial guards! They're taking the tea master!" Scared to death, the little man ran into the night, toward the temple.

Burke imagined himself springing to his feet. In his mind's eye he picked up a fallen sword and ran toward the hut. The tea master was lying face down while armed men kicked and beat him. Burke surprised his enemy. He killed three of the guards, but there were too many. He retreated into the dark maze of hanging roots, the Imperial soldiers in close pursuit. He fought them off, one by one.

Burke sat drenched in sweat, swaying back and forth, his eyes clamped tight. He heard the screams of more men in the night. It was the old peasant man who had been so kind. He listened to his pitiful cries. Burke fought the impulse to jump to his feet. He sat rooted and battled.

An hour later it was light. He opened his eyes to the dawn and struggled to straighten his cramped legs. When he could manage to stand, he stumbled to the tea master's little hut. It was empty. The master was gone. Burke searched, calling out through the maze of trees. All was silence and emptiness. He retraced his footprints back to the temple.

Shi-Lun listened with concern, but the monk's face told Burke he understood nothing. Burke used his hands, feverishly acting out the events of the night. Without the help of his guide, it was useless. Frustrated and alone, he found the dirt road and followed it back toward the mountain pass. Peace, it seemed, had eluded him. A deep sense of loss lodged in his chest, making it difficult to breathe.

He had passed Jerusalem; and been but a day's walk to Mecca. His holy pilgrimage instead brought him to the other side of the world, to the Temple of the Six Banyan Trees. It made his failure all the more wretched.

When he reached the crest of the hill and looked back to the valley, he saw the peasant following him. The old man was carrying the black and white bowls in which he'd brought the rice and tea the night before. Burke waved for the peasant to catch up. They walked together in silence through the mountains, seeking the valley below, and a boat to carry them downriver.

Mason was overjoyed and relieved to tears when he saw Burke's silhouette emerge from a long low sampan. Mason jumped onto the floating gangway, nearly sinking it.

"Mason, my fine fellow, you look like you haven't slept in days!" It was close to the truth. It was the longest wait of Mason's life, sitting on the little ship, powerless. "I'm sorry for the distress I've caused. But it couldn't be helped." When Burke saw the look in Mason's eyes, he was deeply ashamed. "I swear, if I leave you again, it won't be on an earthly errand."

"My lord, don't trouble yourself on my behalf." Mason began to confess to the dozens of times he had nearly struck out in search of him, but Burke stopped him, having guessed as much.

Ma'mar came running up. "My lord!"

Burke thought he saw Na'ila raise her head just above the ship's deck, from her aft cabin.

The Journey Home

Teaism is . . . . essentially a worship of the imperfect,
as it is a tender attempt to accomplish something
possible in this impossible thing we know as life.
—Okakura Kakuso

Al-Waddu was grateful to have Burke back aboard. They went immediately below, where he opened the black wax seal of a large clay pot. Giant ceramic pots were stacked three high and two deep, lashed to port and to starboard for balance. The emir removed an elegant blue and white porcelain cup and blew off the packing straw to show his friend.

"From the Ru kiln, in Hebei Province. It's famous throughout the world for adding agate into the glaze, giving a creamy texture like that of jade. We've traded a king's treasure for that of an emperor. Find your sword. We best be on our guard until we are well away." He carefully placed the cup back inside the clay pot and resealed the lid.

"Why not use wood crates?" Burke wondered.

"The Chinese believe these pots are the safest way to transport their goods. They're very solid, but to be honest, I don't care for the extra weight."

The emir took the rest of the afternoon to conclude his business with the port master, paying his demurrage fees in full. He bowed low, thanking the honorable gentleman for his gracious hospitality. The port master wished them an auspicious wind at their back and a safe journey home. He said nothing but wondered how they would leave with neither tide nor wind. The crew grumbled under their breath when the emir ordered the men to launch the skiffs and man the oars. The two rowboats were launched and cables tied to the bow of the ship.

"Cast off!" the emir shouted his orders. The men pulled at their oars until the heavily laden boat nudged slowly away from the pier and out into deeper water. They crawled slowly past the massive junks anchored side by side in the harbor. Many Chinese sailors and their families stood watching them slowly pass.

The emir watched from the deck. His men would earn their salt today. They carried a much larger crew, including women and children returning south with the season. The winds might prove too weak or erratic to carry them straight across the China Sea. He knew better than to speak of his concerns, but they could ill afford to wait for conditions to improve. They needed a couple of weeks of favorable winds, and then they would be safe.

Burke joined the emir on the captain's deck and took in the clean air of the open sea. It made Burke feel young again to shed the crowded smell and chaos of the harbor for the simple life aboard ship.

A plate of food was brought to both men. Burke's meal featured a large moonfish stuffed with lemongrass and spices over saffron rice. "I see you found a new cook for our return journey. My congratulations." It was the best food Burke had tasted since departing Ceylon.

"Thank you, but we've the same cook since Kalah Bar."

Burke gave the emir a look of surprise. "Wang cooked this?"

"Perhaps your stature has risen." The emir lightly offered up his explanation. "As you can see, my food is the same as yesterday."

Burke took another bite from his perfectly prepared fish. "I thought Wang called me the white devil?"

"Since then, my friend, you've been to the six banyans."

"At least my pilgrimage was successful in one small way."

"Bringing aboard our new crew member also seems to have raised your prestige." The emir pointed to the little peasant manning an oar in the farthest launch.

"Yes, he helped me at the six banyans after my guide ran off. He organized my passage downriver. The poor man must be alone and without family. I don't even know his name." Burke thought for a moment. "Does he know Wang?"

"I don't believe so." The emir felt the beginnings of a breeze. He barked out orders to the first mate.

The boats returned to the ship, and the crew thankfully stowed their oars and raised the sails.

Burke watched the old man brushing the deck. "Does anyone on the ship know him?"

"His name is P'O. He is, or was, the tea master of the Temple of the Six Banyan Trees. You seriously didn't know?" The emir shook his head and smiled. "They say when he's cut, he bleeds tea."

"Are you quite sure?"

"I checked his story with the port master before our departure. There's no doubt."

Burke stared at the little man. It was difficult to tell his age. He was not young, but he moved like a young man. Burke recalled the strange events of the past week. The little peasant had spoken the truth. The tea master was making ready for his departure from the six banyans. The peasant had told him if he sat through the night in peace, he would see the tea master the following day. This also turned out to be the truth. Now Burke wondered if the last thing the little man said would come true—that he could become a man of peace. He felt a burden lift from his chest. The sense of failure that accompanied him downriver drifted away. He smiled and bowed toward the tea master. The little man bowed low in return.

Mason, drenched in sweat from his time at the oars, joined Burke by the helm. "My lord, may I ask about the Temple of the Six Banyan Trees?" Mason imagined massive columns.

"What would you like to know?" Burke always enjoyed it when Mason broke his silence with questions.

"Of what manner of stone was it made?"

"I'm sorry to disappoint. It was entirely of wood, but in a most elegant design."

"Why wood?" Mason was disappointed.

"When I questioned the monk, Shi-Lun, on this point, he explained that the spirit within the temple was everlasting, so the building didn't need to be."

Mason pondered this in silence.

Only two days into their voyage, an unexpected squall came upon their wooden ship. A thick curtain closed off the bright sun of the afternoon.

The emir felt a sudden flaw of wind on the back of his neck. "Hand the sail!"

Quickly, the heavy sea changed from choppy gray to moving black cliffs that crashed over the gunnels. Towering dark clouds sent a torrent of wind, and rain engulfed them. A great gust sliced through a shroud and shredded the mainsail before it could be furled. A piece of rigging crashed down on Malik's head, killing him. Whatever wasn't tied down rolled and shifted. The deck was awash; the barefoot crew slipped and scurried about to restore order.

The emir turned the ship into the wind and put two men on the helm. "Rahim, cut away that rigging! Haul up a piece of canvas any way you can!" The emir needed some sail to help them come about and ride out the storm.

They were heavily loaded and taking on water. Those below deck bailed the bilge.

"Batten the aft hatch!" the emir yelled over the torn canvas slashing about in the high wind. He knelt over Malik and whispered a quick prayer before ordering him committed to the sea.

Na'ila took charge below deck, organizing the women to help bail. She tended to a sailor who had been injured by a large pot that had broken loose and crushed his leg.

The emir employed every option before jettisoning his cargo. He ordered two barrels of fresh water dumped and Wang's cooking wood.

The lashing wind abruptly ceased, leaving them rolling in the waves. A deep trough cradled them until a violent crash shook everything wooden and flesh.

The emir knew if the sea timed it just right, all was lost. He barked his orders.

Mason immediately understood. He slid down the ladder and cut the lashing and began heaving the heavy clay pots of porcelain onto the deck. From there, it took two men to hurl them overboard.

HERBIE

Having picked some tea, he drank it,
Then he sprouted wings,
And flew to a fairy mansion,
To escape the emptiness of the world.
—Chiao Jen

Uncle Herbie was a large jovial man of Polynesian stock who could never quite manage to wait until one was close. He was said to be from a royal family, the Ma'afu chiefs. As soon as Herbie caught sight of a friend, he would enthusiastically yell all manner of things from a distance. Figas seldom could make out the words, but after a while he understood it was just Herbie softening you up, marinating you and tuning you to his frequency. Within normal conversational range, he kept it up until you gave up and agreed to play along with his jokes and jests.

It took some reflection for Figas to realize Herbie Ma'afu was one of the most serious people he'd ever met. He was a giant sylvan of the wood, full of stories about the trees and the animals. Everyday anecdotes from Herbie seemed more interesting than the most profound moments of his own life. Figas would anticipate Herbie, and Herbie, in his own way, would return the favor. Figas joked that this altered the time-space continuum.

"You're an agent of the profound, Herbie," Figas said in earnest.

Herbie laughed so hard Figas worried he might be choking.

"More like agent of da profane!" Herbie replied, cracking himself up even more.

Herbie's job for many years had been to oversee the tea workers in the fields. He did little on the harvesting side, concerning himself mainly with new plantings. He had an uncanny way of knowing who was working hard and who was doing too much of nothing. He believed in getting the work done, while working hard at enjoying oneself. His management style was a complex system of carrots and sticks. Everyone received the same pay, but the hardest workers received plenty of perks. A large chunk of smoked sea bass would show up at their doorstep, or they would be given a week off to go fishing when the tuna were running. A lazy bugger worked Saturdays.

None of this was strange, except that Herbie seldom visited the fields. The various crew members might see him first thing in the morning, but then he was off to visit one of the farther terraces. How Herbie knew what was getting done, or by whom, was a mystery. The one thing everyone agreed was that Herbie was fair, and always knew who was working hard and who wasn't. This accuracy only enhanced his reputation as an effective boss. When Herbie asked a member of his crew to do something, that person was enthusiastic about getting it done. Not to say that Herbie didn't enjoy shooting the breeze, or as he put it, de-bris.

It took Figas a while to work out Herbie's little secret. One day he followed his boss home and waited until after dark. He heard the big man call out to the trees as he set off into the night. Figas followed a safe distance behind watching Herbie disappear into one of the tool sheds nestled among the plantings. Figas crept up and peeked through a knothole.

Herbie lit a lantern and carefully inspected each tool, jotting detailed notes in a little black book. A shiny digging bar told a story. Herbie knew every implement and to whom it belonged. A rusty blade had a lazy owner. The higher the polish, the greater the effort behind a handle. Despite the secrecy of his midnight visit, Herbie whispered vociferously to the various tools, sharing news of the island to which they otherwise might not be privy.

Figas began to giggle and retreated lest he give himself away.

It had been agreed early on that Figas would work in the accounting office, but Es-sahra believed he also needed to be out in the tea to get reacquainted. When she told Herbie he would need to make room for Figas on his crew, the big man laughed until he was out of breath. He sat down and crossed his tree-trunk-size legs.

"Whose idea, dimlightened one?" Herbie loved to tease Uncle Sun, reminding him that the closer one thought one had gotten to "da P'O," the farther away one was. Herbie's called this phenomenon *dimlightenment*. Many a fool he had witnessed drinking the nectar of the gods, only to become "da dimlightened one."

"No, Herbie. This is all my doing." Es-sahra was comfortable taking the credit.

"Sista, why you want to plow da field with a razor? Ha-ha! It gonna get dull quick. Da field? It just laugh."

Es-sahra explained all the myriad things Figas had missed out on during his many years away.

"Okay, I take on da boy. But no one gonna say nawting about how me handle da job."

"Deal. You know I wouldn't dream of it." Es-sahra shook on it.

Figas enjoyed planting tea, though the digging not so much. The crew teased him mercilessly about what kind an asshole he must have been in his previous lives to merit being Hu's personal *ass*-istant.

The crusty Hu would flirt with any woman he came across.

The women, in return, were never shy with their response.

"Under model!" Es-Mira declared, sending the crew into hysterics.

When Hu was out of earshot, Figas asked Es-Mira what she'd said.

"Me said," she shouted again, "Hu, you no underwear model!"

The crew roared a second time.

Figas couldn't imagine working for two more different people. He much preferred Herbie's boundless energy to Hu's fixated personality. Herbie never wasted energy making the pieces of life fit together, while Hu continually reconciled and reexamined everything. One was pleased with his efforts; the other looked over his shoulder never pleased, even though the office figures were child's play for him. Figas worked on the most basic accounts, while Hu oversaw all the overseas accounts. Over time, Figas gleaned enough about the books to guess what was in those international accounts. By his estimates, a great deal of money had been made over the years. Viridis, it turned out, was a very wealthy place—not that it helped much with the blisters on his hands.

Herbie immediately noticed how much Figas struggled both physically with the work and also socially. Too much book learning left him defenseless against the torments that rained down on him every day in the fields.

"So, Es-Mira, do you know how to confuse a math prodigy?" Gema asked.

"No. How?" Es-Mira acted clueless.

"Line three shovels against the wall, then ask Figas to take his pick."

The fact that it took Figas a while to work out the joke, though he was swinging his pick at the time, had the crew rolling. It wouldn't have been so bad if he had thought of a witty reply. But eventually he did have his day.

After he discovered Herbie's secret method, it was easy. He brought a bag of salt to work and mixed a pinch in a bucket of water. He dipped Es-Mira's shovel and her friend's tools in the brine at the end of each day, causing them to rust overnight. Es-Mira and her gang were soon very lazy in Herbie's eyes. Inexplicably to them, they were now working longer hours, as well as Saturdays. Meanwhile, Figas received all the perks.

After months of physical work, Figas was in better shape and able to carry his own water. He became impervious to all forms of abuse from his tormentors, knowing all the while he was getting the better of them.

Late one afternoon, he cut himself trimming some undergrowth. Herbie showed up right on cue. Figas squeezed his bleeding finger and held it up to show his boss.

"Come to da shed." There, Herbie opened the first-aid box. He shook a bottle of Mercurochrome and uncorked the rubber stopper, rubbing the glass dropper over the cut. It turned Figas's finger iridescent red.

"What is this stuff?" Figas read the brittle label. "A bit out of date, Uncle. March, 1968."

"Mercury lasts fah-eva." Nurse Herbie's feelings were hurt. "You want da finger to drop off?"

"Thanks, Herbie, heavy metals are good for you."

Herbie wrapped gauze and tape firmly but not too tightly around the glowing finger. "I got to tell you, little braddah." He lowered his voice. "You had me going brining dem shovels. You clevah! Rusty buggahs. Ha-ha! Mess up da system!" Herbie held his index finger to his lips. "Tell nawting."

"You know I would never breathe a word, Herbie. It gets rough in the trenches." The unwritten portion of the rules had given him trouble and grief.

"Geevum! Was genius, really." Herbie slapped Figas on the back to let him know all was forgiven.

"To coin a phrase, every dog will have his day."

"You coined the phrase to coin a phrase. You be doin' my job soon."

"Can I ask you something, Herbie?"

"Fire away, little braddah."

"I know our tea is top quality, but what makes it so special?"

"Da tea runs hard in ya veins." Herbie chuckled. "Tomorrow, little braddah, come plenty early. New boss, yea."

Water from a Stone

Tea is liquid wisdom.
—Anonymous

The black polish of the sky slowly dulled to a gray whisper. The thick weather of the past days gave way to clear blue skies and a scorching calm. Their healthy stock of provisions was of little comfort without fresh water. All onboard became sick, surviving on only a few mouthfuls of water from the torn sails spread over the deck at night to catch the dew. The young crewman whose leg had been crushed died of a fever. Wang had to guard his vinegar to keep the delirious crew from drinking it and becoming ill. The children were strangely quiet, too weak to cry. They lay below deck in a sleep bordering death.

"Ah, but it's a wet thirst." Burke cast an eye over the watery horizon. He searched the rough sailcloth for a pocket of moisture. He glanced at the emir, who was leaning against the rail. It worried Burke that the captain had not charted their course for several days. "I've the scratchy tongue of a house cat." Burke licked the sailcloth.

"What cat would want your tongue?" The emir pretended not to appreciate Burke's dark wit. Why had they not sighted land? The storm could not have driven them that far to the east. He prayed to Allah for a wind. With a trimmed sail they had ridden the wind for a week. Through a miracle they had stayed afloat. The emir dozed off in the afternoon heat.

After three days and nights of lying in the doldrums they woke to an afternoon breeze. A sweet zephyr filled their loose sails. The emir had no voice left to bark out orders. He found a wooden pin and beat it against the deck to draw the crew's attention. The few who were physically able manned their posts, quietly carrying out their duties. The old tea master ended his meditation and helped secure the lines. For the first time in days, they began to make sail.

When the boatswain spotted tall cliffs on the horizon, he wasn't sure if his eyes were turning vapor into mineral. He called down to the emir, who smiled with cracked lips and reassured the boatswain that the cliffs were real.

"Land ho!"

The emir could smell land, but what drove them full sail was fresh water. He approached the island cautiously, leaving room to beat back against the current if necessary. It wouldn't do to be too eager and be dashed against the cliffs.

Evening was close upon them. Without a chart, it was madness to sail along an unknown coast. Two of the children below deck were burning up with fever. They needed water if they were to make it till morning. They sailed in the offing of the high cliffs until almost sunset. Then the emir dropped anchor near dark stains on the rock's sheer face, traces of an old waterfall. They heaved to, just beyond the shore breakers. Divers were sent to set the anchors, lest they drift closer.

The emir chose Burke to lead the shore party. Mason and three oarsmen loaded two empty barrels into the launch. The rest of the ship's company watched at the rail. The small craft waited, counting the swells, feeling for a calm moment. Burke gave the order, and the men pulled through the pounding surf, toward the steep pebbled beach. Each wave bore the power of their undoing. The crew let out a hoarse cheer when they saw the landing party drag the launch up the beach.

Burke led the men to the cliff's edge, where water had flowed not long before. Though the rock was damp to the touch, no water was to be seen. The men looked up at the massive cliff, which was too high to climb. The three oarsmen knelt facing Mecca and began to pray. Burke looked at Mason. The big man was breathing hard and seemed too weary to focus on the problem at hand.

"My lord, we must return to the ship."

"If we return without water, Mason . . ."

"No, my lord. I need tools."

"Get up!" Burke drove the sailors back into the boat. He grabbed an oar and ordered the men to pull. Mason gave the skiff a powerful push into the surf and jumped in behind them. The oarsmen gained faith from the determined look in Burke's eyes. He was no ordinary man. He wore the king's ring. The emir treated him as an equal.

When they came alongside the ship, Mason climbed aboard, leaving the skiff to dance like a cork on the waves. He stuffed a canvas bag full of odds and ends and tossed it down to Burke. Then he climbed down the rigging and back into the launch, the extra bulk settling them up to the gunnels. Again they pulled their way to the pebbled shore.

By now, all light had faded in the west behind them. Two lanterns were lit.

Mason took a hammer and a star-shaped chisel from the canvas bag. He stood on an empty barrel and placed the chisel against a long vertical crack in the cliff's face. His hammer stroke rang like a bell through the thin breeze. He pounded, turning the chisel a quarter turn in rhythm. The chisel quickly ate its way into the rock with Mason's seemingly light touch. He tapped and turned until he held the very end of the chisel by the tips of his thumb and finger. He pulled out the chisel and blew into the hole, sending stone dust into his parched mouth. He held up the lantern in the crepuscular light, but there was nothing to see. He climbed off the barrel, and hung his head.

Burke climbed up and took a look himself. "It was a good idea, Mason." He addressed the landing party. "We'll sleep here tonight and hope for a light tide. Signal the ship." They leaned against the cliff wall. Images of dying children filled their fitful sleep.

The next morning Burke opened his eyes to faintly lit clouds. Mason was standing on the barrel.

"My lord!" Mason pointed to the drip under the hole he had made.

"It's a start."

Mason climbed off the barrel, turned it over and twisted out its wooden tap. He climbed back up and used his knife to whittle the end of the tap, fitting it to the size of the hole. He pounded the tap into the rock with his fist. Burke smiled and nodded as the big man slowly turned the spigot and the first drops ran out. The men tried to cheer, but could only cough through their raspy throats.

Mason stepped aside and Burke put his mouth under the tap. Sweet water ran down his throat, almost choking him.

"My gentle giant, you've saved us again." Burke lay back against the cool rock face as the men lined up to drink and fill their containers. "A fonte puro pura defuit aqua."

"My lord?"

"From a clear spring, clear water flows."

Lijuan, Mother of Viridis

Where there's tea there's hope.
—Arthur W. Pinero

Through good fortune, no lives were lost during the night. With a fresh supply of water, they weighed anchor and continued up the island's coastline. The emir was forced to set course due west, back out to sea, beating against the wind. A rocky point jutted out from the shore, accented by two high sea stacks.

Rahim hung on the webbing near the bow and dropped the lead weight, calling out the soundings. By late afternoon, they had rounded the point and entered the safety of deeper water. In the early evening, they discovered what would later be called Salm Bay.

Ma'mar dove from the bow and helped Rahim set the anchor chains around large coral heads. The crew drew straws for who would stay aboard. The rest of the company set about exploring the island on foot. For three weeks they laid up, replenishing themselves with fresh provisions. They gathered and dried a fibrous plant. Using a two-pronged lucet, they braided massive coils of rope to build a swinging bridge across the chasm between the thumb-shaped ridge and the lush upper regions of the island. When the hanging bridge was complete, the explorers wandered through the pristine landscape, enchanted by its simple, unspoiled beauty.

The emir looked down from the top of the high cliff at his ship, a child's toy anchored in the turquoise bay. The earth felt good under his feet. The more time he spent on the island, the less he felt the pull of the sea. He had lost a king's treasure; worse still; he'd ordered it thrown overboard. If he returned to Sicily, he'd be hung in the piazza.

Burke and Mason, having sworn an oath to protect the cargo with their lives, had little reason to believe they would fare much differently.

For the crew, the unspoiled landscape opened their eyes to a new world in which they could be landowners. Although several men had wives and children aboard, Na'ila and the four young widows were the only women in the company.

The tea master crossed the rope bridge and ventured alone into the mountains, without a word to anyone.

Without speaking of it aloud, the ship's crew had become a group of settlers. The emir called a meeting to decide what should be done. He assured the would-be colonists that he could sail safely back to Canton and fetch family members and any supplies needed to prosper on the island. Those who had no wish to settle could return to port with him. No one raised any objections; everyone wanted to stay.

Trees were felled. Homes and shelters began to take shape around the bay. Men began to fight over the choicest pieces of land. Although the emir ran a tight ship, he was not a governor. He decided he would let things fall as they may, up to a point. Burke noticed the Chinese and Arab crew members who worked seamlessly together aboard ship now began to take sides against one another.

In the early evening, Master P'O crossed the swinging bridge and climbed down the ridge to the bay. When he heard raised voices, he followed the light of the ship's lanterns, which were hung under a massive tree. A lively meeting was taking place. He waited in the darkness and listened.

A brisk-tongued Chinese sailor complained how he'd staked four corners of land only to return and find Rahim had removed his wooden posts. Rahim jumped to his feet in protest, arguing that he had laid claim to the land on the very first day. Rahim halted in midsentence when he saw Master P'O emerge from the shadows in a green ceremonial robe. The meeting drew silent.

Master P'O bowed and sat motionless in the middle of the gathering until everyone was calm. When he stood up, he had everyone's attention.

The master explained that he had traveled to the heart of the island and found a place of great peace. "For five days, I sat there and listened. I sensed a quiet presence. I built a fire and made tea. I poured tea into my black bowl and placed it on a small rock, inviting my unseen guest to join me. I sipped my own tea and waited. All the while, I could sense a presence, though I saw no one. Dawn came. I rose and gathered the tea bowl. It was empty. I looked about, but my footprints were the only ones to be seen in the sand."

The crowd looked at one another, unsure how to interpret the master's words.

Burke was the first to speak. "Are you saying, Master P'O, that we are not alone on this island?"

"Yes."

"Who else is here?"

"I don't know."

No one doubted the master's sincerity. He spoke only the truth.

The emir stood up and addressed the gathering. "I believe this changes everything."

A grunt of approval filled the night air.

The emir turned to P'O, "What should we do, master?"

The tea master cleared his throat. "We have behaved poorly. We have not acted respectfully. We assumed we were alone and acted as if the island belonged to us." He looked around at each and every face. "With your permission, emir, I will now return to your ship."

The emir was confused. "Of course. But then what, master?"

"Wait."

"I don't understand, wait for what?"

"For a sign."

Being of a superstitious nature, many of the sailors nodded in agreement. Others failed to see the wisdom of the master's proposal. They were happy to be on the island and had no desire to return to the ship, or anywhere else, for that matter. Soon the crowd were on their feet and arguing with one another.

"If there are natives here, let's seek them out!"

"I say let's form a search party. The rest can defend the shelters."

"Hold on! Perhaps we should wait on the ship. The master knows what he saw."

"I saw nothing. I say we make our own presence known here!"

Burke leaned close and spoke in the emir's ear. "You must act decisively, my friend."

"Quiet!" The emir held his hands up. "We will return to the ship tonight."

Though most did not understood what the master had seen, no one spoke out against the emir's order.

With quiet efficiency, the would-be settlers packed up their belongings and returned to the ship just before dawn. Once aboard, the emir was the supreme law. He gave orders that no one was to go ashore for any reason. To disobey meant death.

The next day was long and hot, with little for the crew to do but scrub the deck. And complain under their breath. The emir confided in Burke that they were in deep trouble. The ship's company were honest, hardworking men, but every man had a breaking point. Mixed with the men's prayers were dark whisperings.

Burke understood that they would not last many more days like this. Nor were they in any condition to return to Canton. He and Mason both wore their swords and stayed close to the emir.

On the third day of the wait, Master P'O asked the emir to assemble the crew for a brief ceremony.

They all gathered in a circle on the deck at high noon. The women and children were at the outer edge. Standing in the middle, the master bowed to each of them. He took a wooden bucket and some rocks that Wang had placed under his cookstove at the bottom. Then he shoveled hot coals from Wang's cookstove on top. He poured water into a pot, which he suspended over the coals. Then he sat down and waited for the water to boil. The men stood in silence. When the water boiled, he filled his black tea bowl halfway and sprinkled in some dried tea leaves. After a long silence, he stood and walked to the leeward rail and held the bowl up to the sky. Then, bowing toward the island, he poured three small offerings into the sea. He chanted softly, cupping the black bowl in his hands. He held the bowl briefly to his heart, then leaned forward and dropped it into the bay.

A collective gasp rose from the ship's company as they rushed to the rail. The dark shape was already out of sight.

The tea master retired below deck.

The next day the mood was unbearable. The crew could no longer make sense of the situation. They stared toward the cool shade of the palms that lined the shore. Were they to remain on ship and die like rats? Indeed, the rats themselves had long since smelled land, crawled down the anchor chains and swam for shore.

Sensing the desperate feeling in the air, Burke took it upon himself to come up with a plan. He stood at the railing for an hour, staring into the water. He reflected on the tea master's actions. Burke realized he was relieved when the precious porcelain had been thrown overboard. He wasn't sure of his commitment to guard it. Would he take a life to protect a collection of teacups? A weight had lifted. The tea master's black tea bowl lay on the bottom on the bay. He turned the ring on his finger. He knew what he had to do. He went to the emir and asked for permission to address the ship's company.

"By all means, my friend. If you can think of something worthwhile to say, all the better." The emir knew they were very close to mutiny.

Burke stood at the center of the deck and called out, "Friends, please come closer!"

Mason could hear the added resonance in his master's voice.

The crew ceased their activities and gathered round. The women and children followed.

When everyone became quiet, Burke began. "This silver ring was given to me by Roger, King of Sicily." He slid the ring off his finger and held it up for all to see. Master P'O smiled as he listened from the back of the crowd. "On this ring, as many of you have seen, is the map of the world. It has provided me safe passage across many lands and seas across the world. To its very edge."

A soft murmur filled the air as Burke passed the ring around for everyone to hold and gaze upon the map. All knew Burke to be no ordinary man. He was said to have defeated a small army with his sword. Even master P'O had been seen to bow low to him. This silver ring was legendary, and considered magical.

Mason was the last to receive the ring. He returned it to his master without looking at it.

Burke thanked his friend. "I give my word," he announced, "the first among you to find this ring will be its new owner!" He took a step forward and heaved the ring high into the air.

In the shocked silence, a tiny splash was heard. Everyone stood frozen. A child spoke, and then there was frenzy. Sailors dove overboard in wild abandonment in hopes of adding the ring to the many amulets they wore about their necks for luck. The boys and girls followed without waiting permission. Shouts of encouragement rang out from those who could not swim. The hopes and dreams of everyone aboard came back to life.

Na'ila watched Burke from her place by the rail. Their eyes met. He had never seen her so radiant.

The melee lasted well past sunset. No one had found the ring. Everyone was exhausted and fell asleep amid laughter and excitement, eager for the morning sun to rise. Where the ring had entered, the water was not more than five fathoms, though it dropped off deeper near the stern. Someone would surely find the ring the next day.

From dawn till dusk, for three days Burke watched men, women, and children diving off the ship's rail. Without the ring he felt light, thankfully released from his sworn oath. He had no more stomach for killing, certainly not over a bunch of cups and saucers. They dove, jumped, swam, and dove again. Yet, despite diving as deep and wide as they could, no one had found the ring. In the meantime, food supplies were dwindling and fresh water once again had to be rationed.

A Chinese sailor below deck whispered, "It must have been a trick. Burke must have thrown a coin or pebble into the water."

"No man throws away a treasure for no reason," Rahim agreed.

"Aye!" said the other. "We've been tricked. Are you ready to swim to land?"

"If tomorrow brings more of the same."

Early the next morning, Lijuan, daughter of the ship's carpenter, Li Zhang, came up from her dive screaming. Her father dove after her and brought her aboard. She was trembling from head to toe.

Her mother asked, "Has someone drowned?"

The girl shook her head. "Master P'O," she mumbled.

The master was summoned from his meditation. "Speak, child. Don't be afraid," he said softly as he brushed the wet hair from her face.

"I saw it."

"You saw the ring?"

"No. I mean yes. I saw your tea bowl."

"Wonderful. How is it doing?" The master giggled.

"It's inside!" The young girl became hysterical.

"Be still, calm yourself. What is my tea bowl inside of, child?"

Lijuan shook her head. "No. The ring. I saw the ring. It's inside your black bowl."

The ship's company, who had all gathered on deck by this time, gasped in unison. That was impossible.

"Can you dive and bring them to me, Lijuan?"

"Yes." The girl settled herself down and climbed onto the stern rail and made a perfect dive into the deepest part of the bay.

The entire crew held their breath. Li Zhang was not the only one concerned when it seemed too much time had passed. At last, bubbles floated to the surface and sounds of hope filled the ship. Ma'mar climbed down the rigging to the water's edge and waited. He twisted the rigging, and wiped tears from his eyes. When she broke the surface, he caught and held her steady.

In her right hand was the tea bowl, in the other she clasped the ring.

Cheers went up to heaven. Men jumped overboard in celebration. They carried Lijuan up the rigging on their shoulders.

She placed the ring inside the tea bowl and handed it to Master P'O. "This is how I found it," she said, still out of breath. "It was sitting on a ledge of white coral."

No one spoke.

Burke felt the hairs rise on the back of his head. He looked at the emir, who was smiling and shaking his head in disbelief. Both men were thankful they had listened to Master P'O. They had waited for seven long days. On the morning of the eighth day, they understood that the spirit of the island had answered them.

Burke unfastened the chain from his neck and threaded the ring through it. He put the chain around Lijuan's neck and kissed the top of her head. He bowed on one knee, and without a word, everyone went down on their knees and bowed to Lijuan.

When their prayers ended, the emir gave his orders. "Make ready to go ashore. Take only with you what you cherish most." He spoke soft and intimately. It was clear to everyone that he was not addressing which cargo was to be loaded into the shore boats, but to bring only the best part of themselves to the new lives that awaited them.

Walking on the sand felt different under their feet. Alive. This time, the island invited and welcomed them.

Burke asked, "Master P'O, is it possible to have tea with a spirit?"

The master held his hands out as the first drops of a sweet rain lifted the smell of the soil into the air. "If you are unsure, gather this sweet blessing in a cup and make tea."

During the months that followed, Burke and Master P'O became the two men to whom everyone looked for leadership. The emir remained the ruler of the seas, which pleased him greatly. With the expertise of the Li Zhang, they built two new ships from tall, straight trees. The following spring, the emir sailed the small fleet of three ships back to Canton. He traded the two new boats for twelve large clay pots, filled with the same fine porcelain they had cast into the sea the year before.

The emir caught the returning monsoon winds, successfully delivering his cargo to Palermo, two years late, restoring and enhancing his reputation. Before his death, he made nine more such journeys from Sicily to China, and back to Green Island.

Burke gave up the great challenges of travel and adventure for the smaller ones that came from living under the same roof as Na'ila. It seemed only natural because Ma'mar was like a son to him. Na'ila loved Burke. She understood when he promised to love her, but said he would not convert to Islam. She knew this meant she would be unclean in the eyes of the prophet and his followers. She prayed to Allah for forgiveness. Her faith comforted her. She trusted that Allah could match the love and mercy of any mortal tenfold. And she also prayed to the spirit of the island, which she had come to recognize as the embodiment of compassion.

Mason built houses of stone all over the island, and married Aasiyah. They had two sons.

Ma'mar and Lijuan were married and had two sons and three beautiful daughters. Lijuan started island school under the largest monkeypod. She called the massive tree the mother tree.

Master P'O planted tea from the seeds he had brought in his pockets. The many varieties grew well and proved to be of excellent quality. The tea's reputation also grew, becoming a favorite in the markets of Canton and beyond. It was the beginning of the golden age of tea and spices.

When Burke passed away, Lijuan became a strong leader of her people. She put Mason to work building a small library next to where Burke's house stood. When the work was complete Na'ila carried her husband's books next door and placed them on the new shelves. She worked as the island's first librarian building up a fine collection.

Lijuan lived to be eighty-eight and had twenty-seven grandchildren and ten great-grandchildren. Surrounded by her loving family, Lijuan let out a sigh just before she passed away. Stories are told about how the island herself trembled with the loss of one of her first daughters. Hard years followed, which found the tea markets in Canton flooded with tea reputed to be from Green Island, rendering the authentic island tea almost worthless.

Ma'mar and Lijuan's oldest son, Zoraida, grew to be a master craftsman like his grandfather, Li Zhang. Zoraida fashioned the first small wooden tea chest, using his mother's ring as a signet wax seal. This method of authenticity lasted for nearly two hundred years, creating prosperity for the island.

In 1631, the Dutch ship *Batavian* entered Salm Bay. The reputation of the island's tea had reached the ears of Jan Coen, the ruthless director of the Dutch East India Company. A ship was sent to secure the rights to the tea. The Dutch captain was treated cordially by the islanders, but all his offers were politely refused. After the captain had replenished his provisions, he demanded his ship be loaded with tea or the town would be leveled.

The islanders ran for higher ground, cutting the rope bridge behind them. They watched helplessly from above as the broadsides from twenty-four canons smashed their homes to splinters.

To make matters worse, the chests and the seal were counterfeited and mass-produced, making it once again impossible to find a market for genuine Green Island tea.

The generations that followed lived in poverty. Many were forced to emigrate with their entire families to find work.

Tea master Xu was said to have a dream in which he heard Lijuan's sigh when he opened a tea chest. It is unknown who brought master Xu's dream of Sighing Woman Tea into the waking world, ushering in hundreds of years of prosperity for the island.

A Silver Veil

*A teapicker has a sprig of wisteria stuck
in the basket carried on her back.*
—Kyoroku

Half an hour before dawn, Figas approached the potting shed on the damp side of Kuten ridge. He saw someone waiting. His smile froze when Beba turned around.

Figas stood with his mouth open. "Good morning." Since coming home, he'd lost all ability to anticipate events.

"Morning." Beba's eyes hid her thoughts.

"Herbie asked me to meet someone here for the . . . I don't know."

"Yea, Figas, that would be me. For the . . . I do know. Are you ready? Good. Let's go." Beba started off at a quick pace, leaving him standing there in the dark.

He raced up the path, but she was gone. He found her an hour later, with the help of the morning sun, sitting on a mossy rock. He barely recognized the tall teenage girl with hunched shoulders, Cedar's older sister. He remembered the little plays she made Cedar and him take part in. He once had to play an aardvark. Now she was a woman. Her long black hair was pulled up under a no-nonsense hat. The smooth pores of her neck caught the light.

She pretended not to hear him coming up the hill.

"Look, Beba, I'm sorry. I didn't know I was meeting you."

"It's fine," she said stiffly. "That's Herbie, he didn't tell me squat either."

Figas looked in her eyes, one toward green, the other gray and clear as a cirque lake. He was used to being able to predict events, which gave him time to plan what to do and say. He'd practiced meeting Beba a hundred times, but always under better circumstances.

"I was going to come and see you as soon as I got home. I guess I got . . ."

"It's fine. No big deal, Figas."

"Can you quit saying 'it's fine'! I'm saying I'm sorry, Beba. It's great to see you. Apology accepted?"

"Sure, Figas. Nothing to be sorry for," she said without feeling.

A deep shame overwhelmed him. He stood there unable to respond.

Beba seemed to sense it. She was fierce, but she knew when to let things be. She'd never been off island, and was proud of it. She'd never admit how it cut both ways. Her father went abroad to work when she was five. She never saw or heard from him again. Her mother always spoke well of him. For all she knew, he was still alive. The world outside was a big place; it could swallow things completely, and forever.

The thin wings of a dragonfly buzzed above them, casting a surprisingly large shadow. She reached down and picked a fragrant sprig from a low shrub and stuffed it into her shoulder bag. She walked up the hill and snipped another stalk with shears she kept in a sheath on her hip.

Figas followed close behind as she abandoned the path, heading straight up the saddle ridge. Every few steps, she paused to clip more little bunches of leaves. She looked completely at home in the woods. Figas wondered if she remembered that he was even there. They rested on a small rise that overlooked the green tea terraces and the blue ocean. Beba checked the moss for dampness before she knelt down and dumped out her satchel, spreading out her wild gatherings. She held her finger to her lips, signaling for him not to speak. She pointed to her eyes and gestured for him to pay close attention. She handed him each plant specimen to examine. She wondered if he saw the plants or perceived patterns of symbols and numbers.

"What is this one . . ."

"Try not to talk, Figas. Look at all the plants and try to remember them." She held up the last wild stem for him to examine. "Come on, now it's your turn."

He followed her down the hill the way they'd come up.

She pointed back up the hill. "Let's see the genius at work."

He got out his Swiss Army knife, unfolded the little scissors and snipped bits of leaves and stems as he went, stuffing them into his pack, just as she had done.

Beba kept a straight face. When they reached the spot where they'd rested before, he dumped out his pack next to Beba's earlier collection. Without waiting for instructions, he began matching what he'd picked. He was pleased to find three identical specimens. The other couple dozen were a bluff that didn't seem to be panning out. He was greatly relieved to hear her laugh.

"Sweet tea!" she seemed tickled. "Were you trying to pick that many different ones?" She looked to see if he was playing a joke on her. "I'm not sure you could randomly miss this many if you were blindfolded." She was more zesty than upset.

"Maybe if you told me the names of the plants . . ."

She was on her feet and down the hill. "Tomorrow by the potting shed. Only earlier!" she yelled without turning around.

"I can't make it," he yelled back before he had time to think. He examined the plants she had picked and crawled around the hillside finding matches until it was too dark to see. He created a grid in his head. The numbered column went up the slope, the letters ran east to west. Without names, he struggled, so he assigned reference numbers. He stuffed B3 into his pack and headed home.

At dinner, he asked Uncle if Beba was supposed to teach him about teaism. Uncle's belly laugh was accompanied by a smile that neither refuted nor denied his suspicions.

The following morning, Figas arrived at the potting shed well before first light.

Beba was already there. "Change your mind?" she asked.

"Yep."

"With all that brain power, it must be like turning an oceanliner around."

"Very funny." He wasn't awake enough to argue.

She took him to a different spot on the ridge, repeating their exercise. Like an alphabet without any vowels, he struggled to interpret her. He felt as if he were back in one of the many make-believe productions she had created as a child. As she rooted around a tree trunk with her shears, her dark hair fell from under her hat.

"Did you find something?" He thought she was trying to trick him by not letting him see what plant she was picking.

"Look at the tree, Figas. What do you see?"

A silver veil covered the leaves. "I see the vine covering the tree."

"It's ylang-ylang, an invasive creeper. It's blocking the light and will eventually suffocate the tree. When I come across it, I clip the main feeders at the base. It's not a solution, but it helps a little." She looked at all the seedpods blowing in the breeze.

Figas looked down the ridge. With his newly acquired vision, he spotted several trees with a silver covering. He was slightly embarrassed that he hadn't noticed them before, but decided not to say anything.

When Beba finished, she dumped out her satchel. Along with all the leaves and stems were a few paper plumes.

He unfolded one. It had KISSES in blue lettering. He gave her a look, but she stonewalled. He studied each plant silently and then without retracing their steps, began snipping little stems and stalks, carefully omitting any mention of his Bingo card method. He spread out his collection. It matched Beba's nearly perfectly.

She smiled without changing her mouth.

He took it as high praise. After a brief rest, they ranged farther up the mountain. Just as before, Beba picked a wide assortment from the changing environment. Figas did his best to emulate. He soon learned it was not enough to pick the same plants; Beba wanted them from the same small environ. She taught him that Viridis was home to a wider variety of microclimates for its size than was any place on earth. If a plant was edible or useful, Beba explained how to prepare or use it. If a plant had been brought by boat, it was likely to be invasive and spread like wildfire. If a plant was native to Viridis, it was indigenous. If it was an indigenous plant that only grew on the island, it was an endemic species.

They rested on a soft termite-eaten log overlooking a small stream. Figas thought of all the patterns in nature: the veins of a leaf, the ripples of the stream. A bumblebee landed in front them on a patch of powdery earth. Its fuzzy body was soon covered, resembling a walking dirt clod. It made Beba laugh.

"Once you learn about the plants, Figas, they're here for free. You can use them your whole life. Isn't that amazing?"

"It is. Thanks for sharing them with me, Beba. I know it might seem strange to you, but numbers are like that for me. Once you learn them, they're free to use forever."

Crossing a maze of deep ravines using a vast system of narrow swinging bridges, Figas became familiar with places he had only heard about as a child. After a month, they had finished exploring the inner mountain region. He wondered what would be next. He spent the beginning of the week catching up on the tea accounts for Hu. On Thursday morning, he again met Beba just after sunrise in front of the potting shed.

"You're late." She pulled a light-colored strand of hair off his pack and held it up in an accusing way. "Tall blonde?"

"Yeah. I'd say so," he admitted. "In the neighborhood of fourteen hands."

"Who has fourteen hands?" Beba imagined her father walking arm and arm with a tall blonde her long curls falling over her shoulders like cascading heliconia, the woven panicles filled with sweet nectar.

Figas could tell Beba's mood wasn't improving. "Shiva has lots of hands."

"Is Shiva blonde?"

"Relax, Beba. It's only Uncle's viola bow shedding."

"You mean this is from a horse's tail?" She held the long strand up to the light.

"From a Mongolian horse whose name is . . . Shiva."

She rolled her eyes. Reaching into her own shoulder bag, she handed him a small variegated leave.

"Not just the plant, but where it grows, right?" he asked, guessing what she wanted.

"Maybe you're not too old to learn."

Figas was enjoying her playful mood. He took the leaf and headed up the path, trying his best to leave her in the dust. To his surprise, he led them right to where the little variegated plant grew.

Beba was pleased. "It's called hetch. It only grows right here. As far as we know, it's an endemic species to Viridis."

"I'm glad you told me the name, Beba." He let out a sigh of relief. He wanted to confess about the grid method. It made him crazy not having a designation to apply. They were now standing in J-57. He doubted she'd approve. "Can I ask you what this one is called?" He pointed to a nearby flower.

"Lantana. It's pretty stinky." She warned him against touching it.

"Is that why they call Auntie Lan 'Auntie Lantana'?"

She allowed herself a guilty giggle, then held up her hands. "You didn't hear that from me."

He wondered what had changed. "Look, Beba, why tell me the names now?"

"Have you heard the story of Leonardo da Vinci's housekeeper? She couldn't read, so the master painted beautiful little fruits and vegetables to use as her grocery list."

"So you sent me shopping with an orange so I'd bring back an orange?"

"Something like that. It's how I was taught when I was a girl. You're an islander, you should know that the most important things cannot be approached directly. This way you receive the essence of the plants, without confusing the names with the plants themselves.

I know it seems backwards, but now you know all of them. You just need to learn their names."

"Why's it so important I learn every plant?"

"If you are going to do a proper job of it, you need to realize that the tea isn't just tea."

"So I've been told since I was a baby." He held up a variegated leaf of hetch. "What have all these plants to do with tea?"

"Silly Figas! Did you fall on your head? Do I have to spell it out for you?"

"Definitely."

"Every plant plays its part. Not all the characters in a play have lines, but that isn't to say they're not as important as the lead." Beba had a sweet laugh when she let herself. "Our tea is a blend. Everything goes into it—from the tiniest pinch of hetch to our thoughts when we are picking it." She carefully picked a small leaf at the tip of the stem.

For a moment he could see inside her eyes. Her folds of contradiction faded away. The cool moon was suddenly close and tingling on his skin. "Beba . . ." He was about to confess about the grid. He wanted to touch her.

"Yes?" She stared at him, standing under the chestnut and for once not looking out of place. She sensed he finally understood what she'd been trying to show him. "This is how the world is, Figas. The sublime hidden in plain view. Can you see it? I know you can," she wanted to say. All at once it occurred to her it was more personal. She blushed.

He saw the color in her face. He told himself it wasn't anger. He fought the urge to run. Every plant might be called something, but there wasn't a name for what he saw in her eyes. He was pretty sure he was shaking. Against all better judgment, he reached out and touched her cheek.

Daughter of the Island

She loved coffee and I loved tea, and that
was the reason we couldn't agree.
—Mother Goose

After morning break, Mrs. Morris rang the bell and waited for the children to settle in their seats. Emma worked with the older children in the back of the room. They had just read *The Memoirs of Thomas Burke*. Emma had prepared a list of questions. "When Thomas Burke visited the temple of the Six Banyans, he met the tea master named P'O. What happened?" she asked.

Fletcher Kim raised her hand and answered, "Master P'O disguised himself as a peasant."

"Why did he not simply tell Lord Burke that he was the tea master? Was he not less than truthful to pretend otherwise?"

"The tea master was waiting for just the right moment to reveal himself," Fletcher explained.

"So he lied?"

"He used *upaya*, skillfull means, to help Lord Burke on his path."

"He tricked him?"

"He used skillfull means."

Mrs. Morris finished sorting through the graded papers on her desk and stood up to address the younger students. "We're coming to the end of our unit on our island forebears. It's parent night this Friday. Your assignment is to write a one-page essay on the legacy of Lijuan. Your essays will be on display for your parents to enjoy. Do you have any questions?" Na'ila raised her hand and Mrs. Morris called on her.

"Why did Lijuan sigh?"

"Why do you think?"

"I think because she was happy. She was very old and was playing with her grandchildren, and then heaved a sigh before she died."

"Very interesting, Na'ila. What do you think, Victor?"

"I think she sighed because she was sad. She was surrounded by her family and didn't want to leave the people she loved."

"Another interesting point of view. I can tell, Victor, that you've thought about this before. And you, Tsani, what do you think?"

"I think she was content. She knew she was breathing her last few breaths, and so she remembered all the wonderful things she had experienced in her life, and let out a sigh without thinking about it."

"Thank you, Tsani. Of course, no one is alive to tell us what happened so many years ago, so there are no right or wrong answers. We can't even be sure what Mae is thinking right now with her sigh." She pointed to a girl in the front row. "That was more of a silent yawn, wasn't it?"

The children laughed and Mrs. Morris winked at Mae to let her know she was teasing. "What is a sigh? Anyone? Come on."

"It's breath." Tsani answered without being called on.

"And what is breath?"

"It's from the Latin, *spiritus*," the older Gao answered from the back of the class.

"Excellent. Not simply air, but breath––spirit. Lijuan is often associated with the spirit of the island. Why are there so many stories about her, do you think?"

"She is the goddess of the tea," Fletcher Kim called from the back of the class.

"A goddess or a real person? Or could she have been both? And why do we remember her after all these years?" Mrs. Morris explained that Lijuan was the daughter of Viridis and also the mother of Viridis. She was a goddess and also a living girl who grew up and founded their school. She was a teacher, and a mother, and grandmother. Then she caught herself: she didn't want to steal the thunder from their essays. "The hardest part of writing your assignment might be fitting everything you have to say on one sheet of paper."

OVER AND INWARD
VISITOR'S VISA

Wouldn't it be dreadful to live in a country
where they didn't drink tea?
—Noel Coward

Harbormaster Grimmes had drawn a little map showing how to get to the Council of Visitors office and gone over it very carefully so Fioré wouldn't get lost. When Fioré reached the office, he was delighted to find a young and fresh-faced woman behind the desk.

"Hello. My name is Michael Fioré." He was surprised that the young woman neither smiled nor offered to shake hands.

"I know who you are. It is a small island. Please have a seat."

"And you are—" Fioré asked.

"That's very observant. I am." The no-nonsense woman didn't look up from the paperwork in front of her. "What is the purpose of your visit?"

"I'm here to shoot a documentary about your wonderful island."

"We received a request from you last February. Our records show you were sent a letter in March denying your request. Here is a copy of the letter. Did you receive it?"

"Well, yes, I did. So I decided the best thing to do was to come here and apply in person."

"I'm sorry, Mr. Fioré, that you've traveled such a long way." She stamped the letter with the date and put her signature beside it. "All

I'm able to offer is an updated version of the same letter, denying your request."

"Please call me Michael. May I ask why you don't want me to make a film?" Fioré was trying to stay upbeat.

"Certainly." A long silence followed.

"So why not?" Fioré was trying hard not to laugh, or grimace. Clearly she wasn't going to show him any of her cards.

"Are you presenting your case for why you should be allowed to film?"

"Have you seen any of my films, miss?" He wanted to at least know her name. "I sent my résumé and DVDs of all my pictures."

Fioré knew in his heart that he walked a clean path. His intentions were good. It wasn't as if he was interested in exposing the *truth*. He had learned how to get out of the way and let the camera lens tell the story. It was true he hadn't done anything remarkable in several years, but his last film, on the American buffalo, had won several awards, he reminded himself. "I'm very excited to share your beautiful island, the wonderful people, and your unique culture with the rest of the world. I'm not talking about an interpretation here; it's a documentary film."

He wasn't getting any read from the young woman, so he went on to explain that he would pay a reasonable fee, but he wasn't going to offer any preview. He had a very strict policy regarding anything to do with editing or censoring of his work. He would never take money from a producer if he thought they wanted their fingers in the pie. He would rather not embark on a project if it meant giving away the keys to the car. "May I start by knowing your name?"

"Miss Montri."

"Your first name?"

"Diya."

Fioré stood up and shook Diya's hand, trying to start over. "It's a pleasure to meet you." He bowed a little and looked straight into her eyes.

Diya looked back, nonplussed. "I should probably confess, Mr. Fioré." She didn't sound contrite.

"What is it?"

"I did see *The B Grade Celebrity Guide* when it first came out."

Fioré kept the smile on his face. It was his first film, and by far his worst, a biopic about a college prank that went awry. While in grad school at UCLA, he and a classmate named Jessica went to a party in Malibu where Sting was supposed to show up, but didn't. By 2:00 a.m., both drunk, they went to his apartment and ended up sleeping together. The next morning, they consoled themselves by recalling there had been a couple of fashion models at the party, along with a bunch of wannabes. They decided to make a class project on how to become a B-grade celebrity. They were convinced there was a formula. They were successful beyond their wildest dreams. What started out as a joke ended up earning them top grades in sociology, and more importantly, invitations to Hollywood parties where they did meet famous actors. Jessica fell in love with her new glamorous persona and all the attention that came with it. Fioré warned her about taking it too far. Within a year Jessica had committed suicide. She was twenty-three.

When he was accepted into film school, Fioré made an exploitation film based on Jessica's life. It became a cult classic. He used the money he earned from that film to bankroll his first full-length documentary. His career was built on his lover's grave.

Diya waited through the silence, pretending to file papers. Maybe, she thought, she'd been a bit insensitive.

Fioré was too lost in thought to notice the long silence. "You can't fire me, God—I quit." Bill Maher had said something along those lines about taking one's own life.

Diya coughed.

"So what's our next step, then?" Fioré regathered himself.

"To sum up, Mr. Fioré, your second request to film on Green Island has been denied. Your request for a sixty-day visitor's visa was sent over yesterday. The board is currently reviewing it. It should take about a week to process. In the meantime, you're welcome to enjoy Salm Bay or to take the visitors' tour of the tea plantation. However, the upper tea terraces are off limits without a visitor's visa. If you have questions about lodging, please take a pamphlet before you leave. Thank you for coming in." She didn't get up to see him out.

"Why don't you want me to make my film?"

"I can assure you," Diya laughed, "that decision is not mine to make."

"If it were your decision?"

"If it were my decision? Well . . ." Diya thought for a moment. "The question I'd ask myself is why wouldn't I prefer a Green Islander to make a film about Green Island? Who knows our story better than we do?"

Fioré took in the flush animating her high cheekbones. He thanked her and left the small office, feeling a glimmer of hope.

The Middle Way

*The sounds of tea being made invite the peach
blossoms to peep in through the window.*
—Uson

Beba asked Figas to stop by her mother's house to lend a hand.
He smiled when he noticed the trail of wadded paper plumes. He
remembered some spilling out of Beba's backpack. He picked up
and unraveled one of the inside wrappers. KISSES® in blue lettering.
Accustomed to putting together odd bits of information, he came up
with a likely explanation.

Es-sahra answered the door. "You just missed her."

"She told me you needed help with your persimmon tree."

"Thank you, dear. I've already picked them, but you could carry
them to the sunshine market. That would be a blessing."

"Certainly."

He picked up the two flats and followed her to town. Though
spry for her years, the elegant woman picked her footfalls carefully.
As they walked downhill, he almost bumped into her. "Please slow
down, Auntie!" he exclaimed. "I can't keep up with you."

Es-sahra smiled at being treated so respectfully. "How have you
been since you've come home?"

"Fine, I think. Every night I have vivid dreams. They wake me
up sometimes."

"What kind of dreams?"

"Last night I felt a pain under my skin, an eruption. I woke up thinking I was bleeding to death, but there was no blood. What do you think that means?"

"I think you're a very intuitive young man. It's one of your many gifts."

"But why was I bleeding to death?"

"Life can become dangerous when we ignore what's been given to us."

Figas wanted to ask what she meant, but they had reached town. Uncle was carousing with the Italian director in front of the post office. He was convulsing, holding his stomach in pain. Figas heard him exclaim, "An Italian Buddhist! Very good!" Figas was dying to race over and hear the joke. As politely and quickly as he could, he helped Auntie lay out her fruit.

She peeled one for him. "Here try it. It's not the soft, mushy kind."

"Thanks, Auntie. Very tasty."

She glanced at Uncle, who was still carrying on. "Thank you, my dear. I can manage from here. Run off and check your mail." She winked.

He hugged her and hurried across the square.

Uncle saw him coming and did a little jig. Figas recognized the comic impersonation of himself. Uncle was on a roll.

"Figas, meet my friend Michael Fioré."

"So, this is the young man I've heard so much about? Happy to finally meet you."

"A pleasure." Figas bowed.

"I had the good fortune of sailing with Captain Martin aboard the *Lady Slipper*," Fioré explained. "I understand you're responsible for the game of Volta do Mar?"

"I'd forgotten about that." Figas's favorite job onboard had been working in the galley. The ship's cook continually teased him about being an egghead. "You some kind of genius. But you work for *me!*" Cook said. Figas explained that almost anything was possible in the empirical universe, with some obvious exceptions. For instance, it was impossible to have too much butter on freshly baked bread.

The galley was so undersized that the crew had to eat in shifts. He would set the table, only to see the silverware dance to the floor from the continuous vibrations of the *Lady's* old diesel engine. He soon devised a way to put those vibrations to good use. He took apart an old wooden packing crate and made a shallow box that fit snugly over the red Naugahyde tabletop. Inside the box, he painted a map with a labyrinth running through it. Warnings of "hic abundant leones," "the ocean gyres," and "volta do mar" were depicted in colorful detail across the game board. Each player chose an origami: the Koi; the Crane; the Crab; or the odds-on favorite, Sailing Ship. The crew would place their bets during the week. Friday at six, the race was broadcast live through the ship's raspy intercom. Rebus, the official referee, dropped the adventurers on the board from his flaming fingertips. The *Lady's* vibrations propelled the paper travelers through jungles, over high mountain passes, and across vast oceans. The crew hollered and screamed encouragement, as if it were the World Cup finals.

Captain Martin had watched his crew, wondering why no one had thought of this game before. "Who could-a-figa?" Not enough youth about anymore, he concluded. The Sailing Ship bounced off the Elephant sending the crew into hysterics. The sweat dripped off the flames of the referee's forehead. Rebus had bet his wages on the paper Trident, which was currently stuck on a sand bar. "Perhaps it's not that terribly different," the captain mused. "It pays to keep an eye to the horizon, even when traveling with one's imagination. The inner shoals can cut your ribs, as quickly as a reef a ship's timber."

"Tell Dr. Sun about the daily double," Fioré said to Figas, snapping him back into the moment.

"What's a daily double?" Uncle turned to his nephew.

Before Figas could respond, Fioré filled in the details. "A Volta do Mar player has the option to lay down a side bet before the game begins. Figas wrote down his picks for who would come in first and who would come in last, and sealed this information in an envelope. Rebus held the bets. You'd get ten times your winnings if you came in first and also matched Figas's pick."

"Why is that?"

"It seems the boy wonder picked both the winner and loser every week, even though the game was impossible to rig. He was the ship's good luck charm."

"I don't remember that at all." Figas's face turned bright red.

"I understand you also play guitar, Figas, and your uncle plays viola."

"I play a little guitar."

"Why choose viola, Dr. Sun?" Fioré had met many violin players.

"The Buddha would play viola," Uncle explained. "It's the middle way."

CEDAR

This morning's tea makes yesterday distant.
—Anonymous

"It's safe. Come on, Figas, you sound like a colicky baby." Beba held him firmly by the wrist of his right arm, and was pulling him down the steep steps to the stream below Cairo's mill.

He resisted as much as he dared, without his arm leaving its socket. He felt cold and hot. Ever since he'd decided to come back to Viridis, he had known it meant going back to *the spot*. He honestly couldn't remember if it had been his idea to play down in the ravine all those years ago, or Cedar's. Not that it mattered now.

Until recently he could recall very little of what happened when he was a young child. Being on the island had brought back so much. Including that dreadful day. Now he could even remember his fingers. They had been completely smooth, polished like a piece of driftwood, when the search party found him. They could have dusted the crime scene for prints and found none. Not that it mattered. The verdict was never in doubt. Guilty. His sentence was life.

Beba was tired of his inability to move on, to free himself from that sentence. She should have insisted that he to go down the ravine to face his pain years ago, when they were teenagers. But she hadn't. Their fight last night had finally forced the issue.

"We all have things happen to us, Figas," she told him, after they had been arguing in circles for over an hour. The sun had gone down, and they were sitting on the dark porch. "And they're not all wonderful things. We move on. At some point, we have to accept that it's our life. Right?"

She wanted him to snap out of it. As if it were a mood he'd put himself in. "It didn't happen to you!" He set the record straight.

"It didn't happen to me? Well, it didn't happen to you, either, Figas. It happened to all of us. It happened to all of us!" He had never seen her so upset. "I'm telling you right now, I'm not into the Ophelia thing at all," she said, and stomped off.

She is a drama major, he reminded himself. "It's not like I'm moping around the castle talking to myself," he said aloud. When he was honest with himself, he had to admit he'd been compulsive since about age nine. At that age, he spent all his time after school building earthen and twig dams across a small creek. By the time he was twelve, he had made hundreds of them and earned quite a reputation for his little engineering feats.

A crowd would show up to watch the dams collapse. One auntie made the prediction that he would grow up to be an engineer and build real dams and bridges. She joked that she was scalping tickets before the event.

He devised a method to keep track of each component he used to construct the scale models, and kept meticulous notes about how each structure eventually succumbed to the pressure of the water. He was most interested in the first signs of demise. By the time he was fifteen, he had developed a working mathematical model of all the variables. He eventually was able to predict the collapse just before the tipping point.

Figas recalled the first time he read René Thom and Christopher Zeeman. "Small changes in certain parameters of a nonlinear system can cause equilibria to appear or disappear . . ." He constructed some of his dams using the same size pieces, such as new pencils and chop sticks; others were constructed with mixed sizes. He carefully labeled the diameter, length, and weight of each piece. He became extremely accurate at guessing the weight of small objects. He studied everything on prediction theory that he could find published. Auntie Anjou ordered every book he requested from the library. At sixteen, he was invited to attend summer classes at Princeton, based on the strength of a paper he'd submitted.

Now, as they approached the stream, it seemed to him that his inability to let things go had created opportunities. Not accepting things had been his means to a higher education, his work and everything he had become. "If you're so good at accepting things, you can start by accepting me as I am," he grumbled under his breath.

Beba gave him another firm tug, almost sending him head first down the final steps into the ravine. "Come on, Figas, it's not like when you were nine. They keep it neat as a pin down here. Anyway, most of the water is diverted to Cairo's mill."

"You can let go now," he said as they reached the stream. She released her hold, and he let his arm dangle. His right now felt about six inches longer than his left. His heartbeat and breathing were on different schedules.

He looked up and down the ravine. A shallow stream with soft banks flowed easily in the sunlight; the trees and shrubs were well pruned on either side. He remembered it being dark and brambly. Somehow he thought they would find the exact spot where it had happened, but nothing looked the same.

"Did you bring it?" she asked.

"Yes." He pulled an envelope from his back pocket. Inside were a poem and a pressed blue flower. Blue was Cedar's favorite color. He unfolded the sheet of paper and held it close to his face. Suddenly his eyes felt swollen and his vision blurred.

Beba held his hand and squeezed.

He trembled and then began the poem from memory.

> Love sees Love,
> *I know you.*
> I recognize you, as well,
> Have we met?
> *I tumbled out of reach,*
> *You were bigger then.*
> Yes, just so,
> And very young.
> Love sees Love,
> *You could drown a Universe*
> *with that smile.*
> Love sees Love,
> Again and again,
> inherits without asking.

Beba hugged Figas and held him for a long time. When they separated, he could see her gray eyes were also swollen with tears. He read the poem one more time, silently to himself, then folded it into a paper ship. The stream beside them was making its own verse, meandering between soft edges of light sand, over dark mud, and beneath a thin luster of shiny green. Peaceful, gurgling water, unknowingly heading toward the edge of the cliff. He searched for a rock to stand on, then bent down and set the paper ship into the shallow water. They walked beside the slow craft until it reached a wire fence that stopped them short of the edge.

When he was nine, a violent rainstorm high in the mountains had sent a torrent down this narrow ravine. The water quickly built up behind an old logjam upstream, and when it broke through the dam, a wall of water surged through the canyon.

Cedar screamed, "Run!"

He scrambled up the slope, but his foot caught in a root and when he turned to pull her up with him, he was trapped. He watched helplessly as she was swept by. She reached out to him and smiled. They looked at each other and knew. He managed to hold his head above the rising water with the help of a bobbing green limb. Over the years, he imagined which stick or branch might have given way first, sending the wall of water, changing their lives forever. More than that, he had asked himself why she smiled.

It was a smile that ran in the family. Here now was her big sister, with a smile as strong as any green limb.

When the half-submerged paper ship rolled over the cliff, Figas lost muscle control. He let out a cry, but no sound came out. All he knew was the shadowy sinews wrapped around his ankles that dragged him under the wire and over the ledge. He fell through the void in perfect unison. For hours, he lay on the ground in a cold sweat, his heart tumbling within the pounding surf.

He woke up in the dark, drenched. Beba was sitting beside him, her knees up to her chin. Even with the absence of light, he knew she'd been crying.

She kept her head down. She was twelve. It was her job to watch her little sister that afternoon. Would it have been any easier if they found her body? She didn't have an army of numbers to hide behind, like Figas did with his pretend clay soldiers. When she looked up, he had awoken. She wanted to reach out and comfort him, but she was drowning in her own pain, angry that he had failed to save Cedar all those years ago, sad at being still alive while her little sister was gone.

He sat up and moved closer and looked into her eyes.

In that instant, she understood it wasn't Figas who had let her down. She was doing a fine job of it without his help.

Figas grabbed her hand and pulled her into his arms, lifting her out of the rushing torrent of emotions flooding through her. "I'm sorry, Beba," he whispered. "I didn't mean that it didn't happen to you. I don't know why I said that." He started to break down again. "I'm an idiot."

"No, Figas, it's me." She smoothed his hair from his face. "I'm the idiot." She kissed his forehead, exonerating them both.

UPWISE

*Study the tea business until you're old; you'll
never learn the names of all the teas!*
—Japanese saying

After receiving his long-awaited visitor's visa, Fioré was invited Upwise by Diya Montri to participate in picking tea with a crew. The week before, he had taken the visitors' tour of the tea plantation. It was a short loop around some pitiful tea plants at the top of the Thumb. Some faded signs introduced the varieties of tea. All in all, it was the most boring, lackluster event imaginable. He was having serious doubts about his film project.

Diya explained that he must show up early at Teagate's swinging bridge to meet the foreman of the tea picking crew. "His name is Zeno."

"Is that it?"

"Wear comfortably fitting clothes, long pants and long sleeves. Not to worry, you won't be able to miss Zeno." "If you want to know about the real Viridis," she thought, "you're about to get more than you bargained for." She felt a little pity for him. "Look, Mr. Fioré," she was close to saying, "don't show any weakness. Don't take offense to anything they say or do. If they punch, counterpunch. If they ignore you, it's too late." Instead she simply said, "Good luck."

Halfway up the stone steps of the Thumb, Fioré heard the none-too-delicate sound of Zeno's scratchy voice. The unmannerly young man was fooling around with his fellow tea workers. They had been waiting close to an hour for the newbie. They chuckled when they caught sight of the director's outfit. His pants looked a size too small. Zeno reached out and shook hands, quickly introducing everyone.

It went by too fast for Fioré. The thick local accent seemed to leave things out, like a badly dubbed film. Zeno followed behind Fioré and shook hands with the crew, pretending he was also meeting them for the first time. When he came to Fioré, he shook hands again and said, "Two shakes!" Zeno rubbed his face in delight. "Cha. Two shakes!" He turned to the crew and pointed up the hill. "I go. You go. We go. Viggo."

As they crossed the swinging bridge, they passed old man Teagate. The carved wooden panels of the bridgeman's home reminded Fioré of the small tea chests. He remembered the first time he had experienced Sighing Woman Tea, in a fine Genoa teahouse. He was asked to remove his shoes before being led to a private room. He walked carefully on the tatami mat and settled on a zabuton cushion by a low sandalwood table. A shoji door silently slid open and a beautiful young woman emerged. She bowed and offered a warm towel for his hands. Then she left and returned carrying a tray with a small carved tea chest. He was left alone in the quiet to break the red wax seal.

He held the small chest close to his ear and slowly opened the lid. He clearly heard the faint sigh of woman. It raised the hairs on the back of his neck. The invigorating fragrance of the tea ran through him. The shoji door slid open without a sound. An older Asian woman, dressed in fine silk, knelt gracefully beside him and prepared tea. The cranes on her carved hairpin matched the ones on her silk sash. She ceremoniously folded the tea towel and cleansed the tea bowl before pouring. She set the bowl in front of him in an accomplished hush.

From the first small taste on his lips, he found an abundant stillness. His head rested gently against the bosom of the madonna. A sense of peace and comfort overwhelmed him. He looked back over his whole life without judgment or criticism and saw it was simply a progression, a series of choices he had made.

That golden moment of timelessness in the Genoa teahouse had set in motion a series of beginnings that led him to the famous Ryoanji Zen garden. There he sat, again finding stillness, contemplating the careful placement of the rocks in an empty sea of raked gravel. He overheard an older gentleman refer to a grouping of rocks as the mythical islands of the immortals: Horai, Tsuru, and Kame.

Fioré paused on the swinging bridge and let the tea workers go ahead. He looked over the rope rail at the shallow stream meandering across wide gravel banks a thousand feet below. He wanted to pinch himself. Perhaps it was all of those weeks of being stuck in Salm Bay, but his heart raced as he neared the mythic shores of Upwise. He was finally crossing into the realm of his vision.

He was out of breath when he caught up with the tea-picking crew. He looked about in wonder as they passed through the manicured terraces filled with the most famous tea in the world just as the mist was lifting. It was nothing like the visitors' tour. Soon they reached a high plateau and rested beside a well-fashioned hut. Inside, hanging in perfect order, was every manner of tool and implement. Fioré was impressed by the high quality of the tools. He could have been at a photo shoot for a Japanese gardening catalog.

A young woman handed him a fine woven basket to hang over his shoulder. Anchara was a soft-spoken island girl with dark almond eyes. He followed her into the thick middle of the tea terrace. She explained that all the baskets and tools were made locally. Fioré watched as she showed him how to gently pinch the new green flush from the tips of the branches, careful not to bruise the tender leaves.

"You can tell how happy the tea is by the wonderful sheen of the leaves. See?" Anchara explained that the new flush was ready to pick every seven days.

"What is that flower on your scarf?" he asked.

"A camellia blossom. The tea around you is camellia sinensis."

"I didn't know tea was in the camellia family." He asked her the names of the crew. "Is that Viggo?"

"Yes."

"Is that his real name?" He wondered if there was another Italian on the island.

"It's what everyone calls him. He hates it, so that keeps it alive. You probably noticed that big dimple on his chin, like the actor in *The Lord of the Rings*. Don't ask me." She shrugged. "Zeno just loves saying, 'I go. You go. We go. Viggo.'"

"Can I ask what Zeno meant by 'two shakes'?" It was the local man's ominous laugh that had gotten to Fioré.

"You mean besides making a pun? It was his way of placing a wager with his friends." She held up her slim shoulders to let him know she wasn't a part of it. "He's betting you won't last long."

Zeno yelled over, interrupting, "Ninety percent of picking tea correctly is half mental!"

Fioré laughed. As a Yankees fan, he was a great admirer of Yogi Berra. He was getting a kick out of watching Zeno clown around. Just then, a large local smacked Zeno on the back of his head.

"Did you see that, Pistachio?" Zeno complained to Fioré.

A small argument ensued, the outcome being that the man, named Freight, would buy Zeno a tall cold one at O'Sullivan's after work. A moment later, Zeno remembered that he couldn't go because he had to go to help his auntie. He reached over and smacked Fioré hard on the back of his head.

"I'll tell you what, Pistachio," Zeno said, "you can drink my pint! Cha!"

After the shock had worn off and the laughter died down, Fioré realized the subtle or not-so-subtle complexities of Zeno's prank.

Fioré felt an immediate bond with the crew, and they also seemed to delight in his fresh company. By late morning they were all calling him Pistachio. Anchara warned him to steer clear of the Girth and the Mirth, as she called Zeno and Freight.

Fioré swatted at the swarm of mosquitoes flying around his head.

"Don't worry," Anchara explained. "They're not after you. They're tea mosquitoes. They bite the stems and leaves. See these little red spots?"

Fioré smiled. "Better the tea than me."

He had his second basket almost full when the rain came. The pickers ran to the potting shed and took cover under its generous eaves. Though not quite midday, bento boxes soon appeared in abundance. Fioré had not thought of packing lunch, but was soon offered an assortment of sushi, generously laid out on a fresh banana leaf on a wood plank. He sat down on a long bench between Anchara and Zeno.

"Don't mind her." Zeno pointed at Anchara. "She's off with the fairies most of the time."

Fioré found the sushi rolls amazing. He was about to ask about the kind of fish when Anchara screamed. A small frog jumped out of her bento box.

"The sushi is terribly fresh today!" Zeno used a haughty British accent and fell over laughing at his latest inspiration. "Cha! Amphibious assault. Get it?" No one laughed. "May a wreath of tea be bestowed upon thine brow," he uttered, clearly disappointed at the lack of appreciation.

"Too far this time." Freight lifted Zeno off the bench with one hand. Leaving him to finish his meal standing out in the rain.

Fioré chatted with Viggo. The youth was so thin he looked as if he could walk between the raindrops.

After their meal, the sun broke out again. It was immediately hot and humid. Fioré slung an empty basket over his shoulder, ready to pick more tea. As he did so, Viggo tipped the split-bamboo gutter on the shed's low overhang. His timing was perfect. A thick stream of rainwater poured straight down the back of Fioré's collar.

He yelped and jumped around while the crew giggled. He sat back on the bench and pulled his boots off one at a time, pouring the water out. He could see he was seriously out matched. These were hardened professionals. He was going to have to step up his game if he wanted to live to tell the tale. Zeno remained doubled over in pain, nearly crying. Fioré couldn't help but crack a smile, though he was miffed.

In the late afternoon, they carried their full baskets to the drying barn. Old Sali and his crew helped them carefully spread the tea on the drying racks. Zeno hugged Sali and flirted with the aunties before pointing toward town. "I go. You go. We go. Viggo." He signaled the end of the workday.

As they crossed Teagate's bridge, Zeno cracked Fioré on the back. "Abyssinia!"

Freight translated. "He means 'I'll be seeing you.'" The big man mimicked downing a pint, reminding Fioré of their date.

Fioré was knackered, not being used to physical labor. He didn't care for beer, but graciously accepted the invitation anyway.

O'Sullivan's Tavern was busy. The wharfies were carousing at their usual tables. The big man and Fioré pulled a couple of chairs up to a middle table. The room grew noticeably quieter. Blair, the barkeep, set down a couple of coasters and looked at them.

Freight looked back.

Fioré was hoping for a menu. He knew better than to order wine. "Whiskey, please."

"Rum," Blair stated.

"Wonderful."

His big companion must have nodded imperceptibly. Fioré watched the wharfies at their back booth. A small black man with European features stared back at him. Fioré rubbed the back of his neck. It was cold. He had the feeling he might wake up tomorrow with a chill.

Two rums arrived in well-used shot glasses. Blair stacked the unused coasters and stuffed them in his apron pocket.

"Who's the man with the umbrella in the corner?" Fioré asked the barkeep.

"Dutch Moreno. He runs the wharf."

"Touch Hole." Freight corrected the barman. "Stroking his scepter, as usual."

The black man had both hands around the ebony root handle of his Smith and Sons umbrella. The whalebone ribs were fossilized yellow, and the black alpaca skin was well cared for. The barman explained that Dutch held court most evenings with his crew. They were good customers, but weren't to be trifled with.

Freight laughed at Blair's description and ordered another round.

Nothing came or went from the island without Moreno's say-so. When the fresh drinks arrived, Freight held up his glass to the back table, smiled, and downed his shot.

Dutch studied the Italian dandy and wondered what he was doing drinking with Freight.

Fioré nursed his shot. It was just what he needed to chase away the chill. He turned to his companion. "Why is everyone calling me Pistachio?"

"Cracked and green." The big man's chest heaved a couple of times in a silent laugh. He stood up and padded Fioré hard on the back, then signaled to Blair on the way out to let him know the drinks were on him.

"A man of few words," Fioré said to his drink.

Blair opened a book behind the bar and scratched a note in the ledger. As soon as the big man was out the door, the room regained its lively volume.

Fioré sipped his drink and pulled at a loose copper thread on the seam of his shrunken jeans. An old Chinese man swept under the empty tables and leered each time he passed Fioré's table. It had the prerequisite folded matchbook choked under the shortest leg. Fioré drew comfort knowing that some things were universal.

Blair returned, steadying himself on the chairs as he went, his limp almost unnoticeable. He looked at the dark stains on his new customer's fingertips. "You Upwise today?"

Fioré nodded.

The lines in Blair's forehead rose as he picked his words: "Different world."

The barman's blunt observation was followed by a look that told Fioré he'd better watch his step. He emptied his glass and waited for the burning sensation in his throat to subside before he took his tired bones down the street.

Fioré woke up early, got dressed, and puffed up the Thumb in the dark. When the locals saw him in his designer jeans and boots, they snorted their approval.

"Ah, the dark-tongued one," Zeno intoned.

Fioré shrugged, not knowing why he'd picked up another pet name. In fact, he had the unfortunate habit of licking his fingers, forgetting the green sap from the tea turned them black. Unbeknownst to him, by late afternoon his tongue was also tar black.

In the weeks that followed, a routine set in for Fioré and the crew. He began to hold his own, receiving only minor dings and bruises. His clothes were a different matter: his Giorgio Brutini boots became completely unrecognizable.

One day as they were picking, Fioré asked Anchara, "What kind of name is Zeno? It sounds Greek."

"Mr. Lance, our midgrade instructor, gave it to him."

"I have to hear that story."

She explained that on top of turning every assignment into a joke, Zeno was always late for class. Mr. Lance warned him not to be late again. The next day, he was late again, but he wore a black paste-on mustache. He looked like Charlie Chaplin's Tramp. Mr. Lance was not amused, and demanded to know why he was late. So Zeno played dumb. He said, "Who, me? I'm not late. The Tramp is!" This sent Mr. Lance into a fury. He cried, "You think you can pretend to come here incognito? The only thing incognito, Mr. Baines, is your brain from your body!"

"What happened after?" Fioré was connecting the dots.

"For the rest of the semester he was known as Zero-cognito, which eventually morphed into Zeno-cognito, and finally Zeno."

Shortly after that, the crew settled on the bench for lunch. Zeno peeled a tiny banana and held it up. Everyone giggled at how small it was.

"Hey, Pistachio," he taunted. "Missing something?"

It was early to bed, early to rise. The working weeks turned into months. Fioré was getting a picture of what old Viridis was really like. He spent his evenings planning site locations and camera angles. When his official paperwork went through, he would be ready.

One night, well after midnight, Fioré opened his eyes and turned on the light.

Two men wearing black masks stood over him. Neither spoke. They gestured for him to get dressed. Their outfits gave them the appearance of underpaid ninjas, which kept Fioré from becoming too frightened.

He followed them through the sleeping town and up the steps of the Thumb. A small shoji lantern was burning in Teagate's house as they passed. When they reach the other side, his companions gently placed a hood over Fioré's head and led him blind for two hours, up and down the footpaths.

When at last they pulled off his hood, his eyes adjusted slowly. A young waxing moon, a thin inverted bowl, floated in the western sky. Dampness from a fresh rain bent the leaves downward so their undersides shimmered in the silver light. They rounded a bend in the path, and came upon a narrow suspension bridge swaying in the early morning breeze. Fioré's knees buckled at the sight of it. Its missing planks and rotted rope were enough to cement his feet to the ground. His nerves took on the feel of the fatigued fibers holding the bridge together. The ravine was less than thirty feet across. He couldn't see the bottom, but his stomach felt the river running deep below. To his relief, his hooded companions retreated back the way they had come. He followed them on shaky legs.

After half a mile, the taller motley ninja placed the hood back over his head. It was done with a reverence that helped put Fioré's legs back under him. He understood the *what*, but he couldn't for the life of him work out the *why*. Was it a warning? Was he getting too close to something? Was it a challenge?

A short distance farther, his two companions let go of his elbows. Their footsteps receded in the distance He waited for a few more minutes, then pulled the hood from his head. He was alone, fifty feet from Teagate's bridge.

He walked straight to O'Sullivan's. It was early morning. The tavern's door was unlocked, but the place was empty. No lights were on.

Blair appeared from the backroom and regarded Fioré for a moment. "You all right?"

"I'm in the pink," Fioré lied.

Blair set a shot glass and a half-full bottle of rum in front of him, and managed not to say, "I told you so." Which Fioré greatly appreciated. He wanted to ask Blair the names of the local cognoscenti responsible; instead he gathered up his liquid breakfast and walked home.

On so many occasions when he'd sat for meditation, his mind would not shut up. Now, without a single thought streaming through his head, he climbed the backstairs and got into bed. After several stinging draughts from the unlabeled bottle, he fell asleep.

When he awoke, it was dinnertime. He fixed some plain pasta with garlic and olive oil, sprinkled a few red pepper flakes on top and turned his fork. Then he went back to bed, propped up a pillow and ate. He was asleep again before the bowl was empty.

The following morning, the crew greeted him with their usual teasing, lightly punching and shoving him around. As they did, he studied every hand and shoelace, the way each man walked and gestured.

He could see Zeno's eyes were more bloodshot than usual. "Late night?"

"Yeah, my other job."

"And what is that?" Fioré tried to pressure his nemesis.

Zeno leaned in close so the Italian could smell his morning breath. "Automatic car-wash attendant. Cha!"

The afternoon turned hot and humid. The crew poked around for Fioré's lost sense of humor, but it made him all the more quiet.

At the end of the workday, he walked straight to Diya Montri's office, arriving just as she closed the door to leave. He asked if there was any news regarding his permit. She informed him there was nothing new, and that he should probably be realistic about his situation. He thanked her for her time and frankness.

On the walk home, he decided he would sail on the *Lady Slipper* when she returned to port. Until then he would keep his decision to himself.

ONE STEP TOO MANY

Remember the tea kettle—it is always up to
its neck in hot water, yet it still sings!
—Anonymous

In the middle of night, without the help of his Rolex, Fioré awoke. Again, two masked men stood beside his bed. As before, he threw on clothes and followed the men down his back steps and up the long steps of the Thumb. He watched the way they walked, but though he noticed some vaguely familiar traits, he was no closer to guessing whom he was following. After they crossed Teagate's bridge, the smaller of the two men handed him a hood, which he put over his head. It smelled badly of mildew, and he complained. In response, the masked men walked to either side of him, took both his arms, and led him along the path. The musty hood muffled his sneezes.

After two hours, his legs were beginning to lose their ability to adjust to uneven ground. The shorter guide removed the hood and handed him a black wool mask identical to the ones they wore. With it, Fioré felt like a full-fledged ninja. It was a blessed relief to be able to breathe easily again.

The taller man addressed Fioré in a somber tone. "If you wish to turn around, you may do so now."

Fioré remained silent.

"If you decide to proceed, your personal safety will not be guaranteed. If you make it to the other side of the bridge . . ." The man hesitated.

"You will be a Green Islander," the other filled in.

"Then I can make my film?"

"Yes," said the tall one.

"At any time you can walk away without dishonor or shame," the other added. "Many good people have done so with dignity. But if you turn back, you forfeit your chance."

The two men walked ahead. Fioré followed.

They soon met a group of seven masked shadows. Fioré was sure two were women. As they neared the canyon, a gust of wind made the frail bridge billow like a threadbare sheet. Fioré's skin felt icy, though he knew it was an unusually warm evening. He wondered who was standing beside him. He thought he recognized a posture, the way the man's head sat on his shoulders.

A short, stocky figure was the first to step onto the swaying bridge. The man's weight ironed out some of the twisting effect of the wind. He proceeded halfway and then passed into darkness. Another brave soul, who Fioré felt certain was a woman, started across. Then a third approached and waited. Fioré, without thinking, found himself falling in line. When he felt it to be his turn, he tested the first plank; it seemed to swim under his weight. He figured that by now the others had safely reached the other side. He crept slowly, inching his way, stepping over broken and missing planks. The bridge swung side to side like a long hammock. He reached the sagging middle and began to climb towards the otherside. Thinking he could see the dark ground, he relaxed, knowing he was going to make it.

Just then there was a loud crack and the bridge shook, nearly knocking him backward. A woman screamed. His hands locked onto the railing rope as he turned his head. She had not waited to cross, and now her foot had broken through a rotted plank and she was struggling to keep her whole body from slipping through. The more she flailed, the more the bridge pitched and groaned. A line snapped. The bridge began to list side-to-side, sagging steeply in the middle. The woman's shrieks cut through the low groan of the unwinding bridge. Why wasn't anyone helping her? Where had they all gone?

All Fioré had to do was lunge forward and he could still make it to solid ground. But his muscles wouldn't listen. "It's okay! I'm coming to get you." He turned himself around, using his hands to support himself between the rope railings. He awkwardly swung himself back the way he had come, trying to remember which planks had been most secure.

The woman sobbed, but stopped struggling. She was slipping lower, the strength leaving her limbs. He could hear the ropes strumming lower and lower. He reached her just before she would have slipped too far for him to pull her back.

"Hold onto me," he whispered, out of breath, as he strained to lift her out of the lash-up before they both fell to certain death.

They clung to each other, waiting for the bridge to stop swinging so violently. There was only one direction to go. He half-pulled, half-dragged her to safety.

When they reached the sweet ground, they both collapsed. She was crying, trembling, unable to let go of him. They were completely alone.

He tore off his mask and threw it down. "You're fine," he said. "Rest for a bit. We'll go into town and have a nice cup of hot tea. You'll be right as rain." He gently pulled off her mask.

It was Anchara.

He cried at the sight of her. "What's the matter, Anchara?" he asked in a severe tone. "Did you see a frog or something?"

They both laughed a little, letting the shock wear off. He leaned his head against the ground. "Well," he said, with a mix of relief and resignation. "I almost made it to the other side."

Anchara giggled. "Fior-ray!" She leaned back and joined him in looking up at the starless night. "You proved yourself tonight," she said and squeezed his hand.

It was growing light as they made their way down the trail. They began to meet people. Each one stopped and bowed low. Old man Teagate was waiting on the Upwise side of his bridge for them. He handed Fioré a newly finished tea chest. Fioré was in no hurry to set foot on a swinging bridge again, but the firm grip of the old bridgeman settled his nerves.

When they reached the other side, Anchara kissed his cheek and whispered into his ear, "Pistachio, listen to me. You mustn't tell a soul about what happened tonight."

"Everyone already seems to know." He studied the small tea chest and held it up to smell its contents.

"No, they don't. Not really." She squeezed his hand tight. "And they mustn't ever know. Trust me. Don't tell anyone or you'll spoil everything." She bowed and ran back across the bridge.

Fioré made it home and flopped on his bed. He stared at the ceiling. Where had everyone gone? Why hadn't they tried to help Anchara? What kind of madness was it to send people over a decrepit rotted bridge? It bordered on the grotesque. When he found the people responsible—and he already had his suspicions—he'd let them have it.

Fioré slept all through Saturday into the early evening. He got up and made a bowl of hot cereal and fell asleep again. He woke before dawn and got dressed. He climbed the Thumb and tried to retrace their steps from two nights before. In the late afternoon, he came to a familiar sight: a thread-worn bridge. It hung ten feet above a deep, lazy pool. He noticed a rope swing tied to a high branch, from which children jumped on hot days.

"Porca troia!" Those bastards!" Fioré's mind raced. He had been tricked. Twice. Now he really wanted to rip someone's head off. He knew he couldn't mention anything of what had happened or he would be back to square one.

He walked into town and past the cemetery. The bell was ringing in the small Church of St. Clare. He entered and waited for his eyes to adjust before bending his knee. It was Sunday morning but the church was empty.

"In the name of the Father and the Son and the Holy Spirit. Amen." He sat alone in the second pew and prayed.

Father Murray came in quietly and waited. He knew Fioré was a perfectionist, especially about his appearance. By the looks of his muddy clothes and his hair, he had spent the night down the rabbit hole. He didn't smell like alcohol.

Fioré looked up and saw the young priest.

"May I join you, Michael?"

"Please."

The two sat in silence.

"May I ask you a question, father?"

"Yes, of course. That's not to say I'll know the answer."

"Father, are Green Islanders religious people?"

Father Murray gestured to the empty pews. "Perhaps you should ask them."

"I have. They usually just giggle."

The young priest smiled as he remembered some of the replies he had received over the years. He knew that Fioré had spent a long night. He wondered what they had put him through, but knew better than to ask.

"They seem far from agnostic."

"I completely agree. As I understand it, teaism is similar to a religion in some respects." And not for the faint hearted, he said to himself. "But to be honest, Michael, I'm more comfortable discussing my own faith than trying to put words into other people's mouths."

"Fair enough. I was hoping you could give me some place to start."

"I'd say you've done that quite nicely on your own."

"I meant to start to figure out what goes on around here."

"That's what I thought you meant." The priest smiled again and left him to finish his prayers.

On his way back through town, Fioré stopped to get a shave. That always had a way of changing the day for the better.

The smiling barber snapped his white linen just as Fioré hit the lumpy stool.

"Just a shave today, please, Fa Shi."

"Sha' thing."

The hot towel on his face relaxed his whole body. "Can I ask you something?"

"Sha' thing."

"Do you believe in God?"

"Ah yes." This got the barber giggling. "The divine very important. At the center of everything."

"So, you're a person of faith?"

"No faith."

Fioré waited for the barber's laugh to die down.

"Faith not necessary. We're all a part. I'm a part, you're a part of it."

"Of the divine?"

Fa Shi nodded.

Fioré sat still while the razor scrapped against his throat. "Interesting," he thought, "can it be called a religion if there is no leap of faith?" After the shave, he stood up and set his money on the counter. He was out the door before his big tip could cause the barber to protest out of politeness.

When Fioré got home, he flopped in his chair and wrestled off his boots. An envelope was on the table beside him. He absentmindedly tore it open and dropped the contents onto the table. He stared at his film permit, stamped and dated.

NO RETURN
THE KINGFISHER

A simple cup of tea is far from a simple matter.
—Mary Lou Heiss

Twin Honda BF250 outboards propelled the three high-speed Zodiac Hurricanes at a steady forty knots over the calm water. Lieutenant Peters studied the thousand-foot high cliffs through his night-vision scope. It was imperative they secure the bridge. If their intel was correct, they would not encounter resistance. During the briefing, it had been clear that any insurgents likely would go to ground. It was imperative to take control of the high ground as soon as possible. When they were two clicks away, Peters signaled to cut the engines. The commandos paddled the three Zodiacs silently to their landing coordinates.

The Recon Team of the 125th Expeditionary Force comprised thirty-six men, twelve to a vessel. Peter's smaller red team headed northwest, landing their boat on the small beach behind the thumb-shaped ridge. They dragged their Zodiac into the trees and covered it with fallen palm fronds.

Sergeant Clanahan's larger blue team beached their two inflatables behind the stone boathouses in Salm Bay. Their mission was to secure the town.

Peters scanned the steps of the independent ridge with his night scope and signaled his point man, Private Stewart Saunders, to proceed with caution. The team silently made their approach up the steps to the swinging bridge. Peters found a good angle and used his scope to survey the bridge. Two snipers found positions to cover the team while they made their traverse.

Saunders picked his way across, briefly pausing beside the small structure in the middle of the bridge before proceeding. When he reached the far side, he signaled the all clear. Peters and five men made their way silently across the swinging planks, while the snipers scanned for any movement.

Teagate awoke from the floor, and in one fluid movement, found the wooden lever beside his sleeping matt. In all his years as bridgeman, he'd never had cause to use the lever. He called out a challenge: "Who's there?" When he heard no reply, he shouted, "Stop! You have no permit to cross."

The snipers saw the old man in their scopes, standing just inside the little structure. He was frail and unarmed.

Peters sprinted toward the old man, his men close behind. "Freeze! Hands above your head!"

The old man ignored their warning. Gripping the lever with both hands, he pulled as hard as he could. The bridge shuddered. The wooden pin that held the little teahouse in place slid from its mortise. It fluttered and fell to earth, releasing the entire web to gravity. A thunderous crash echoed against the canyon walls.

Clanahan's radio clicked as he heard the distant boom. He signaled to his men to take cover down a back alley.

"Blue Leader, Blue Leader. This is Red Sierra Tango." Saunders's voice was trembling.

"Copy, Red 5. Status?"

"Lieutenant Peters and half the team are down. I repeat, down. We've lost the bridge!"

"Copy that, Sierra Tango. What's your 20?"

"I'm topside. Repeat, six men are down . . . Reeves has secured the approach."

"All right, Red 5, stay frosty. Proceed to Whiskey Foxtrot Zulu. Reeves, get your men dug in. Defend the approach."

"Roger that. Sierra Tango out."

Stewart Saunders climbed the hill alone. His legs were shaking. He looked down at his GPS and headed west, over an open grassy area. He was to locate and secure a large wooden structure. It was easy enough to find. He pulled the barn door open. It was full of pungent dry tea, and to his relief, void of a living soul. Saunders radioed his position and status. His orders were to guard the entrance and bar entry until he was relieved. He wondered, considering the bridge was down, when that would be. He told himself he was in for a long haul.

Dawn lit the eastern sky like city lights.

Old Sali as he was affectionately known—was the first to work that morning. Private Saunders barked out a challenge and pointed his gun.

Sali, though not frightened, was completely disoriented. "Who are you?" The old man's routine had not been interrupted in a generation.

When the young soldier explained that he had orders not to allow entry, Sali tried his best to laugh, as he sat down in front of the soldier. "My father brought me to work with him when I was seven years old. That was seventy-seven years ago, and haven't missed a day since!"

Saunders watched the old man for twenty minutes, sitting there.

Slowly, a smile returned to Sali's face. He understood. "I've taken the tea for granted." He thanked the soldier and walked away.

Saunders could hear bells in the distance in rhythmic burst. He listened closely. It wasn't Morse code. He spotted the old man coming out of the trees, this time accompanied by several other old people. "Halt! Stop where you are!" Saunders cocked his assault rifle in an exaggerated fashion.

All the old people stopped in their tracks, except one little bald man.

Uncle Sun stepped forward and paused several feet in front of the man in uniform. While calmly looking down the barrel of the rifle, he explained about the death of their dear friend, Master Teagate. "You see, young man, now it is up to us—his friends and family—to prepare his funeral. It is necessary to have tea from our barn to bury our friend with honor. Do you understand?"

Saunders had watched helplessly as the old man fell to his death, along with his commanding officer and half his team. He thought about Lieutenant Peters, and his wife and two boys. A long silence ensued.

Uncle was used to things taking time.

"Please stand over there with the others and I will radio in your request," Saunders said finally. "Thank you."

Uncle Sun unfolded a small bamboo mat and sat down in front of the soldier.

Several minutes later, Saunders received a reply. "Roger that, Red 5. You have orders to allow entry and the removal of one bundle of tea. Repeat, one bundle. Over."

"I copy that, Sparks. Entry into location for one bundle. Red 5 out." The young private motioned to the little man to stand up. He explained the orders.

Uncle Sun smiled and nodded in agreement. Leaving his mat where it was, he went over to the group of locals and relayed the information.

An hour later, many aunties began to show up, each carrying a mat. Saunders thought they all seemed pretty chipper considering the circumstances. They smiled and bowed as they passed by him into the barn. He hadn't been shown so much respect since he graduated as a cadet.

Each woman carried a woven mat under her arm. Some of the women arranged their mats next to Uncle's mat, and then sat cross-legged in front of the soldier. Saunders allowed the other women to pass into the barn to collect their tea. "Only one bundle, you understand?" he clarified.

Yes, they agreed. Only one bundle.

Es-sahra arrived last, carrying a basket. She knelt down on a corner of Uncle's matt and produced a tea setting. She poured Saunders a hot, steaming cup and bowed.

This must be the local tea, Saunders thought, about which he had heard so much. It did smell great. But he respectfully declined, tapping his gun to remind them he was at work.

Meanwhile, the women in the barn wove their mats end-to-end until they had covered the entire length of the barn. Then they wrapped the dry tea into tight bundles with raffia and arranged them lengthwise on the long bamboo mat. An hour later, the tightly wrapped bundle was ready to be lifted.

China came running from the forest, carrying something huge.

"Halt!" Saunders pointed his rifle.

Uncle stood up and laughed.

"It's only a boy carrying a paper dragon's head."

As the boy drew closer, Saunders could see the features of the paper dragon. He shifted his gun across his arms, relieved he hadn't shot the kid to pieces. His earlier adrenalin rush was wearing off and his attention had begun to wander.

The barn door opened and the boy ran straight inside, without looking at the gunman. A few minutes later, the head of the dragon emerged, flashing comically side to side. Saunders recognized the boy's feet beneath. Attached to the head was a long cylindrical body, carried by the old aunties. They smiled as they passed.

At first Saunders smiled back.

Uncle sat on his little mat, smiling and nodding.

The big roll just kept coming and coming. Saunders began to sink in his boots. "Hold on. Wait!" He held up his M-4 carbine, attempting to make them stop. "You can't take . . . Hold on a minute!"

Uncle Sun stood and held up one finger. "One, yes. Only one bundle."

The roll kept coming out of the barn door. Saunders clicked his radio open, then thought better of it. He had already called in. He was following orders. He decided he'd shoot anyone carrying a second bundle, even a small one. Finally, the last auntie passed, shouldering the tapered end of the dragon's tail. After Saunders watched them disappear into the forest, he looked into the barn. It was empty.

"When the ostiary of our two worlds meets the final porter of the next, what will they have to say to one another?" Uncle began his solemn remarks with a question.

Before them, on the north side of the riverbank, the wreckage of the teahouse and the remnants of the suspension bridge had been arranged with great care. Atop the tangle was the immense coil of dried tea, and lining the sides of the funeral pyre were hundreds of carved tea chests. Master Teagate's washed body was wrapped in a feather mantle of kingfisher plumes and laid at peace on the dried tea. A hot bowl of tea was placed above his head, and a full bottle of rum at his feet.

There were no flowers. The natural walls of the canyon became a massive ustrinum. The shallow, meandering stream, a reflecting pool.

"The rivers will not run against you. Can they forget they were once your tears?" Uncle quoted from the "Ballad of Jiao." "To each of us, he was more than flesh and blood." He paused while loved ones uttered their sorrow. "He was the kingfisher, his nest suspended above the worlds. We will not pass him again in this lifetime, but our relationship lives on. Our love is stronger than ever, our bond unbreakable. Love forms a bridge to places unseen by those of us standing on the ground. The bridgeman's bridge remains untouched, just as the tether connecting our body and our spirit is made of a cord unaltered by time, wind or rain. Teagate's life was a gift, so we could sleep and dream safely in our beds. Now, absent his protection, we must learn to live without fear, never wasting a moment in doubt." Uncle turned and looked to where the men in uniform stood watching.

"It's time for us to become the bridge and help our bridgeman cross over. Please join hands." Uncle's voice made a semiquaver. "There is no doubt he'll make the transit whole. Yes, our lives are forever changed. It's difficult not to want to turn back to yesterday, to the days of our bountiful Sighing Woman." Uncle lit a small bundle of tea stems with an oil lamp and ignited the pyre.

"May the light of this flame speed our friend on his journey." His voice was a hoarse whisper. "And illuminate our unseen way."

The crowd retreated quickly as the mountain of tea blazed, engulfing the body that lay waiting. A bright orange bolt shot up the canyon walls.

Uncle watched the essence of his lifelong friend blend with the smoke from an entire year's tea harvest. The intense heat dried his tears as they rolled down his cheeks. All the love that had gone into planting, tending, and picking the tea now accompanied the spirit of the bridgeman into the heavens.

Commander Prescott watched from a distance, his head slightly bowed to show respect. He could feel the updraft sucking the air around them. He regretted the loss of life. Six body bags lay in the Zodiac. Six letters to write to the wives, mothers, and fathers. Had all gone according to plan, they would have caught any potential opposition off-guard. For now, the upper portion of the island was sealed off. Bridge repairs would commence at 0600 hours.

Sali, steeped in the old ways, cleared his voice and began a bardic tea song. He sang of the first gatekeeper, the beautiful Jiao. He sang of her children, and of every gatekeeper who came after. The hardwood from the carved tea chests crackled in the fire as the children sat close and listened to Sali's voice rise and fall.

"A black ship, a black ship on the horizon.

Run for your lives my children.

Thunder to the East, a pillar of fire."

Uncle watched Hu in the shadows. His face was empty. Their entire fortune of tea was evaporating into a pillar of fire.

Uncle whispered to Es-sahra. Hard decisions needed to be made.

Figas watched as the fiery ash shot a thousand feet into the air. It was already floating down, covering everything, even the children. Their colorful cheeks a pale ashen gray. He rubbed his eyes. They burned. Though he was scorching from the flames, he shivered involuntarily. He felt his ankles sink into the solid earth. He picked up his feet to defy the perception, relieved to know it wasn't real. He closed his eyes and tried to erase the children's faces covered in ash.

On Kuten Ridge, Freight and Zeno watched the smoke rise from the south. They had managed to slip away with a small group of men, thanks to old man Teagate. They had cut every rope bridge behind them and hid any trace. They wept silently, cut off and banished, left to imagine what was happening miles away with their families. The soldiers' boots, they were told, had barely set foot on Teagate's bridge before the old man pulled the pin.

Zeno smiled. He was ready to pull the pin. Hiding from the center of the action was already eating at him. He looked up the ridge at the men he was in charge of keeping safe. All had tears in their eyes. He played the game out in his head, for now they needed to watch and wait. It was going to take courage.

"Listen to me." The big man gestured for the men to gather around. "I've made fun of old man Teagate my whole life. I'd cross his bridge and call him old woman. I didn't know under that wrinkled skin he had the heart of a warrior. I thought I was a man. Now I understand what a man is."

UNCLE AND COMMANDER

A true warrior, like tea, shows his strength in hot water.
—Chinese proverb

The next day, rope for a new bridge was slung across the gap between the thumb-shaped ridge and the upper region of the island. A soft tether once again joined the two disparate halves of Viridis.

Uncle Sun crossed the arched stone bridge at Cairo's mill on his way to a meeting with Commander Prescott. Small squadrons of white egrets rose from their nesting tree over the reservoir and made for higher ground. He admired the tiny ferns growing in the shady cracks of the bridge abutment. Three children were sitting on the grassy bank of the millpond. Uncle remembered it was Saturday, no school. They were sitting unusually still, giggling to themselves. It made his heart full to see them playing without a care in the world, after the events of the last few days. They called to him. "Come quickly, Uncle. Hurry!"

He approached. "What is it?"

"Look, Uncle. Our feet are all mixed up together!" Tsani said in her most earnest tone. They crossed their legs under the water and wiggled their toes just above the surface, pretending not to know which toes were which.

"Hmm." Uncle scratched his head. "Don't panic. I'll be right back." He retraced his steps and found a long, dry stick under a thicket, then hurried back to the little rapscallions. He poked the stick under the water, tickling the tops of their feet one by one. They screamed and leaped out of the water, jumping around him on the bank like grasshoppers.

"Don't thank me. I'm always happy to help."

Tsani tried to splash him, but the old man proved too spry.

He walked up the hill to the old post office, now Prescott's new field office. Staff Sergeant French greeted him with an efficient smile before leading him into the back office.

"Good morning, mein General." Uncle Sun used a German accent to goad the man in uniform before taking a seat. It was their second meeting in two days. The islanders had entrusted their fate to him, and he wasn't about to betray it.

"Dark sarcasm doesn't suit you, Dr. Sun. May I suggest that in future you refer to me by my rank?" The commander pulled his right sleeve out to match his left. "We have a great deal of work ahead of us. I need your help."

French poured coffee and then shut the door behind him.

"I continue to hear from the islanders that you're a good man, kind and fair," Prescott said.

"They lie."

"That wasn't meant as an insult." Prescott frowned. This was supposed to be a brief meeting to accomplish what they had failed to accomplish at the last meeting. Earlier, he had promised to scan and email all the requisite signatures by noon. In time to beat the international dateline. Time was at a premium . . . "All right. Let's take a mulligan, shall we?"

"Excuse me?" Uncle Sun wasn't familiar with the phrase.

"Let's have a fresh start." Prescott sipped his black coffee.

"Very well." Uncle Sun looked into the commander's eyes. "Quis custodiet ipsos custodes?"

"The guardians will guard themselves against themselves," Prescott said drily.

"Is that what you're doing here, commander?"

"Among other things. What are you doing here, Dr. Sun?" Prescott tried to turn the tables.

"I thought it was clear by now. I'm in charge of the unwelcoming committee." Under different circumstances, Uncle would have felt empathy for a military man. The thought of kenneling your soul and papering the entire universe with regulations seemed a terrible sacrifice indeed. Was it noble? Perhaps, but he could easily think of nobler pursuits.

"I need your help concerning the dockworkers. The port is run by this thug named Moreno, who refuses to . . ."

"Not my problem."

Prescott was through with small talk. He placed a document squarely on the table. "Please review this and sign here. And the next page, too." Prescott pointed to the yellow plastic arrows that French had thoughtfully attached. The commander explained that the current global government community could no longer tolerate little backwaters. Geographic regions not officially recognized were subject to international supervision, especially remote areas. The swamps of the world would be drained. There would be no places left to organize and train terrorists.

Uncle perused the first page. "I see this has to do with your invasion."

"There's been no invasion," the commander said, frustrated. "We've been over this already. We're here for your protection."

"I'm sorry, occupation."

"Again I must clarify, this is a temporary deployment, not an occupation."

"Now whose dark sarcasm, commander?"

"We need to look at this as a partnership. I don't want us being here to impede the working day of the law-abiding citizen."

"Spare me the platitudes. Forgive me for not sharing in your noble lie. Don't think for a moment that you can claim terra nullius. This territory belongs to us, its inhabitants for centuries. You're here illegally, a fact you're keenly aware of."

"Hold on! You think I'm here without authority?" Prescott slammed his hands against the table and stood up. "French, bring me a copy of the A/RES/66/282, as well as the latest goddamn global protocols!" He stared down at the little man. "Do you know what the threat assessments are for this region? I didn't think so."

French set two large three-ring binders next to the document with the plastic yellow arrows. "Here is the A/RES/66/282." He went in search of the other documents.

Uncle ignored the binders. "Knowing your fondness for paperwork, I've also prepared a document for your signature. It's merely a description of the events of the past week. I assure you there's been no attempt to interpret the facts." Uncle pulled a folder from his shoulder bag and arranged the papers in front of the commander.

"We are full of humor this morning, Dr. Sun. Now, if you could sign at the bottom and initial here?"

"Shall we both sign on the count of three, commander?"

Prescott looked hard into the old man's eyes. He needed to wear his diplomatic hat. He knew that. He sat back down and took a sip of lukewarm coffee. This local official blistered his patience. He wanted to be dealing with the man at the top, but the islanders didn't seem to have progressed very far in terms of a governing body. Luckily he had brought the wherewithal to organize the place. "If anyone is going to count to three, it won't be you, Dr. Sun. We can discuss the finer points of sovereignty later, but for the present, I'm the new administrator of Green Island. Your cooperation is both appreciated and vital if we are to avoid any further misunderstandings."

"You have a strange understanding of civics, commander. By misunderstandings, are you referring to the death of my friend Master Teagate?" Uncle lost his detached veneer. "Instead of signing papers, you can demonstrate cooperation by throwing your weapons into the bay. Or perhaps that degree of courage is beyond your rank?" Uncle could see Prescott using all his powers to hide his rage.

"I'll disregard that comment, since you're obviously ignorant of military culture. Let's not quibble—"

"Your ignorance is unfortunately impossible to ignore. For a Green Islander to hide behind a gun is to be a coward. To do another's bidding, with the mistaken notion one can avoid responsibility for one's actions—that is to be both a coward and a fool."

"You're overstepping the mark, Dr. Sun. I won't tolerate this."

"You can stack paper to the ceiling. It justifies nothing. There is no terrorist threat, and you know it. Therefore you have no legal justification for your presence."

"If that's the case, have all your men come out of hiding. Let's have a look at them."

"No one is in hiding. We've been over this before. Perhaps you are unaware of the island custom for young men to gain life and work experience abroad."

"Do you expect me to believe that nearly every adult male is working abroad?"

"I'm not concerned with your beliefs, only with your departure."

Prescott restacked the papers in front of him in an attempt to regain self-composure. A heavy downpour could be heard on the roof and through the open windows. He raised his voice over the roar. "I see you're both naïve and ungrateful." Prescott was seething. "I'm not a politician or a diplomat, just a soldier following orders. I expected more from a man of your years."

Uncle chuckled at the thought of being naïve. "You still haven't provided any substantive justification for being here."

"You mean aside from my direct orders?"

"It may be naïve to believe we could agree on anything. But the naïveté of a child is a precious thing. Can we at least agree on that?"

Prescott smiled. He had wanted to be a soldier since he was a child. He nudged the documents closer to the stubborn old man. The death of the six servicemen under his command weighed heavily on him. They hadn't been deployed to the middle of nowhere to spectate. "During times of instability, it is a good idea to have common goals, to maintain the peace, to protect the population, to allow for regular commerce . . ."

"To keep the trains running on time?" Uncle couldn't resist the Mussolini comparison. "You realize this document amounts to de facto martial law? We're not willing to accept your presence here, let alone agree to changes in our system of law. We've taken good care of each other for a very long time. We've no need for your unexamined good intentions, or those of your superiors."

The reserves of Prescott's patience were exhausted. "You're hereby informed of a general curfew between the hours of 10:00 p.m. and 5:00 a.m. Any persons in violation will be subject to military detention. If anyone in violation attempts to flee, he may be shot. Public meetings of more than eight individuals will require a permit, to be issued by my office forty-eight hours prior to . . ."

Uncle didn't wait for the commander to finish. He strode to the door and walked out into the rain.

THE COUNCIL OF VIRIDIS

*Some people will tell you there is a great deal of
poetry and fine sentiment in a chest of tea.*
—Ralph Waldo Emerson

Later that night, well past Prescott's curfew, Freight stood lookout.
The next patrol wasn't expected for two hours. Inside the drying barn
sat a diverse group of eleven community leaders—six women and five
men. Figas, though not on the council, had been invited to take part.
The security and sovereignty of their beloved island hung by a thread.

Es-sahra opened the meeting with a long moment of silence to
honor Master Teagate. She then called on Vaughn Chan, who gave
a brief and grim assessment of their situation. Never before had they
faced this type of military challenge. Chan updated the council
on his success contacting international officials who might be in a
position to confirm the military action. "I regret that I've been unable
to slice through very much red tape. The officials I've talked to thus
far don't know much."

The chairwoman thanked Mr. Chan. "I recommend we send
two representatives to New York with documented proof of military
action on our soil as soon as the *Lady Slipper* returns."

The recommendation received unanimous approval.

"I would also like to put forth a recommendation that we invite
Mr. Moreno to our next meeting. He could prove a valuable ally."

The motion was seconded by Mr. Chan and then immediately
voted down. The Chairwoman bowed, and then turned the meeting
over to Dr. Sun.

Uncle greeted each person with his eyes before speaking. "Commander Prescott has paper ears." Snorts and chuckles greeted his opening observation. "He suffers from a deep self-induced ignorance. I suppose we should be grateful that they haven't held Salm Bay for ransom, as the Dutch VOC tried to do. Above all, we are grateful to Master Teagate for giving his life. He traded it for the time we needed to deliver our young men from harm and to prepare our defense. I'd like to extend my apologies to my nephew, Thomas Burke, who predicted this tragic turn of events, and thoughtfully returned home to warn us. For his trouble he was both ignored, and in retrospect, abused."

Figas, who was sitting in the back with sewing machine leg, stood up to speak.

Uncle recognized him and gave him the floor.

Figas bowed and tried to organize his thoughts. When Christopher Elant had told him the price of the tea had skyrocketed, the probabilities were too clear to be ignored. Upon his return home, he had been hyper-vigilant, unable to sleep. An elaborate hoax had sent him jumping off Stony Point. Nevertheless, Uncle's not-too-subtle methods had changed his life for the better. With Beba's help, he had put an end to the cycle of blame he had created for himself. He was grateful, but he had let down his guard down.

"Thank you for including me in this council. Looking back, my concerns did seem a little absurd. I wish they had remained so. Only now am I beginning to fully understand what Christopher Elant was talking about. The surge in wealth and accompanying attention to our island was bound to bring changes, but I never imagined a military intervention." As a mathematician, Figas always began with a neutral slate, neither positive nor negative. Zero. Of course, real places were seldom if ever neutral. The rules of empirical physics had their limitations. A protective instinct resembling anger took hold of him. "I believe the troops were sent in error. To be fair to Commander Prescott, he could be acting in good faith, but on faulty intelligence. As soon as the people at the top realize their mistake, they'll be rushing to make amends. Until then, I'm not sure what I can do, but I'm willing to help in whatever way I can." Figas bowed and sat down.

Jin Morris, the schoolteacher, rose to speak. She had a quiet integrity that welcomed respect beyond her years. "This is my first council. Thank you for inviting me. Though I grew up learning the roles we were to play in the event of an invasion," she paused to swallow and steady her voice, "I can't help but wonder how a plan drafted in the distant past will help us now. What chance do we have against these soldiers?" She paused while the sounds of approval died down. "This isn't a group of ragtag mercenaries; they're elite special forces. I'm wondering if we comprehend how dangerous our situation is." She realized her voice was shaking out of control. "I hope Figas is right and that this is all a big mistake. But with all the men of fighting age hidden away, don't we appear guilty? Or worse, does it give the impression we're organizing to fight?" Jin sat down and looked at the floor. She didn't know if her words had done more harm than good. When she had the courage to look up at the dimly lit faces, they met her with looks of encouragement.

Uncle nodded his approval, giggling in an understanding way that made her feel listened to and taken seriously. He knew Jin was the voice of many of the young people. He looked at Zeno, who was rocking back in forth like a coiled cobra. "Zeno, do you agree, or perhaps you—"

"Yes!" he boomed before Uncle could finish his sentence, not realizing Uncle had baited him into participating. It was well known that Zeno thought the council a bunch of old women who wagged their chins and did lots of nothing. "Why do you want to water the weeds?" he complained. The sardonic smile on his face came across like a badly spelled tattoo.

"It makes the weeds easier to pull out by their roots." Uncle retorted, before turning back to Jin. "All good points, Jin. Thank you. So, you believe it's impossible to bell the cat? Yes, it's true these soldiers have real claws. No one here is under the impression that they are not well armed. It's all very well for me to stand here and say we have nothing to fear. If someone points a gun to your head, are you afraid? Perhaps yes. Perhaps no. But what if someone points a gun at your mother? Yes, it becomes more difficult." He turned back to Zeno. "Your friend Freight is guarding us. What happens if he is fighting an adversary and becomes afraid?"

"He loses."

"Why?"

"By becoming afraid, he ceases to be himself," Zeno made it sound simple. "And so cannot hope to win."

"And, my friend, when outnumbered by your opponents, what would you do?" Uncle's delivery was smooth and round, void of corners.

Zeno hesitated even though he felt sure of his answer. It reflected the essence of the island's planned for defense, crafted years ago by the council. "I would win by not losing."

"I agree with that approach." Uncle paused for effect.

"I don't remember agreeing to anything." Zeno wasn't going to let himself be trapped. He knew how wily Uncle could be.

"Listen, Zeno, have I ever lied to you?

"Many times." Zeno's deadpan expression gave the group a good chance to laugh and relieve their stress.

"Trickery hardly counts." Uncle pretended to be hurt. "Seriously, do you remember me ever being dishonest with you about anything important?"

"Never." Zeno shrugged his massive shoulders at the absurdity of the question.

"Make no mistake, my friend, I need your help. We all need you. We need each other. Your important moment will come. I promise you that. Trust me when I tell you, we are far from defenseless. We are this place. We are Viridis. The spirit within each of us is our strength. I'm not trying to sugarcoat our situation. Real sacrifice is in the offing." He knew inspiration was the greatest source of hope. "We'll continue to take away our natural bounty, our Sighing Woman Tea. The soldiers themselves have broken the seal. When they realize the only profit in remaining here is bitter tea, they'll leave. I can't promise when or at what cost."

"And what about Jin's point, that by hiding in the bush we seem like we're organizing to resist?" Zeno asked.

"I agree that the commander is paranoid, and he's very concerned that all of you have gone missing. That's why I believe he'll put the bulk of his resources into finding you. Therefore, our priority must be that he doesn't. We want to avoid any kind of direct confrontation. They're counting on an altercation, which they will use to justify their presence. I'm meeting with the church leaders tomorrow. I will do my best to convince bin Abu to keep a low profile. Yes, these troops are well trained, but they follow the most wooden of doctrines. They can never match our hearts. They've never met anything like our quiet fierceness. We'll fight them in the shadows where they're blind, and from what I have seen, they have blind spots aplenty. As unwelcomed guests, I see no reason any of them should enjoy a good night's sleep or a moment's rest while they remain here." Uncle looked around at the young men and women. He knew there were grave risks to any strategy. He looked over to the chairwoman.

Es-sahra thanked Uncle Sun. "I can see your mischievous imagination is running like a footie through the night." She raised her hands. "So, let's get to work updating our plans."

The meeting broke out in a muted roar. Everyone began to talk at once. An unbridled excitement mingled with the fine tea dust that filled the air in the drying barn.

"It's time to show these boys a real Green Island welcome!" Auntie Lan's sharp voice cut through the crowd. She was clearly looking forward to sticking a pin.

Figas almost felt sorry for the soldiers. Better to be shot and killed than death by a thousand cuts from Auntie.

By unanimous vote, their counteroffense was readily named Bengafly. The pesky fly best characterized their Lilliputian efforts. They were small, fast and left a nasty bite. In the morning, the young boys could busy themselves catching large stashes and sneaking them under the soldiers' tent flaps.

The following day, Uncle met again with the commander. When he arrived, Prescott was sitting at his desk, toying with the lid of an empty tea chest, holding it to his ear, opening and closing it. He felt around the wooden hinges. "These chests make a little sigh when they're first opened," he said, without offering his guest a chair. "How's that done exactly?"

"I'm here to discuss your departure." Uncle was terse. How could one explain a sigh anyway?

"What produces the sound? Is it a small bit of bamboo? I should very much like to meet the cleaver fellow who makes these things."

"Some of your clever fellows met him on the bridge. His name was Teagate. You are behind the times, commander. There is no more Sighing Woman Tea. It fell to earth the night your storm troopers arrived. You've failed. There's no more tea, no product to protect or to sell. Your mission, your reason for being here, is finished."

"Surely more than one person knows how to make these things? What do you call them?"

"I can give you an answer." Uncle took his pen and wrote the Hanzi character for *answer.* 答 "This symbol combines bamboo, 竹 with the character for fit, or join 合." Uncle wrote the radicals separately to show what he meant.

The commander thought he understood. The little chests were made of bamboo and the tea was made to fit inside. Pretty simple, really. "What are they called in English?"

"As I've just explained, you're holding an answer." Uncle smiled.

"There must be someone else who knows how to make these little boxes," the commander persisted. Trying to carry on a conversation with this old fool was like transporting a wheelbarrow full of frogs on a hot summer day.

"I assure you it was fully our intention that only one person have the artistry necessary to carve a tea chest. That was the point."

Now it was Prescott's turn not to bite. He knew that others must have the skill, and he would soon find out who they were. Perhaps the man on the bridge had a son or daughter. "What was the real name of the man you call Teagate?" Prescott asked.

The bridgeman had many names: the kingfisher, the guardian, the ferryman. "Peng," Uncle said. "His name is Peng."

"Mr. Peng?" A last name. It was a place to start. He would get French right on it. "I regret the loss of life, as I've stated." Prescott's voice tried to correspond to the meaning of the words. "Peng's family must be devastated. Perhaps it would be best if I personally delivered my condolences."

Uncle wasn't biting, either. "Condolences or not, we both know your men were ready to fire on an unarmed old man the night of your failed invasion. Your intentions from the beginning have been to secure the tea and the tea fields. Don't think we're simpleminded just because we have a simple lifestyle."

"You have a vivid imagination. I'll give you that much," Prescott scoffed.

Uncle picked up the little tea chest. It was probably the only one left on the island. He put it to his ear and slowly opened and closed the lid. For a minute he considered putting it under his foot and bringing his heel down hard. It would be interesting to see Prescott's reaction. But, as he recalled, the council had agreed to avoid altercations. He placed it back on the desk. "Your facts are spinning, commander. When they stop," he said, "you'll realize you don't understand where you've landed." Then he walked out.

YES

Truth lies in a bowl of tea.
—Nambo Sokei

"Uncle, I thought it is your intention to affirm all things?" Figas watched as Uncle swept his kitchen floor.

"It is."

"How do you explain saying yes to all things, and then saying no to these soldiers?"

"I'm glad you had the presence of mind not to ask me any questions at the council last night."

"That's all you are going to say on the subject?"

"Yes."

"Okay, let me rephrase." Figas looked up to the rafters to focus. "So what you're saying is yes to no?"

"Yes."

"Thought so."

"Look, nephew, don't take this the wrong way, I'm not a monk or ascetic. I'm definitely not a nihilist. If anything, I'm a musician." Uncle swept the threshold, pretending to hold the broom like his viola bow.

"Musician or arranger?"

"They've had their sixteen bars of *Drums and Bugles*. Now it's time to end the parade."

"Isn't that a bit too easy of an answer?"

Uncle set down his broom. "I guess you have a point. They aren't about to stop on their own."

"Good. I don't like the soldiers being here at all. In fact, I hate them."

"You know, I wouldn't harm a hair on their shorn little heads. And I doubt very much you could, either. That said, unwelcomed guests with guns? They're going to have the table set for them differently. Yes?"

THE ECUMENICAL COUNCIL

Teas vary as much in appearance as the different faces of men.
—Hui-tsung

The annual Ecumenical Council meeting had been moved up two months due to the military crisis. Dr. Sun was invited to represent the indigenous laity. He joined the local church leaders—Father Barrett, the young Muslim cleric Ali bin Abu, Rabbi Morton Schmuken, and the chairwoman, Reverend Betty Keller, who was representing the Methodist Church. Ecumenical Council meetings were traditionally held at the neutral location of the island school. The students' desks were moved to the far end, and folding tables and chairs were set up in a semicircle.

"Buongiorno," Uncle greeted Father Barrett with a flourish and his best fake Italian accent. The old priest had no Italian ancestry and never understood why the locals thought he spoke Italian. He did love Latin and was devastated by Vatican II. Mass wasn't truly Mass unless intoned in the original language.

Pleasantries were exchanged, and the meeting was called to order.

Uncle did his best to lie in the weeds. That is, until Ali was recognized. Ali had taken the place of the much-beloved mufti, bin Fahim, who had died three years earlier. To Uncle, bin Fahim's younger protégé had an outward understanding of inward things.

Uncle stood up, interrupting Ali.

"Sit down, Dr. Sun. I have the floor." Ali looked toward Betty for support. She kept silent.

"I have the right to be recognized, Mr. Abu. I would just like to remind you, in case you didn't realize, Commander Prescott is licking his chops waiting for someone to openly challenge his authority. If that person happens to be a Muslim, he will regard it as a gift from heaven."

"And what is your point, Mr. Sun?" He wished the old fool had not been invited. "What can you claim to represent? Not a thing. Nothing!"

"Precisely, Mr. Abu." Uncle giggled. He couldn't have put it better himself.

Ali stared at Uncle. "Do you not see Satan's hand in all this?"

"Are you suggesting we should be frightened like children?" Reverend Betty shot Uncle a withering look. He tried to soften his approach. "Bin Fahim often shared stories from the Qu'ran. I recall him speaking about Iblis."

"Yes, Iblis was the Lord's favorite angel, but was cast from heaven."

"Why was he cast from heaven?" Uncle pretended to have forgotten the story.

"He refused to bow to man."

"Interesting. So he didn't refuse to bow to the creator, but to the creation—to humankind. Is that right?"

"Yes." It pleased Ali that even an unlearned man like Mr. Sun knew that much.

"And what was his punishment for not bowing to humankind?"

"As I said, he was cast from heaven."

Uncle gave the young cleric a satisfied smile. "I think I'm beginning to understand. Separation from the divine is a terrible penance indeed. Still, I'm not sure the idea would frighten many children today."

"So you would let these soldiers take our island? Kill our young men? Steal our children's future? Can you not see the devil at work?" Ali raised his arms, ready to rain down justice from the heavens.

"Gentlemen, please. Order!" Betty stood up and held out her hands. She had let things go on long enough. "Please sit down, Dr. Sun. Bin Abu, this is not the time to rabble-rouse. I believe we've agreed on this point in previous discussions. We've called this meeting for the express purpose of protecting the peace and to guard against unlawful behavior the troops may be tempted to take part in. Foremost in our minds is the protection of our young women. Need I remind you, a society that does not protect its women and children cannot call itself a society. I'm not sure what our best approach should be. However, I can clearly state that we will not raise an army to defeat an army."

Rabbi Morton stood up in agreement. Father Barrett stood up because he didn't like being the only one sitting down.

The meeting was going much better than Uncle had expected. He was unabashedly having the time of his life. He often joked with the young priest, Father Murray, that their situation was not unlike the classic Pandava of the Mahabharata. The two priests, the rabbi, Bin Abu, and he made up the five brothers of the Pandava. All were married and joined to the same woman, Draupadi. Or in this case the Rev. Betty. She calmly motioned for her spouses to sit down.

Uncle had met Betty in private before the meeting to brief her. They had been friends for many years, and he trusted her. She grew up in Northern California, came of age in the late fifties, and witnessed and took part in the counterculture of the early sixties. His nickname for her was Summer, short for Summer of Love. Their first encounter made an instant impression on both of them. He was given the task of showing her to the rectory when she first arrived on the island twenty-eight years before. The Viridis Council, by way of introduction, had given her the most rustic accommodations available. Rotted posts on uneven ground supported a small hut with a patched, rusted roof. The windows were missing panes, and the screens were rusted and torn. The front door, lacking a bottom hinge, fell open against the dirt floor when Uncle turned the knob. He kept a straight face.

The young woman entered and looked around. "I grew up across the Golden Gate from San Francisco, under the penumbra of the young gods of Tamalpais. They've helped me recognize that chopping wood and carrying water are little miracles of their own." She looked around the little room. "I love it."

"Does Gary Snyder make your pantheon of young deities?"

"You've heard of Snyder?" The young woman was amazed.

"I met him on the green paths overlooking the Golden Gate. We sat and watched a ship gliding into the bay. The bridge workers were on their scaffold, painting. I asked your Mr. Snyder if it were true that a drop of orange paint had landed on a seagull's head, prompting a new breed of seagulls to be declared. He laughed and said if it wasn't true, it should be."

Though Uncle fell well short of embracing the good news message the young Methodist brought with her, they nonetheless managed an enthusiastic conversation that had lasted nearly thirty years. They agreed on all the important points: one could access the divine directly without the need of a priest or go-between, and little miracles in nature were proof enough of the divine. He allowed that she might have different names for the workings of nature. For her part, Betty never backed down or conceded a thing. Her hard work in the community became an integral thread that ran through of the fabric of the island.

Though Father Barrett, Rabbi Morton, and Reverend Betty had all lived and worked on the island for many years, Saturdays and Sundays found their places of worship mostly empty. Betty never took it personally. She marveled at how the island culture melded the three Abrahamic faiths, while the religions of the East blended into a unique form of teaism. For an islander, the teachings of one prophet didn't conflict with the teachings of another. Nor did East seem to clash with the West, but both were steeped in peaceful harmony.

To the other church leaders, Uncle had offered no mention of his meeting in the drying barn two nights before nor of his ongoing talks with the military. Rabbi Morton hosted a lively Tuesday night mah-jongg gathering at his synagogue. It was usually the only time anyone came to temple. Now he looked around the room at the other church leaders. It was time to step forward and get serious. Rabbi Morton surprised everyone by standing up. "I suggest we make it our priority to get out into the community and raise our profiles. Each of us should meet with this Commander Prescott and make an effort to reach out to the troops. Let's invite them to synagogue, mosque, and church."

The remainder of the meeting was spent reviewing the guidelines set forth by the island's Non-Proselytizing Agreement. They could welcome and invite potential parishioners, but never actively sell their wares. Their good work was to speak for itself. Marketing their faith was a one-way ticket off the island. The rules of the Non-Proselytizing Agreement, however, were not clear with regard to servicemen.

WILMA

Make tea, not war.
--Monty Python

Corporal Fields used his laser rangefinder to measure the distance to the top of the ridge. Yellow survey flags formed a zigzag line up the steep green slope. The cammo-painted D9 Cat rumbled out of the amphibious landing craft utility and squeaked and chugged its way up the sandy beach. The locals were cordoned off from the area by a tall fabric fence and rolls of concertina wire. It was impossible to miss the heavy troop presence.

When Uncle Herbie learned about the bulldozer, he organized a protest. Three hundred islanders filled every step of the Thumb, which overlooked the opposite slope where the road was about to be cut in. The protestors held homemade signs and sang songs about their beloved old trees.

Figas found his tea boss in the crowd and joined him on the twenty-seventh step. "It's not looking so good, Herbie."

"Makes ya wonder how long befa we all work for some new, bigga boss."

Although Herbie was technically one of his bosses, Figas had not thought much about their chain of command. "That's a good point, Uncle."

Herbie wasn't listening. He was thinking about the trees. He wasn't going to stand by and let his loved ones be harmed.

Uncle warned the commander that going ahead with their plans to build a road without local consent was a provocation that would not be forgotten.

"You can't stand in the way of progress, Dr. Sun." Commander Prescott was nonplussed as he proudly watched his men at work.

"By progress, do you mean become a sentient being?"

"A road built for free? Surely you realize how this will benefit the island." Not to mention, he thought, how much easier it will make my job. "What you have now is a small town below and basically rural poverty everywhere above. Soon you'll have a wide road that reaches across the island." The commander was proud of how succinctly he was able to explain the obvious. Fields, the company engineer, had crunched the numbers. The most efficient way to gain access to the upper region of the island was to build a road. "You'll be able to achieve things in the interior with almost the same ease as in Salm Bay. That equals jobs, growth, and prosperity."

"We have jobs," Uncle pointed out.

"Oh, my mistake. I heard you say recently that the young men had to leave the island for work."

"You have no justification for bulldozing our island."

"Nonsense. You'll see." He couldn't understand what the fuss was about. Armies had built roads since the days of Julius Caesar. Plus, what was the point of having an army if you had to ask permission every time you wanted to implement a positive change? The old codger would thank him before it was all said and done. "Perhaps you'd prefer to live in the mud. That's fine. But other citizens might prefer to join the twentieth century."

"You mean the twenty-first century?" Uncle hated quoting Hu.

"So you've heard of it?" Prescott turned his back and walked to a better vantage point to view the machinery doing its work. Watching the D9 Cat was like watching an entire armored division cross the North African desert, challenging Rommel's best panzer division. The smell of diesel filled him with hope.

"It's our island, Prescott! We're the ones to decide what's to be built or not built." Uncle felt the boot on the back of his neck. He wondered how much longer he could lie down and take it. He had to admit, however, that more people now lived in Salm Bay than Upwise. This had changed slowly over the years. The traditional lifestyle was dying along with the oldest generation. He was witnessing the last days of old Viridis. "You'll regret this, Prescott."

The locals screamed their protest against the wind, drowned out by the din of the earthmover. A coat of fine dust settled on the green leaves around them. Uncle couldn't stand to watch the bulldozer cut its way up farther the slope. He grimaced as he imagined what would be destroyed when the machine reached the tea terraces and monkeypod trees.

He hurried to Vaughn Chan's office. "Hava, I need you to download some schematics."

"I'm already on it."

All through the night, footies carried messages. Time was of the essence. The bulldozer had chewed halfway up the rise and was resting for the night atop the rocks and dirt it had pushed over the green hillside. The larger boulders had rolled down into the back alleys of Salm Bay. Generators fed a bank of lights strung along poles up the steep slope. Outside the wire perimeter, night patrols crisscrossed the boundaries.

The commander slept soundly through the night. Soon he would be able to drive to his upper command post. How ridiculous to walk wherever one went. If he never saw another long stairway or set of switchbacks, it would be too soon. Sitting behind a desk for so many hours a day sometimes made it difficult to see how one was making a difference. It was occasions like this that made it all worthwhile. A few more hours and they would christen Prescott Memorial Highway.

Early the next morning, Private Collins turned the key and waited for the glow plugs of the diesel to heat up. His helper, Private Shaw, backed the all-wheel drive fuel rig close behind the Cat. When he was finished, Shaw climbed out from underneath and brushed off his coveralls.

"She's all fueled. The beast is greased," Shaw announced in his South Texan drawl. He wiped around the fuel cap like a butler polishing the silver.

The ready light came on, and Collins fired her up. "I'll let Wilma warm up for a tad. Shaw, you best roll your gas can off my sand pile till I'm topside." Collins pointed to the crest. He did love his job.

"Good luck, Collie!" Shaw pocketed his rag. "Will you look at that cloud? It looks like it could talk." A giant thundercloud darkened the eastern sky as Shaw drove the fuel rig back the bumpy, narrow tract, giving the D9 Cat room to move.

Collins pushed both sticks forward, sending the heavy machine lurching forward. The outside left track reeled off on the ground and lay there like a thick slab of bacon. An important cotter pin had gone missing. The right inside track gripped, abruptly spinning the big machine ninety degrees. Collins pulled the right stick back, keeping the left stick forward, unable to comprehend why she wasn't responding. He barely had time to curse before leaping. He watched as his beautiful Wilma made a slow-motion swan dive. She pitched forward, leaving huge divots where she rolled.

Herbie led the cheers that went up from the steps of the Thumb as the crowd of islanders jumped up and down in sheer joy. Herbie had a wide grin and a gleam in his eye as he watched Wilma gather speed. She tumbled end for end and ripped through the fabric and wire barricade. She crashed through the backside of Lang's Green Dragon Works and came to rest in the middle of the stone carver's shop. A muffled pop could be heard as the engine let out its last gasp from her crimped exhaust stack.

The protesters danced on the steps and hugged each other. The storm that had been brewing to the West opened up, pounding the dry ground with a massive downpour. The dusty leaves once again turned a deep green.

The commander felt the ground rumble. He heard the radio message come in to French before the staff sergeant burst through the door.

Uncle was waiting in front of Lang's, getting soaked to the bone as the commander and French rushed up. Prescott's temples were bulging, testing the tinsel strength of his wire-rimmed glasses as he tried to force the door. It wouldn't budge. French grabbed a length of pipe leaning against the building and jimmied it open. A thick cloud of stone dust filled the warehouse and spewed out into the street.

Uncle followed the two men inside. He could barely hear the commander's string of curses over the rain pounding on the roof. The entire back wall was flattened. A section of the roof was hanging like a felled metal bough. Shafts of light poured in with the rain.

The three men stood looking at the twisted heap smoking and hissing.

Uncle looked at Prescott and shook his head. "I hope you sprang for the damage waiver."

FIFTEEN CANDLES
AND A QUILT

We haven't had any tea for a week . . .
The bottom is out of the Universe!
—Rudyard Kipling

Sergeant Clanahan heard voices and laughter coming from a neighborhood house as he and his men passed on the lane. He gave hand signals to the others as if preparing for a surprise attack on an enemy compound. His adrenalin kicked his heart rate up as he crept up to the house like a cat. He listened at the front door before signaling his men to burst in.

The laughter of the birthday party turned to screams. About a dozen small children huddled in a corner around their mothers.

"This is an unlawful assembly. A permit is required prior to any public meeting." The sergeant didn't write the law; he was just informing them of their apparent ignorance.

"But it's just a birthday party," an old auntie stated the obvious as she shielded her granddaughter's face from the intruders.

Clanahan looked over the group. Again, no men over sixteen or under sixty. He walked up to the cake and counted fifteen candles. He yanked a candle out and tasted the frosting. He tilted his head, like a food critic about to deliver his opinion. He stared at the cake momentarily before smashing his whole face into it and taking a big bite.

225

Muted screams and angry groans rose from the family members and friends. The birthday boy, Deoden, lunged at the sergeant, but his mother grabbed his wrist and pulled him back.

Clanahan laughed as he wiped the frosting from his face. "Finally, one person on this island with balls. Happy birthday!" He held out his hand, as if to shake with the boy.

Deoden glared back, breathing hard, hands tight behind his back.

His grandfather stood up. "It's time for you to leave."

"Sit down and shut up." Clanahan pushed the old man back into his chair.

Deoden slipped from his mother's grip and grabbed the sergeant from behind.

A moment later, the boy was writhing in agony on the floor, his leg pinned by the sergeant's boot.

"Arrest this man!" Clanahan declared. Two men grabbed Deoden and carried him out the door, two steps behind the sergeant.

The whole family ran after them, protesting all the way to the soldiers' encampment.

The guard at the gate stopped them. "Go home. You can come back tomorrow and get the boy." He did his best to explain it would be useless to hang around the gate all night, making his life miserable.

Bells of every timbre could be heard coming from the lower valley and beyond. The camp was put on high alert, and searchlights began sweeping the areas outside the perimeter. More and more locals gathered, setting their lanterns in an ever-widening circle outside the fence. They began to chant, "Deo, Deo, Deo, Deo."

Staff Sergeant French had the unenviable task of waking Commander Prescott from his sleep.

"What is it, French? I don't hear gunfire. This better bloody well be important." He heard the bells from every direction. His staff sergeant gave him a brief outline of the situation. Prescott cursed Clanahan under his breath, then ordered French to radio the guard at the gate. "Have him tell the crowd the boy will be released in the morning. Everyone better go back to bed, or they'll spend the night in the brig as well."

"That's just what the locals have been told, sir, but tensions are running high. The situation's escalating."

"Very well."

The commander was not happy when he approached the security gate. "What's that they're saying, French? Deo? As in 'in excelsis deo?'"

"No, sir. It's the boy's name."

"Get me Clanahan. And let's see this little terrorist. ASAP!"

When the commander saw the boy and the swelling on the left side of his face, he knew it was time for some damage control. "You all right, son?" he asked.

Deoden nodded.

The commander led the boy into his barracks office and gave him the chair behind his desk. "You like hot cocoa, son?"

The boy shook his head.

"Get his parents in here, French!"

The staff sergeant had already ordered the parents to be found and brought.

When Clanahan reported, Prescott got two inches from his face and screamed with all his fury, while the boy's mother and grandparents watched. "What kind of an idiot picks a fight with a child?"

The sergeant stood at attention, unflinching.

"Well?" Prescott wanted an answer.

The sergeant stared at his commanding officer with a look that said "I'm not an idiot."

The commander had heard it all a thousand times. "I suppose you want to tell me you're not an idiot, that it takes real brains to do this good of an impersonation?" For the better part of an hour, Prescott abused his sergeant. He then apologized profusely to the boy's parents, promising it had all been a big mistake and assuring them that nothing like this would ever happen again. They had his word on it.

Deoden's mother and grandparents listened without smiling or acknowledging anything the commander said. They took the boy and left. The large crowd at the gate cheered when they saw Deoden emerge. When they saw his swollen face, they began to shout, "Get off our island, off our island! Get off our island, off our island!"

Over the next week, the protests became a daily and nightly vigil, organized so at least fifty people were always at the security gate. The loudest and worst singers were asked to come after midnight.

A group of women got together and shared their old fabrics. They organized quilt blocks to be made by everyone. Zeno contributed a particularly graphic two by two, as did many of the young men in hiding. Freight refused. Not that anyone had asked him. When the women had enough blocks, they set about quilting them altogether. They worked all night in shifts.

The following morning, the commander was forced to rise early. "What is it now, French?"

"I think it's best if you come see for yourself, sir."

When the commander looked out, he saw a fabric ring encircling the encampment. He stared at it. "What is this thing, French?"

The islanders booed and jeered as loudly as they could. Prescott smiled and waved, like the villain in a melodrama, trying to get the audience to behave. But it was gas on the flames.

"It looks to be fabric, if I had to guess, sir."

"I can see that! Get Dr. Sun down here before this takes a turn for the worse."

The returning patrols weren't sure about stepping on the quilt that blocked the gate. They were ordered to do back-to-back patrols until the situation was remedied.

When Dr. Sun arrived, Prescott went to the gate to discuss the matter. "What is this mess?" he yelled over the fabric barrier and the din of the hostile crowd.

"If I had to guess, I would say it's a giant peace quilt."

"What's it doing here?"

Uncle Sun thought Prescott would make a great straight man when his military service ended.

"I'll give you twenty minutes to remove this mess."

Uncle looked over at the women shouting at them. "I for one am not sticking my nose in this hornets' nest." He turned and walked away.

Prescott put his left hand on the pearl handle of his revolver and clicked off the safety. As the devil would have it, shooting Sun in the back wasn't an option. He likewise thought better of marching his men over the handsome quilt, knowing their muddy trail would provide more unnecessary ill will. He thought about cutting or going underneath it, but decided that would be too undignified.

"Sergeant, have your men bring out some bed rolls and lay a path across this——whatever it is." He turned and marched back to his office. "Get Doogan down here on the double. Have him clear away this mess! Find a damn seam or something!"

ALISON STEVENS-FOWLING

Though I cannot flee
From the world of corruption,
I can prepare tea
With water from a mountain stream
And put my heart to rest.
—Ueda Akinari

Alison Stevens-Fowling of ACUGO, multinational commodities corporation, arrived by the company yacht, *Starry Night*, a seventy-six-foot Lazzara. A leggy woman in her midthirties, she stood like Botticelli's Venus in the stern of the sleek runabout, which glided effortlessly over the foam.

Dutch Moreno and a half-dozen wharfies gathered around the graceful mahogany craft as she docked. Her engine purred gently as a crewman jumped onto the floating pier and fastened the line to the dock's bollard. The wooden boat's classic curved lines were out of an old movie. The wharfies were speechless. The glimmer of the mahogany surpassed even Blair's polished bar top, and that was saying something. The boss of the wharf offered the lovely Alison Stevens-Fowling a hand.

The silver heel of her sling-back stiletto pumps touched down on the dock. "Why, thank you," she said breathlessly. "Could one of you strong gentlemen tell me where I might find the port authority?"

"Follow me, miss." Dutch escorted her up the rolling gangway and across the street, with his umbrella under his arm and his hat in the other. He held the glass door open.

She thanked him and squeezed his hand in an affectionate way that let him know his services were no longer required. Then she rang the little bell on the glass counter and waited for the harbormaster. When Grimmes emerged from his back office, she presented her card.

Grimmes squinted. It appeared the young woman was an attorney. "You'll have to come back tomorrow."

Alison Stevens-Fowling reached out her lily white hand.

The harbormaster felt the smoothness of her touch.

She had never seen such a cute building. "Why," she exclaimed, "it looks like an old ship!" She lightly scratched the inside of his palm with her long red nail. "Are you a ship's captain?" she asked, batting her long lashes.

The harbormaster felt himself trapped in a strong current drifting toward the shoals. He pulled his hand away as he remembered not being just a ship's captain but also a fleet admiral. "First thing in the morning I will have your paperwork ready. Thank you and good-bye." He pretended to be hard of hearing, which was becoming easier and easier as the years progressed.

The next day, the harbormaster used his standard techniques to stall her, but Alison managed to close every loophole he invented.

When she left the port authority office, Uncle Sun was waiting for her on the floating pier beside the Hacker-Craft launch. He was watching a white cigarette butt with bright red lipstick stain bobbing up and down on the surface of the water.

She grabbed her phone from her oversized handbag.

"I'm sorry, you won't get any reception here," he thoughtfully explained.

Alison regarded Uncle as one might a homeless man and politely informed him, "I will. It's called a sat phone." She speed-dialed and spoke with authority. Toward the end of the call, she noticed a tiny imperfection on the end of one of her long nails.

When she finished her chat, Uncle was standing in front of her. "A sat phone? I've never heard of such a thing. May I see it for a second?" he asked sweetly.

"I suppose so, but be careful, it's the newest . . ."

He promptly fumbled and dropped it into the bay. "Terribly sorry!" Uncle bowed and apologized profusely.

She let out a small "Eek!" and nearly clubbed him with her Coach handbag. She stepped aboard the launch, taking a hand from one of the crewmen, and was whisked away to the *Starry Night*.

The young wharfie named China ran down the dock and dove in. He came up a moment later smiling, with the phone in his hand. Uncle promptly brought to it Vaughn Chan, who disassembled it and carefully dried each component. He did a thorough search of all the phone numbers on the SIM card, careful not to activate the GPS feature, knowing it could be tracked.

The following morning, Alison was disappointed to find a woman, Diya Montri, in charge of visitors' visas.

Diya had been warned by Uncle Sun not to underestimate Miss Stevens-Fowling. The young attorney wore a short multipleated skirt that made her look younger and less dangerous than she really was. Diya was disturbed by the sharpness of the woman's incisors when she flashed her fake smile. Diya took two straight pins from her desk drawer and wove them between the top visitors' form, a well-used piece of carbon paper and the copy sheet beneath. She pressed down hard with a black ballpoint pen, then licked her thumb to peel up the top sheets to check if the copy was working.

Alison Stevens-Fowling watched with horror. What century was this?

"Last name, please?"

"Stevens-Fowling."

"Spell that, please . . ." Diya milked it for three hours before Stevens-Fowling marched out, her stiletto heels denting the hardwood.

"She was impressive. I'll give her that," Diya later confided to Uncle when he stopped by for a report.

"How so?" Uncle looked down at the cookie drawer.

"She put her lipstick on without a mirror. And it was perfect. That tells me she's an experienced woman used to being on the go.

She wanted to apply for a business license. And to talk to a property agent. She wants to speak to a man, I'm certain about that. How about you, Uncle? You're her type." Diya allowed herself a little giggle as she imagined the young temptress rubbing his bald head.

"We've met, and yes, there was a spark."

"I explained there are no property agents, and only citizens can own land. She wanted to know about citizenship applications. This woman moves fast. She asked about leases. Long term. Short term. I told her I didn't know if someone with a temporary visa could do any of that. She punched lots of notes into her phone after I said that."

"So she has a new phone already." Uncle smiled.

"She acted as if she would sue if I didn't say the correct thing. Is there an international law that requires us to comply with her requests?"

Uncle shook his head. "It's still our island, though I can't help but wonder for how long. Our Miss Stevens-Fowling also went to see the commander. I understand he's agreed to help her acquire a business license. I don't think it would be wise for us to deny her the license. Probably our best hope is to make the process long and tedious."

"That won't be hard."

"By the way, the carbon paper was brilliant! Grimmes was in hysterics when I described the straight pins. If Stevens-Fowling gets a straight no, she'll simply maneuver Prescott into giving her carte blanche. It wouldn't surprise me if there's been collusion from the start. That is what my nephew was warning about, but I was too pigheaded to listen. Now it may be too late." He cast another glance at the drawer. "Remember to lock all the originals in the safe. Starting tomorrow, old Sali will stay the night in the building."

"Isn't that a bit much? What do we have that's worth stealing?"

"It's important we keep records of the legal process. To be honest, I'm not sure anymore. We just have to stay strong and do the best we can to navigate the current. I'll see you tomorrow."

She reached into her bottom drawer for a cinnamon crunch. She held it up for Uncle. To her surprise, he was gone.

In the early hours of the morning, Freight stood watch outside the drying barn while Uncle addressed the Viridis Council. He described how a lawyer hired by ACUGO was pressuring them into allowing international companies to do business on Green Island. To make matters worse, Commander Prescott was facilitating her efforts, if not complicit from the beginning. By calling the numbers in Alison Stevens-Fowling's phone, Hava had discovered that ACUGO had no real assets of its own and was merely the shell company for an unknown equity firm.

"She certainly has the bona fides," Vaughn added. "Including a master's in global business law. I was able to contact several of her superiors in the company. Their CFO informed me, in no uncertain terms, that ACUGO is not required by law to disclose the identities of its investors."

"So we don't know who's behind all this?" Jin Morris asked.

"That's right," Uncle replied.

"If there's no Sighing Woman Tea, what interest do they pursue?" Es-sahra had a firm grasp of the most important aspect of their strategy.

"That's what I've been going over in my mind. One possibility is they plan to grow tea under their own label, claiming it to be Green Island tea. Which it would be."

"So we're going to be treated as an agricultural zone, like the European appellation d'origine contolée?" Es-sahra was well aware of the protected designation of origin. Every Green Islander learned in school how Charles VI granted the people of Roquefort-sur-Soulzon a monopoly on their sheep milk blue cheese. That was a hundred and fifty years after Li Zhang's grandson, Zoraida, carved the first tea chest.

"It's clear they mean to set up their own tea operation and will do whatever's necessary to get what they want. We've led them to believe the goose that laid the golden egg is dead. They've called our bluff. They'll not try to imitate our tea but to compete with it by leasing or buying land to grow their own Green Island tea."

The council members understood that no corporation knew the secret of the tea chest or what made their tea special. But quality was not the only important factor. It was the story that swayed and held people's imaginations. One only needed to have eyes and ears to know that the illusion of the truth was as good as, if not better than, the truth itself. Certainly, any tea from the island would carry with it a significant reputation.

"It is safe to say we're being outmaneuvered on every front," Uncle conceded. "Our young men can't be expected to hide in the bush indefinitely."

DOOGAN

Bread and water can so easily be toast and tea.
—Anonymous

Private Doogan McPhearson made his way through the security gate of the encampment and the mass of protestors. They reminded him of soccer fans at a match holding up homemade signs and shouting. Their naturally smiling faces seemed to undermine their purpose. He climbed up the hill to the temporary headquarters of Commander Prescott, the small stone building that had been the island post office. Its strategic location hadn't gone unnoticed. He pulled at the scar tissue on what remained of his left ear, as was his habit when deep in thought. The top half had been torn off in a bar fight when he first joined the service; now what remained glowed red from his unconscious attentions.

The morning summons had a familiar ring to Doogan. His seventeen-year military career had been chock-full of such appointments. The reason could be any of a dozen. He had felt something in the wind the last few days. Still, he didn't remember anything particularly egregious of late. "It has to be that feckin' eegit, Can o' ham."

He came through the open door and saluted. He noticed the staff sergeant had used all the open mail slots to organize his mountains of paperwork. He followed the paper warrior into the back office, where his commanding officer was waiting. Prescott slapped a packet of Stevia against the corner of the desk before tearing it open and stirring it into his black coffee. The staff sergeant disappeared, closing the door behind him.

The CO completely ignored the PFC, who remained at attention, his ear itching like the tag on a cheap T-shirt.

"At ease, private," Prescott said at last, without looking up.

"Sir."

Prescott switched on his desk lamp and then stood up and tugged on the chain of the ceiling fan. He walked over to the makeshift countertop and flipped on the stainless steel coffee maker.

Doogan heard the generator outside kick into a higher gear. "Brilliant," he thought. "Now French can't hear what's being said. That could be a good thing, or maybe not? Anyway, maybe this Prescott's not the bean counter I thought he was." It was easy to imagine the commander's head having that perfect jarhead shape in his youth. Now his gray hair, which was the length of two-day stubble, did precious little to hide the pack of franks on the back of his neck. Doogan thought there was too much chin below where the heavenly father had placed the commander's undersized mouth. Bent wire-rimmed glasses had worn a groove on either side of his pudgy temples.

Even the heavenly father would have had second thoughts before Prescott. The chain of command trumped anything Moses brought down from the mountain. His uniform was impeccable, his long-sleeve khaki shirt pressed and stiff as his rigid view of the world.

He finally looked up. "Sit down, McPhearson."

"Permission to remain standing, sir." He found it best in these cases.

"Yes, I was informed you were incapable of following even simple instruction." Prescott reminded himself it was necessary to scrape the bottom of the barrel. A great deal of subtlety had been lost in his command structure when Lieutenant Peters was killed in action. "I didn't invite you here to chew the fat, so I'll get straight to the point. I'm going to ask you a few questions. Answer honest and directly."

"Yes, sir." A powerful thirst overtook him. "My horse for a bit of the barley water," he bartered with himself.

Prescott opened a manila folder. "Where are you from, soldier?"

"Ireland, sir."

"It says here Northern Ireland."

"Yes, sir."

"I see you've been in and out of trouble, mostly in. You've seen your share of action. It looks like you could have made sergeant a couple of times. I wonder why you haven't?"

Doogan had heard this sort of rhetorical phrase before and decided not to respond.

"You're a fuckup, McPhearson!"

"Yes, surr." He knew the answer to that one. "Your coffee's a boilin'."

"Shut it, private! I did not ask you a question."

"Sir!"

"You pronounce your sergeant's name Can of ham. That's insubordination."

"Yes, sir." Maybe I was right, thought Doogan. He is a bean counter.

"I see your mother was Irish, and your father Scottish." The commander paused and looked at Doogan over his glasses. "How was that, private?"

"Sir?"

"Your upbringing? Answer the question."

"The coal was short, but there was always plenty of sod to burn."

"And your family life?"

"Well, sir. Me mother, bless her heart, was usually with the Vicar when the fightin' broke out. And me father was a drunken bastard. God rest his soul."

Prescott gestured for him to continue.

"When the paddies weren't kickin' the shat out of me, the micks were."

"It says here you joined the service when you were seventeen. Why?"

"Well, sir. To get a bit a peace and quiet, really." Doogan delivered the punch line flawlessly.

"You have a mouth on you, private."

Doogan pressed his lips together and shuffled his feet, as if to say, "You asked!"

Prescott read through an incident report from Bosnia. McPhearson was reported to have broken a superior officer's collarbone in a barroom brawl. He was cleared of all charges after the arresting MP testified that Sergeant Pheely had thrown the first punch. The report indicated that one week prior, McPhearson had witnessed

Pheely beating an older civilian man who had refused to get out of his way. The seventy-one-year-old civilian had suffered a broken collarbone in the altercation. The similarity of the two injuries didn't go unrecognized by the convening authority nor by Prescott. He closed the manila folder and looked hard at the PFC.

"Off the record, I want your assessment of our present situation. First in regard to our company."

Doogan just stood there.

"Begin, private."

"The men are well trained." Doogan searched for the right words. "And are very well equipped."

"Go on."

"And though I'm ignorant of our mission, the men are—off the record, sir—are very young, with little, well . . . no combat experience. The population is, you know, made up of civilians."

"Spit it out, private!"

"To sum up, in the event of a disturbance, well, sir, someone's gonna get shot, aren't they?" Doogan regarded the population as completely docile. The post boxes he saw coming in didn't even have doors, let alone locks. He wondered if the islanders locked their doors at night. He doubted it.

"Hmm, all right, private. Good. Now about your sergeant, what's your assessment?"

Doogan's face turned red. He couldn't bring himself to say the first or second thing that entered his mind.

"Answer the damn question, man!"

"Well, sir, he's a . . . well, he's a killing machine, sir."

"Would you trust him in a combat situation? Off the record."

"I would trust him to kill anything in his path, yes, sir."

"So he instills respect?"

Doogan involuntarily spit while stifling a derisive laugh. "Sorry, sir."

"Okay, let's move on. What do you think of our strategic position?"

"We are very well positioned, sir."

"And?"

"That is to say, we're in complete control of the known habitable parts of the island. But this story of the all the young lads being off working somewhere? I think it's a load of bullocks sir."

"So do I. That's why I want you to find them."

"Whah, me, sir?"

"Do I stutter, private?"

"No, sir!"

"Let's get this straight. You're a fuckup, McPhearson! You haven't got a lick of sense, that is, common sense. What you have is a troublesome stubbornness that's well-suited to this assignment." Cunning was the word he wanted to use, but thought better of saying it out loud. "Consider yourself on special assignment. Somewhere on this rock the young men are holed up. I want you to ferret them out. You can use your own judgment. Report on your progress directly to me, no one else. Am I clear? Now unplug the damn coffee maker and pour me a fresh cup."

The generator kicked down to an idle. Doogan poured the coffee and stood at attention, his back as straight as he could make it.

"Report here tomorrow, 0800 hours, to Staff Sergeant French to receive your new orders. You'll have the temporary rank of acting sergeant. If you successfully complete your mission, I'll make the stripes permanent. Dismissed."

"Sir."

Doogan kept a straight face until he was halfway down the hill. "Phear,"—the pet name he used when pleased with himself—"McFeckin-McPhearsome! Ya Legend! I always said you were some kind of genius. Jasuz, Joosheph, and Meerie! Phear, you're foockin' massive." He congratulated himself all the way back to camp.

TRIO

Strange how a teapot can represent at the same time the comforts of solitude and the pleasures of company.
—Anonymous

"I don't know what you see in skinny, little Figas." Es-Mira reached down and pulled the strap of her gel sandal back over her ankle. They were on their way home in the late afternoon after attending a rehearsal of Beba's new play.

"You don't know him, that's all. He's kind, and deep like a . . ." Beba looked up in the direction of her favorite star, knowing it was there beyond the blue glow of the sky.

"There's deep, and then there's knee-deep."

"Fair enough." As frustrating as Figas was at times, she very much enjoyed his company. "He's a work in progress. I'll give you that."

"Sistah, if want to put in that much overtime." Mira moved her neck side to side like a hip-hop dancer. "I've never seen you take the gloves off for anybody." Mira had a hard time thinking of any eligible man on the island who wasn't intimidated by Beba. "You're gonna have to take your mitts off if you want to put that skinny worm on the hook," she said to herself.

Beba loved Es-Mira and trusted her insight, though neither had much experience with relationships. She dug in her bag and found a couple of Hershey's Kisses. She tossed one to Es-Mira. It was true Figas wasn't giving her what she needed, but what choice did she have but to be patient? She hoped he would surprise her. As a playwright, she was familiar with traveling into the unknown. One thing was certain: she had a better chance of finishing her play than figuring out the Figas. She tried to change the subject. "You're just upset because you want Jala to have more lines. You should be happy you got a lead part."

"Forgive me, Miss Playwright, but doesn't a lead part usually have lines?"

"You know what Master P'O said: 'Don't rely words.'"

"Can you imagine sitting through a play by Master P'O?" Es-Mira fell into character. "'O, look on the horizon. Clouds!' Wait, here's the exciting bit." She cupped her ear. "'Listen to the rain.'" Es-Mira waved her hands, acting out the clouds and the rain falling.

"Do not saw the air too much with your hand thus, but use all gently." Beba gave Hamlet's advice to all stage actors.

Coming down the hill toward them, right on cue, was Commander Prescott, flanked by Emma Carroll and Michael Fioré.

"My, my." Beba was still using her stage voice, her hands on her hips. "Look, if it isn't the lion, the bitch, and the wardrobe!"

Es-Mira's high laugh was like a squeaky drawer. "A lion among ladies is a most dreadful thing." She pointed at Fioré.

"Wait, isn't he the wardrobe?" Beba pretended to be confused.

The oncoming trio gave the two local women a collective stare as they passed.

Emma recognized Es-sahra's daughter, Beba. Fear grabbed hold of her for a moment. She imagined the tall, elegant auntie's face pressed against the ground by a soldier's boot. She struggled to free herself of the image, telling herself it wasn't real, and forced her lips into a smile. So far, she'd handled Prescott with her "history student" story, but she was realistic. He couldn't be as stupid as he appeared. Or maybe he was. Having studied two of the greatest amphibious battles in history, she had more than a few questions about his botched landing operation—seven dead—against a completely unarmed civilian population. That didn't engender a great deal of confidence. She hoped the pleasant demeanor he was exhibiting wasn't a sign of his being sweet on her. She pushed the thought from her mind. She needed freedom to complete her research, no matter what the political situation was. She had just taken on the ridiculous local bureaucracy; now it seemed, she needed to start all over.

Fioré didn't hear what the local girls said as they passed, but by the look of the two of them, it wasn't complimentary. He was having a hard time not feeling beaten down. Less than a week after he'd received permission to film, it had all gone up in smoke when the military landed. Not that the troop's arrival didn't add a compelling complexity to the situation. The fact was that all his equipment was under lock and key. He'd have to charm this military throwback from the fifties into trusting him. Perhaps he could pad his résumé with some propaganda pieces.

The commander looked at Emma out of the corner of his eye. He wished there was a restaurant nearby where he could take this charming young lady to dinner. The Stevens-Fowling woman was beautiful, but that much ambition never looked good on a woman, no matter how physically attractive. Something about Miss Carroll reminded him of his wife when she was younger. Maybe French could rustle up a bottle of wine. Unfortunately, that would have to wait: he needed time to prepare before Stevens-Fowling arrived that evening. He shook Emma's hand gently and nodded to Fioré. "Now if you'll excuse me, the island won't run itself."

Emma gave Fioré a knowing look after the commander was out of earshot. "What a pompous ass."

Fioré was glad to have a moment alone with her. "I've missed you, Emma," he gushed. Her long orange dress made him think of a tall mango lassi. "You look fantastic."

"Thank you."

"How are you holding up with all this?"

"I'm fine," she said simply. "Diya said you were granted permission to make your film."

"Not that it will do me any good now. That stuffed shirt made it pretty clear he's not going to allow any filming until all the subversives have been located."

"What subversives?"

"Exactly. He's upset all the young men managed to go into hiding. And even more upset he hasn't been able to find a single one of them. You have to admit, it is suspicious."

"Are you kidding?" She couldn't believe he was buying into Prescott's paranoia.

"Of course I know there isn't any threat. The whole situation is absurd."

"If I didn't know better, I'd think it was one of Dr. Sun's tricks."

Emma sounded like she meant it. Had something happened to her? He felt the urge to tell her about what took place on the bridge. But he remembered Anchara's warning. He could never tell a soul. "What did Dr. Sun do to you?" he asked.

"I don't want to talk about it."

"I understand. I didn't mean to press," he said. He wanted to draw her out. He missed her. "Hey, why don't we go to my place? I'll make some pasta and . . ."

"I don't think that's such a good idea, Michael."

"Why not? You must be hungry."

"Look," she said, spouting the first excuse that came to mind, "you don't want to make Prescott jealous, do you? Or you'll never get to make your film."

"Very funny."

"Look, I've got to go. I'll see you later, okay?"

"Hold on, why the rush? Are you avoiding me?"

"Of course not. I'm just busy. You're not the only one who's here to work."

"I know. I'm sorry," he said, hoping to stall her. "How's your research going?"

"Pretty well until recently. Now I'll have to go through the paper mill all over again."

"I'm in the same predicament. Are you sure you won't have a bite with me?"

"Sorry, I can't. Maybe you should swim to the yacht in the harbor and call on Miss Sexy Attorney?" Emma bounced her eyebrows up and down.

"That's hardly fair, Emma."

"Tell me you haven't noticed her shoes."

Fioré glanced down at Emma's flat sandals, the same pair she had worn when they met, and bit his tongue.

"I'll take a rain check on dinner. Good-bye, Michael." She kissed his cheek and walked away.

He watched her, knowing he'd been one step behind the entire conversation.

O'SULLIVAN'S

Its liquor is like the sweetest dew from Heaven.
—Lu Yu

"Don't stand there with curlers in your hair, Stu. We haven't got all night. Onward and bevward!" Doogan took off downhill toward the one horse town. He'd never heard of a place with only one pub. "Adam's Ale for two freckin' weeks straight!"

The ever-thirsty Stewart Saunders couldn't agree more. "I'm seriously gummin' for a pint!" He had been fighting with a book of damp matches to light his cigarette. The day had been a scorcher, but as Doogan said, "The island is of the feminine persuasion, she's forever changing her mind." Now the rain was bucketing down.

Their first time at O'Sullivan's Tavern hadn't gone so well. Doogan had asked the proprietor, Blair, a simple enough question. "What's in that clean-skinned jar there?" He pointed at a jug with no label, hoping it was whiskey.

"That's the local cream. It's rum."

"Oh, a lady's drink," Doogan said, brokenhearted. He turned his head as several chairs scraped the floor behind them.

"That's an opinion better felt than expressed." Blair did his best with what he had to work with. He lifted his eyes as a means of introduction.

Doogan and Stu turned around to meet Dutch Moreno and his crew.

"I was just saying to my friend Stu here," Doogan said in his sweetest singsong voice, "we thought cream was cow juice, ya know.

245

And the ladies really love you know . . . ahh hell!" Doogan gave up. He turned to Blair and pointed to the jug in question. "Decorate the mahogany!"

A low growl of approval swept over the place. Blair had the shot glasses brimming in the time it took Doogan to look up. He held up his glass and downed his shot.

"Tastes like a bag of cats!" Doogan sucked in air to ease the pain. Moreno glared at him.

"Good though!" he added quickly.

It turned out to be a great way to meet the local wharfies, Stu admitted. Still, this time he was hoping for a nice tall pint. Or a stubbie, even better.

"Jaysus, it's lashing outside!" Doogan stomped through the doorway into O'Sullivan's and rubbed the rain off his head. He nodded his greeting to Blair and pointed two fingers at the tap.

The barkeep pulled two pints, not bothering to be neat, and set them down just as Stu came through the door.

"Pull up a pew," Doogan advised, without turning around. "Down the hatch."

Stu grabbed his pint and they both took a long, deep tug. Doogan wiped his mouth with his sleeve in an exaggerated gesture of happiness.

"Oh, the sergeant. He was up to ninety!" Stu said gleefully.

Doogan pointed at the tap again. "Can you believe Can-a-ham?" He shook his head with utter distain at the sergeant's last rant.

"Asino Morto!" Stu shouted into his empty pint.

"Aithne chin."

"What's that?" Stu didn't know any Irish.

"'He knows every sheep.' Don't they teach ya anythin' in school Down Under?"

Stu tipped his second pint, draining all the lingering froth. "The aforementioned asshole," Stu stated flatly, "is clearly not human." Stu had heard what Clanahan said during morning drill: "McPhearson, what's that? Gaelic for missing a pair?" The whole company roared with laughter.

"Frickin' eejit, dumber than a rock." Doogan capped off his second glass. Two fresh pints arrived. "Face like a bulldog licking piss off a nettle!" he testified, catching Stu off guard with a fresh mouthful of ale. He watched his friend closely. "Are you going to make it?" he asked sarcastically.

Stu managed to swallow, sucking in a big breath, only mildly irrigating his nostrils.

Blair set another round on fresh coasters and mopped off the long mahogany bar. Stu noticed a small discrepancy between the two new pints. Doogan's was full and overflowing, whereas the froth on his own barely reached the rim of the glass.

Doogan read his companion's look of concern. "And the Baby Jesus cried," he added drily, before launching into a story about a priest, a rabbi, and a farmer. He was working his way to the punch line when he noticed Stu still obsessing over the inequality of the pints. "For pity's sake, Saunders!" Doogan reached over and took a big swig out of the shorter pour and slid his own brimming pint in front of Stu. "You sure you're not Scottish?"

"So, how's your special assignment going?" Stu instantly recovered from his melancholia.

"Could tell ya, but then I'd have to kill ya."

"With your Irish wit?" Stu had that one waiting.

"If need be. We don't want you dead quite yet, do we? Not till you've paid for the round."

"Aren't we suddenly the tall poppy? Nice!"

"Don't get all bunched up. Like I told you, when I get an angle, I'll bring you in. I'll ask the bean counter himself. Tell him I need your help."

"Not that feckle face! I meant the crack about me buying this round. It was me the last time!" Stu was outraged.

"You are tighter than nun's knickers! A Scottish nun!" It was true that O'Sullivan's wasn't cheap. "Beer on a champagne budget," as Doogan keenly observed.

Both men turned at the same instant and pointed at the tap, and Blair pulled them two more fresh pints. He didn't mind. Customers were customers. And these two reminded him of a couple of homely babies, with their nearly bald heads and accompanying gurgling noises.

"It's like this, Stu." Doogan sounded as serious as he could after several pints of bitter. "Every time I find a well-used path, it leads up some steep brae, with a fat little Buddha covered by flowers and wrapped-up rocks and things. Ya look over the edge. It shrinks your willie. The cliff edges are soft and sandy. If you get too close, you're the buzzies all the way to the bottom."

"What are you fossicking about for, anyway?"

"A way 'round the place, ya cabbage! The young men have to be somewheres, don't they?" Doogan had met border collies with more God-given sense than Saunders had. No wonder Stu didn't stay in Australia, too much competition in the job market. He chuckled, lit Stu's cigarette and then his own, lifting his pint as if it were a choreographed move, while Blair mopped up under their glasses and replaced soggy coasters.

That morning, Doogan had taken Corporal Fields, the company engineer, up to the end of the path, where a weathered bronze figure sat overlooking a deep ravine. Two local women were praying. The younger got off her knees and poured a small bowl of sweet tea over the statue. They wore broad woven hats and tangerine-colored scarves that concealed all but their eyes. Doogan thought they might be on their way to pick in the fields. He wasn't at all surprised when they didn't turn their heads. He was used to being ignored by the locals.

Out of habit, he doffed an imaginary cap and used his singsong brogue. "Good marning, ladies." Talking louder than he needed to, he asked Fields what he thought of the layout.

"The soil's very sandy and well drained. I would guess the substructure is similar to what we saw coming up the trail. A thin layer of hard pan sits above a deep layer of softer material."

"Can you build a bridge across the ravine?" Doogan pointed to the other side of the canyon.

"Given enough time and materials, of course."

"Don't piss me about!" Remembering the women, Doogan lowered his voice. "Realistically, Fields, with the time and resources at hand?"

Fields picked up a perfect throwing rock, did a little crow hop, and hurled the stone as far as he could. They both listened as it hit the far canyon wall, sending a small echo to the unseen bottom.

"That didn't have much hair on it." Doogan expected more from the young man's throwing arm.

"It's a pretty high ridge over there."

"Higher than a giraffe's balls. So what do you think?"

"I'd need to do some field tests."

"Mind the puns."

Fields kicked at the loose, decomposed sandstone with his boots. "Shooting from the hip, I'd say constructing a bridge would take serious resources—namely concrete. More than we have on hand."

"That's what I thought." Doogan remembered helping his dad pour a patio. They mixed the mud on a board and shoveled it with the sod spade, then waited an hour for the mud to dry before they could do the final toweling. His dad had shown him the secret. "Son, press yer thumb right here. When it leaves a clear fingerprint, it's ready to trowel smooth."

Their devotion ended, the two women gathered their baskets. Doogan admired the recurve shape of her shoulder yoke as the younger woman balanced her load and followed the other woman down the track.

Doogan waited till they'd disappeared. He stepped around the assorted offerings and tapped on the statue's fat belly. It rang like a cast bell. The bronze was shiny from the sweet tea the women had just poured on it. "Hollow. Too bad," he grumbled.

Fields guffawed in disbelief. He considered Acting Sergeant Doogan a primitive. In his mind's eye, he could see the fool securing a rope around the statue's neck, then tumbling down the ravine like a cartoon coyote, with the Buddha in tow. He couldn't shake off the urge to laugh. Out of desperation, he faked a cough. It didn't matter—Doogan was deep in thought, eyebrows pulled down, tugging on his dog-eared lobe. Unfortunately for Fields, this amplified the coyote effect. He went from coughing to choking.

On their way down the slope, the two soldiers passed an old man carrying a basket of offerings.

"Pardon me, sir. What do you call that fellow sitting on the edge of the ravine?"

"Yes, yes." The old man's eyes lit up. "That is our old tea master."

"Can you tell us how he came to be sitting so near the ledge?"

The old man smiled, looking a little more closely into Doogan's eyes, impressed by his question. "Our Master P'O is a bit of a trickster. With one of his long stories, he gets you right on the edge." The old man gestured with his wrinkled hands, mimicking the razor's edge.

"Then what?" Doogan wondered.

"He conjures a strong wind!"

Fields headed down the trail, clearly irritated at the absurdity of the old man's story.

This made the old man chuckle.

Doogan, on the other hand, prospered in the absence of facts. He swam through the waters of absurd contradiction refreshed—a quality that didn't go unnoticed by the old man. "What were the ladies pouring over his Lordship?" Doogan asked.

"Sweet tea. When our ancestors returned to the island, there was a sweet rain that fell. Now we pour sweet tea over the master to show our respect."

"Returned to the island, you say?" Doogan wondered from where, but the old man had picked up his load and was heading up the hill.

LINGERIE

*Life is like making tea. Boil your ego, evaporate
your thoughts, dilute your sorrows, filter your
mistakes and get a taste of happiness.*
—Anonymous

A steady drizzle had been falling all morning. Figas crossed the stone bridge below Cairo's mill. He looked down and saw a trail of paper plumes leading into the south entrance. It made him smile.

He could feel the vibration of the wooden gears as he approached the open door. When he stepped inside the windowless room, he stopped and waited for his eyes to adjust to the darkness. The moving machinery reminded him of working in the hole with Rebus. He tucked in his T-shirt and stuck his hands in his pockets. He could hear a man's scratchy voice mixed with the low growling of the gears. He was expecting to find Beba. The doors to the pit wheel were open and he could see the lignum vitae mechanism turning below. Keeping clear of the grasshopper escapement, he craned his head into the pit room below. There was a young man in the far corner. It was Zeno. He was speaking with someone, but Figas couldn't see who without risking falling through the hole.

"That's easy for you to say. You're sleeping in your own bed. I don't care what they fucking say. I haven't done anything wrong."

Figas knew Zeno was supposed to be on the other side of the island in hiding. He couldn't make out what the other person said.

"I don't want to hear it, Beba! You just show up and do you part."

Figas felt a twinge. He hadn't planned on eavesdropping or spying on anyone. What were they up to? He felt like he was aboard the sinking *Walter Scott*. It took him a minute to realize he was trembling. The whole puncheon floor was vibrating. He held his hand up and admitted it wasn't the millstone that had ground down his nerves.

"I'm not asking, Beba. You be there with bells on, or shit's gonna hit the fan!" Zeno turned around and looked up. "Hey!"

Figas rolled over, ducking out of sight. He got up and ran out the way he'd come in. He wasn't sure why he was running. He wasn't exactly the enemy. He ran back across Cairo's bridge and up the hill toward home.

The clouds lifted and he caught sight of Auntie Es-sahra's clothes on the line. Behind it, he spotted a patrol on the move. He quickly headed into a shelterbelt of trees, where he crouched behind a log. His hands were still shaking. When the troops first landed, he had decided to stay put and continue working in Hu's office. He didn't feel threatened; then again, he wasn't planning on taking them head on.

Doogan's patrol rounded the saddle of a sunny ridge, near a nicely kept cottage. He held up his fist, signaling the patrol to halt. He admired the way the goats were tethered. A long rope was staked parallel to the path. A shorter tether was tied to a ring that glided freely, providing the animals with a long swath so they could keep the darnel nicely groomed. Doogan looked down at the small reservoir and Cairo's mill and dozens of perfect tea terraces rolling to the sea. The new flush glowed like green electric filaments in the mist. A gentle rain had been falling all morning. He looked up at the little house and was about to signal the patrol to advance.

"Hold on a tick, Peevers." Doogan pulled on his torn earlobe. "It's interesting how everything is so tidy around this place. So why do they have their clothes hanging out in this drow?" Doogan had a thing for laundry hung on a line. And it wasn't just about a woman's knickers.

"Drow, sir?" Corporal Foster had trouble with the Irishman's accent. Not to mention, he didn't care much for being called Peevers.

"In this pissing rain!" Doogan clarified. A white nanny goat, seizing the moment, sampled the right sleeve of his uniform. Doogan looked down at the goat. "Go and tell the billy there are owls in the moss." He turned toward the corporal. "I want you to write down how many bits of laundry are hanging on that line. The size and color as well."

Foster thought he must be joking.

"Wait till we're well past the house. You got it?" Doogan pointed up ahead.

"Yes, sir." Peevers got out his notebook. "Every time?"

"Jaysuz, Jooseph, and Meerie! Yes, every time, Peevers! Otherwise what would be the feckin' point?" he said in a loud whisper, shaking his head at the nibbling goat. "Can you believe the glut of talent I'm surrounded by?" He pointed to his head and shook it from side to side.

The nanny wasn't following.

Doogan patiently explained how you take an old shoe polish tin and fill it with little rocks to make a shuffle piece to play peevers. "Maybe you call it hopscotch around here." He could see in the corner of the goat's eyes that she understood. Besides having rocks in his head, Peevers wasn't worth his salt. On top of that, he had witnessed the young corporal shoving an older man out of the way on a narrow bend of the trail.

"Nothing worse than young people mistreating old people, 'cepting maybe the other way around," he reminded the nanny goat. She had nearly succeeded in nibbling off the shiny button on his cuff. He pointed to his temporary stripes. "Now the boot's on the other foot." He wasn't going to tolerate boys being boys.

For the next week, Doogan checked Peever's laundry list against a count of the returning men on patrol. The numbers didn't correlate. Next, he cross-checked the colors. The following morning, he decided that a red item meant ten; blue, five; and a white item, one. A black item signaled they had passed by and would be returning. He checked his theory out for another week. When a patrol of twelve men passed the small house, nothing was on the line. Upon their return, a red item with two white items was waving, along with a black item.

"Downy little buggers," he said to himself. He knew the clothesline was visible from a distance like flag semaphore. He thought of all the little houses with clotheslines they passed. The locals were keeping careful track of where the patrols were going and how many men it was composed of. He was convinced an early warning system was in place. No wonder they couldn't find a soul. The deep ravines every two clicks didn't help.

As part of his thorough research, he visited O'Sullivan's that evening. After his requisite six pints, he took a moment to study the froth on the top of his freshly poured seventh. "Did you know," he asked the barkeep, "the secret to a creamy head atop the ale is in the peptides?"

"I did not know that," Blair answered with the patience of a man who listens to inebriated people for a living.

"Tons of kinds of foam. You know the black stuff, Guinness in a can? They use a widget with nitrogen. You could say I'm of a student of the foam." Doogan winked at the barkeep. "There's a whole parlance you have to master."

"You don't say?"

"Foamin-clature, they call it."

"I did not know that." Blair kept a straight face. "Wheels within wheels," he muttered to himself.

Doogan reached into his front pocket and pulled out the remainder of his wages and slammed the bills and miscellaneous change on the bar top. "I'm in the market for a little information."

"Sounds like you've got a handle on the big stuff." Blair turned around and finished washing the glasses he'd left soaking in the sink.

The following morning, Doogan was out bright and early. He met a young girl on her way to school. "Top of the marning to you." He tipped his imaginary cap. "What's your name?" he asked in his singsong voice.

"Tsani."

"Hello, Tsani. You're shiny as a new button. And how old are you, then?"

"Nine years old." She tried to match his melodic way of talking.

He noticed her woven bag with three pearls sewn in a loop. "What's for lunch today?"

"Fish with rice and some bananas. It's share day."

"Sounds fun. Can I see your little bag you have there?"

She held it up proudly.

"Pretty as you please. Where's your dad today?" He slipped in the question.

"He's in Commurran."

"Oh, where's that?"

"It's an island."

"Oh? By chance have you been there?"

'Noo! I'm in school." She laughed and ran down the road before breaking into a practiced skip. Her three-pearl bag swung side to side.

Contest of Champions

A butterfly fluttered over the lively teakettle.
—Issa

"Nonsense. It will be a great way to break the ice."

Prescott's idea of a contest of champions caused Uncle Sun to grimace. The commander's clumsy plan to flush out the local men in hiding might have unfortunate consequences.

"Have one of your young lads come and take a crack at one of my men, all in good fun, you understand. Boxing. Wrestling. Whatever you do around here. What do you say, Dr. Sun?"

"A brawl?"

"I can see you're not the man to ask. I'll have some of my men put the word out at the local drinking establishment. Let's make it for next Saturday."

Uncle left Prescott's office knowing the idea of a contest might prove too great a temptation for Zeno. He could easily see the prideful young man showing up to fight the sergeant. When he thought of the two men on the same little island, it was only a matter of time before the inevitable occurred.

Saturday morning arrived on a cold wind from the South, which blasted against Figas's cheeks. A dark wall of clouds to the East gave the dawn second thoughts. Figas watched for Zeno's arrival. He was worried about Beba. He wanted to ask her what they were planning, but how could he without admitting he'd been eavesdropping?

An old woman limped toward the gathering crowd.

Figas thought she wore a traditional Portuguese fisherwoman's shawl, but as she moved closer, fear suddenly grabbed the back of his neck with icy hands. What he thought was pure white lace was really tiny rows of shark's teeth carefully sewn into her gown. One row was set in one direction, while the next ran opposite like a shimmering coat of ivory chain mail. The slippery sound of the pearly teeth contrasted with her mock smile of black and filmy yellow. Her head was set slightly off center, helping her balance the rusted iron kettle she carried in her left hand. Scars covered her neck like a poorly wrapped scarf. The left side of her face was bruised and pitted like a pustular clove of garlic. She was hideous. Figas felt her presence in his stomach. Whether from fascination or an uncontrollable freezing of his will, he couldn't avert his eyes. The whole crowd seemed likewise paralyzed.

Pressed into the middle of the onlookers, Doogan heard an auntie whispering to her friend, "She boils her tea with salt water." He found it hard to think of the old woman as real. He decided it must be because her spirit had flown many years before. The part of her that remained limped slowly by, in between realms, breathing the dust of the dry earth.

"What? This is your challenger?" The commander stomped the ground and cursed. "Impossible! My sergeant can't be expected to tussle with an old lady." He searched out Dr. Sun and grabbed him by the arm. "There must be one young man out there with some backbone!"

Uncle removed Prescott's hand and continued searching the crowd for Zeno. He noticed his nephew was the only one not looking directly at the old she-wolf of the sea.

She stood inches away from the man in uniform, looking up at his face.

Uncle wondered if his nephew knew something he didn't.

Clanahan remained motionless.

The old woman lifted the lid off her kettle and dropped it ceremoniously on the ground in front of the sergeant. She turned slowly counterclockwise, relishing the moment.

Her high-pitch mumbling felt like slivers inside Clanahan's ears.

The old woman put the kettle to her wrinkled lips and swallowed with a disgusting gurgle. She took a moment to look around. No one was willing to meet her brackish gaze. She stared at Prescott.

He sneered back before turning to Dr. Sun, "What's in that pot? I won't have my men poisoned!"

"I don't know, but by all means help yourself," Uncle suggested unapologetically.

The old woman held the kettle out to the sergeant, spilling some of its contents on his polished boots.

He came out of his wooden pose and glanced over to his CO. "If this old hag can eat this muck . . .," he said to himself.

Prescott gave an imperceptible nod.

Clanahan grabbed the kettle. It looked small in his hand. He tipped it back and took a long swallow and then resumed his previous stance of attention.

Everyone stood still, not believing what they were seeing, waiting for what would happen next.

Figas mumbled the opening of Yeats's "Second Coming," "The ceremony of innocence is drowned."

The sergeant's face and neck flushed red. Beads of sweat rose on his temples like fetid droplets. His mouth and throat burned out of control. He needed to cough, but he held himself in check.

The old woman's laugh was a low rhythmic shriek that grew higher and higher.

"Was there ever a more agreeable couple?" Doogan intoned his question like a prayer. "A match made in hell." He unconsciously genuflected.

Clanahan's face began to contort.

The old woman pried the kettle out of his grip.

Her shagreen touch sent shivers throughout the sergeant's body. The world hurled into shadow. He doubled over in a full body spasm, attempting to vomit, gasping for air.

She bent down and put the lid back on the kettle and slid slowly away, the victor.

No one applauded or seemed willing to celebrate. The crowd regarded the sergeant as they might a child who stuck his hand in fire, knowing full well it would burn.

Clanahan kept his feet, but he was swaying. His knuckles were bright red, his hands clamped to his knees.

Doogan lingered. He looked into the cloud-filled sky. He held his palms together like an altar boy. "I don't know which of ya up there to thank. So thank ya's one and all. Tears before bedtime, to be sure."

Prescott watched as the remaining islanders milled about uncomfortably. He was waiting for a derisive cheer, but it never came. One by one, the locals went their way. This was not what he'd envisioned. He wasn't sure what had just happened, but decidedly it was not what he had hoped for.

Ramona Rai

Drinking a daily cup of tea will surely starve the apothecary.
—Chinese proverb

Uncle dropped a spoon into the washbasin hoping to wake Figas. He couldn't believe how late into the morning the young could lie in bed.

"I'm awake, Uncle. No further need for crashes and collisions," Figas yelled from his little house in the back.

"The sun has been up for nearly an hour. Your tea is stone cold."

Figas pulled on a pair of shorts without unbuttoning them. He came in and sat on the bamboo matt across from Uncle while steaming hot tea was poured.

"Umm, stone cold?" He combed his hair flat with his fingers.

Two loud thumps were heard on the front door before a woman let herself in.

"Good morning, doctor." Uncle changed his tone to light and sweet.

Figas stood up.

"Do you know Dr. Ramona Rai?" Uncle introduced their guest.

"I've yet to have the pleasure. Nice to meet you." Figas shook the woman's soft hand and offered her his seat. "Please have a cup of hot tea."

"I'd love to, but I've twenty-nine temporary cots filled with special forces shitting their brains out with IVs stuffed in their arms. You wouldn't know anything about that, would you, Dr. Sun?"

Figas had never seen anyone dress down Uncle before.

Uncle sipped his tea in a way that told Figas he probably did know something. Now that he thought about it, he remembered something at the emergency council meeting about using little armies to fight larger ones.

"*Entamoeba histolytica*. Ring any bells?" The doctor stared down at Uncle, but he didn't seem concerned. "I've enough nitazoxanide for a couple of weeks, after that some of these boys could die. If I find out . . ."

"Calm down, Ramona. The tea is just the perfect temperature." He poured another cup and waited for her to sit.

"You know I didn't come here to play military hospital nurse. I've got a serious study underway."

"I know, Mona."

"Don't give me your line. I'm not stupid, and we're definitely not on a first name basis." She sat down and took a quick sip of tea.

"Are you finished?" Uncle tried to turn it into a joke.

"Yes. No. Of course I'm not finished!"

He managed to get the crack of a smile, but she wasn't having it. "I know what you've been up to, Mowgli and your gang."

"Can you give me a little more to go on?" Uncle continued to act innocent.

"Look, if one of those boys dies . . ."

"Now, now, that's not going to happen." He could tell she was exhausted. "I'll find you some more help." He looked over at Figas and smiled.

"Seriously?" Figas knew who was going to be left holding the bag.

"Fine, it's settled. You can both help at the infirmary this afternoon. That idiot commander refuses to see what's going on. Well, it's going to stop!" She stared at Uncle before she got to her feet and left without closing the door behind her.

Uncle laughed a little to clear the air. He explained to Figas that Dr. Rai had arrived three years earlier from Iceland. The pharmaceutical company she was working for was sued for publishing private DNA information without permission. She'd written a new grant and was receiving the bulk of her funding through the University of Washington's genetics, genomics, and bioinformatics program.

"She didn't sound much like a scientist." Figas meant it.

261

"She's quite brilliant. You'll see."

"Why did she choose Green Island for her study?"

"The greatest concentration of talented people per cubic meter."

"Funny."

"Think about it. A small, isolated gene pool, very similar to that of Iceland, in that most who live here were born here. Not much new blood in a few centuries."

"That goes a long way to explain some things."

After breakfast, they made their way to the infirmary. When they lifted the tent flap, the smell knocked Figas back. He steadied himself and took in the situation. There was a groaning military man in every cot.

Dr. Rai was arguing with the only man in uniform in an upright position. "Paperwork? I don't give a damn what your commander says! You go and get as much toilet paper as you can carry. That's the kind of paperwork we need right now. Bring fresh linens and towels while you're at it. Unbelievable!" She pointed the way Figas and Uncle had just come in.

Uncle made his way from cot to cot, talking to the soldiers, asking if they needed anything. Most were not capable of making it to the temporary latrine themselves. Figas rolled up his sleeves and followed suit, helping the best he could. After a full shift of eight hours, more volunteers arrived.

Dr. Rai invited Uncle and his nephew into her lab to clean up.

Figas's eyes widened when he entered the small laboratory packed with high-quality equipment. "What's that?"

"Look but don't touch. It's a thermal cycler."

"And this?"

"A microplate centrifuge. We're separating the intrinsic from the extrinsic fluctuations . . . I'm sorry. Basically, I'm looking at the outer events from within."

"Gotcha." Figas played along. "And this little baby?" He pointed to the largest, most impressive machine. Multicolored lights flickered on and off.

"An automated DNA sequencer."

"So is that what you're doing—sequencing DNA?"

"I already have." Dr. Rai looked over at Uncle. "One of my conquests."

"We're all cut from the same cloth," Uncle said simply.

"Most of us are," she admitted. "You're sui generis. One of a kind."

"Inhabit whichever story you're most comfortable with, Mona. We're all children of the cosmos. Where else would we come from or be going? We have small differences, I'll grant you that, but our similarities outweigh any measure."

Dr. Rai ignored the philosophical banter. "The human genome is three billion bases long. It's arranged on twenty-three pairs of chromosomes, so we're looking at fragments or sections."

Figas nodded his head as if he were following what she was saying. "Does the law of total expectation come into play?" He took a shot in the dark.

"No, but the law of total variance does have applications." Figas suddenly showed up on Dr. Rai's scope. She walked over to him with the walk of a woman. "So what do you know about probability theory?" she asked softly.

He wanted to blurt out that he rewrote it, but knew how pompous that would sound, even if to some extent it were true. "I'm familiar with Bayes' theorem."

"What about the hidden Markov model?"

"Oh yeah."

Uncle'd had enough. "I'm leaving you geeks in wonderland. Good-bye."

Without turning around, Dr. Rai held up her right hand and rotated it in a quasi-royal toodle-oo, dismissing him from his duties while she trained set her sights on Figas. "I could use another hand around here." She raised her delicate eyebrows. "How are you with sensitive lab equipment?"

"I don't know." Figas returned her intense gaze and felt the heat. "I'm more of a numbers man."

"I'm serious, if you're interested. Do you have a job?"

"I have a couple of jobs." The curves under her lab coat were influencing more than the fabric. "But I might be able to carve out some time."

"Wonderful," she said quickly. "Call me Mona." They shook hands. She held his hand a little longer than was comfortable.

He had just watched her roll over Uncle with ease. He didn't need a DNA sequencer to know what his chances were. Like it or not, he found her interesting.

On his way out, he stopped to help Corporeal Foster make it to the latrine and back, holding up his saline IV. If it weren't for the assault rifle under his cot, he might have had some pity for Peevers.

Beba walked up quietly behind Figas. "I hear you're working with Dr. Rai?"

"That was quick." He snapped his head around. He had only left the infirmary an hour ago. It was a small island.

Beba ran her fingers through her hair, suddenly aware of Figas's gaze. Dr. Rai had that certain something men loved. Her hair gleamed like a fox on a sunny hillside.

"Jealous?" Figas teased.

"If you think she can pass the bitch-alizer test, don't let me slow you down." She punched him in the shoulder and ran off to sulk.

"He is such an idiot!" she told herself. "He believes he can explain nature with a formula." For years, she'd read the newspaper clippings Auntie Anjou collected. There was a thick binder of clippings and articles in the library about Figas. Beba read every one. Though she wasn't able to follow the math formulas, she understood the concepts well enough. She knew he was special. She tried to be happy for his success.

To her, numbers were cold, impersonal, inanimate. She believed in her five senses. To understand nature was to unite with and become a part of the whole. "The divine is always here, waiting," she said to herself, "like your oldest, closest friend." Symbols and abstractions were at best a shabby overlay. Mathematics poked holes in the lid, confident that it was capturing life in a jar.

People were more than bits of proteins aligned on a double helix. Beba looked at the cirrus clouds moving overhead. "Is it any wonder we're in so much trouble, with so many stupid-smart people running around?"

Fa Shi

*Tea's proper use is to amuse the idle, and relax the
studious, and dilute the full meals of those who
cannot use exercise, and will not use abstinence.*
—Samuel Johnson

A week later, Acting Sergeant McPhearson stood under the
shade of a large tulip tree and fooled with his torn ear. He counted his
lucky stars that he hadn't gotten the shits. It confirmed his belief that
man was not meant to drink plain water. He watched the goings-on
up and down Lantern Street, the main drag of Salm Bay. A steady
but slow flurry of late morning commerce passed in front of him. He
jiggled the key in the lock. He had marched over most of the back
bush of the island and come up empty. He knew the bean counter
was doing what he did best: counting the days since he began his
special assignment.

"Prescott puts the butter on with a feather and takes it off with a
razor," he confided to a local woman, who ignored him as she passed
by. "These feckin' Greenwegians!" He cursed under his breath.

The tall, blonde European woman came out of the shoe repair
shop with her silly handbag over her shoulder like David's sling. She
passed Foster, who turned and whistled as he watched her walked
away. He crossed the street to Doogan.

"Ka panga panga!" Foster rocked his head from side to side to
illustrate his meaning. "Top heavy as a Swedish man o' war."

Doogan ignored Peevers. He would never forget his visit to the
Vasamuseet, the museum in Stockholm where the *Vasa* had been

carefully restored. She had sunk on her maiden voyage only a mile from port. Her sixty-four bronze cannons had proven top-heavy indeed.

The shoe repairman came out of his shop with a pair of newly repaired sandals in his hand. He walked down the block and set the sandals in front of the barber's shop and returned to his own business.

Doogan always enjoyed getting familiar with a place and meeting the occasional character who would climb out of the woodwork. He began to wonder how many eccentric inmates one little island could hold. "Owls in the moss," he said to himself. He crossed the street just as the barber came out to inspect the reinforced straps on his sandals.

"Good marning, sir." Doogan tipped his imaginary cap.

The barber slipped on his sandals, made a quick bow, and hurried back into his shop with Doogan in tow.

"High and tight, no shave, if you please."

"Sha' thing."

Doogan sat down on the better of the two lumpy stools. The barber wrapped the Irishman's neck with a soft towel before snapping a white sheet over him and fastening it tightly in the back with a worn silver clip. Doogan smelled witch hazel on the old barber's hands.

"You want high and tight fade?"

"Sounds good." Doogan relaxed in the chair. He'd been trying to work out the local way of doing business. A kind of all-inclusive barter system, he reasoned. "Looks like the cobbler's been at your shoes?" This didn't nudge the barber's tongue. "Is he any good? I need my belt done up." He involuntarily jumped when the barber clicked on the loud shears. Doogan wasn't thrilled when he saw the man's hand shaking. "Careful of my good ear!" he said in all seriousness.

"Sha' thing."

Doogan stared at the long, scraggly white beard. "In the blacksmith's house, the ornaments are made of wood," he reminded himself. "That Sullivan sure pulls a mean pint." Doogan had to practically shout to hear himself over the vibrating clippers.

"Sullivan dead."

"Really. When?"

"Thirty-five, thirty-six years ago."

"Who's the barkeep then?"

"Blair."

"Oh well, he talks too much."

"Yes, yes." The old man's giggles began to run away from him.

"Are you the barber, or is he dead too?"

"Yes, yes."

"If you're not the barber, that takes a bit of the shine off." Doogan was good at one-sided conversation. He pictured himself on a hand-levered draisine, pumping himself down the tracks. "What's your name? I'm Doogan."

"Yes, yes, I know."

Doogan decided not to wait for the coals to die down. "What is it I call you then?"

"I am Fa Shi." The old man bowed.

"Pleased ta meet cha." Doogan could never get used to this bowing. He would always proffer a good old-fashioned handshake. "Say, Mr. Fa Shi, what can you tell me about this shark lady?"

The barber shrugged, unwilling to gossip.

"I can tell you, she makes a knee-buckling fish chowder."

Fa Shi unfastened the white linen and lifted it with a flourish, then brushed his customer's shoulders with a stiff brush before unwrapping the towel around his neck.

"What do I owe you?"

The barber pointed to Doogan's 9mm Browning on his hip. "Throw gun in bay."

"Spending the rest of my life in the brig might be a wee bit dear for a haircut. What ya think?"

Fa Shi chuckled in agreement. "Okay." He smiled broadly, tapping on his gold tooth.

Doogan realized he should have bartered first then gotten the trim. "How 'bout a coupla rounds at Sullivan's?" He took out his wallet. "I could murder a pint right now," he said under his breath.

The barber shook his head.

"A trade then?" Doogan reached in his pocket and pulled out his folding knife.

"Too much. Tell you what, Mr. Duggan, you bring two bar of soap next time."

"Deal!" Doogan pretended to spit in his hand. They shook and sealed the bargain.

The Irishman walked out into the bright morning, feeling he had learned an important piece of the puzzle. Like a tusic idiot, he had been holding the wrong end of the stick. If he wanted information, he needed leverage. Being good cop to Can-a-ham's bad cop wasn't going to be enough to gain the locals' trust.

He felt the newly bristled hair on the back of his head and pulled at his torn earlobe.

Farther up the street, three off-duty enlisted men were teasing the young wharfie, China. They had pushed him to the ground and were taunting him.

Doogan ran up the street. He remembered the boy, a simple lad. His ma would say the boy was touched. "What's this?" Doogan barked. He picked the boy up and dusted him off. "You okay?"

China smiled.

"Off you go then." Doogan watched the boy's Yankees cap fly off as he ran down to the pier, but he was too terrified to stop and retrieve it.

The barber, the shoe man, and the other shopkeepers were all outside their businesses watching.

"Sometimes it's just a shame to be in uniform," Doogan muttered. He had the urge to fight all three on the spot. "Ya molly-cuddlin' bastards are on report." He pointed to his temporary stripes.

The enlisted men groaned in unison.

"Yeah, surprise, surprise."

"You're lucky you've got those stripes to hide behind," the biggest of the three said under his breath.

"More's the pity." Doogan stared until the three decided to cut their losses.

The shopkeepers went back inside.

Doogan walked over and picked up the boy's cap. He found him at the end of the wharf, watching the small crabs chase one another around the wooden piers. "Where'd you come by the cap?"

"Uncle Fioré gave it to me."

"A tad loose, don't ya think? Come with me."

They returned to Fa Shi's shop. Doogan leafed through a magazine and ripped out an ad. He folded the thick paper neatly into fours and fit it behind the sweatband inside the hat. "Try it now."

The cap fit snugly.

JAMILA

If you are cold, tea will warm you. If you are too heated, it will cool you. If you are depressed, it will cheer you. If you are excited, it will calm you.
—William Ewart Gladstone

"Slowly, damn it!"

Just beyond the bronze statue of P'O, Stu and Corporal Fields lowered Doogan over the steep sandy edge.

Doogan realized he needed to go alone if he had a chance of befriending any islanders. "Well, Phear, at least the bean counter put his best man on the problem," he reminded himself.

Twenty-eight feet of rope and Doogan felt a narrow ledge. He pulled on the rope twice and yelled up for them to wait. He unwrapped the figure-eight loop and took off his climbing harness. The sun felt blistering. The rocky path led down to the welcome sight of shade trees.

He followed a cascading stream. The steep sides of the canyon began to widen out into a low valley. Large boulders fostered deep, clear pools between them. A finely stacked rock wall covered with thick white lichen lined the opposite bank. The one-armed man who lived outside his grandparent's village of Billina was the only mason Doogan knew with the skill and patience to dry-stack a rock wall so perfectly. "This is the work of the old ones, back when they believed the stones had powers," he told himself. As a boy, he often played about ancient stones. The Dolmen of the Four Maols was just outside the village. He remembered asking the four stones if they cared much for being bare naked. "Wouldn't yas rather be covered in dirt? Can yas even breathe all surrounded by air?" He wondered if atop the earth they could hear their brethren deep underground. At least the Dolmen had each other for company. He wasn't sure about magic powers. Maybe he couldn't explain it, but he'd never deny the stones gave off a feeling of their own.

He walked softly down the valley, watching and listening. The back of his neck tingled, and the feeling grew, along with the height of the stone wall. He began to wonder if he shouldn't turn around.

At the shore, the stream gathered behind a wide sandbar before reconciling with the salty surf. He waded through the shallow freshwater that spilled over the sand. It looked to be low tide. The sand ran thick through shallow stream, obscuring the bottom. When his boot went under, he managed to regain his balance. He picked his way carefully and successfully leaped over the deepest part of the channel.

Halfway down the white crescent beach, an old man and a boy were pushing a canoe. Doogan whistled to announce his approach.

The boy jumped, but the old man just leaned against the gunnels of the canoe to rest.

Doogan waved and smiled as he walked up to them slowly.

"Hey there. Need a hand?"

The two locals watched him approach.

"I was taking a bit of a nature walk, you know, and I might have gotten turned around." Doogan sat down and unlaced his boot and emptied out the water. "Looks like a canoe for five or six." He kept up his one-sided banter.

The faded hull was badly checked. A deep crack along the bow was expertly filled while other repairs were makeshift. The canoe was nearly thirty feet long and sat on a rack of lashed poles. The thin dark-skinned boy looked to be maybe thirteen. His face was twisted tight. He tried to bore into the white stranger with his eyes. The grandfather was bony, short of teeth, and well past the age of hard work. He was breathing hard and didn't look up at the soldier.

Doogan laced up his boot and got to his feet. "The name's Doogan. Pleased ta meet cha." He extended his hand to shake.

Neither the boy nor the old man moved.

Doogan recovered by making an awkward bow. "It's my day off. Thought I'd wander about, see the sights." He knew his uniform was the kiss of death. Or was it his sidearm? "Looks like the old girl could use a wee bit of TLC." He nodded toward the canoe. "Anywhoodles . . . have you another oar?"

The boy's face lit up. He ran up into the thicket and soon returned with a long hand-carved paddle.

"Okay, on three, let's push," Doogan said.

"No." The boy pointed to the waves breaking. "Wait."

A full five minutes passed in silence. The three watched and counted waves.

Doogan saw three big rollers coming in. The first reached way up the sand.

"Now!" the boy yelled. The momentum they gathered sliding off the wood rack ended when they met the wet sand. The next wave crashed and lifted the bow. They ran her easily into the shallow surf. Doogan stumbled and hit his face on the outrigger before he could flop himself into the middle of the boat.

The boy let out a high-pitched scream and then yelled, "Paddle!"

The old man in the stern steered them straight into the next wave. They sliced through the surf and into the small bay.

Doogan let out a joyful yelp of his own. The blood from his split lip tasted salty sweet as he leaned back, palms burning against the oars. He was back in his childhood. He could smell the Cavendish tobacco from his grandfather's pipe and see his grandma bent over, collecting seaweed on the beach, which they used to fertilize their field.

Cool water siphoned through the midsection of the canoe like a sieve, threatening to refill Doogan's boots.

The boy tossed back a plastic pail without looking.

It hit Doogan on his right knuckle as he shifted his paddle. "Jaysuz, Joseph, and Meerie!" he testified. He grabbed the pail and began bailing water over the side. He was barely able to stay ahead of the steady leak. The cool water felt good on his swollen knuckle.

The old man and the boy rested their paddles as they glided into the deepest part of the bay. The old man leaned back to catch his breath. The boy gathered his net in both hands and balanced his bare feet on the gunnels. He remained motionless, like a heron patiently watching the fish under the surface, awaiting his moment.

Then the net flew in a perfect arc. The boy quickly gathered it in. The canoe lurched forward.

Doogan helped the youth roll the teeming net into the boat. The outrigger lifted high out of the water as they nearly tipped. The sharp spine of a fish stung Doogan's hand. "Feck!" He sucked on another swelling finger.

The old man and his grandson let out a long, pleasurable laugh.

Doogan resumed his job bailing the rising water. With the added weight of their catch, they pulled for shore with the gunnels riding just above the waves. They lingered a stone's throw from the beach and waited for the boy's signal.

"Paddle!"

A big wave lifted their stern, sending them high up the polish. The boy caught Doogan climbing out the wrong side just in the nick of time—his legs almost crushed as the surf rushed the angled canoe up the sand. The three pulled the loaded craft up the beach with the help of another big wave. Digging their paddles into the sand, they levered the long canoe on top of the wooden rack.

Doogan felt his numb lip and sucked on his throbbing, salty fingers. It was the most fun he'd had in years. He bailed the remaining water out of the dugout. He imagined the tall, straight tree it must have come from. A series of intricate knots and joints held the thin gunnels to the main hull. He had admired the crisply made canoes that covered the beaches near Salm Bay. This boat, on the other hand, belonged in a museum.

The two islanders had cleaned half the fish before Doogan came out of his reverie. He pulled out his pocketknife. "Which of these little bastards has the sharp spines?"

The boy playfully held up the likely offender. "It's a dogfish. You can have it. They're tasty."

"Hello, Mr. Tasty. A pleasure." The Irishman doffed an imaginary cap and then turned to the boy. "And you, my young friend. What's your name?" Doogan held out his hand.

"Wasil, they call me Wuz. This is my grandfather." The boy dropped the fish in a plastic five-gallon bucket and gave Doogan a big handshake. "I've never talked to a soldier before."

"Pleasure to meet you, Wuz. Not to worry. But you're right, it's never a bad idea to keep clear of men in uniform."

Doogan shook hands with the old man and then helped them carry their catch up the path through the trees. He counted five little structures as they walked through terraces of rice. Their modest home relied on the natural protection of a black basalt cliff behind it and a large monkeypod tree to its windward side.

A young woman dressed in lavender lifted her head and stared at Doogan.

He stuttered and hoped she didn't notice. Thick lashes hid her thoughts from him. He wanted to grab at his earlobe but only managed to stand there mute, his mind jaywalking.

Wuz mercifully interrupted as he showed off his catch. "One cast, Jamila! This is Dugun. He tried to break our boat with his mouth." This caused everyone to laugh.

Doogan's lip felt heavier on his lower left.

"This is my sister, Jamila." Wuz looked at her in a way that said, "Make tea."

The movement of her shoulders told him that the tea was hot.

Doogan was loath to leave but knew it was past time to report in. "'Tis an honor and privilege to meet ya. My apologies. I'm due back. May I come back for tea another time?"

Jamila smiled and bowed with her eyes.

The old man tapped Doogan lightly on the shoulder and walked off into the trees to relieve himself.

Wuz followed his new friend back up the canyon. "Come early in the morning before the wind kicks up. The sea is calmer."

"First thing in the marning then. I promise."

"See ya t'morra." Wuz slurred his speech, pretending to have a fat lip, before running back down the path.

"Pull! Pull me up, for feck sake!" Doogan was in a temper.

"What happened to you?" Stu was concerned but had a telltale smile on his face.

"Shut it, Saunders!" Doogan wrestled his climbing harness off.

"You should see the other guy, right?" Stu was enjoying himself at his friend's expense.

"As I outrank you Saunders, schut yer cake hole!" Doogan's lip had continued to swell, giving him a lisp.

Fields was choking as he fought back his laugh.

"You got a hairball or something, corporal?"

"No, sir."

When Doogan calmed down, he ordered Fields to construct a twenty-eight foot rope ladder. "I need it by zero six hundred, corporal. Understood? You and funny man here clean up this mess. On the double!" Doogan walked off, trying to retain a small shred of dignity.

Dog Fish

Tea! thou soft, thou sober, sage, and venerable liquid.
—Colley Cibbe

In the late afternoon, Sergeant Clanahan found himself off duty. It was a rare event. He roamed Lantern Street and scoured the back streets of Salm Bay for a sailor's chance at sweet and brief companionship. The Chinese laundry had turned out to be nothing but that—a laundry. There certainly were more women than men everywhere one went, which improved his chances. He couldn't ask the wharfies after the way he had treated their weaselly boss.

He noticed a local girl crossing the street. Her gray eyes held his until she was close.

"Looking for a good time?" she asked.

"You could say that." Clanahan couldn't believe his luck.

"Meet me by the anchor at sunset. Bring cash." Beba rubbed her fingers against her thumb, using universal sign language. She had argued with Zeno over her involvement but now found herself enjoying the role. Deoden getting beat up had been the final straw. The sergeant stank of cheap aftershave.

"Why wait?" he asked and tried to grab her arm.

"What's your hurry?" She slapped his hand away. Her red lips smiled in anticipation. Her short, tight skirt hiked up her thighs as she crossed the street.

Clanahan stared at her shapely behind, putting what little imagination he possessed to use.

He spent the remainder of the afternoon in the little park that held a massive anchor. Most island cultures lacked knowledge of metallurgy. It had been common practice for islanders to dive at night and cut the thick braided anchor cable of their early European visitors. After the ship sailed, they hauled ashore the massive anchor, from which they made everything from nails to weapons. Near the rusty anchor, two windswept poinciana trees faced the long sand beach. An autograph tree in the back of the park had the names of young lovers scratched on its waxy green leaves. Under its canopy was a wooden bench. "This will do nicely in a pinch," he said to himself.

He found a vantage point behind a rack of fishing nets that had a clear view in all directions. He stood watch, surveying the bay, where fishing canoes lined the arc of sand like fifty-caliber machine gun cartridges. He tapped on his sidearm, as if he were an impatient customer at a store counter.

Without giving notice, the sun slipped into the ocean. The light dialed down to a muted orange and gray. Clanahan swatted a bengafly that landed on his neck. He'd started out somewhat incredulous but couldn't get the image of the woman out of his mind. He wondered how long he would wait, not that he needed to report back until twenty-three hundred.

The unmistakable outline of a man running down the beach with an M4 carbine spiked Clanahan's adrenaline. He immediately charged toward the man with the gun. His boots dug through the deep, loose sand until he reached the surf line.

The running figure spotted him and immediately threw his weapon into a fishing canoe and launched it into the calm bay.

"Stop, or I'll fire!" Clanahan yelled but didn't stop to take aim. It was too long a shot with a pistol. He chose a small canoe of his own and shoved it into the waves. He put his back into catching the boat, still within sight. It would be completely dark soon. He cursed that he had not brought his radio.

Zeno looked back briefly and was surprised to see the soldier gaining on him. He dug his paddle in for all he was worth. He'd hunted since he was a boy but had never been hunted. He was the cheese, but envisioned himself the boar. Whatever happened, he'd do his part like a warrior. Beba had played her part to perfection, now it was his turn.

As soon as they rounded Fletch's Point, big waves began to toss their canoes about.

Clanahan struggled to keep his heading. The big swells momentarily hid the outline of the man's silhouette against the horizon. A dark cloud in the West suddenly cut off any remaining light. The sergeant's intense focus was interrupted by cool water rising around his boots. The canoe grew slower and heavier by the minute. Fish guts and tangled fishing line floated around his ankles. His canoe was rapidly sinking.

The large swell had turned him around, and he had lost his direction back to land. He set down the paddle and quickly unlaced his boots, knowing they would be too heavy to swim in. He stripped down to his black boxers and took his 9mm Browning out of his holster. He held onto the floating outrigger with his other hand and balanced on the submerged hull, riding the swells up and down. He could feel a current carrying him out to sea. The swell widened in the quiet.

A white searchlight flickered and disappeared. He clicked the safety off his Browning and discharged a round in the air. The ringing in his ears sharpened his focus. His sense of relief vanished when he didn't hear a motor.

The searchlight blinded him.

"Hold your weapon up so we can see it!" Zeno shouted.

Clanahan thought for a moment and then held up his pistol.

The boat inched closer.

"Throw your pistol forward, high enough for us to see."

He fired two quick shots at the rescue light. It went out. His eyes began to adjust again to the dark. He listened, floating.

"You're not alone. Do you feel them bumping your legs? The fish guts in your boat chummed the water. You can use all your bullets on the sharks. But you might want to save the last round."

Since Clanahan's encounter with the witch, he'd experienced vivid nightmares of giant sharks. The rough touch of her shagreen skin buckled his knees. He knew his best chance was to surrender. It didn't matter. He would kill them all later with his KA-BAR or bare hands.

"If you throw your gun away, I give you my word, you won't be harmed. If you fire on us again, we will leave you here with your friends."

"All right!"

The searchlight found him. He held the pistol up and heaved it in front of him. The splash was distinctive in the quiet.

"We're throwing you a rope with a loop. Put it around you. Keep your knife. You're going to need it. We're pulling you to safety. If you try and reach our boat, we'll cut the line and you will be lost. Understood?"

"Yes."

Hours later, with the light of dawn, he made out a canoe with six paddlers and a rectangular sail fifteen meters away. He guessed they were making between fifteen to eighteen knots traveling southeast. He heard a metallic sound and looked up to see a canteen on a metal ring bobbing its way down the rope toward him. More than once he had lost concentration, swallowing saltwater. His throat was raw from hacking. When the canteen reached him, he took a small swallow. It was sweet but burned all the way down.

He rolled over, floating on his back. The rope had burned through the skin under his arms. He hoped there was no blood.

He leaned back and watched as flying fish jumped out of the water to either side of him. They flew trying to avoid their predators. What was he now but a giant shark lure? He kept his arms in and moved only when necessary.

Late in the afternoon, he came out of a blistering daydream. The rope went slack. He pulled on it. It gave no resistance.

"I apologize for your means of travel. We guessed the only thing you'd surrender to would be the ocean, and for obvious reasons, we couldn't trust you aboard our canoe. Swim toward the sound of the surf. Mind the coral, or you'll be reef meat. Use your knife," the voice instructed. "Cut four short lengths of rope. Tie them around your hands and feet. That should help you reach the shore relatively unharmed. Once onshore, you'll find fresh water, clothes, and some food. I've loaned you my fishing pole and some tackle. Please take care of it, and it will take care of you. Good luck."

Clanahan rubbed the saltwater from his eyes. The canoe was in the direction of the sun. He couldn't make out a face. "I'll kill you! I'll kill all of you!"

"Yes, we know. Good-bye."

LONG BOW

When life gives you lemons, add sweet tea.
—Anonymous

No matter which way Figas worked the problem, he came up with the same conclusion. If he could figure it out, then what was preventing Prescott? The soldiers were forcibly entering every home carrying out an island-wide search.

The day Clanahan disappeared, Beba was seen talking to him. To top it off, Figas heard she was wearing a short dress and had on bright red lipstick. When he asked her about it, she said it was a costume for a dress rehearsal for an upcoming play. He remembered the conversation he'd overheard in Cairo's mill. Zeno had said, "Be there with bells on." At the time, Figas thought it was only a figure of speech.

When Figas asked Uncle about it, he was mute on the subject. But Fa Shi told him that Zeno was bragging about how he had rid the island of the soldier who beat up young Deoden. No one knew if he had killed the soldier or was holding him prisoner.

For Figas, the pattern stood out like a billboard. He could feel the tension ratcheting up everywhere around him as the grid search continued. He feared the sergeant's body would be found and a clue would lead back to Beba.

He waited in the shadows after dark under the wooden footbridge near her house. The new moon slowly rose over Kuten Ridge. She had told him that sometimes she carried messages late at night. He knew she'd have to cross the bridge.

Just past three in the morning, he was awakened by footfalls on the planks above. He shook off the cold. As Beba passed, he saw she was carrying two pails on a thin yoke balanced across her shoulders. A footie bag was slung over her shoulder. He followed well behind as she headed up the East Ridge to the end of the path, where the statue of P'O sat. There, she met Es-Mira. Figas crouched behind a boulder and watched.

Beba unclipped her buckets and hugged Es-Mira. Both of them knelt in front of the tea master and appeared to be offering prayers for some endeavor. Figas fought the urge to crawl closer. Beba got to her feet and bowed then gently poured her two buckets of sweet tea over the master. She picked up her yoke, which Figas could see was actually a long bow, and together, the women strung it with string from Beba's footie bag. "What are they up to?" Figas whispered.

Beba took a reel of twine from her bag and tied it to a long, blunt arrow that Es-Mira found stashed behind the statue. Beba pulled on a pair of goatskin gloves and sat on the ground, facing the deep ravine. She slipped both feet into the handle of the bow, then pulled with all her strength as Es-Mira notched the arrow with the twine attached and stepped away, holding tightly to the reel. Beba aimed high across the canyon and let loose.

Figas heard the string pop and listened to the twine reeling to the far canyon rim.

Beba got up and brushed herself off. Like a fisherman waiting for a nibble, Es-Mira held the line between her fingers. A moment later, with some effort, she began gathering in the twine. Soon, she was holding a thick rope that had been sent over. It took both women to pull the braided rope around the thick bronze base of the statue. Beba tied a bowline knot and tugged on the rope three times.

Figas could hear the rope being ratcheted tight from the far canyon rim.

Beba slipped a small pulley over the taunt line and looped it around her bow, which she had unstrung. She slung her footie bag over her shoulder and straddled the bow between her legs like a T-bar seat.

Before Figas could react, Es-Mira gave Beba a big push, sending her over the chasm.

Freight caught Beba just as she was about to slam into the rock face that held the piton and the rope. He groped her backside as he set her feet on the ground.

She slapped his hands away. "Try that again, and next time, I'll kick you in your two little brains!"

Freight pouted out his lips. "Maybe next time I'll just let you kiss the rock."

"Girls, girls, knock it off!" Zeno interrupted. "So, Beba, what's the latest from civilization?"

She took a letter from her inside coat pocket and handed it to him without a word. The men hadn't spent much time around a woman in a while. She could smell the testosterone.

Zeno ripped open the envelope and read the letter. "So Prescott replaced Clanahan with a drunk private?" He spit on the ground.

"Did you skim the part where it says not to underestimate the Irishman?"

"You reading my mail? Do you think the beer monkey can fly?" Zeno looked across the canyon.

"You got your fat ass over here, so I wouldn't be too cocky." She meant it.

"It's a good thing for your sake you're not a man," Zeno mumbled.

"How's your food holding out?" She changed her tone.

"We can live on sweet tea."

"I wasn't suggesting you couldn't."

"The spearfishing out past Tap Rock is choice, lots of big lazy parrot fish. And we've plenty of rice. Vittles are not the problem."

Beba handed her footie bag to Zeno. "Here's the rest of the mail. I've got to get back."

Zeno grabbed her hand instead of the bag. "You did a great job with Clanahan!"

"I did it for Deo." She slammed the bag into his hands and pulled away. "Please be careful, Zeno. Stop messing around and stick to the plan for once. They're turning the island upside down looking for you." She looked around at the young men who had gathered around them and who were smirking at her concern. It made her nervous and mad to see how much fun Zeno was having. "This is serious."

Freight wedged a long forked limb under the rope, changing the incline to help with her return trip. Beba zipped up her coat and climbed back on the T-bar. Freight squeezed her left cheek as he pushed her back across.

She yelled over her shoulder, "Next time!"

Saw the Lady in Two

All true tea lovers not only like their tea strong, but like it a little stronger with each year that passes.
—George Orwell

Doogan had been put in charge of the grid search. He tried to be as polite as possible, but he wasn't making many new friends by barging into one house after another, searching for Clanahan. He prayed to the heavenly father that if he did find the bastard, he'd already be dead.

After two weeks, Prescott decided it was a bad idea to have McPhearson looking for a man he despised. He promoted the only female in the company to sergeant and gave her the assignment. He didn't do this because he liked her—he could do without a woman in his command—but as hard as it was to stomach, Reeves was a good soldier.

Doogan was happy to be reassigned. On his first day of resuming his previous assignment of searching for insurgents, he climbed down the rope ladder and made his way to the sleepy cove. With the help of French, he had requisitioned a saw, epoxy glue, and marine caulk. He presented Wuz, Jamila, and their grandfather with a rough drawing of his plan.

"Have you ever done anything like this before?" Jamila asked.

"I've fixed my share of things, but never any then like this. My da, my father, was a pretty decent chippy. I picked up a few things from him. I think it'll work."

The old man smiled with his gums and tapped Doogan on the shoulder. Together, Doogan and Wuz blocked up the canoe rack until it was level. Doogan used his pocketknife to cut the old coir that held on the thin gunnels. After they removed the outrigger, they turn the rotted hull over. Doogan carefully drew a long, angled pencil line near the stern and then used a stick to measure a corresponding line toward the bow.

"Ladies and gentlemen." Doogan feigned perfect posture and the air of a professional magician. "Watch closely. I will saw the beautiful lady in two." He could almost hear the startled murmur of a crowd. He acted with exaggerated confidence, as if trying to convince himself and his audience that he could indeed put the girl back together again. For two hours, he followed the thick pencil line, fighting to keep the saw blade straight. When he'd finished sawing the canoe in half, he sat in the shade and rested. He drained his canteen and realized he wasn't as young as he used to be.

As he started to cut the middle section out, the muscles on the back of his right arm burned so badly he had to take another break. It took the rest of the afternoon to finish the second long cut. When he'd finished, Grandfather helped him roll the rotten middle section off the rack and onto the sand. The saturated hull split apart like an overripe melon.

Wuz helped Doogan lift the eight-foot bow to the corresponding eight feet of the stern. The two saw cuts were hardly a match. Doogan was disappointed. "Not to worry, we just keep at it till they fit," he said.

Doogan kept up his positive banter, but inside he was nervous as a cat. "Phear, you've just destroyed the family's most valuable possession," he muttered to himself. But there wasn't any going back. He lashed the two sections loosely together with twine and took two steps back. The canoe looked like a badly rolled cigarette.

"We'll have to line her up straight. Wuz, have you got a coupla nails?"

The boy ran off and quickly returned with a small can of rusty used nails.

Doogan straightened a nail and centered it on the bow and then did the same on the stern. He tied a string tightly between them, which provided the straight line they needed. He used small wedges under the hull to adjust the two sections until they were in perfect alignment.

Over the next two days, Doogan worked on the long angle cuts until they began touching in places. He ran the sharp handsaw again and again through the long joints. As the sun was setting on the second day, the kerf of the saw teeth finally began to take a taste from both sides, creating a finely matched joint. That evening they mixed epoxy glue and wrapped the mended sections tightly together with layers of coir twine.

The following morning, when the glue had dried, they unwrapped the coir. Using rasps and sandpaper on the inside and outside of the hull, they fine-tuned the new joint. Doogan brushed the dust from the hull, revealing a thin scar—a souvenir of the amateur magician's scalpel. The old man cut dozens of small butterfly-shaped pieces from a plank of dense black wood. Wuz held a black butterfly over the joint as Grandfather traced around it with a sharp knife. Using a sharpened screwdriver and a heavy wooden mallet, the old man slowly chiseled out the shape. Over the rest of the week, Grandfather fit the dark butterfly patches all along the angled joint.

Taking a guess at its proper length, Doogan and Wuz cut a curved limb from a standing dead snag and began making a shorter outrigger.

"You know the boy China?" Doogan asked his young helper.

"Everyone knows China. He's my friend."

"What's wrong with him, exactly? It's like the birds eat up the breadcrumbs before he finds his way to what he's saying."

"Nothing's wrong with him." Wuz looked down and folded the sheet of sandpaper in half again. "Everyone's good at something. China, well he's just . . . good."

"Everyone's good at something—like being an asshole," Doogan said to himself. "Right you are, Wuz. Poor choice of words on my part. Forgive me?"

"What's to forgive? Everyone knows you're a bit slow to put things together."

Doogan grabbed the boy and rubbed his knuckles hard into his scalp until the boy cried out to stop. They stood back and looked at the boat. She was now a full seven feet shorter with the rotted midsection gone. Most importantly, she was now lighter and easier to handle.

Jamila boiled tree nuts and made a clear oil. When they were through sanding, she rubbed the oil into the thirsty grain, changing the wood from silver gray to a chestnut brown.

"Beautimus," Doogan declared.

They decided to wait a day to let everything dry and cure. If the weather proved calm, they would take her out the following morning for a test run.

Instead, the following morning found Doogan in front of his angry CO.

"You've really screwed the pooch this time, McPhearson! I took you off the grid search for you to look for the men in the mountains. According to your report—if you call this parrot cage liner a report—the farthest you've gotten this week is to a valley that can be reached by Zodiac in fifteen minutes. The three residents there include a twenty-three-year-old girl, who has already been interviewed." Prescott raised one eyebrow and paused. "She's living with her grandfather and younger brother." He threw the report on his desk in disbelief. "If this company had an ass, I would put you in charge of it."

Doogan stood at attention, waiting for the gale to blow over. He knew if he gained the trust of even one local person, it could lead to good things. Instead of going out to find people who didn't want to be found, they would come to him.

"Give me one good reason I should believe you'll begin doing your job? Are you even a hair's width closer to finding a single man in the bush?" The commander was too disgusted to continue.

"Excuse me, sir, but I believe I am."

"How so, private? Please explain."

Doogan noticed he was once again a private. "You ordered me to find the men, sir. And to do it in my own way. If all goes according to plan today, I'll have gained the trust and confidence of three local people. From there—"

"One of which is a twenty-three-year-old girl!" the commander interrupted.

"And a radiant raven-haired colleen," Doogan added to himself with pride. "Yes, sir, that's true. But . . ." His face turned bright red. "If ya give me a little more time, I think . . ."

"You *better* think, private! About one thing—your mission! I want daily reports. And I want them to look like they were written by an adult."

"Yes, surr!"

"Now get the hell out of my office!"

GREEN CREEK

The first cup moistens my lips and throat. The second cup breaks my loneliness. The third cup searches my barren entrails only to find therein some thousand volumes of odd ideographs. The fourth cup raises a slight perspiration—all the wrongs of life pass out through my pores. At the fifth cup, I am purified. The sixth cup calls me to the realms of the immortals. The seventh cup—ah, but I could take no more! I only feel the breath of the cool wind that raises in my sleeves.
—Lu Tung

Figas watched a dark blue jumping spider hop across the low table, stalking unseen prey. Many times he'd witnessed Uncle use his ratty old broom to gather up a spider and its web, then shake them loose outside. Jumping spiders, for some unknown reason, avoided deportation.

Figas waited for Uncle to finish his meal before bringing up the topic he wanted to address. "How well did you know my father?"

"We were good friends in school. He was a decent violinist. We played in the school band together. It may come as no surprise that he was very good with numbers. He graduated with an engineering degree, but preferred working with his hands. Your mother worried about his fingers and scolded him for working with machinery. He told her that what really scared him was office furniture."

"My mother said my father worked in a mill. Was it Cairo's?"

"It was a lumber mill. Do you remember your father at all?"

"Not really."

"You were probably too young. He was a millwright, the person in charge of operating the mill."

"I've only seen black-and-white photos of men sawing lumber. Which mill?"

"He went to Tasmania to work when you were a baby. He had the top job running an operation in a place called Green Creek. My sister—your mother—would read his letters to me. Aside from maintaining the mechanical equipment, his most important task was to listen to fluctuations in the timbre of the two-story high bandsaw blade."

"Why did that matter?" Figas enjoyed hearing about his father as a young man.

"Just before the weld would break on the giant bandsaw blade, it would change pitch. It was a dangerous situation, especially because there was a great deal of pressure not to halt production." Uncle paused. He had heard loud and clear the question behind Figas's question. Evidently, no one had ever explained what had happened to his father. "Your father came to work at 5:00 a.m. every day," he began, his voice more somber than usual. "One day, he was checking on the green chain where the freshly cut lumber was handled. A millworker saw him take his tuning fork out of his pocket and hold it up to his ear, as he did periodically throughout the day. The next second, he was running to the emergency shutoff. He never got there. The weld broke, flinging the blade across the room like a giant uncoiling spring."

"He was killed by the blade?"

"Yes, nephew. I'm afraid your mother never recovered from the shock." Uncle poured tea.

Figas couldn't think of anything to say. The tiny blue jumping spider pounced on an unseen speck near his cup.

GUNSLINGER

May you always have walls for the winds, a roof for the rain, tea beside the fire, laughter to cheer you, those you love near you, and all your heart might desire.
—Irish blessing

Doogan felt a mixture of relief and panic as he raced down the path toward the sea. It was already late afternoon. He couldn't help feeling he'd missed the moment. When he looked down the beach, he saw his new friends sitting beside the flower-adorned vessel. They had waited for him to begin the blessing.

The four sat silently in a circle and sipped warm tea without speaking.

Doogan was still out of breath.

The old man stood up and poured the remainder of his tea over the bow.

Doogan got to his feet and splashed the remainder of his cup across the new seam.

The old man nodded and smiled.

Doogan held up his empty cup and made a toast quietly to himself. "To her second virgin voyage." Then he looked up into the clouds. "Sorry, father." The wind had picked up and was adding some chop to the heavy rollers coming in. "It looks pretty rough right now."

Grandfather nodded his head in agreement and picked up his long paddle.

"Well, Phear," Doogan said under his breath, "either she'll snap in half like an old twig and you'll have destroyed their only means to feed themselves, or the old tub will be born anew." He wondered how well a goat could swim.

Grandfather's wrinkled hands rubbed a butterfly patch as they waited. A big wave crashed and retreated.

Wuz let out his high-pitched call. They slid her off the wooden rack and hit the water in perfect rhythm as another big wave slammed into the bow, waking up their paddles. The patch held. In a few clean strokes, they sliced through the surf and into the rolling sea.

No one spoke. A serious rhythm set in, driving them far from shore. Doogan searched the long seam for a leak. It still held. When Grandfather called out, they switched hands. The water from the ends of their paddles pooled in the belly of the canoe. When they broke tempo, the old man brought them about in a gentle arc. The dark cliffs of Viridis stood out against the clouds. They floated in a somber stillness.

Doogan swayed side to side and felt the boat respond. The few miles they had just paddled seemed the farthest he'd ever traveled. No one broke the sweet silence. He looked at Jamila, her dark hair covering her brown shoulders.

At last, Grandfather broke the silence with something the Irishman couldn't understand.

Wuz burst out laughing and then replied in local pidgin. They all laughed, except Doogan.

"Did he say good job?" he asked.

"No," Wasil explained, "Grandfather said you should try this same miracle repair on your ear, add a bit of something back on. So I asked where you'd get that little something. He said, 'Where you can least afford it.'"

"All right. All right." Doogan's face flashed red. He wanted to correct the old man about how much extra he could afford but kept his tongue. He always tried to be a gentleman in mixed company.

"Then Grandfather said that maybe you already did that miracle repair using a bit of something from down there," Wuz had comic timing. "But the patch didn't hold."

Doogan scratched. "What's so funny?"

Jamila covered her mouth and put her head down on her knees.

"Grandfather said . . ."—Wuz gathered another mouthful of air and used his imitation Irish accent—"that makes it cleere why you're always pulling on your ear!"

Doogan self-consciously brought his hand down to his side. "I see." He reached over Jamila and grabbed the boy under the arm and tossed him overboard. "Paddle!"

Wuz swam after them, but was no match for the speed of the canoe.

Doogan looked back at the old man's toothless smile. "Ya should be in the drink, the boath of yas."

The old culprit pointed with his wrinkled finger at the squall coming their way.

They waited for Wuz to climb back in then paddled hard for three hours against a stiff wind and sheets of rain. They found their way back in the dark—hungry, thirsty, and exhausted. They beached the canoe, easily pulling her up the sand and onto the oversized rack.

"I'll make a cover to keep the rain out, Grandfather." Jamila was happy to have thought of another way to contribute.

On his subsequent visit to Sullivan's, Doogan was thanked for his good deed. Stu had saved his favorite pew. The place was quiet, considering how many wharfies were in the back. Doogan pointed at the tap and looked around, trying to figure out what was going on. When he reached up and tugged at his ear, the place erupted into a roar.

"Very fecking funny! Clever clogs," Doogan shouted, but nobody could hear. He drank his pint, but it didn't taste good. "Saunders, this island's too damn small."

Stu looked over at him, confused.

"Another round for my friend here," Doogan yelled over at Blair.

Stu was even more confused.

"At least it wasn't you," he said, wondering if it was the boy or the old man who had betrayed him. He caught his left hand going up and pulled it down slowly, like a gunslinger away from his six-shooter.

Another chorus of laughter broke out.

"It's going to be a long night," the Irishman said, but no one heard him over the din.

THE PAYOFF

Tea doesn't cheat you, but it's people who cheat.
—Chen Zhi-tong

Doogan, keen to look his best, made it to his predawn appointment for a hot shave and a trim. Fa Shi's shop was full. A cadre of nonagenarians filled the chairs against the back wall. They looked up in unison from their old issues of *The Standard* and *The Times of India*. Doogan bowed awkwardly and gave his signature "good marning." He slapped his payment of two bars of soap on the counter and took the lumpier pew. The crusty old Hu was occupying his favorite stool by the window.

Fa Shi wrapped a hot towel around the Irishman's face and pumped up the chair. He drew the edge of his razor out on the wide leather strap and waited for Hu to finish his story.

Hu hated being interrupted by rude youths. He continued, "You know the little ones. The sting is worse than the big ones."

The king's court grunted in agreement.

Fa Shi brought Doogan up to speed by mimicking the legs of the dreaded local centipede.

"I'm in bed asleep and this little one stings me on my cock!"

This sent the court into hysterics.

"It swelled up! My *gau* never been so big!"

Fa Shi's soprano giggle made Doogan laugh.

"It was a little bugger!" Hu held up his fingers two inches apart.

"My mistake." Doogan's timing was perfect. "This whole time I thought you was talking about the centipede."

"Turtle eggs!" Hu's outrage made it even funnier. He stormed out without paying.

The old men held up their fingers two inches apart and laughed themselves to tears.

Fa Shi snapped his towel to let whoever was next know there was an empty chair. "Mr. Hu has left upset," Fa Shi explained.

"That's about the size of it." Doogan added a final touch.

All freshly trimmed and smelling of witch hazel, Doogan hurried down the beach and waited by the canoe, watching for the burning disc to emerge from the metallic water. Clouds on the horizon frustrated his hopes. Still, it was a fantastic morning. When Wuz didn't show up, he walked up to the house and gave a shout to give Jamila warning. He tapped at the door and let himself in.

The old man was lying on a bamboo mat. Jamila was sponging his forehead with a damp towel. She didn't look up.

"Where's Wasil?" Doogan asked softly.

Jamila made a gesture with her head that said he would be back in a minute.

When the boy came in, Doogan knew he had been crying. He grabbed him by the neck and hugged him.

"You need a doctor?" Doogan tried to make it sound like a question.

The old man opened his eyes and looked at Doogan and mumbled something.

"What'd he say?"

Jamila smiled. "Grandfather said he's old."

"And?"

"And is your head packed with clover?"

"Is that a crack at me being Irish?"

The old man's chest went up and down as if he were laughing, but no sound came out.

"The only thing that's old and tired is your sense of humor. Tomorrow, we'll go out and catch some fish!"

The old man smiled with his eyes closed.

Doogan went outside.

Wasil sat beside his grandfather to give his sister a break. She found Doogan leaning against the monkeypod, picking at the bark.

"Is there anything I can do?" he asked.

"I don't know. I think he needs to rest. He's worn himself out."

"It's my fault, if I hadn't . . ."

"If you hadn't come to help us, he would . . ." Jamila didn't want to think about the future or the past. The two just stood there in silence.

"Are you sure there isn't anything I can do?"

"I was going to gather some eggs, but I would rather stay close if Grandfather needs me. If you want, you can take a bucket to the cliffs and climb the ladder. But be careful, make sure it's steady before you climb up."

"Yes, I know. I've helped Wuz collect eggs a time or two."

Doogan was happy to have something to do to help. He followed the trail to the base of the sea cliffs. He found the rickety ladder, which was tied to a root near the top rung to keep it from blowing off the face of the rock. The frigate birds came and went from their nests above. He set the plastic bucket down and wedged a flat rock under the shorter wooden rail. As he tested the ladder, a gust of wind swept the plastic pail down the embankment. "Feck!"

He picked his way down the green slope. The clumpy grass and moss was silky soft, glowing like the green down of the little local birds. He grabbed the bucket and scampered back up the hill. A large rock near the top of the path caught his attention. The moss around it was brown, as if it had recently been disturbed.

"What do we have here?" He tilted the boulder forward and exposed a small canvas bag, half covered with sand. He pulled it out. It was extremely heavy for its size. He untied its long strings. It opened like a parachute, revealing dozens of tiny pockets. He reached in and pulled out a thick gold coin. "Jaysuz, Joseph, and Meerie!"

The queen was on one side and the Canadian maple leaf on the other. He squinted and read "One oz. pur 9999." He bit down hard, wondering if there was any truth that the real thing was soft. It wasn't. Without thinking, he pocketed the coin and reached into another compartment. That gold coin was also new. Chinese writing surrounded a rabbit. He could make out "Hong Kong."

Doogan pushed his head back against the mossy hillside. He felt like he was slipping downhill. He was light-headed, unable to make the motion in his head stop, as if he'd had a few too many at the pub the night before. He fought the temptation to tip the bag upside down. He rubbed the shiny coin between his fingers and tried to think. A series of questions scrolled through his mind, adding to his motion sickness: "Whose gold is it? How did it get here? Does Jamila know? How can they be so poor with a fortune buried in their backyard?"

He went through a hundred scenarios and concluded the gold must have been stashed after the troops landed. He sat up and reached into his pocket and withdrew the thick gold coin. "So how's it gonna be?" He flipped it high in the air. "Tails!"

Jamila smiled, wondering what had taken him so long. "Did you find any eggs? I almost came looking for you."

"No." Doogan showed her the empty bucket.

She shrugged. "Grandfather's sleeping. He just needs to rest."

"And Wuz? Is he okay?"

"He's fine. We're fine." Jamila poured tea.

"I've got to get back. Tell the old man to quit . . . I mean, tell him to rest up and get better. Good-bye, Jamila."

"Let's go, Doogan. Onward to beveraging." Stu used his hands like a cone to announce the charge. "Bev-ward!"

"You go ahead."

"What?" Stu felt Doogan's forehead.

The Irishman slapped his hand away.

"Just checking to see if you have a temperature." It was the first time he'd known Doogan to pass up O'Sullivan's on an off-duty night.

"I've got to finish my report to the bean counter."

"See you afterward?"

"Yea, sure."

Well past last call, Doogan checked out a pair of night-vision glasses and informed the duty officer of his night op. "Radio Reeves not to shoot me."

"The grid search is in the northwestern quadrant, steer clear and you shouldn't run into any patrols."

"Thanks."

Half an hour later, Doogan made his way down the rope ladder and retraced his steps to the hiding place on the mossy slope. He rolled the rock back and felt for the canvas bag. "Feck!" Doogan cursed as quietly as he could. It was gone. He leaned back against the moss and then turned and punched it like an insomniac's pillow.

He silently approached the little house and checked the area with his night scope. Everything was still. He waited. He hoped the old man was feeling better. He felt he couldn't face Jamila.

An hour before dawn, he made his way back to his cot.

He woke up in the late morning, grabbed two bars of soap, and headed for Fa Shi's shop. All the chairs were empty. He slapped the two bars of soap on the counter. "A shave if you please, Sweeney."

"Sha' thing." The barber cranked back his chair and pumped it to the perfect height. He didn't speak, but his look said, "What happened to you?"

Doogan ignored him and enjoyed being pampered. The hot towel felt comforting.

When the barber was finished, he splashed witch hazel on Doogan's clean face. It stung in a refreshing way that buoyed Doogan's dismal mood.

Fa Shi gave him another look. "You have twin brother?" Fa Shi had never seen Doogan when he wasn't babbling.

"Can I ask you a question?"

"Sha' thing. First one free."

"You ever wish you were rich?"

Doogan's look was so earnest, it tickled the barber's funny bone. "I'm serious. You ever think about it?"

"Everyone think about it."

Doogan knew the old barber was aware of everything that went on. He heard it all, knew it all. "What do you want in life, Fa Shi?"

The old man giggled. No one had asked him that since he was a child.

Doogan knew he couldn't bribe or coerce the old man into telling him a thing.

"You want high and tight fade?" Fa Shi's warn silver clippers were at the ready.

"Yea sure, why not?"

After Doogan left, Uncle came in and sat in the barber's chair. He looked into the mirror on the front wall, seeing the mirror on the back wall into infinity, enjoying the illusion.

"You want trim?"

Uncle rubbed his completely bald head. "Nice job on the soap."

"Take it. Don't come back unless you paying customer." Fa Shi pointed to the door.

"Get some new magazines!" Uncle barked back.

"You mean comics?"

Uncle pocketed the two bars of soap. "So did he say anything at all?"

"Asked if I want to be rich."

"You may as well. You're not good-looking or funny." Uncle pulled open the door.

"Out!"

Uncle stopped by the school and left the two bars of soap with Mrs. Morris. She blinked. Her shoulders went up in mischievous anticipation.

That night, she carefully steamed open the ends of the wax paper wrappers. She melted down the bars, stirring in the essence of *C. fargesii* to lure the bengafly. She recast the bars in molds she had made. When they cooled, she sealed them back inside their wax paper wrappers. The next morning, she dropped by Fa Shi's shop and left a bag on the counter and enjoyed a laugh with the barber. They secretly took pleasure in watching the passing soldiers swat at bengaflies wherever they went.

SOUTH
BUTTERNUT SQUASH
FESTIVAL

Better to be deprived of food for three days, than tea for one.
—Chinese proverb

In light of the tea plants being ripped up terrace by terrace and replaced with food crops, the annual Butternut Squash Festival took on superhuman proportions. After seven months of occupation, the Viridis Council set aside extra funds to promote a new direction away from the traditional crop of tea. It was to be a statement that let the occupying troops know they had not succeeded in dampening local spirits.

Winston, the festival's organizer, signed up a dozen volunteers to make giant papier-mâché butternut squashes. Winston tied a string around the giant inflated weather balloon, a little above center, and choked it until it mimicked the correct hourglass shape. When he was satisfied, he mixed the paint to match the golden brown of a ripe butternut squash.

Beba mixed sticky rice flour and water and helped Figas dip strips of newspaper over the rubber balloon molds.

"Here we are papering over our old holiday with a new one. How much more traditional can you get?" Winston joked. He felt the volunteers' sense of loss as plainly as his own. The Autumn Tea

Festival was in their bones and couldn't be ignored any more than the seasons could fail to recall the tilt of the earth.

When the paper had cured over night, Figas and Beba cut holes in the bottom of the giant gourds for the feet. They sanded the edges smooth. Winston traced a single small eyehole, an oculus, to see through.

"What about arms?" Beba asked.

"No arms. Butternut squash don't have arms!"

This didn't make sense to Beba; squash didn't have feet either, but she knew it was way easier to just agree with Winston and compliment him on his artistic vision. Including the height of the operator's legs, the largest of the gourds stood ten feet tall. They were somewhere between a costume and a float.

On the morning of the festival parade, Doogan passed by the preparations and stopped to watch. Father Murray was helping to load a giant squash, tipping the bulbous shape to its feet.

"Easy, vicar! This baby is a bit top-heavy," a small voice yelled from inside.

"Don't they know the difference between a vicar and a priest around here, father?" the Irishman asked, his curiosity brimming.

"Oh, they know perfectly well," the young priest explained. "It's more that they believe in wringing as much out of things as humanly possible."

"At your expense."

"My meaning exactly. I corrected them for years before I caught on."

Doogan pointed over the priest's shoulder at a large wayward shape careening over a small rock wall. Father Murray rushed over too late. Doogan followed and helped him tip the giant gourd back on its feet.

Looking into the crowd, the Irishman noticed the little bald man he had seen coming out of the bean counter's office on several occasions. He wondered if he was the mayor.

Just then, Auntie Lan sliced through the throng, nearly cutting the legs out from under Father Barrett as she passed, as if they were thin sticks of butter. She confronted the little bald man. "A squash festival with everything that's been going on? Really, Red, have you gone completely mad?"

"I only wish it had been my idea," he confessed.

"Where's that idiot Winston hiding?" Auntie Lan continued to needle her way around the event.

Doogan came up behind the little bald man. "The heart of a lion and the mind of a fox."

"Indeed." Uncle gave the soldier an understanding look. Both took a moment to size the other up. With Clanahan safely tucked away and knowing Prescott's limited imagination, Uncle knew where his greatest challenge lay. Without effort, he feigned an expression of fear as he watched Auntie Lan making her rounds, chiding and reminding the festival participants of their duties.

Doogan watched the old man closely from the corner of his eye. He wondered if the bean counter ran this little fella around as easily as this old auntie had just done. He felt a soft spot coming on for little baldy. "The name's Doogan." He reached out to shake hands.

"My name is Sun." Uncle bowed. "A pleasure to meet you."

"You and the black thorn, I see you've something special together?"

"Black thorn. Yes. I like that very much." Uncle beamed.

"Fancy a wee swallow of something down at 'Sullivan's after the revelry?"

"Thought you would never ask," Father Murray answered from well behind them.

"And will you join me, as well, Mr. Sun?" Doogan asked before turning to recognize the priest's good ears and sticky beak.

"Of course, after the event." Uncle made a small bow. "Now, if you'll excuse me, Mr. Doogan, I must go and help with the band."

Uncle collected the members of the small marching ensemble. He rigged a rope around China's neck, helping the young wharfie carry the bass drum while he marched. Two trumpet players joined the young girl, Tsani, who played cymbals.

Islanders lined both sides of Lantern Street all the way through Salm Bay. An obstacle course was laid out for the giant squashes. Hurdles were arranged in the form of low shrubs in pots for a steeple chase. A unicycle was at the ready.

Tsani crashed her cymbals, signaling the first baby squash to begin the ballet of the gourds. Expression was somewhat limited due to the un-limber nature of the participating vegetables. Winston's choreography did a nice job of introducing the movement and left the rest to the festival goers' imagination.

When the parade reached the end of town, the finale of skipping rope drew the biggest cheers. Excitement broke out when the most nimble gourd stayed alive during double Dutch. She recited her favorite rhyme. The crowd clapped in time. *"Bake a pudding. Bake a pie. Did you ever tell a lie? Yes, you did. You know you did. You broke your mother's teapot lid."*

All the grief and loss was transmuted into joy for a brief moment.

The parade ended at the school's soccer field. A long line formed in back of the bleachers, where green tea Jell-O with a sweet black bean base was served. An impromptu match was held: the home team against the visitors. The crowd poured into the stands—the locals on the home side, and the troops on the opposite visitors' side. The grass on the field was thick and wet.

Winston took off his smock, revealing zebra stripes. He blew his referee whistle incessantly, directing the festival crew to wrap green ribbons around six of the giant gourds playing for the home team. Pieces of camouflage cloth were randomly taped on the visiting team. The three remaining gourds were outfitted with red pom-poms so they could lead the hometown cheers.

The two bleachers heckled each other and screamed encouragement to their players, giving free advice on how to exploit the other team's defenses. Off-duty soldiers placed bets, claiming that maybe their team wasn't as big, but they were faster, stronger and by far more physical.

Winston placed the ball in the middle of the field. The players took their positions. The whistle blew. The ball was successfully kicked once before the two teams collided with a series of hollow cracks, splitting one gourd in two and knocking over all the players except one. Winston, running full speed backward, blew his whistle and signaled a penalty before bouncing off the last remaining player and toppling them both. Legs wiggled in the air across the field of play like freshly dug worms.

Winston recovered and began handing out yellow penalty cards.

Commander Prescott stood near the goal line and watched the ridiculous proceedings with a scowl. The match was thankfully over. A draw. He searched the crowd for anyone who might have been responsible for the disappearance of his sergeant. He noticed that Dutch Moreno and his dockworkers were not in attendance. The island-wide grid search was still underway. Those responsible would pay dearly.

Uncle walked past and announced to anyone who might be listening, "I've heard of killing for oil. We've seen killing over tea. But butternut squash?"

The Dipsas

Tea—the cups that cheer but not inebriate.
—William Cowper

Uncle and the young priest nabbed a table outside O'Sullivan's while the Irishman wedged himself inside the front door to order the drinks. A roar exploded out of the pub door. It was standing room only. Doogan hadn't realized how much he'd missed his old watering hole. He held up three fingers for Blair, who didn't see him. He found himself behind Figas and Beba, who were also trying to get served. He'd met the young couple on a previous visit to the island's only pub. "Well, if it isn't the mathematical wizard and the lovely Miss Beba." Doogan cracked Figas on the back. "Did you know," he quoted, "*there was a young fellow from Trinity who solved the square root of infinity. But it gave him such fidgets, to count up the digits. He dropped math and took up divinity.*"

Figas, whose voice didn't carry like Doogan's, yelled in the soldier's good ear with a quote of his own: "*A limerick packs laughs anatomical into space that is quite economical. But the good ones I've seen so seldom are clean. And the clean ones so seldom are comical.*"

Doogan chuckled in deep satisfaction and held up five fingers to the barkeep.

When Blair finally sighted him, he pointed to both ale taps and sliced his throat with his finger, indicating they were dry. It was rum or nothing.

Doogan nodded and pointed to the outside tables.

Blair nodded back.

Despite his long absence, Doogan retained his well-worn slate at Sullivan's. "Come and join us outside." He used his sweet singsong voice.

"Thanks, Doogan, but we're meeting some friends," Beba lied. She'd never partied with a cave dweller, but she was okay with a rain check.

Reverend Betty watched Figas negotiate with the Irish private. "Look, Morty."

The rabbi cocked his head but remained vigilant to garner the bartender's attention. He guessed she meant the local kid who earned a PhD before he was twenty.

"He's like a young soup." Her shoulders rose and fell as she sighed. "With a little time, he'll sozzle into a nice young man."

"Hot things don't sozzle, Elizabeth. Cold things sozzle. That's why I'm always telling you not to gulp your Manhattan."

"Very funny, Morty."

Doogan worked his way through the crowd and ran smack into Fioré.

The director leaned in close to what remained of Doogan's ear. "I loved you in Blue Velvet."

"What?"

"Have you seen Emma?"

"Huh?"

"The tall woman with the little handbag."

"Oh yeah. No." Doogan squeezed out the door and pulled up a pew between Uncle Sun and the young priest. He was unaware that his banter remained at the same volume as when he was inside ordering drinks. Sheer panic overcame him when the server came out with a tray holding three teacups. He set them on the table without explanation while leering at Doogan.

The Irishman picked up his cup and smelled it. "Jayzus! Close one. I thought for a moment it was tea. Cheers. May your soul be in heaven an hour before the devil knows you're dead. At least Blair got out the good delph for Sunday tay." He emptied his cup. "Around this time of day, I always get a bite from the dipsas."

"What's a dipsas?" Uncle asked.

"'Tis a snake that bites ya and ya die of thirst."

"My grandfather claimed that was why St. Patrick banished all snakes from the old country," the young priest added.

"Where'd you say you were from, father?" Doogan thought he detected a bit of an accent.

"My parents were from Lisdoonarna, County Clare. I was born in Boston."

"Oh, a Yankee?"

"Yes." It was funny to Father Murray how the Irish thought of everyone from America as Yankees, no matter their ethnic background. He could be a Sikh from Alabama wearing a turban and he would still be a Yankee. "I've never seen you here before, Uncle." The priest was curious if Uncle Sun drank anything but tea.

"Yeah, Mr. Sun," Doogan broke in, "what's it you do exactly?"

"I used to teach music. For many years I worked in the tea." Uncle took a small sip. "Now I'm between jobs."

"So you get by?" The Irishmen tilted his cup, hoping for a lingering drop.

"I started out with nothing and still have most of it left." Uncle stood up. "I'll get the next round." He bowed and pushed his way inside the crowded front door.

"See if you can squeeze some ale out of the barman while you're at it." Doogan yelled after him. Doogan turned to the priest. "Funny little fella. Is he some kind of muckety-muck?"

"Hmm. I'm not sure we have those." Murray remembered a little joke the locals told: it wasn't so much the pedigree but the verdigris that mattered. He always felt at a loss when trying to explain Green Islanders.

"So he's not the mayor?"

"He doesn't hold office formally." The priest explained that the local connotation of the word *formal* was to be or act suspicious. Similarly, *pious* was synonymous with creepy, which made his job that much more of an uphill climb. If the islanders believed in anything, it was informal spontaneity. Life was best experienced as a beautiful accident.

"Do you have much of a flock here, or do they go the way of the heathen?"

"They believe in many things, but proselytizing isn't among them."

"No knocking on doors, eh?"

"Just so."

Figuring the priest had had a few by now, Doogan felt confident this was the opportune time to pump him for intel. "So, what can you tell me about our Mr. Sun?"

"He is straight out of the P'O school."

"Which means?"

"When I arrived on the island seven years ago, I asked Uncle Sun how I might best become a part of the community. He replied, 'Stand aside and let the world work. It's been doing it a long time.'" The priest explained that this statement initially baffled him, but it proved to be sound advice. If he were forced to try to capture the venerable Dr. Sun in words, he would say the old man was nestled in the moment. "So," he concluded, "are you a practicing Catholic?"

"I didn't know you were on the clock father."

"I'm just curious. Are you?"

"Not anymore."

"Why's that?"

"Here's the short version. I suppose, given your day job, you've buried a few people. So there you are, staring into the coffin. I'll wager you were never worried about a one of them. You're more concerned about the people they've left behind."

"Well, I'm concerned about the souls of the departed."

"Why is that?"

"Eternal damnation."

Doogan shook his head. That was the crux of it, wasn't it? Everything came down to the threat of damnation. "Sorry, father, but I don't believe in hell."

"That's fair enough." Murray picked up his cup to take a swig, only to realize it was already empty. "Truth be told, I'm not convinced I believe in it either, but that's no reason to walk away from God's grace. And I'm convinced our actions and our choices lead us away from the light or toward it."

"You'll get no argument from me on that last little bit about choices, so let's leave it at that."

Just then, Uncle squeezed out of the tightly packed pub with an unopened bottle of rum.

Doogan pushed his chair out and stood up, as if a lady were passing. "How the hell did you manage that? An unopened bottle? Jayzus!" He was seriously impressed. "What happened in there anyway? Did someone die?" He had noticed a hush in the bar, though the roar was once again gathering steam.

"I think someone was giving a toast just now." Uncle managed a small fib. In fact, the islanders had never seen the tea master in the pub before. They were shocked into silence and parted like the Red Sea as he approached Blair. The barkeep handed him an unopened bottle and wanted to say, "It's on the house," but his jaw went slack.

The cork made a loud pop as Uncle pulled it out ceremoniously with his teeth. He liberally refilled their teacups. "Mr. Blair owed me a small favor." Another fib. "I'm sorry it isn't ale, Mr. Doogan."

"All's forgiven. I've seen this before." Doogan felt himself to be a bit of an expert pub-wise. "The place gets busy, and it's faster to pour shots of liquor or hand over an unopened bottle than to pull a proper pint of ale. Plus it adds up quicker on the slate."

"I've grown fond of the local cream," Murray confessed. He was starting to get lit. Uncle refilled the young priest's cup.

"Yeah, there's 'melts in your mouth.' And there's 'melts the inside of your mouth,'" Doogan complained, albeit in a grateful way.

To Murray, drinking the distilled spirits of the island was like being hit on the head with a hammer made by God's favorite angel—feather light, but divinely effective. He held up his cup to make a toast. "Cheers! I best be off. I promised Winston I'd help him clean up. And you know how he gets. Good-bye."

Dutch Moreno at the next table shouted after him, "Candy is dandy, but the vicar is quicker!" A wave of laughter washed the tipsy priest down Lantern Street.

Hu walked by and gave Uncle Sun an earful. "Foolish youth. Drinking liquor with the riffraff."

Dutch Moreno held his fingers up two inches apart. "Look, if it isn't the little centipede!" The rest of the outside tables held their fingers two inches apart and roared.

Hu scurried across the street. "Turtle eggs!"

Uncle Sun refilled Doogan's cup to the brim and sipped his own rum as if it were hot tea. Master P'O's way was to "anticipate the difficult by managing the easy." Uncle wondered if it would work the other way around as well. He waited until they were near the bottom of the bottle, by which time the crowd had thinned. Then he asked Doogan about his present situation.

"We're the 125ᵗʰ Expeditionary Force." The Irishman took another long pull from the short teacup. He was getting seriously drunk, though remained nimble of tongue.

"Never heard of such a thing." Uncle kept up his local yokel wide-eyed charm. He pointed to Doogan's uniform. "You don't have your own insignia?"

"Funny you should ask. SSI, shoulder sleeve insignia are too brightly colored and therefore are not worn by recon forces in the theater of operations." Doogan topped off both their cups. "Now it's my turn, mo chara." He leaned three inches from Uncle's face. "You know a colleen named Jamila? How about a lad named Wasil and his grand da?"

"Yes, they the family you've been helping."

"You know about that?"

"Do you think I drink with just anyone?" Uncle laughed and managed to get a smile from the drunk Irishman.

"How's the grand da?" Doogan was worried about the old man.

"He's still kicking."

Doogan wanted to ask the gray fox if the whole thing had somehow been staged. He wanted to believe Jamila was real, at least. But if he tipped his hand too soon, he might lose his chance. He knew old baldy thought he was drunk. And he was. But he wanted to learn a few things before he passed out. As his grandma used to say, "The truth is the thing people don't want to know."

"I found a bag." Doogan hesitated.

"Oh?"

"A special kind of bag."

"What was special about it?"

"I was about to take a bite of the cheese."

"What cheese?"

"You know what I'm talking about."

"I'm not following."

Doogan leaned in again. "Did you know that a fox is a wolf who sends flowers?"

Uncle erupted into a cheery giggle.

The next morning, Doogan awoke to Stu's voice pounding through his skull. "I heard an old man from the village had you licking the peanut shells last night, McPhearson!"

"There's not a tittle of truth in that!"

"Are you going to lie in the fart sack all day?" A hangover meant the Doogan he knew was back. Stu was elated.

Shimmering Dome

Cake and tea or death?
--Eddie Izzard

The full moon rose over the notch in Kuten Ridge. It was yellow orange. Herbie passed by Millie, the big tree near Flute Rock, and asked, "Sista. Why da moon bigger near da horizon?"

Her leaves rustled in response and reflected the white light down to him with ten thousand tiny mirrors.

He grunted, letting her know he was thinking about what she meant. He had one more stop on his late night rounds to the toolsheds, checking up on his crew's activities and making notes. "Who's been busy, and who's been busy with nawting."

He had been told about the grid search but brushed it off as unimportant. He was good at ignoring everything to do with the occupation. He wasn't going to let it change things. Maybe they were growing vegetables instead of tea, but farming was farming. Had he bothered to inquire, he would have known he was walking straight into a patrol.

By the time he heard them coming, they were right on top of him. Herbie was in great shape for a man of his years. He could hike all day long, but he couldn't really run. He whispered to Millie, "Sista! This da chase. They still plenty upset over da big machine they lost."

"Stop! Hands over your head, or we'll shoot!" Reeves called out.

Herbie looked up through Millie's shimmering dome. He raised his hands toward her canopy, as if reaching into a transcendent sphere. "Sista," he called, "liff me up!" Then he closed his eyes and began his ars moriendi.

The Caprice Theater

A cup of tea excels the real.
—Lian Ya Tang

"Hot places do freeze over." Commander Prescott was pleasantly surprised to receive a formal invitation from the production company of Insta-Gators. The letterhead portrayed a tilting box with a picture of an alligator. The little caption read, "Just add water." And the letter said, "Please join us for the premier performance of the original play *The General and the Mousetrap* this evening."

"Perhaps these yokels are finally getting used to the idea of me being in charge," he confided to French. "After all, it's not like they don't need some structure, by god."

French explained, "Dr. Sun will join you and interpret."

"Splendid." Prescott was grateful for the thaw after nothing but the cold shoulder for months on end.

The following Tuesday arrived hot, with not a breeze to be found. The evening settled in with a merciful cushion of cool air rolling down from Kuten Ridge.

The natural amphitheater was rendered from the blue and gray porkbelly sandstone. The high canyon wall backstopped the stage, helping to amplify the actor's voices and holding the heat of the sun long into the evening. The thick bench seats and steps flowed in a freeform curve. Two polished slabs of dark slate stood upright like menhirs, towering twenty feet high to either side of the stage. The megalithic coulisse functioned like the traditional wings of a theater, while also serving as two giant gray chalkboards. The effect was a magnificent multidimensional set. With the help of five talented chalk artists, Winston had created the illusion of a massive army camp.

Uncle handed Prescott a program and led him to their seats near the back of the theater. As he looked out over the hall, he could see just about every Green Islander. Except Herbie. But then, Herbie was known for running on his own time.

The commander read the back of the program first. He noticed Dr. Sun had written and arranged the musical score. On the front, under the play's title, the fine script read, "By very kind arrangement, this play is sponsored in part by Immaculate Cold Storage."

"Interesting name for a business," Prescott remarked.

Uncle, dressed in his worn cashmere, quickly related the story of how several years ago a young woman named Iris purchased the business from a crusty old man named Chu, who died before the transaction was complete. After signing the property deal with Chu's younger brother, she entered the walk-in freezer and found a small jar labeled *For Iris*. A little note from old man explained this was the only way they could have children together now that he was dead. The story got around quickly. With decided humor, she named her newborn business Immaculate Cold Storage.

Figas sat beside Es-sahra and carefully watched the bellowing fabric scrim. He was hoping to catch a glimpse of Beba behind the scenes. She had written the play with help from Auntie Lan and Winston.

"Auntie, what does a backstage manager do?" he asked.

"I imagine right now Beba is helping the actors with their cues and their lines, but most of all bucking their confidence. Many of them have never been in a play before. It is a great loss that so many fathers aren't here to see and encourage them."

"I wish I could be with her."

"She wants you to enjoy the play. You wouldn't see much from backstage."

"Have you been in a play, Auntie?"

"Not me. Unless you include the theater of the absurd. The council meetings with your uncle can be quite fantastical." She held her program over her mouth to muffle her laugh.

"I wonder why Beba never goes to those. She has such strong feelings about things," he mused.

"She does indeed, but I'm not sure wild horses could drag her to a council meeting."

"I guess writing plays is more her thing. But I still think she'd be a natural at community organizing. I know she's proud of you as council leader."

Es-sahra's face relaxed. "Sweet of you to sit with an old woman." She patted his wrist. "Tell me, what is it like to be back? Are you adjusting well?"

Figas's back straightened.

"I don't mean to pry. It's just that I've never been away and come back."

"I would say one big difference between living abroad and living here is that if you have difficulty with a certain person or situation living in a city, you can simply walk away. That strategy doesn't work here for long."

"I see." She thought Hu was probably the one he was having difficulty with. Or perhaps Beba, for all she knew. Her daughter was a complete mystery. She seemed happiest when she was in nature.

The corner of the fabric caught on a rampart. Figas caught a glimpse of Beba. She had tried to explain to him that words on stage transcended their everyday meanings. When her mind wasn't trying to organize her heart, her imagination was busy casting her friends and family as their cosmic ancestors, with nature as the backdrop. The names and the people changed, but the roles remained surprisingly similar through the ages.

The last light departed over the canyon wall, leaving behind warm shadows. Figas turned around and was glad to see the theater now packed. Maybe they would finally get the show started.

Es-sahra studied the young man in the waning light. She was happy her daughter was finding her way past her anger. She knew her oldest had conflated the absence of her father and transferred onto her young man the offences of everyone who had abandoned her. The wound started with the disappearance of her father, then burned deeper with the tragic loss of her sister. Es-sahra realized she was telling all this to Cedar in her mind. Most of the time her habit of talking silently to her youngest went unnoticed. Her reverie ended abruptly as two young aspiring actors stepped forward to warm up the crowd.

"Look, Pompie, have you read this new haiku?"

"No. I'm waiting for the movie to come out." Pompie had a unibrow penciled in that gave him the necessary gravitas to carry off his important message.

"Is it a summer blockbuster?"

"Um-hmmm."

"What's it called?"

"The Murder of Gonzago."

"A comedy?"

"Most assuredly."

"Sounds like an awfully long haiku. So, Pompie, you must be a Buddhist?"

"No. A Psueddhist."

"Never heard of it. What's that?"

"A fake Buddhist. Psueddism is the fastest, fattest growing religion in the world."

"Quite an unleavened thought! How do you know, Pompie?"

"Just do."

"I guess you think you're right."

"Of course. Can't really help it."

"You always have to be right."

"No I don't."

"Ya think?"

"No. I know."

"About what? Can you please remind me?

"About *not having* to be right all the time."

Two more youths entered the stage. The short boy asked the tall, thin boy in drag, "What you been up to, Ed?"

"Touring with my one-man show."

"What's it about?"

"Getting along with other people."

"Makes sense."

"I play myself. Eddie Puss Rex, torch singer extraordinaire!" He put his hands on his hips, with his knees locked, kicking out his skinny left fanny cheek. His long, paste-on lashes fanned.

A big cheer went up. Down from the sky came a young demigod dressed in a white toga. He landed effortlessly. With a light gesture, he quieted Eddie and the crowd. His gentle smile turned to a cold stare as he walked to the front of the stage and milked the silence.

"If we offend, it is with our good will. Thou should think, we come not to offend, but with good will. To show our simple skill, that is the true beginning of our end."

He was whisked up and out of sight. The audience clapped with noticeable relief, recognizing the voice of the bard from the prologue of the play within a play. The green show was thankfully over. The young actors bowed, hamming it up like a command performance. Blowing kisses. The demigod and the wharfie China came out and took a bow together. China, though mentally vulnerable, was well known for his light touch on the hand-operated rope boom, his day job. The overused deus ex machina gag was always a popular way to warm up the crowd.

As the audience gave them a standing ovation, the commander remained sitting.

Uncle chuckled as he glanced at the dour commander, imagining him as a fat house cat in uniform. Neutered of all humor.

Soft filtered gels interrupted Uncle's thoughts and brought to life the exquisite chalk drawings of the slate coulisse. A massive army made camp across two sides of a slow, meandering river. Thousands of tents covered the landscape to the far horizon. Perfect pyramids of black-painted coconut were cannonballs, stacked at the ready. Two guards stood at attention, guarding a large white tent in the middle of the encampment. The lights dimmed. On the scrim, a few stars were barely visible. Crickets chirped.

Fioré sat close beside Emma, already extremely impressed by the quality and diction of the presentation. The crowd's impatient low murmur filled the air with electricity. The light from within the tent lit the stage like a large shoji lantern, complete with soft gray shadows. The tent flaps were drawn open by some invisible means, revealing a general and his aid. The crowd involuntarily booed. Emma and

Fioré noticed Prescott squirming in his seat. Fioré whispered in her ear. "They say boos on the road are like cheers at home."

The loyal aid, Briggs, helped the old general remove his heavy uniform. It was part armor, part uniform, and part holy mantle. Each article was laid out and folded, as carefully as a patriot folding a flag at sunset. Flag bunting was draped over the wooden headboard. Briggs helped the aging warrior into his bed and slowly tucked him in. The tent lights dimmed, leaving only a spotlight on the general's gray features.

"Sometimes it's not enough to kill with kindness, Briggs. Sometimes it's necessary to kill kindness," the general lamented. "There comes a moment when the rope needs to be knotted. Knotted and pulled."

"I understand, sir."

The general faded into sleep. Briggs brushed aside his fine gray hair, as if from an innocent child's face. Tender music swelled as the light faded from the dreaming general.

Briggs walked to the edge of the stage. "On the night before the Ides of March, the heavy restless sleep of Caesar."

Uncle's orchestra score went from light and sentimental to stormy and uncertain. Then the swelling strings were overtaken by the harmonious rhythms of a farming village. The lights on the fresh scene revealed a trio of young girls pounding bark into a fine brown tapa cloth. They lifted the fragile fibers together. The audience was just able to see the three joyful faces through the gossamer texture. They sang a sweet morning song of blessing.

Hiding behind stalks of grain, the rising sun's yellow light shown on three young boys with bent curved tools. They begin a dance, bending their knees, scything in perfect unison through crisp golden stalks of grain. This produced a sound so ancient and authentic that Uncle believed even one who had never heard it before would recognize it. Three old women with stone pestles answered by grinding a low chord, like an earthen cello accompanying the three girl's high voices.

From a high platform suspended above the stage, a young man with a clear voice recited from the third book of the *Mahabharata*, the *Aranyaka Parva*, Book of the Forest. "Those seeds of grain they call rice and so forth are all alive, good brahmin, what do you think of that . . . Come to think of it, no one fails here to hurt."

The low thunderclap of a drum startled the villagers. They shaded their eyes and look into the East as a stranger approached. A tall hooded figure clothed in a long robe of animal skins could be seen from the back of the theater, moving through the audience, a bow and full quiver hung from his shoulder. The audience tried to recognize both the face of the actor, whom they must know, and of the character they were about to meet.

Figas watched in fascination from his seat beside the aisle as the ominous stranger passed close by. He was amazed. From which shadows did this stranger emerge—those of the amphitheater or those of his own unconscious? He remained unsure as the hood slid back and the thunder halted. A low hum of recognition and approval filled the evening air.

"I am Haidar the Hunter!" the proud young man boomed.

The villagers came close to study him. His long knife and bow unsettled them.

"I've come to kill the mighty boar who ravages your fields at night and frightens you in your sleep."

An elder man approached the stranger and bowed. "We scare the boar away with our shakers and sacred songs, written in the language of the boar's great grandparents. We've no need of meat, so take rest, drink and be on your way, child."

"I'm not a child. I am a man among old women." He surveyed the passive men standing around him with distain. "I am a warrior." Haidar held up his long knife. "The boar knows the language I speak!"

The villagers gasped and backed away from the sharp blade.

A young girl, Jala, fearing for the life of the boar, dropped her cloth. She walked out of earshot of the villagers to the far corner of the stage and spoke so only the audience could hear. "I must warn the boar."

In the next scene, she crept out of the village and hid in the tall grain. Before she could shake her magic gourd, she snapped a dry reed underfoot. Haidar, who was hiding nearby, loosed an arrow through the night. It passed clean through Jala's throat and struck a faraway tree. Blood spurted from her throat as she slumped onto her side.

Es-sahra's hand found Figas's and squeezed. She put her hands over her eyes so she wouldn't see the dying girl. She had seen her youngest early on that last morning and never again. Now, with her eyes covered, she experienced those moments again.

Figas put his arm around her. "Don't look," he whispered.

Haidar listened in confusion to the arrow strike the tree. He had never before missed his mark. He tracked his quarry and was shocked to find the child lying cold. He gently picked Jala up and carried her back to the village. As the red gel sunrise became more and more intense, he laid Jala in the arms of Salm, her grieving father. The village women shrieked an unearthly broken triad.

Nine feminine figures in black and red emerged, with glowing hibachis balanced on their heads. The red-hot coals lit their faces as they encircled Salm, who cradled his daughter. Handfuls of dry straw were thrown from behind the coulisse and ignited on the red-hot coals. Bright streaks of yellow fire fell about the bare feet of the nine. The villagers moved into shadow. Jala's mother took her child in her arms and pleaded with her husband. Salm's eyes were fire. He heard nothing. A young boy ran up to Salm and handed him the bloody arrow.

Recognizing the fletching, Haidar fell to his knees and bared his chest.

Jala's mother slapped her husband's face. But he didn't see his wife or feel her hand. "Salm, do not do this! Wake up from your madness. Salm! You'll kill us all."

Salm approached Haidar, cradling the arrow as careful as he had his only daughter. The young hunter reached out and took his arrow. The two men look at each other in silence. The nine figures circled closer. The old women shrieked. Haidar held the arrow above his head, both hands grasping the shaft. The nine froze. Silence.

Haidar thrust the arrow into his bare chest, hitting a rib. Salm reached with a quick thrust and drove the sharp barbed tip through Haidar's heart.

The nine figures of fire closed around the boy's body, hiding him from view. Jets of cool water rained down from behind the coulisse. The drowning coals hissed, and a dense smoke choked the theater. The crowd was doused with streams of cool water and screamed in protest. Dozens of dancers in green flooded the stage, waving long blue ribbons, creating the impression of a rushing river. The fire-red caulk ran down the tall slates. The lights faded to black. The audience applauded in sober appreciation as the houselights were brought up for intermission.

Figas offered his long-sleeve shirt to help dry Es-sahra. "Are you all right, Auntie?" He could feel her shaking. Her eyes were red.

"I'm fine. Just a little chilly."

She noticed his eyes were red, too and reached out to brush some drops off his hair.

Beba peeked from behind the scrim and watched them drying each other. She was glad she'd gone along with Winston's crazy idea to douse the audience before intermission.

"What do you think so far?" Es-sahra asked.

"It's incredible. A real gift. Beba has turned herself inside out for all of us to see." Figas put his head in his hands and stared at his feet. "It's a healthier response to all that's happened than I've been able to manage."

"I feel the same." She hugged him.

"I'll find us something hot to drink." Figas squeezed her hand before letting go.

Beba watched, wondering what they were saying to each other.

"So, I'm Haidar, I suppose." The commander made a statement of his question.

"I'd be more inclined to suggest a colossal bore." The opening Prescott left proved too great a temptation for Uncle. "Yes, commander, you're the hunter. And if you're lucky, also young Jala, Salm her father and Jala's mother, as well."

Prescott chose not to respond to the absurd reply. He made a note on the back of his program next to the name of the youth playing Haidar. He looked at least eighteen.

Figas returned to his seat with two cups of hot tea. Es-sahra smiled to let him know she was all right.

An old woman in tapa cloth stood on the raised platform and gently rolled a large gourd wrapped with a web of tiny shells. The sound was like a steep beach of tiny pebbles lapped by small, quick waves.

The audience quietly found their seats. The house lights dimmed for a moment, then cool white gels illuminated Jala alone, center stage, wrapped in a gold and silver cloth. Her flowing dark hair was a weave of maidenhair ferns and tiny white baby's breath. The small white flowers stood out against the black shiny stems of the delicate fern. A cool mist covered her pale skin, the tiny droplets reflecting the bright lights.

Figas held Es-sahra's hand tightly.

Villagers brought flowers and placed them around her in silence. The entire stage was quickly filled with color. The villagers surrounded the area around the stage, standing among the audience, with their heads down.

Figas could feel Es-sahra's diaphragm knot and catch.

Prescott wondered how the play would continue. There was no longer room on the stage for the actors to stand. Slowly the flowers began to slide toward the back corner and roll off the stage. A rug was literally being pulled over the edge. Jala tumbled off the back of the stage with a hard thud. The audience gasped. The lights faded into darkness.

On the high platform a shaman beat his drum. A spotlight found the dark figure in torn furs, turning slowly counterclockwise. The yellow creases of his eyes cut through the audience. The violinists dragged their bows, making the sound of hissing teeth. The shaman's face grimaced into a satisfied black smile. With every solemn beat of his drum, he conveyed how easily he could see inside of each person present, entering at will.

A red sun rose on the bellowing scrim. Yellow gels brought morning to the small village. Two young girls sang and pounded the brown tapa cloth. Three boys cut the stalks of grain, and the old women ground the grain. The shaman's drumbeat pounded, drowning out the sounds of the waking village.

A giant thunder drum announced the imposing figure of Haidar's father, the hunter chieftain. He didn't look to be a man who'd inherited his position but taken it from another. His voice was a low, splintered reed, each syllable a guttural thrust. His arms and thick shoulders carried his meaning. The gist of his grunts and gestures were plain. Prescott recognized it was the same actor who played the old sleeping general.

"You have killed my son. My wife is too old to bear another. I will take another wife, many wives." The villagers greatly outnumbered the hunters. It didn't matter. No one could kill this chieftain.

It became clear all the men of the village who could leave would take what remained of their families and go. They would start again. They understood if they wished to survive, they would have to learn to defend themselves.

The lights faded for the stage crew to set up the last scene. Prescott looked at Uncle and tried to form his question.

"Having trouble with the island accent?" Uncle tried to be helpful.

Prescott explained that he understood the words plainly enough, but it was as if they were being intoned by a different species.

"I couldn't agree more. They are actors, after all." Uncle's mind drifted. He thought of Shakyamuni Buddha being asked by a follower if there were a spirit. The Buddha replied with a question: "What would you do if you were shot with a poison arrow?" The disciple replied. "Pull it out as quickly as possible."

Out of nowhere, someone screamed.

The lights flared as black coconut cannonballs crashed onto the wooden stage. The audience screamed. Sheet metal was being pounded all around them. Babies and small children began to wail. Parents shielded their family and yelled in protest. Figas held his hands over Es-sahra's head as a black coconut passed over them and struck someone two rows in front of them. Screams filled the night.

"Enough is enough!" Prescott stood up and barked.

More coconut cannonballs rained down on the audience. They begin to get tossed and batted around like beach balls. It became clear they were made paper balloons. The agitated crowd let out a collective sigh of relief. A lull followed as people settled back down. Parents comforted their children by giving them the paper balloons as toys to keep.

Prescott sat down, unhappy with the prank.

"Not long ago, some theatergoers were treated for minor injuries. I believe it was the same director," Uncle whispered.

Onstage stood the old general in his dress uniform, Briggs by his side. The stage was covered with black coconut cannonballs, mixed with paper munitions. "It's lashing outside, Briggs," the general said casually.

"Yes, sir." Briggs kicked a cannonball beside his commanding officer's shin.

"Cats and dogs, I daresay."

Behind them, the farmers were wearing suits and ties. Skyscrapers filled the slate horizon. They had built a great city, surrounded by a high wall, with soldiers guarding the battlements. A finely robed priest stood on the front steps of the temple and argued with a poorly dressed man from the countryside.

"Nature?" the priest asked. "Tell me, what has nature ever done for me?" This sent the audience into fits of laughter. He had to wait for quiet before continuing. "I can explain nature to you. Human nature. It's about the getting and the keeping!"

An old woman passed a soldier and asked, "What is this new war about, young man?"

"You don't you know? It's the war to end terror."

"I'm sorry," the old woman said. "Fear and terror are emotions. So I don't suffer your meaning."

"Then we will interrogate your imagination until you do," he promised.

The stage went black. Prescott began to fidget, clearly frustrated. He grumbled that he was unable to follow the plot. He was relieved when the stage lights went up on the old general's familiar tent. The two guards stood at attention. The coconut cannonballs were once again stacked in perfect pyramids. Inside the tent, Briggs was helping the general into his heavy dress uniform.

"Did you sleep well, sir?"

"Well, as can be expected these days. I had a strange dream, very strange indeed."

"What was it about, sir?"

"I don't quite remember." The old warrior looked off into the predawn light. "I was dressed in a long robe of animal hides . . . I can't remember anything else. That's too bad."

The stage lights slowly faded, and the house lights were brought up. The audience stood and applauded while the actors took their bows. Mira, who played Jala, received a huge burst of applause. Winston did his best to act reluctant when the actors dragged him onstage. When Beba came out, the crowd went into a frenzy. Figas whistled and cheered until his throat was hoarse. Flowers were thrown until the stage was once again covered. Beba looked down at Figas and her mother standing next to one another and smiled.

After most of the audience had left and the cast party was under way, Beba found a quiet corner to sit with her mother.

"So, what did you think?"

"Of your brilliant play or your young man?"

"He's not my young man."

"If you say so." Es-sahra folded her hands and waited.

"Was he nice to you?"

"You're two peas in a pod."

"No, we're not!" Beba was stung by the comparison.

"He's quite the intuitive type."

"Mom, he runs on numbers and figures. He created a grid over the whole forest and thought I wouldn't notice. He's a total geek."

"If you say so," Es-sahra repeated. Her oldest had never been easy to read. Watching the play had provided an extraordinary glimpse into how she viewed the world. She watched her daughter scan the empty seats of the theater, as if combing the shore after a storm, searching for the gifts the sea had left behind. "The only real valuable thing is intuition. Guess who said that."

"Give up."

"Albert Einstein. He was a numbers geek too, if memory serves."

God's Not Dead,
Just Asleep

Outside the window a voice selling tea. Inside,
the monk startled from his slumber.
—Gido Shushin

"Namaste." Uncle placed his palms together in front of his heart in the traditional Hindu manner.

"Good morning," Prescott barked. He was not in the mood for local customs.

"When are you releasing Mr. Ma'afu?" When Herbie failed to turn up the morning after Beba's play, Uncle had put two and two together. "Are you detaining Mr. Ma'afu?"

"Yes, he was caught sneaking about well after curfew. I've been aware of your clandestine activities. I've turned a blind eye for far too long. When I receive information on the whereabouts of my missing officer, Sergeant Clanahan, I'll consider your request."

"Your men are your responsibility. If you misplaced one, it has nothing to do with me or Mr. Ma'afu." Uncle raised his brows.

"You know full well that my sergeant can take care of himself. He didn't go missing without help."

It was pointless to reply. Uncle chose the waiting game.

Prescott lifted his stapler and wiped under it with a paper napkin. "Dr. Sun, since we went to that play—if you can call it that—whenever

I go out, people hold their fingers up in a *V.* Are they giving me the peace sign, or is this an obscene gesture?"

Sometimes the boar forgets the songs of his great grandparents, Uncle reminded himself. "I assure you it is not the peace sign."

"What then?"

"It's a *V.*" Uncle pause for effect. "For Vishnu."

"Meaning what exactly?"

"I think it would be best if you did some research, commander. You know what they say: when you're through learning, you're through." He let Prescott boil for another minute. "May I at least be allowed to visit Mr. Ma'afu?"

Prescott scowled. He was in the mood to lock someone else in the brig.

"You may find the story of Varaha relevant, if not too boaring." The many-layered pun unfolded like a lotus. Prescott was a South African Boer. "You'll have to trust me when I say it's not a slander to be associated with a Hindu deity. So, about my visiting rights?"

"Very well." He called out to French to begin the paperwork. Then he tried a fresh line of inquiry. "I gather you're not a medical doctor. What is your field, Dr. Sun?"

"Questions at last, commander. I knew you were a curious man at heart. I'll tell you what. Let's walk down to the harbor. You throw your pearl-handled revolver into the bay. And I'll tell you my life's story. Deal?"

"Have a good day, Dr. Sun."

The MP unlocked the chain around the wire gate. Inside the tent was a chain-link dog kennel. Herbie appeared to have grown larger on the prison food. The cot bent in the middle where he sat.

"What are you doing in there?" Uncle sounded nonchalant.

"Braddah! Da question be, wat you doing out dare!" Herbie gave off a whallop of a laugh.

"Well played, Herbie David."

"You come ta fetch me out?"

"I've always been opposed to prisoners having the vote."

Herbie's smile faded a little. Uncle looked over his shoulder at the MP, then lowered his voice. "I'm supposed to trade you for a big guy with a bullet-shaped head. Have you seen him?"

"No."

"Can I bring you anything?"

"Tell me da news."

Later that afternoon, French turned in copies of the research the commander had assigned to him as urgent after Uncle's visit.

Prescott scanned the materials, grunting to himself as he turned the pages. So Vishnu was the deity in charge of preserving the world. Between the various eons, he lay asleep in the cosmic ocean. Sleeping, it struck the commander, was an odd way of keeping watch.

Prescott let out more grunts of frustration as he read on. Vishnu at one point turned himself into the great boar, Varaha, to save the world. The commander recalled the villagers in the play worshiping the boar. "Not unlike these outdated islanders. It wouldn't surprise me if they had a golden pig statue hidden in the shrubbery."

When the world had been cast to the bottom of the ocean, Vishnu, as the avatar Varaha, lifted it from the depths of the ocean's floor with his great tusks.

Prescott threw the stapled papers in the trash and took off his glasses. A bengafly bit the back of his neck. He slapped at it too late. The more time he spent on the island, the less the place made sense.

The Buddha Flu

Tea is water bewitched.
—Lu-Wah

Figas woke just before the sun made it over the gap in Kuten Ridge. He rubbed the sleep from his eyes. He braced himself and waited for Uncle to chide him about how late he had slept. For the first time he could recall, he actually considered staying under the covers. He could just skip the day, pick things up tomorrow. But eventually he forced himself to get up. He entered the back door. Uncle was still in bed.

"Uncle, the sun has beaten you out of bed. Are you sick? Or dead? Come on, fossil bones, get a move on," Figas teased.

"You make tea. But wait for the water to get hot. A rolling boiling."

Figas had never seen Uncle sleep in. He sounded full of piss and vinegar, but Figas was worried. Later, after making tea, when he got to the lab, he told Ramona about how strange Uncle was acting, even for him.

That evening, when Figas arrived home, Uncle was in his study in the dark, meditating. No food was cooking. Figas washed some rice and went out to pick young bok choy and peas. He rinsed the vegetables and put them in the bamboo steamer. When dinner was ready, he tapped the wooden spoon on the rice cooker, as Uncle did when it was time to sit down and eat.

Uncle came out of the dark room. He looked pale.

"You feeling all right, Uncle?"

"Yes. Why?"

"No reason, just that . . ."

"Good, let's eat."

They ate in silence, and Figas wondered how he might go about getting Uncle to the infirmary. "Ramona asked if you could come in to help tomorrow. Another wave of dysentery, I'm afraid."

"Yes, yes. Thank you for dinner. Now I have some things to attend to. Good night, Figas."

"Good night, Uncle. I'll clean up."

The next morning, Uncle rolled out of bed when he heard the younger man's door slide open. They spent the morning in silence. They walked all the way to the infirmary without a single jest, bad pun, or biting remark from Uncle.

"Where are all the sick soldiers?" Uncle was upset when he saw the empty cots.

Ramona came over and felt Uncle's forehead. "Sit down, you old fool. You have a fever."

"I have no such thing."

"Fine. Since you don't believe me, you won't mind if I take your temperature. Stick this under your fat tongue, and see if you can give it a rest." She bullied him long enough to show him the digital readout. "One hundred and three degrees. Guess whose world you're in now? No arguing. Lie down on this cot. Right now. No. No talking!" Ramona pointed to the cot until Uncle was in it. "You're officially checked into the hospital. Doctor's orders. Figas, you stand guard. Rest, sleep, no talking!" Dr. Rai went off and came back with a wet rag and some ice.

Uncle curled up on the hard cot. "Infirmary? More like a stalag."

Ramona gently washed Uncle's bald head and neck. She softly chided him for running himself down. What did he expect when he took the weight of the whole island on his shoulders?

Uncle was too tired to think of a reply. He drifted into an uncomfortable sleep.

"What do you think it is?" Figas asked Ramona.

"It's too soon to tell. I'll do some tests. Hopefully it passes overnight."

The next day, Uncle's fever remained high. Ramona was concerned and wondered why no one else was sick. She examined him for insect bites. Besides his temperature, he had no other symptoms. His blood test didn't show anything unusual; in fact, the opposite. Uncle was in very good shape for someone close to eighty.

Figas slept in the cot beside him and kept watch and periodically washed his forehead with a small damp cloth.

On the third day, Hu visited. "Get up, lazy youth. You can't lie around while everyone else does all the heavy lifting." Hu tried his best, but even Figas could tell his heart was not into what he was saying. His old friend just lay there in a kind of sleep.

"Don't come into work this week, Thomas. I don't need you messing up my books."

"Yes, Uncle Hu. Thank you."

Holding his hands uncomfortably at his side, Uncle's oldest friend left without a good-bye.

Figas dipped the towel in cool water and squeezed it then gently washed Uncle's arms and feet.

The next morning, Dr. Rai and Figas pored over Uncle's chart, searching for a clue.

"The thing I don't understand," Ramona said, looking at Uncle's blood work, "is if this is the flu, why is Uncle the only case on the island? Pyrexia without a cough or any congestion, this rules out . . ."

"I'm sorry, I'm not following you."

Ramona explained that Uncle had a high fever, so she had given him an antipyretic, paracetamol. It should have reduced his fever by now. "The pyrogens I've isolated," she said, "are similar to some of the superantigens I have in my reference books, but I've been unable to isolate the strain of the influenza yet."

"Sorry, Ramona, you're just wasting your time trying to explain this to me. Just let me know what I can do to help."

"We're lucky to have a TEM microscope. You can help me prepare a few specimen trays."

Late that evening, Beba came into the lab. Figas was surprised, considering the way she felt about Ramona.

"I need to talk to you." She tried to get his attention, but he was glued to the TEM scope.

"I'm pretty busy right now."

"I didn't say I wanted to talk."

"All right. I'm listening."

"Not here."

They went into the infirmary tent were Uncle was sleeping.

"How is he?"

"He has a high fever. We still don't know why."

"Is he awake?"

"We're not sure if he's fully conscious."

"Let's go outside. I'm not sure he should hear this." They went out into the dark. She held both Figas's hands. "Hava received a radio transmission. The *Lady Slipper* is missing."

"Missing?"

She whispered, "A distress call was made two days ago by Captain Martin. A reconnaissance plane flew over their last known position in international waters in the South China Sea. There's no sign of survivors. The *Lady* is considered lost at sea with all hands. I'm so sorry, Figas." She held him close, and they both wept.

Figas was grateful Beba had thought to whisper. This was the last news Uncle needed right now.

"Have you eaten anything today?" she asked.

"We haven't stopped since this morning."

"I'll bring you both some dinner."

The next morning, Uncle was upright, sitting in meditation on his cot.

Dr. Rai took his temperature, but she was unable to get him to respond. He seemed to go from a mild coma into a sitting trance.

His fever was a steady hundred and three. She admonished him for being such a pain in the ass. "You're by far the worst patient I've ever had." She missed his mischievous smile and ridiculous cheery giggle.

Later that afternoon, she called Figas over to the TEM scope. "I'm noticing some remarkable results for the viral strain in his blood. You have to remember that one thing we know about the flu virus is its ability to mutate, potentially killing millions. The Center for Disease Control keeps a close watch on all strains so they can stay ahead of a possible pandemic. When Uncle got here, I introduced the virus to different blood samples. They didn't replicate."

"Meaning?"

"Well, in simple terms, this is the opposite of a pandemic. This virus is only interested in Red."

"Have you heard of anything like this before?"

Ramona powered down the scope and retied her ponytail. "No. I'm going to contact the CDC. And I think you should go home and get some sleep."

"Thanks. I think I'll sleep here again tonight."

The next day, Uncle was still upright on his cot. His fever had dropped to a steady a hundred and one degrees.

"This is a hopeful sign." Ramona checked the thermometer. "I don't think it's anything we've done, just the virus taking its course. Let's hope it's an isolated case."

Figas started to pour cool water into a basin to wash Uncle's forehead. When Ramona turned around, he had fainted and fell to the floor.

She managed to lift him onto a cot.

All through the day, patients arrived with high fevers. By the following morning, every cot was filled, with more patients coming in every hour. Ramona laid woven mats on the ground to accommodate the overflow.

Uncle remained in a state of meditation for six days and nights. In the early morning hours of the seventh day, his fever broke and he opened his eyes. Soldiers and islanders lay all around him, side by side, filling the infirmary. Volunteers did what they could to keep the burning fevers down.

Ramona noticed Uncle from the corner of her eye trying to stand up. She rushed over. "Sit for a few minutes and rub your legs to help the blood circulate." She sat beside him. "How are you feeling? You know, you've been a great deal of trouble."

"The worst patient you've ever had?" Uncle asked.

"Far and away."

She shared with Uncle the CDC epidemiologist's report, which had raised the possibility that the virus could have been engineered to interact specifically with his blood cells. They didn't know how such a thing could have been achieved, only that it seemed unlikely to be explained by coincidence. She showed him a picture of a single virion. It looked like the wheel of dharma.

"The CDC has specialized equipment that enabled them to track your virus very closely. They witnessed very minor mutations taking place over the last several days. They warned that your virus would eventually become contagious. And it did."

Uncle described his inner experience of the past week to Dr. Rai. When he'd regained consciousness, he had created a safe harbor for himself. He went into a state of deep meditation and focused his intention on his burning body. He directed the light from its inner flames to penetrate the veil of his physical body. He imagined compassion as a cool breeze inhabiting a body of pure consciousness. He understood the *other* as himself. Obstacles and differences were no longer recognizable.

Dr. Rai listened patiently, but she had no reference point to help her follow the old man's poetic description. She was a woman of science, of fact and of proof—the kind of proof you could create, witness, and recreate.

When Uncle saw the look on her face, he laughed his most heartfelt laugh. She felt a weight lifted from her, even though the burning bodies of a hundred women, children, and men lay all around them. She imagined Uncle's compassion intervening, inhabiting the round virions, the little wheels of dharma.

When the first soldier awoke from his fever, he got up and left the tent, leaving his assault rifle under his cot. One by one, the patients' fevers dropped, and they regained consciousness. They thanked Dr.

Rai, claiming they felt better than ever. It wasn't until later that day that she noticed all the weapons left under the cots.

Figas felt the pillow under his head being adjusted. "How's my Figas doing?" a soft voice near his ear said. He opened his eyes. To his surprise, it was Uncle sitting beside him. "Uncle, where did you come from? Where's Ramona?"

"I've been here for days, nephew."

"Where's everyone?"

"Everyone who?"

"All the people with fever, the soldiers. Tsani. She was lying right here." He looked for her pearl bag.

Ramona came in and felt his forehead with the back of her hand and took his pulse. "You scared the crap out of us, Figas. You've had a high fever for the last three days. It looks like you're on the other side of it now."

"I know. But what about everyone else, the epidemic?"

"You may have been dreaming. A high fever can have a hallucinogenic effect."

"If it was a dream, it was so real."

"Please, Figas, tell us about your dream." Uncle wanted the details before Figas was fully awake. "Start at the beginning, right after you passed out and we brought you to the hospital."

"You brought me? No. I tricked you into coming." Figas corrected him.

"How believable is that?" Uncle laughed.

"You slept in, Uncle."

"What!"

"I dreamed you had a high fever. Someone was trying to assassinate you, but you beat them at their own game. They designed a special virus that only infected you. You sat in meditation for six days and eventually controlled your fever. Your focused intention changed the virus, infusing it with compassion and pure consciousness."

"Indeed?" Uncle was impressed with all he was able to do.

"I remember when I was nine, you told me people were like horses—they smell fear and run. You explained how when horses are frightened, their fear ripples across their skin. It's their early warning broadcast system and they run to safety. You told me people have a similar warning system. That's why fear is contagious. In my dream, people woke up from fear. The soldiers left their guns under their cots. Compassion became infectious. A pandemic. A contagious higher consciousness."

"Sweet tea. The Buddha flu! What an imagination?" Uncle felt Figas's forehead. "You still seem a little hot under the hood. The world could use your Buddha flu. I think you should patent it."

"Don't tease me, Uncle. I'm serious."

"So am I, nephew."

The young man had never seen this look in his mentor's eyes before. He realized he must have been sick enough to frighten Uncle. He really had caused everyone a great deal of trouble.

"I dreamed the *Lady Slipper* had been lost at sea."

Uncle looked into the young man's eyes. "Beba was here all last night. She thought you were dying. She's been here beside you, talking to you for days. She spoke to you from her heart."

"What are you saying? Has the *Lady* been lost at sea?"

"I wish we could all wake up, and it wouldn't be so. There's been no radio contact for forty-eight hours. Search and rescue craft have been unable to find even a life raft."

Figas's head began to swoon. He lay back down, disoriented. Was he still dreaming? "What else have I missed? Please tell me. I know there's something else you're not telling me."

"You should rest."

"Please, Uncle."

"Prescott has signed an agreement with Stevens-Fowling granting ACUGO a business license to operate on Green Island."

"Is that legal?"

"They've contrived to make it so. And it appears we're powerless to prevent them."

The Oracle

The path to heaven passes through a teapot.
—Anonymous

The *Lady Slipper* had been overdue in port for a week. The Viridis Council voted to open the emergency supply warehouse to prevent any panic. A few hundred locals lined the docks on the first morning, toilet paper being the first item on people's minds, followed by sugar and rice. Dutch Marino personally presided over the affair and took every available opportunity to emphasize his importance. Everything coming or going needed to pass through his hands first.

Fioré watched from the floating pier as islanders carrying bags of TP, tins of kerosene, and cartons of cigarettes filed out of the giant warehouse on the wharf. A few he recognized as living Upwise. He assumed their lifestyles were less reliant on imported goods than were those of folks living in town. He spotted Zeno in the queue.

"I thought you were in hiding," Fioré called out.

"Country life isn't for me. I decided to come in from the cold." The young man's face was bruised, and his lips were badly cut. His left eye was swollen shut under his cheap sunglasses, which accounted for why he hadn't seen Fioré coming.

"What happened to you?" Fioré was angry. "Did they torture you?"

"I lost at rock, paper, and scissors." Zeno smiled, showing a missing upper tooth.

"You were beaten!" Fioré was livid.

"Yes, my pompous Pistachio. I just told you, I lost." Zeno pumped his fist three times in slow motion, coming up with a fist for rock.

"Did they interrogate you?"

"Hey, Pist, save my place in line. I gotta piss." He held his abdomen. "My bladder's swollen like a pregnant teenager at a melon-eating contest."

Fioré waited in line, but Zeno never came back.

As the week progressed, the islanders stayed close to their shortwave radios and listened for the latest news updates. Anxiety ran high as the locals added up all the changes.

Figas visited Herbie in military detention. He kept a smile on his face, not wanting to give in and add to Herbie's woes. The big man had lost thirty pounds or more.

"So, Figas, what's da news?" The circles under his eyes were even darker than his dark complexion.

"You were the first to say it, Herbie. How soon before we're all working for someone else?" The first time Figas heard it, it sounded prophetic. Figas filled him in on the bad news. Hu had been meeting with Prescott and Stevens-Fowling, in their words, to fill in the gaps on the new trade policy.

By "news," Herbie meant what was going on under the trees. Not the news of town. He listened to Figas without interrupting.

"There is a council meeting in an hour. I have to go soon."

Herbie could see the boy was about to break down. "You go, little braddah. My meal's just coming." Herbie could tell Figas had no way to say good-bye. "I see ya real soon. Tell da dimlightened one to step up his game alretty."

"I will, Herbie." He shook the big man's hands and hurried out. He tried to hold back his tears until he was out the front gate.

He was halfway up the hill to the drying barn when he spotted Beba near a stand of trees. She was staring at the trees, which were covered by ylang-ylang. The creeping vine was a ghostly silver veil in the sunlight. He ran over to her. The blank expression on her face worried him.

"They say that it was the impact of a giant meteor." Her tone was detached.

"What?"

"The disappearance of the dinosaurs, along with most living creatures in the ocean and on land."

"I'm a gamma ray burst man myself." Figas tried to make light. "Or it could have been those stinky fabric squares they threw in when drying their laundry."

"It's the end, Figas."

He reached out for her hand. It was cold. "Are you all right?" He felt her forehead.

"I read a science paper Auntie Anjou saved. It was called 'The Big Five,' and it predicted the sixth. You were quoted in it."

Figas remembered the article. In it, a prominent paleontologist discussed the variety of microchanges in the environment might have led to the collapse of natural systems in each of the five major mass extinctions.

"Beba, I'm late. There's a meeting."

"I know. This time, I'm coming with you." They held hands and hurried to the drying barn.

Es-sahra was addressing the Council. The chairwoman was shocked into silence by the sight of her daughter in the back of the barn. She motioned for the new arrivals to move closer, then finished reading from the preliminary draft of the new trade policy. She began fielding questions, questions to which she no longer had answers.

An oppressive gloom hung in the room. They had been outmaneuvered on all fronts. A new governing body had been set up, eclipsing their own. They were powerless to change it.

Zeno stood up and started for the door.

Uncle tried to head him off. "Where are you going, Zeno?

"It's time something was done. And since you ladies clearly lack the stones . . ." He pushed the barn door open. It slammed back against the wall, shaking the entire structure. Tea dust rained down from the rafters.

Figas looked for Uncle after the meeting, but he was gone.

The wind gusted savagely all night. Uncle lay in bed, listening to the coiled bursts shredding the leaves of his protected orchard. Cold blasts entered under the doors and through every small crack, grating at the surface of his mind. He climbed out of bed in the early hours, packed his shoulder bag, and headed up Kuten Ridge. He climbed the long switchbacks, as the stiff chilly breeze burned his cheeks.

Kuten Temple had been abandoned for longer than Uncle could remember. He passed the remains of a caretaker's hut, which had been overtaken by a bamboo grove. The gusts of wind brought rustling groans and squeaky whispers from the new inhabitants. Walking through the temple gates, one was cleansed of evil by two ferocious stone guardians to either side. Under a natural rock overhang, a stone Buddha with three heads was seated. The head on the right looked into the past, the one facing forward was in the present and the one looking left gazed into the future.

A short, ratty broom hung behind the entrance gate. Uncle swept the blown debris from the entrance and worked his way to the inner temple's oval-shaped stone floor, known as the cauldron.

Uncle believed the Swiftian approach they'd been taking to solve their problems was having little effect. It was going to take something big if their island was to remain their island. He bent over and swept, trying to clean and calm his mind. He chuckled. It was no use pretending. He was frightened.

Who was Kuten? Uncle's rational mind thought of her as a conscious commonality between earthly cognition and the realm of the unconscious. Past intuition was pure madness. He swept, creating a safe harbor around himself. He chanted, repeating her name.

A yellow sulfur mist escaped through a crack in the cauldron floor. The pungent smell mixed with his aporia. Open to the sky, the stone floor was segmented like an inverted turtle shell. Hundreds of characters written in bone script radiated in a wide spiral from its center. The symbols were bone script, the earliest known pictographs, the bare beginnings of Chinese writing. Just off center of the turtle's chest, an altar stone faced East.

A gust of wind momentarily cleared the air, swirling the debris around Uncle's feet. He reached into the drain curb and removed a handful of rotted leaves. The black pool of water that sat near the base of the altar stone drained away. He felt light-headed. When he was convinced he had done a thorough job, he hung up the broom and took off his shoulder bag. He sneezed twice in rapid succession and rubbed his burning eyes. He could feel a catch from the sulfur mist in the back of his throat.

Toward the top of the curved incline was a round, flat obsidian stone. He sat beside it and wiped the dust from the polished surface with his palm until it reflected like a mirror. Taking a small piece of white chalk from his bag, he wrote his question in the form of three Chinese characters onto the ancient mirror.

A rusted teapot sat inside a small vestibule. Uncle washed and filled the teapot from a leaky rain barrel. Using some kindling he had brought, he built a fire in a pit made of three small stones. He thought of Nargarjuna's causes and conditions, which were in motion, allowing the wood to suddenly become flame. He thought of his old friend Master Teagate. He knew that soon his own body would also be like dry wood.

One evening, Figas had shared with him that science considered water to be older than the earth itself, with the ability to outlast rock. Water, his nephew explained, ironically had been forged in the furnace of ancient suns. Uncle smiled. It made him happy when science happened upon the truth.

When the primordial liquid reached a galloping boil, he sprinkled in some tea. Once the brew reached the perfect temperature, he poured it into the baby-finger deep bowl formed by the obsidian stone, thus amplifying its reflective surface.

His knees on the hard stone floor, he bowed low and chanted her name over and over. He meditated on the original moment of creation, which persevered outside the realm of time. He opened his eyes and peered into the ancient mirror, whose reflection it was believed revealed the shadow self. The thin overlay of human reason evaporated. What remained mixed with Kuten. The masters who had survived the encounter called her the Physical Basis.

Mortal flesh was not born to sojourn to her timeless realm, Uncle thought. Given the choice, he would rather have tea with Auntie Lan every morning for eternity.

A sea of dry hope slowly enveloped him. The island's misfortunes had grown beyond his powers of perception or persuasion. As Master P'O had said, when there was no longer a way forward, one should "become completely still, wait, and listen."

He reached into his bag for the leaves he'd picked along his trek up the mountain. He chewed on a fresh laurel leaf. He walked to the altar stone at the center of the cauldron and spread the other leaves on top. Then he sat on a segment of bone script with the character of the tiger.

He rocked gently and chanted his greeting over and over. His voice dropped into a low growl. The sulfur mist coated his throat and burned his eyes. The wind generated a deep drone as it circled the cauldron. Above the lowest note, Uncle could hear a higher overtone. Within the eerie, high-pitched whirring was a perfect fifth.

Spirit sifted downward in between time, as the wind swirled around the cauldron and gathered the leaves into the air. They circled like tea leaves settling in the bottom of a bowl. An awning of heavy clouds granted the chilly mountain air an advantage. The wind held the gold and red tipped leaves in a suspended coil.

The safe harbor dissolved. The frame around everything was gone. Uncle was naked and alone.

The floating offerings were released. Exonerated, they all drifted away, save two. The pair floated down and settled on two segments with sacred script. The present moment indicated what was to soon follow.

Sacrifice. Uncle's breath slowed and then stopped. He collapsed on his side, cold and unconscious.

NOWHERE TO RUN

The perfect temperature for tea is two
degrees hotter than just right.
—Terri Guillemets

White egrets alighted from their nesting tree, which hung over the south bank of Cairo's reservoir. They flew over Saunders's head, making their way to higher ground to feed. He looked up, daydreaming. He found patrol to be only slightly less boring than guard duty; it was certainly no way to start off a Monday morning. What was the point of patrol anyway when the locals' idea of trouble was a bunch of leather lungs singing off-key outside their barracks while he tried to sleep? It was bad enough that the only means of transport was Shanks's pony, using one's legs.

He sorely missed Doogan. He couldn't understand what happened to his best friend. The Irishman volunteered for night patrols and slept all day. After Doogan lost his temporary stripes, he stopped going to the pub altogether. Without him, O'Sullivan's had all the life of a funeral parlor.

Two nights ago, Saunders had bought a round for the wharfies. It made him cringe to spend that kind of cash, especially when Dutch hardly glanced over without so much as a thank-you or an invitation to join them.

He finished his routine pass down Lantern Street. He could hear the children's high-pitched voices as he started to slog up the wet hillside toward the giant monkeypod in the center of the schoolyard. He looked up and caught the glimmer from the assault rifle Zeno was carrying. The two men froze for an instant and looked at each other, neither sure what to do.

Saunders tried to yell out to stop, but Zeno was already racing up the hill. Saunders ran after him and fumbled with his radio. The muddy grass on the slope slowed him considerably. "Bravo Echo Charlie! This is Sierra Tango Uniform. I have a hostile. Repeat. I have a hostile heading north toward the school. I'm in pursuit. Requesting backup. Over!"

"Roger that, Sierra Tango. Are you sure, Saunders?"

"Yes, I'm sure, Sparks. God damn it! He's carrying a bang stick. Over."

"Blue 7. I copy that, Sierra Tango. I'm two clicks from your twenty," Reeves responded.

"Stay frosty, Saunders. Help's on the way. Over."

"The hostile is in the school. I repeat. Unfriendly has entered the school."

"Roger that, Sierra Tango. Hold your position, and watch your six. Over."

"Copy that."

Acting Sergeant Reeves, the only woman of the company, and Corporal Porter joined Saunders behind the trunk of the big monkeypod. Within the hour, a field command center had been set up. Prescott arrived to coordinate the operation and was briefed by Reeves. As of yet, Dr. Sun couldn't be located. The local authorities—if one could call them that—were no-shows. Inside, children could be heard crying. There was no communication from the teacher or the gunman.

The thick hurricane shutters had been locked from the inside, and the heavy front door bolted. The commander ordered Saunders to fetch his equipment in case it became necessary to blow the hinges. The siege was three hours old when he returned with his demolition gear.

A large crowd of parents gathered. Commandos in full combat gear kept them behind a barricade. Ciao, Uncle's dog, squirmed under the blockade, and barked and sniffed at the school door.

Several attempts had been made to open a dialog, but the gunman had not responded. The sound of furniture scrapping the floor and screams of young children frayed everyone's nerves. Ciao continued to scratch and dig at the threshold.

Hu was allowed past the barricade and directed to the field command center, located near the front door. Before he could voice his concerns, Prescott raised his voice, "What's the name of the gunman?"

"Zeno. He is an unstable hothead."

"I remember him. When he was arrested, I interrogated him myself."

"He's dangerous. He eliminated your sergeant without getting a scratch."

"The gunman killed my sergeant? How do you know? Were there witnesses?"

"Can you do something about that little mutt?" Hu protested. Ciao was yapping as he tried to tunnel under the doorway. "I can't hear myself think."

"Listen to me, is the man in the school responsible for the disappearance of my sergeant?"

"Without question."

"Where did he get an M4 carbine? Clanahan's weapon isn't missing."

"What is a carbine?" Hu didn't like being shouted at.

"Where is Dr. Sun?" Prescott was furious.

Hu raised his arms as if to say, "I don't know and I don't care." He had little patience for people who didn't show respect to their elders. "You're speaking to the person in charge."

"I'm the MFWIC!" Prescott corrected the old fool.

The heavy crash of furniture being tipped over startled the soldiers outside the school's bolted entrance. Prescott knew that if he left the gunman inside and something happened, he would be faulted for not taking action. If he risked going in, he would be held accountable for any casualties. He knew he had been assigned to this post for his administrative skills, not his combat experience. All attempts to communicate with the combatant had failed.

Prescott drew up a plan as the evening light faded. Saunders was ordered to place shape charges on the window shutters and the entrance door. If no progress had been made by 0300, he would send in his team. They would enter from every direction. The absence of combatants had burrowed like a worm into the commander's head. Now there was meaning and purpose to the whole catastrophe.

Doogan watched and waited in the dark, his palms sweating. He had objected as strongly as he could to Reeves.

"One more outburst from you, McPhearson, and you're brig meat!" She had no patience for questioning orders.

"Better to be locked up than watch." He pulled on his torn ear until it bled. He hoped the pain would be distracting. Instead, he was back in Bosnia. He was tempted to put a round through the bean counter's forehead before things turned worse. They hadn't been deployed to "spectate"—Prescott's motivational catchphrase.

Doogan knew if he hadn't washed out of his special assignment, the bean counter might listen to him. Now he was back on the bottom of the food chain. Through his night-vision glasses, he watched Saunders place the charges around the windows. He could see Stu's hands shaking as he formed the C4 coils around the hinges and locks and carefully stabbed the detonator wires into the gray putty. Maybe they'd get lucky and manage to capture the assailant without killing any children. He remembered the little girl with the three-pearl bag. He asked Reeves if he could help Saunders.

"Return to your position, private. I won't repeat myself." She couldn't understand how a drunk had made it into the military. That he'd been promoted before her to replace Clanahan was beyond belief.

They waited in the early morning quiet for the commander's signal. Unable to keep his imagination from running ahead of the operation, Fields had already thrown up twice. His head was bent down in a cold sweat. The men adjusted their Kevlar helmets and vests, unused to wearing full combat gear.

On Prescott's signal, the charges blew simultaneously, but with more of a muted fizz than an explosion. The assault teams hit their spots right on time. The C4 burned like a dozen Roman candles, shooting sparks from around the ironwood shutters. Flames darted up to the bare eaves. Reeves yelled for water.

No shots were fired. Floodlights were switched on. Doogan wasn't the only one overwhelmed to see the building go up in flames.

"Get those shutters open! Let's go! Get those children out! Move!"

Flames poured from the cracks around the locked shutters as the soldiers pried at the corners with crowbars. Dense smoke seeped through the slate roof tiles before they collapsed in on themselves. Frenzied screams from inside mingled with the chaos of men running. A pump was located and hoses quickly rolled out. The stream of water was no match for the blaze. A deep anguish kicked the men in their guts as they tried to pull the parents, who had broken through the barricade, away from the flames shooting out of the windows.

Within twenty minutes, the island school was four stonewalls. A gutted mass grave. The wailing from the mothers and fathers was unearthly. Many of the enlisted men fell to the ground and wept.

Prescott was frozen, watching from his position nearby. Reeves was carried away on a stretcher, with multiple burns to her hands.

Doogan looked through the gutted window at where the floor used to be. What was left of the floor joists smoldered. He ordered a spot to be watered down so he could climb inside. He could feel the hot rock of the window well through his leather gloves. His knees burned as he crawled over the deep sill. Corporal Sheppard helped lower him inside.

Doogan kicked at the smoldering coals. The bottom of his boots melted and the smoke became too much. He grabbed Sheppard's hand and climbed out. "Where's Saunders?"

"I don't know, sir."

"Well get some men on it and find him. Now!" Doogan ran around the schoolyard. "Saunders! Stu, where the hell are you!"

Ash-covered mourners wandered around looking for family members. An eerie quiet set in as the shock took hold.

Figas looked around at the ashen faces and remembered his vision from Master Teagate's funeral. His knees gave way, and he curled up in a ball.

China ran up to Doogan and grabbed his sleeve and then ran back the way he had come.

"Hold up! What's going on, lad?"

China signalled to follow him. Doogan ran after the boy. He found Saunders propped against a tree, his service revolver in his mouth. Doogan could see the safety was off. He pointed for China to go.

"Listen to me, Saunders. I'm going to tell you something. If you repeat it to anyone, I'll shoot you myself."

Stu didn't look over. He could taste the gun oil in his mouth. He aimed upward, with his thumb on the trigger.

The following day Islanders arrived by the hundreds. When they encountered a soldier, they overpowered him, held him to the ground, and stripped him of his weapons, ammunition, and radio.

Prescott ordered the troops guarding the camp to open fire if the mob approached the front gate. He was relieved to hear Dr. Sun had been located and would meet him.

Uncle walked into the dark office. Prescott sat in the silence, unaccustomed to playing a losing hand. He did his best to appear indignant, but his words sounded hollow, "I'm counting on you to restore order with your people before we're forced to open fire."

Uncle looked into the officer's eyes with a blank expression. A bloated silence followed. He placed a sheet of paper on the desk without saying a word.

Prescott read down the page. There was to be no negotiation. He would sign an immediate ceasefire and withdraw his troops, or they would forcibly be removed.

"I need time to contact my superiors."

"If by sunrise you don't surrender your weapons, you'll have more innocent blood on your hands." Uncle set a DVD on the desk and walked out.

"French!"

The staff sergeant slid the disk into a metal-clad laptop and waited for it to load. "It's a video, commander."

"I can see that."

The two men watched the black screen fill with the light of dozens of Roman candles illuminating the walls of the school. The building was quickly enveloped in flames.

"Turn it off, French." Prescott put his head in his hands and took off his glasses. He rubbed his eyes and remembered the Italian. Somehow had he managed to film the debacle. "My career is over," he thought. What choice did he have but to sign the withdrawal agreement and resign his commission?

"French, I'm going to need you to send a communiqué. Give me a few minutes, will you?"

"Yes, sir." It troubled the staff sergeant to see all the starch let out of his commander.

Prescott charged through a bottle of scotch while he awaited his orders.

French came in just after midnight with the message. Prescott poured another glass to the brim. "Sit down and take a load off, French. Have a drink with me."

French took a seat and sipped his scotch.

"What does the bloody thing say?"

"Sir, your orders are to double the guards on the perimeter. Shoot to kill anyone attempting to breach the wire. They're sending reinforcements."

REINFORCEMENTS

He was raising a tempest in a teapot.
—Marcus Tullius Cicero

The sound of chopper blades slapped the air as the Dauphin VIP helicopter deployed its landing gear and touched down on the grassy ridge above the old post office. Before the twinjet turbines could wind down, the diminutive Mr. Black opened the rear cockpit door and helped Christopher Elant onto terra firma.

A sigh of relief passed through Figas as he watched Elant walk upright under the whirring blades, heedless as they slowed and dipped. Without a wrinkle in his suit or any sign of wear, the gentleman waved to Figas and Uncle, who were waiting. The senior director of the Lance McCandish Foundation had radioed ahead, announcing their ETA.

"Hello, Thomas. It's good to see you again. This must be Dr. Sun. A pleasure to finally meet you. I'm Christopher Elant. My colleague, Mr. Black." He bowed with great subtlety.

"Welcome to Green Island, Mr. Elant." Uncle returned his bow. "My nephew has spoken of you often."

"I understand you've all been through a great deal. I'm anxious to hear the details. We're here to assist in any way we can."

They walked down the hill to the post office, where Hava had organized an impromptu council meeting.

Es-sahra was waiting with the other council members. She gave a detailed overview of the situation before asking Uncle Sun to brief the council on his latest meeting with the military commander.

Uncle explained that Prescott had been unusually humble. The career officer had shared his new orders and admitted freely that he had made grave errors of judgment. He likely would be replaced when the troop carrier arrived with reinforcements. In the meantime, Prescott had reminded Uncle, orders were orders. If the islanders approached the encampment, they would be shot. As a small concession, no patrols would be sent out. All other negotiations had reached an impasse.

When it was time for Christopher Elant to speak, he took his time. He waited for Figas to refill his teacup and tapped the table with three fingers. An imperceptible hum filled the room. Elant's good manners and lack of hastiness endeared him to the council. "Thank you," he began, "for taking the time to put me in the picture. It's a story that goes back to the early days of the spice trade. The state-sponsored Dutch VOC, the first multinational corporation, was established in 1602. Since then, governments and their militaries have successfully supported business interests in the far-flung reaches of empire. Unfortunately, military power plays are often the rule, rather than the exception. There can be little doubt that vast amounts of money influence the behavior of governing bodies. The concentration of wealth and its corruptive power has long been of concern. Thomas Jefferson, the third president of the United States wrote, 'I hope we shall crush in its birth the aristocracy of our monied corporations, which dare already to challenge our government to a trial by strength, and bid defiance to the laws of our country.'"

Elant paused and took in the room. "With the right legal assistance, you could make a strong case to the International Court of Justice in the Hague. However, I must warn you it could take five years to get a preliminary hearing. Depending on the terrorist threat assessment at the time of your hearing, you could be put off indefinitely from a full assembly vote. Finding a paper trail and proving collusion between a shell company like the ACUGO Corporation and the military, I fear, will be next to impossible."

Zeno and Jin Morris stood up in protest. All the members began talking at once, sending the meeting into disarray.

Es-sahra stood up and held out her hands until there was quiet. "I know many of you are upset. It's true we may have placed too much trust in the International Law Commission. But let's show some manners and respect. Our guest has come a long way. Can we at least give him the courtesy to finish what he has come to say?"

"I agree, it's ridiculous, if not shameful." Elant began anew. "Unfortunately, that's the way the game is played in the current foreign policy environment. The most-favored-nation clause tips the balance of power into the hands of a few. You have the option of petitioning for de jure sovereign status, but that can take generations."

"Do you have another approach in mind, Mr. Elant?" Es-sahra asked.

"What you need is a strong ally to step up and represent your case. Preferably a country with close ties to the secretary general's office. I've been in direct contact with Evelynn Peters of the Canadian State Department. The Canadians carry a great deal of clout around the globe when it comes to international trade. They're willing to send a diplomatic envoy, providing the Viridis Council is willing to consider them an equal trading partner in the future."

Something about the phrase "in the future" tugged at Uncle's memory. He had heard it recently.

"What do they mean by an equal trading partner?" Es-sahra asked. Vaughn leaned over and whispered something in the chairwoman's ear. "Are you saying the Canadians wish us to sign some kind of agreement in exchange for their assistance?"

"That's correct. Evelynn Peters, their special envoy, provided me with a basic Trade and Investment Framework Agreement, the details of which will need to be worked out. Here's the preliminary draft."

Mr. Black produced the document from his attaché case and handed it to the chairwoman.

"Thank you. We'll need some time to look this over."

"Please take all the time you require."

Es-sahra perused the document and asked Vaughn a few questions before passing it around the table. "Mr. Elant, how is this different from our current predicament?" The chairwoman was not new to cake cutting.

"Well, the Canadians are not likely to send boots on the ground. I can safely promise that much."

Several council members laughed at the thought of a Canadian invasion.

"I'm not an attorney, Mr. Elant, but the irony of the situation is not lost of me." The chairwoman was not amused.

"You need help from the international community, and it is my experience that you can trust the Canadian government to be a fair and equitable trading partner. When you meet Evelynn Peters, I think you'll agree she is a person of great integrity. Due to the distance and time constraints, I've been given the authority to act in good faith on her behalf. I'm a Canadian citizen. It's not my bailiwick, but Mr. Black is an attorney specializing in international law."

Es-sahra stood up. "Very well. I move that we reconvene later this evening with a public meeting to vote on who is to lead the trade negotiations."

The senior director arrived early and was surprised to see the drying barn completely empty of tea. The hard dirt floor was covered with a fine powder that kicked up around his feet and began to fill the huge volume of air with a sweet aroma. His eyebrows rose when he saw the dozen large brown papier-mâché gourds propped up in the far corner. Thin shards of light filtered through a giant gable vent, illuminating the swirling tea dust.

Volunteers arrived with ladders and began hanging festival lights from the rafters. A podium was set up, and folding chairs to either side for the speakers.

The assemblage slowly gathered. The islanders spread out woven mats and sat cross-legged. It was standing room only at the back, the crowd spilling out the double doors into the tea fields.

Elant wore a dark suit and tie and sat patiently in his chair to the right of the podium. It began to get very warm inside.

Dutch Mareno made his way through the crowd. Zeno and Freight blocked him.

"If it isn't Tweedledum and Tweedledee." Dutch tapped his umbrella to punctuate his insult.

"I fear you are too rude." Freight showed concern.

"I fear that one or both of you may have children someday," Dutch replied.

Zeno took a couple of steps closer. "My fear is that when I do have kids, Mary Poppins's evil twin will be their governess."

Dutch pushed past them and entered the crowded barn. Finally, he was getting the respect he deserved. He walked to the podium and took his place beside Elant. Dutch had a million stories, and he couldn't keep them in. "I'm Dutch Mareno. I represent the dockworkers."

"Christopher Elant. A pleasure to meet you."

"It may take some time to get the rabble collected."

"I understand. Are you native to the island?"

"I've lived here for going on thirty years. I grew up in Sherwood, Arkansas. The deep south. Ever heard of the Little Rock Nine?"

"Yes, Mr. Mareno. I clearly remember watching the National Guard on TV escorting the children to school."

"I grew up a few miles from there. I had three older sisters and a baby brother. We were dirt poor. At Christmas, we'd go window shopping with our mama. That was the only kind we could do. Not just because we had no money. We weren't allowed in any of the shops. I remember the dolls in the window, all white dolls. And there was this one with dark almond eyes wearing a red silk robe. None of us had seen an Asian person. My sisters wanted that doll real bad. Mama said there wasn't going to be Santa Claus, but she made a deal with us. She said, 'I'll buy that Chinese doll if you promise to all take good care of her and share her.' We promised. We shared and played with that little doll—my sisters, my brother and me. We loved her. A couple years later, I had a fight with my little brother, and we ripped her arm off. You know kids. When I was old enough, I joined the army. Before long, I saw my first real-live Asian person. Man, was I excited. The bad news was, they wanted me to kill him. The white boys in my company wanted to shoot me just bad as they wanted to shoot them Viet Cong."

Es-Sahra stepped up to the podium and asked for quiet.

Dutch picked up the pace. "Nowadays, I live surrounded by Asian people. I love them. I love their food, their language, writing . . . everything." Es-sahra turned her head, and Dutch had to end his story before he was ready.

In her elegant manner, Es-sahra outlined their situation. The task at hand was to choose a representative to address the Canadian proposal. Write-in ballots were passed around, and a quick tally was made.

Mr. Hu was nominated to lead the negotiations. His office had been in charge of tea contracts with the large auction houses going back generations. As Hu stood, several older citizens groaned. They knew they were in for a long-winded speech.

Hu held out his hands to calm the noise and excitement he imagined was taking place in the near silence. Now it was time for the grown-ups to enter the picture. He stared at Uncle Sun with a conspicuously smug look. "In ancient times, there lived an arms trader who made a most magnificent spear. He claimed it could pierce any material. Every warrior desired his spear. He became famous throughout the realm. This same man later produced a shield like no other. He claimed, 'My shield is impenetrable, nothing may pass through it.' A warrior asked, 'What if I use your spear against your shield?' To this day, the characters of spear and shield are used to depict contradiction. You may ask, 'What contradiction?' With light, there is shadow. With youth, follows old age. Our birth ends with our death. We never escape contradiction."

The crowd reverberated in agreement.

"Automatic rifles have replaced spears. Soldiers march over the soil where our tea plants once grew. From the north, our allies bring us a shield." Hu paused to emphasize his point. "If we wish to remain separate from the world, we must open ourselves to become more a part of it. If we desire for things to remain the same, they must change."

More sounds of approval filled the barn.

"I can't promise quick results, but I can pledge to work hard for progress, to salvage something positive from a difficult situation." He looked down again at Uncle as he drew a contrast between his new, progressive approach and Sun's ridiculous wei wu wei. It had been nearly a year of action without action. Everyone was fed up.

Figas was close enough to catch Hu's octogenarian eye roll. His crusty boss went on ad nauseam, explaining that he was confident a mutual understanding could be reached within a few weeks.

Elant stood up and apologized. He explained that he had only three days. On Friday, he was needed elsewhere on another urgent matter.

Es-sahra thanked everyone for coming. The meeting was hastily adjourned.

Hava organized staff to cater to every need of the important visitors. Meals were to be brought to the post office because the meetings would go all day and even into the early morning hours.

Figas awoke to voices. A light was on in the main house. He pulled on a pair of shorts and hurried over to see what was happening.

A footie was giving Uncle a report on the recent developments. Mr. Black had filed a suit against the ACUGO and personally delivered a copy to Alison Stevens-Fowling aboard the *Starry Night*. She was on deck, sunning in her bathing attire, enjoying her third cosmopolitan. Her smile vanished when she read the brief. At 3:00 a.m., the yacht had been heard weighing anchor, sailing on the early morning tide.

Later the next day, the buoyant mood became somber again when reports spread over the island that a large gray troop carrier was entering the bay. Commander Prescott called a meeting with Dr. Sun and explained that his orders had once again been changed. A full-scale troop withdrawal would commence immediately.

Dr. Sun gave the commander firm assurance that the troops would not be confronted as long as they were about the business of leaving.

Locals filled the steps of the Thumb and watched the soldiers methodically dismantle their encampment, striking their tents, and loading gear. Uncle didn't know how, but the Canadians seemed to be pushing all the right buttons.

Figas was waiting outside the military detention tent when Uncle emerged with Herbie. "Did he surrender his sword?" Figas asked.

"I should have thought of that," Uncle lamented.

"He's freed the king from prison! Betta den a sword!" Herbie stretched his hands to the sky.

"Much better, your majesty." Figas could see Herbie was a little unsteady on his feet. He propped his skinny frame under Herbie's meaty shoulder.

Uncle's mind raced ahead. He imagined the twisted heap of the D-9 Cat as a lasting memorial of their struggle. If the road had been built, it would have been the end of old Viridis. The wreck must be well-coated to preserve it for future generations. It was too soon to be counting chickens, though. When he noticed the way Figas was looking at him, he forced a smile. "Prescott ordered a complete withdrawal. Go find Beba and give her the news. Make yourself useful! Herbie and I have work to do."

Twenty-four hours later, French helped the commander into his full dress uniform.

Lantern Street was lined with locals. Prescott held his head high as he strode through Salm Bay, ignoring them. He had one last unpleasant task to face.

Fa Shi was standing in front of the shoe repair shop with his friend the cobbler. The leather craftsman had rendered an oversized boot from thick bull hide and had it prominently displayed at an upward angle. It was the cobbler's silent poetic statement.

Mrs. Li Meis, the mistress of the laundry, and Blair were in front of their businesses. They gave the V sign. This time, it didn't mean Vishnu.

Uncle waited in the small park near the rusty anchor. When Prescott arrived, he handed him a map with the location of the small atoll where Clanahan was marooned. He was reported to be surviving okay, albeit thinner and sunburned.

Prescott was about to voice his outrage over the treatment of his officer when he looked down the beach and saw dozens of children. He pointed. "Who are those children?"

"Oh. They're back from their field trip."

"You lying bastard! I'll see that you go to prison for this, Sun! What kind of man lets another man believe he has killed a hundred children?"

"I never said the children were in the school. I wasn't there. By the way, commander." Uncle paused before he said something he would regret. "As far as your question about when a man is or is not a man, I'll leave that up to you."

"You're lucky that I don't kill you right here with my bare hands." Prescott's temples were bulging.

Uncle looked at the pearl-handled revolver in its holster. "I'm so glad we got to have this little heart to heart." He tried to see Prescott in a new light. "When I was younger, I had trouble with forgiveness. It seemed like such a one-sided affair. Now, here I am, ready to forgive you. But there you are, uninterested in taking part in what I'm suggesting. Fortunately, it doesn't much matter if forgiveness only takes place within me. For many years, I've witnessed the positive effects set into motion with a simple gesture of forgiveness."

"I have no idea what you are talking about. Why am I not surprised?"

Uncle tried putting it in more absolute terms that Prescott could understand. "There are two kinds of people in the world: the kind who forgive and the kind who don't. I forgive you. And I'm not waiting for you to reciprocate. It is my sincere wish that you will find it within yourself, but it's not, shall we say, required." An awkward silence descended. Uncle could feel Prescott's rage reaching across to him. "I'm curious, do you have any idea why the world values our Sighing Woman Tea?"

"I'm a hundred percent sure that I don't give a rat's ass!"

"I know you're a man of action, but I trust on your journey home, you'll take a moment to reflect on your time here."

"Don't flatter yourself. When I leave this place, I doubt I will think of it again. It's a middle of nowhere place, containing nothing of value whatsoever."

"Well, it is pleasant that we finally agree on the main points. Good-bye."

Prescott was too filled with loathing to reply.

Uncle turned his back and walked down the beach toward the children.

Doogan scratched the back of his head against a palm tree. After a long hard separation, a group of fathers joined in a game of stickball with their kids. A boy hit a towering pop-up. The Irishman admired the high arc. "That will bring rain," he forecasted without turning to look at Uncle.

"Tell me, Mr. Doogan, how was it that you first came to suspect?"

"Little things."

Uncle noticed the heliotropic optimism he so admired in the Irishman was gone. "I'm very grateful to you." Uncle bowed low. "We're all grateful you didn't give us away. How did you know?"

"The wet field."

"What do you mean?"

"I played futball as a kid. We were a scrappy team—short, tough street kids— none of us very fast. Our coach would wet down the field the night before a match to slow down the other team, even the odds." Doogan remembered Saunders trying to run up the soggy hillside when he first spotted Zeno. The ground was perfectly dry everywhere else.

"That was the only clue you needed to see through our ruse? Fioré will be disappointed after all his special effect work and careful planning."

Doogan's hand shook as he lit a cigarette. "I've been through a building where people burned to death. I know the look and the smell." Doogan's voice cracked. "I knew you were a wily son of a bitch, but I didn't think you were cruel. Why did you set up my mate? Saunders nearly blew his brains out."

"We trusted he'd never shoot a man just for carrying a gun." Uncle meant it as a compliment.

"Why do you say that?"

"It may not mean much to you, but your friend Stewart Saunders crossed Teagate's bridge unharmed."

"You're right, that doesn't mean much."

Uncle felt a deep responsibility for what had occurred. A sacrifice was called for. He hoped a ritual sacrifice would be enough. Better lives appeared to be lost than real blood spilled. "I'm deeply sorry for your friend's suffering. Perhaps he'll learn an honest trade going forward before more lives are lost." Uncle waited for the sting of his words to wear off. He bowed low. "Please, can you find it in your heart to forgive me?"

"I might have done."

The crack of the bat sent a ball deep into the surf. Three runs scored. The two men watched in silence as the ball was finally recovered. It was important to Uncle to feel the balm of forgiveness, but he knew it was out of his control.

"How much time before you ship out?" Uncle asked.

"Two hours."

"Let's stroll. Please allow me to buy you a cup of tea, with cream if you like."

They walked up Lantern Street to O'Sullivan's without speaking. Blair set a full bottle and two glasses on their table and turned to leave.

"I'm surprised you've any left!" Doogan barked at Blair as he limped back behind the bar. Doogan suspected the accelerant used in the school fire was Blair's homemade hooch. He pulled the cork out with his teeth and poured their shot glasses full, then emptied his glass without looking at Uncle. He overfilled it a second time and downed it. "So how was it done?"

"Let's just call it movie magic. A microphone here, a speaker there."

"The Italian."

"Yes. The children were never in school that morning. No one was meant to be hurt."

"Fair enough. That brings us to the next question—the reason I should break your neck!" Doogan looked straight into the old man's eyes. "Why did you have to bring Jamila into this?"

"I did no such thing." Uncle sipped.

"You bastard, you know you did!" He slammed his glass on the table. "She sent me to the cliffs to fetch eggs that morning." He overpoured another shot. "She pointed me right to the payoff."

"I swear Jamila knew nothing about any payoff. It's true bags of gold coins were hidden around the valley in hopes you'd eventually find one. We knew you're much too pigheaded to take a bribe."

"What do mean?" Doogan was in a temper.

"The wind blowing the plastic bucket over the hillside was an inspiration, don't you think?" Uncle sipped, allowing himself a small moment of pride. He could see Doogan was in no mood to appreciate any part of what had happened. "We hoped you'd take the gold and be satisfied."

"Satisfied? Don't you mean guilty? I'd be so rich with guilt I wouldn't do my job." After that morning he'd lost all interest in finding the young men in hiding, but for different reasons.

"Why didn't you just take the gold?"

"I couldn't honestly say." He had flipped the coin and called tails. It was that simple.

"I want you to know, Mr. McPhearson." Uncle stood up to leave. "I swear to you, Jamila had no knowledge of any schemes. It was my doing. I take full responsibility. If you have a score to settle, settle it with me."

"I might take you up on that."

"You are right about one thing. She is a remarkable woman. Jamila takes good care of her grandfather and brother. And there is much more to her than you know. It's just too bad."

"What's too bad?"

"It's just too bad that you're—how do you say it?— an eejit."

Rennie's Mill

Tea is drunk to forget the din of the world.
—T'ien Yiheng

Elant seemed to be enjoying his long meetings with Hu. "Have you ever been to Vancouver, Mr. Hu? As you may know, it's become the most integrated Asian city in North America. A fantastically vibrant place."

"Yes, I've visited. Many of my friends moved there from Hong Kong prior to the transfer of sovereignty in '97. Unsure of the wind, many transferred their companies and assets abroad."

"I gather you've also been to Hong Kong."

"Many times. I was there just prior to the handover. A most uncertain time."

"Yes, I was working there during the transition, a guest of Sir Edward Heath. I used to stay in Rennie's Mill. Do you know it?"

Hu gave an odd laugh before reminding the senior director that Alfred Rennie was a Canadian who tried his luck in Hong Kong but failed. He later hanged himself.

Elant was used to being ribbed on this point and ignored Hu's off-color humor.

"You understand, Mr. Elant, that we are currently receiving thirty-nine percent of the auction price. Yet your Canadian friends offer only twenty-eight percent. We don't consider this fair treatment."

"I quite understand. But if one is to be truly fair, one must factor in the free cost of shipping, plus the fact that you're currently exporting and selling no tea at present. When one includes the cost

363

of the Canadian Navy keeping a vessel in the region to assist you if necessary, these figures make a great deal of sense."

"You agree we can increase our yield by opening more land to production?" Hu was looking for more positives.

"That seems a common-sense approach. I'm surprised you haven't already done so. A great many shelterbelts could be cleared."

"I'm surrounded by people from the last century."

"By using modern farming techniques, you could increase your yield tenfold."

Hu understood that meant chemical fertilizers, herbicides, and pesticides. Whenever he walked through the tea fields and saw the bug-eaten leaves, it gnawed at him. "Neem trees indeed!"

Elant took a sip of tea and waited for the old man to process the information before moving on. He decided it best to change his tack. "If you'd prefer to negotiate a set price for the tea, we can approach matters from that perspective."

"I'm open to at least hearing a figure. That's not to say we're leaning toward a fixed price." Hu was more than happy to leave the agricultural methods out of the discussion for the moment.

"I don't see why we can't tie our proposal to a deepwater harbor project." Elant had saved the best for last. "A rock jetty could easily be built. I see no reason your port facilities shouldn't be large and deep enough for a modern cargo ship to dock properly."

"I agree with that in principle." Hu was trying hard not to let his enthusiasm show. He had been fighting for port improvements for years.

THE FIVE PILLARS

Kissing is like drinking tea through a tea-
strainer; you're always thirsty afterwards.
—Chinese saying

The pavilion hugged the cliff's edge at the southern tip of the Thumb, where it melded into the rocks and tamarisk. Beba watched the sea stacks below being lashed by huge waves that seemed to move in slow motion. The white guano against the chiaroscuro basalt was repeatedly overtaken by foamy surf. Frigate birds rode effortlessly on the strong breeze.

Figas held her close from behind and watched the morning star weaken. The metallic gray water seemed to be lit from beneath.

According to island tradition, the five stone pillars that held the pavilion's domed roof represented the five senses. Beba turned and touched his cheek.

"See how close I shaved? Just for you."

"Oh? You started shaving?"

"Thanks for that. Yes, and my voice is starting to drop. I've even started to get these urges."

"Really?" She lifted an eyebrow. "What kind of urges?"

"I used to look at your skin. It looked so . . ." Figas lost the handle on what he was saying.

"And?" She didn't care for the pause.

"It's so soft. It's amazing." He felt the buttery smoothness of her neck and shoulder. How could he really feel her softness when his fingertips were rough by comparison?

A small tremor rippled through her body. "Do you ever wonder what would've happened if you hadn't come back?"

"I think about it all the time." He turned her around and pressed her into the stone column behind. He could feel her heart racing. Her gray eyes drank in the new light of the morning. He kissed her.

"I wonder which pillar we're leaning against?" She let her senses wander.

"Taste, I think." He kissed her again, testing his hypothesis: tear-filled eyes make sweet lips.

She pulled him closer.

He came up for air and together they settled on the ground at the foot of the tasting pillar.

It was hard to believe how much had happened in the past year. These last two weeks had been a blur. He had almost died of a fever. Captain Martin and the *Lady Slipper* had been lost at sea. Alison Stevens-Fowling had sailed with the *Starry Night*. Prescott and his troops had packed up and shipped out. Christopher Elant had signed a trade agreement with Hu.

Things would soon be back to normal. With one difference: Green Island would now be open to the world of commerce—and with that, all the many gifts of capitalism. Business entities with power and influence beyond that of a single individual would soon flourish. Something Herbie had said played over and over in his head: "How long before we're all working for somebody else?" Herbie had laughed, but his words seemed eerily prophetic. It was all too much, too fast.

The biggest festival of the year was in three days. It was the anniversary of his homecoming. The whole island would pay tribute to the Original. For some, this was the spirit of the island; for others, it was the first and oldest sentient being. Nearly everyone on the island would spend Saturday night on anything that could float. They had a great deal to be thankful for this year during the Zhu Yong Jiē, the Wait of Courage.

Figas went over it again and again in his mind. Who was responsible for the tragic events of the past year? He reasoned that Prescott and Stevens-Fowling were not pulling the strings. Whoever was responsible must have had help, someone on the inside. Emma Carroll had been rooting through the island's records. Isn't that what an undercover agent would do? Fioré had also acted suspiciously, but he had helped when the chips were down. Everyone Figas could think of seemed beyond reproach. He hated the thought, but it always came back to Hu. He was the most likely candidate. A pain rippled through his body. The vivid dream he'd experienced when delirious with fever had been trying to tell him something. He shuddered.

"What is it, Figas? What's wrong? I know that faraway look. You're chopping everything to bits and assigning letters and numbers."

"Beba, remember how Uncle always jokes around? 'We have met the enemy, and it is us.'" Figas felt like a beetle that had flipped on its back.

"Are you still looking for someone to blame? Oh, sorry, find the causation in your formula." She tried to be patient, but wished he could let things go. If he was going to obsess, let it be about her. "So much for our romantic moment."

"We're not having a romantic moment." He kicked his legs in the air in a futile attempt to right himself. Someone would later come across his inverted empty shell and understand his demise.

"My mistake." She went limp.

"That's not what I meant. It's not a moment. Moments pass. I love you, Beba."

She looked at him in shock.

"I'm sorry, I have to go."

She couldn't believe it. "You have to what?"

"I have to find Hava. There isn't enough time. I need Zeno. I'll see you later." He kissed her.

"Hold on a minute." She reached for his sleeve. "One small flaw in your plan."

"I could have this all wrong. If you haven't noticed, when I make an emotional decision, it's usually a disaster."

"Thanks for that."

"You know what I mean. I get things wrong, really wrong. I don't want you to be involved."

"Sorry if you haven't noticed, but I'm already involved!"

"I just don't want you getting into trouble . . ."

"I can handle it. Why don't you tell me what's going on?"

"If I'm right—and I really hope I'm not—things are more messed up than ever. And it's my fault." He started from the beginning and explained as best he could in plain language, going step by step through his prediction methodology. He left out the mathematical jargon and expressed it conceptually.

She listened closely until he was finished. "What proof do you have? You can't go accusing people without evidence to back it up."

He grabbed his face.

She was worried. "So tell me, what's the smoking gun?" She tried to coax something out of him.

"Isn't it obvious?" But he knew it wasn't. "Okay. I've got a feeling."

She held her hand over her mouth, fighting the urge to burst out laughing. "Are you kidding? You have to admit, that's funny," she said, delighted. "You've got a feeling. What kind of feeling?" Her obvious enjoyment didn't make it any easier.

"I have a gut feeling. All right?"

There was the man she loved, and for once, he wasn't hiding behind an army of clay numbers. "That's good enough for me."

"I know you're enjoying yourself, but this falls into the category of not helpful."

"I'm saying I'm in. I trust you." She kissed him.

He took a minute and looked in her eyes. "Good. Here's what I think we should do. Zeno is probably Upwise somewhere. We need to find a footie."

"Silly Figas!" She shook her head. "You think you're gonna to find a footie who's faster than me?" She put her hands on her hips.

"Of course not. You find Zeno. I'll meet you at Hava's." They kissed and ran in opposite directions.

A Change of Plan

Life is like a cup of tea, It's all in how you make it.
—Irish blessing

Figas came up behind Christopher Elant as he waited on the tarmac for his flight home. "I can't help but wonder, what do you get out all of this?"

"Hello, Thomas."

"What kind of deal did you manage to get?"

"I'm sorry. I'm not at liberty to discuss the negotiations."

"I'm just curious if it was worth it. How much will your share be?"

"I'm not sure I understand."

Figas narrowed his eyes as he stared at the older man. "You set me up. You needed me to come home. You counted on me to sound the alarm. 'The bastards are coming! Watch out!' And they did, didn't they? Prescott and his little army marching right on cue. It's interesting that just when we had them on the ropes, you showed up out of the blue. Your timing was good, very good. When I saw you get out of that chopper, I was so relieved. The guys in the white hats."

"We're the good guys, Thomas."

"You missed something."

"Excuse me?"

"I know all about your little scheme."

"Scheme? I'm not sure what you're implying, but you may wish to go over your facts." Elant patted the young man on the shoulder. "Change is stressful, but I promise it's not always negative. I can safely say we've reached an understanding that will mutually benefit all parties."

Figas shook his head. "It's you who've rushed things. Stevens-Fowling gave up far too easily. Was Hu being his stubborn self? You had to move things along. So with the flip of a switch, the troops packed their bags."

Elant had a puzzled look. "I wish I knew what to say, Thomas."

"I'm sure you do." Figas moved so Elant was looking into the sun. "You're treating our tea like a product kicked out of an assembly line. I don't think you get it. Our whole way of life goes into it. Everything."

"I haven't turned your tea into a product. You Green Islanders have been perfecting the Sighing Woman Tea brand for the last thousand years. Your wealth is based on packaging and marketing: the red wax seal, the tea chest, the Sigh. It's how you've survived and prospered."

Figas couldn't deny there was truth in what Elant said. Green Islanders were responsible, at least in part. Once again, Nagarjuna's observations of causes and conditions were precise: the seed of any action contains within it its own beginning and ending. The complete cycle. Maybe it was hubristic to try to capture the essence of the moment in a box of dried leaves. He stared past Elant.

"Blaming yourself for everything that happens is an unhealthy habit, Thomas."

He spun the wheel of guilt. "Maybe Elant's right," he thought. Ever since he was a child, the world in his head seldom matched the real world. He couldn't help it. He was taking the biggest gamble of his life, and based on what? A feeling. "Feelings come and go," he reminded himself.

"We all like to think we're important, Thomas. And each of us is in our own way. But can we, or should we, take responsibility for things out of our control?"

Figas looked at the man who'd convinced him to come home and went from pressing to second guessing. "I'm not only blaming myself," he thought, "I'm lashing out at the very people who've helped me. Is there anything worse than being ungrateful?"

Elant gave him an understanding look.

The pilot shouted down, "Is everything all right?"

Elant waved back, letting him know there was no cause for concern.

Figas also gave an awkward wave, and looked at the ground. "People here can be a real pain in the ass," Figas admitted. "They can be small, petty, and as vindictive as the next person. They don't always treat each other as they wish to be treated. They do, however, understand about sanctuary. When it comes to tea, they bring the best of themselves. I'm not sure I'm capable of that yet. But I'm working on it." The two looked at each other in silence for a moment. Then Figas squared his shoulders and took a step closer, looking straight into the older man's eyes. "You almost had me again with your weapons-grade bullshit! You know better, and yet you choose to consciously perpetrate evil."

"Evil. Really, Thomas? Do you think it's fair to blame me for an imperfect situation? A situation I didn't create." Elant was disappointed in his young friend.

"That's just the thing. In many ways, you are responsible for creating it. You set all this in motion. Yea, I'm gonna go with evil." If he was right, it didn't make him happy. "Ignorant people are easier to forgive than someone who knows better and chooses to do the immoral thing anyway. That makes you a demagogue."

"Pretty strong stuff. I'm hurt." Elant gave up trying to reason with the young man. "I came here to help, and this is how you repay me?"

"Did you ever wonder why tea leaves settle in the middle of your cup and not around the edges?"

"Can't say I have."

"The pressure gradient takes over the primary flow. High up, the liquid flows outward, but deep down the secondary flow travels inward, bringing the tea leaves to the center."

"That's wonderful, Thomas. Now if you'll excuse me, I have a meeting in twelve hours and a long flight ahead. Perhaps in time you'll come to understand. Everything usually works out for the best." He wanted to ask the young man where he thought the money came from to support the great art of the world. Lemon aid sales? Would we have the paintings of Vermeer and Rembrandt without the Dutch East Indian Company? He didn't have time to explain such complexities to children. In the real world, hard choices have to be made. Compromises. "Good-bye, Thomas. Best of luck."

Mr. Black opened the cabin door as the pilot began his preflight checklist.

Elant turned and waved to Figas before climbing aboard.

The two jet engines cycled on, spinning the props slowly. The two auxiliary fuel tanks were full, *check*. Electrical systems, *check*.

Zeno watched from the ridge.

Main cabin door secured, *check*. Number one turbine, *check*.

Mr. Black poured his employer a Napoleon brandy and adjusted the air temperature in the spacious cabin. He placed the white linen on the serving tray and prepared a small hors d'oeuvre.

Beba joined Figas. They watched the chopper blades beating the grass down flat. "Are we in trouble?" she asked over the loud whir.

"Plenty. And we're about to be in even more."

"He didn't give anything away?"

"Not a thing. He's smooth as glass. Maybe it's for the best. I like the guy." Figas tried to smile.

Beba squeezed his hand in support and watched the chopper lift off. So what if he'd made a mistake? She loved him for taking a chance solely on intuition. Prediction theory models were for getting the five-day weather forecast wrong. She was proud he hadn't even thought of asking Uncle before he took the leap. Maybe he wanted to take all the heat if it turned out he was wrong. One thing was sure: Figas's mathematically perfect universe was breaking down into a whimsical heap of molten chaos. She gave him a kiss.

He gave her a look in return. "I never know what you're going to do or why," he confessed.

"Excuse me, sir." The pilot's voice came through the intercom.

"Yes, Walters. What is it?"

"I have a red light."

"Meaning?"

"There's a small vibration in the tail rotor. It might be a bearing. But if I had to guess, I would say it's a bent rotor blade."

"How could that have happen?"

"No idea, sir. They're made of pure titanium. It looked in perfect condition when I did my preflight inspection."

Zeno watched the chopper. Hava had said, between all the geekspeak, that a small tweak would be sufficient. It was hard not to just snap one of the fucking blades off. Of course, that would have been too obvious. "I'll snap one of Hava's arms off!" He swallowed his next curse as the copter took off, hovered for minute, then headed back to the tarmac.

Walters set the copter back on the ground and slid the dual controls forward, winding the turbines down.

"How long will it take to correct?" The smoothness left Elant's voice.

"No idea, sir. We'll have to fly out a mechanic with the parts. I'll radio and have an estimate inside an hour. The repair itself should only take a few hours, but it will likely be the better part of a week before the mechanic and parts get here."

Elant set his brandy down and straightened his posture. His mind raced through the different scenarios. "Is it safe to fly to the far side of the island?"

"Sorry, sir. I wouldn't risk it." Walters wasn't going against the book on this one.

"Very well. Radio the *Starry Night*. Wijzigen van het plan. A change of plan. Have the captain turn around and wait out past the boundary zone. It won't do for her to be seen. Arranged for a rendezvous late tonight if possible.

Old Friends

I say let the world go to hell, but I should always have my tea.
—Fyodor Dostoyevsky

The *Starry Night* lay concealed eleven miles off the coast, a single green running light on her stern. Mr. Black arranged for some locals to paddle Elant and himself out to meet the yacht in the early hours before dawn. In his signature dark tailored suit and polished leather shoes, Elant stepped from the dry sand into the wooden canoe. Mr. Black secured his black leather briefcase under the woven seat in the bow. The two men were surprised at the speed of the primitive craft.

They were a mile beyond Fletch's Point when their two paddlers abruptly dove into the water.

A high-pitched laugh felt like slivers inside the two men's ears. They turned around to see the horrid black smile of an old woman, wrapped in a Portuguese fisherwoman's shawl, steering them out to sea.

Mr. Black found he was unable to safely step around his employer to get to the old woman in the back of the boat. He decided to lower himself into the water and drag her out, and paddle them to the waiting yacht himself. He pulled off his shoes and removed his suit jacket, folding it neatly. He slipped into the water and held onto the gunnels as he worked his way past Elant.

His employer decided not to turn to watch. He would leave his efficient assistant to do what needed to be done. Elant felt a violent pull and shuddered, closing his eyes. Now that it was done, they could continue on their way. He felt something large strike the wooden hull, and then another bump swiveled the boat abruptly. A high, rhythmic cackle from the back of the canoe carried over the water when they capsized.

The Wait of Courage

The nature of the tea itself is that of no-mind.
—Pojong Sunim

Zeno helped Freight drag an old log across Hong's pasture and onto the sand. Homemade rafts of every size and description were beginning to take shape up and down the long stretch of beach for Zhu Yong Jiē. Wood pieces deemed unworthy of a raft were stacked into vast bonfire piles to be lit at dusk.

Winston walked the beach handing out hanks of rope from a burlap sack. He had never seen such joyful enthusiasm go into an event. It was this sort of rapt intensity that Winston lived for. The first sentient being, the Original, was not celebrated by storytellers, but rather honored at this annual festival. After the year the islanders had just experienced, they woke up to the meaning of their history. A group of drummers pounded out a steady, flowing beat that had the raft makers dancing in the midday heat.

Zeno pointed to a pod of spinner dolphins playing just outside the farthest break. They were jumping high out of the water. "Look at them looking at us!" Zeno shouted to Uncle Sun, who was working on the raft next to him. He tongued the hole of his missing tooth and wondered if the ancestors of these dolphins had watched his forbears return to their ship to wait, hungry, thirsty and unsure.

A big high tide was already helping launch the assorted menageries, adorned with flags and flowers. The loosely affiliated jumbles rolled and rippled with the surface of the water as they were slowly towed to their moorings. The bay became a floating city.

Strings of paper lanterns were stacked near the floating pier, making it nearly impossible to walk. Beba had a tight hold on Figas's hand and wasn't planning to let him out of her sight for any reason until they were safely afloat in their borrowed canoe.

Ramona Rai strolled by holding onto old Sali's arm.

"Hello, you young lovers," the old man said and winked, proud of his lovely escort.

A ship's air horn blasted, and Ramona jumped. A loud cheer rose from the crowd on the beach. An old black cargo ship had just rounded Fletch's Point.

Uncle dropped the end of the rope he was tying and waded into the waves in his clothes. He couldn't fail to recognize the rhythm of the ship's horn. As the ship feathered her way slowly into the crowded bay, he tried to make out the men on deck. He breaststroked and squinted to help his old eyes focus.

China paddled up next to him and lifted Uncle into his outrigger. When they came alongside the ship, Hu was already climbing the ship's ladder.

Capt. Martin yelled down, "I was held up."

"You're four weeks late, Martin!" Hu was annoyed that he unable to get his complaint out first.

Uncle giggled in delight. "Thank you for the ride, China." He climbed out of the boat and onto the ship's ladder. "Have a wonderful time tonight."

"Welcome aboard the *Salamanca*, you roughneck dogleggers!" Martin greeted them in his usual gruff fashion.

"You gave us quite a scare, captain." Despite his soaking wet clothes, he embraced his lifelong friend. "I'm glad you're alive, but I'm a little sore you didn't radio ahead to tell us you were safe."

"There's been so much monkey business of late, I thought it best I make the trip and talk with you in person. I confess, when I knew we could make it in time for the Zhu Yong Jiē, I couldn't resist the surprise." Martin's manner became serious. "I was told in Guangzhou that you've signed a contract with a Canadian shipping company."

Martin and Uncle stared at Hu.

"She looks just like your old ship," Hu said to avoid the question.

"If you mean she has a bow and a stern, then I agree!" Martin was not pleased with the comparison. The *Lady* was the *Lady*, and that was that.

"I see." Hu looked around. "Perhaps this ship isn't built quite as well as your old ship, and she's not nearly as large." Hu knew the captain had to defend the honor of his one and only true love, but this old ship must have been the closest match he could find.

Martin appreciated the ever-antagonistic Hu tempering his remarks. He further cooled when he considered that the *Salamanca* was a full ten meters longer than the *Lady*. Even a landlubber like Hu could tell that much at first blush.

"I think we'll save the tour of the ship for another time," the captain stated.

"First things first." Hu took a fresh bag of tea from his pocket. The two old islanders followed the captain astern to his quarters under the bridge.

Wood brought in the porcupine tea setting after the three were comfortably settled.

The captain explained that before leaving Guangzhou, the *Lady* had taken on a new second engineer, a Mr. Donaldson, because Rebus was down with a stomach ailment. The new engineer should have known better when he changed the oil in the ship's engine without Rebus's supervision. Instead of pouring the used oil into the recycle drum, he added it to the diesel fuel. At the next port of call, Donaldson didn't return to the ship on time, even though he was owed wages. They sailed without him. Three weeks later, they ran straight into the teeth of a tropical storm. The used oil kicked up from the bottom of the fuel tank and fouled their injectors. When they lost engine power, Rebus was quick to discover why but was unable to clean the injectors in time. Without propulsion, they were unable to maneuver. Martin was forced to abandon ship just before she foundered.

"You were reported lost at sea with all hands." Uncle smelled a rat. "Are you going to tell us how you came to safety and where you met your new mistress?"

"I think Hu is going to tell us a story first." Martin was very curious about the new shipping contract.

The veins in Hu's forehead stood out more than usual. There was an awkward silence, mixed with the sounds of revelry on deck.

The first mate knocked and entered. He was carrying a black leather briefcase, which he handed to Martin. "Pardon the interruption, captain, but the forward watch saw an old woman tie this to the rigging before she disappeared under the water. I thought I should bring it to you straight away."

"Child of the deep." Martin's hair tingled on the back of his neck.

Hu recognized the briefcase. It was dented in the middle and had lacerations deep into the leather.

"Ask and ye shall receive." Uncle's eyes gleamed.

Martin plopped the wet briefcase on his desk and scooting it in front of Hu.

Hu took his time, fumbling around with his reading glasses. He wiped them methodically on his silk sleeve and put them on. He stared at the two golden latches.

Uncle marveled at Hu's ability to rankle. He never passed on an opportunity to go against the grain. It was a source of nourishment to the salty man's soul. "Sweet tea and vinegar! I've got a crazy idea," Uncle pleaded. "Why don't you open the thing?"

"Young people have no patience," Hu complained.

"Some of us are just considerably more efficient at being patient." Uncle knew Hu was taking his sweet time simply because it pained Martin and himself. Fate had delivered Elant's briefcase to the right man at the right time. Now they had to wait for Hu to find the courage.

The latches snapped. It was dry inside. The papers were all in perfect order. Hu thumbed through and found the shipping contract. He tossed it across the desk to Martin.

The old seaman scanned the document and turned to the last page, where he found Hu's signature. He stabbed the paper with his index finger.

Uncle leaned over and read through the legal document. He smiled when he got to the signature.

Martin was at a rolling boil.

"This is your handwriting, Hu," Uncle chuckled. "I see how someone not fluent in Cantonese might mistake this seal for your own."

Hu gave Uncle a hard look over the top of his glasses.

"What do you mean?" Martin studied the red seal. "What is this character? It looks to be 'speaking,' or 'talking' . . . and these others? A person's backside?"

Hu began a low rumble of a laugh, which gained speed like a steam locomotive. He pushed his glasses up his nose and pointed to the seal. "Rough English translation is bullocks."

It turned out Hu had not signed away the future at the expense of the past.

Hu couldn't believe people thought him a greedy man. He knew what greedy men looked like, and he wasn't one of them. He did, of course, live in the real world. And in the real world, Sighing Woman Tea was worth a great deal more than twenty-eight percent of auction price.

"So it was all a sham. It's over." Martin let out a sigh of relief.

"I wouldn't be too hasty, captain." Uncle rubbed his bald head. A serious look came over him. "Think of the everlasting joy and happiness you will bring to thousands when your crew throws Hu over the rail. They'll go wild! They'll make you king! No one ever need know what is in this case but the three of us." Uncle was deadpan.

"I like your thinking." Martin was intrigued. "What do you think, Hu?"

"Are you in the shipping business or the entertainment business?" Hu was almost in the mood to have fun.

"Let's be realistic. It's not worth the risk," Martin lamented. "If he drowns, they'll make him a martyr."

"Too late!" Uncle couldn't resist turning the knife.

"If you two sourpusses are done, I'd like to join the festivities." Hu closed the case and snapped the latches, indicating he was finished with serious nonsense and ready for some celebratory nonsense. He took off his reading glasses and replaced them with a pair of lightly shaded ones. They resembled the style of the Dalai Lama's glasses. He took a white scarf from his pocket to make his party costume complete. He flashed a mischievous smile, and even Martin couldn't help but giggle at how ridiculous it was to see Hu mugging the 14th Dalai Lama. It was made all the more silly because Hu's face really did resemble his Holiness.

Martin stood up tipped his cap at Hu's Houdinian knack of getting away with almost anything.

The Indications

Great love affairs start with champagne and end with tisane.
—Honoré de Balzac

The full moon rose from the watery horizon and cast a silver-velvet coating on everything but shadow. Diya and Hava paddled out to the far corner of the bay in hopes of privacy, only to find a dozen other boats anchored, with no sign of a crew.

"Let's park, Vaughn."

"It does look a bit like lovers' lane." He dropped anchor.

Diya took their seat cushions and made a comfortable spot to lean back and watch the fireworks. She pulled him toward her and kissed him on the cheek.

Doogan rubbed a butterfly patch along the new seam of the outrigger. He watched the moon's reflection dance across Jamila's polished brown eyes. Earlier that morning, he had decided to find her. He stopped on his way to pick her some flowers. An auntie rushed out of the house, slamming the screen door behind her. "What are you doing in my flowers?" she yelled.

Doogan turned around with the look of an old yellow lab caught in the neighbor's yard.

"Oh, it's you," she said, coming closer to get a better look. "So you're going to see her after all?"

Doogan wondered who this auntie was, and how she knew him or where he was going.

"Come with me to the back and get some red ones. Girls love red."

Doogan followed. When he got up the nerve to speak, he asked. "Why are you helping me, auntie? I'm a soldier, or I was a couple of days ago." He was still in his uniform, not having any other clothes.

"That was then." She brushed her hands. "I'll make some tea. Come in when you've finished pilfering my flower beds."

He picked until he had an outrageous bouquet. He had sent his letter of resignation with the last postal sack, nearly a month ago. The troop carrier had brought confirmation of his civilian status.

Auntie opened her back door and took the flowers in both hands and placed them in a wide-neck jar with some water. "Come in. Don't be frightened. I'm not as dangerous as I look." She poured tea and then disappeared. She returned with a finely made shirt. "I used to sew before my hands got too bad. I made this for my Guerin. You're about his build. Come. Try it on. You can't go to her dressed like that." She pointed to his drab green uniform.

Doogan acted shy, but caught on that this auntie meant business. The shirt fit perfectly. The buttons were handmade from shells. "Thank you, auntie, it is a fine shirt, but I can't take it."

"Nonsense! Don't argue with your elders! Didn't they teach you anything on your island?"

Doogan had used that line many times on Stu. "Can I ask you how you met your husband?" Doogan guessed she wasn't looking at him in the shirt.

"He worked in Kichiro's hardware store. When I was young I bought some cheap paint from the mistints table to spruce up my newly rented room. A week later I saw him in town. He called over to me, 'Well if it isn't Miss Tints.'"

"You liked his sense of humor?" Doogan felt he could see right into the old woman. She had no defenses.

"He told me he could mix the color I needed. I asked, 'What color would that be?' He said, 'The most beautiful color in the world—the color of your eyes.' I said, 'Brown?'"

"A real charmer?"

"My Guerin could charm the birds out of the trees. Now drink up your tea, nephew, and get a move on," she chided.

He climbed down the rope ladder and hurried through the valley toward the shore. Despite his efforts, he was unable to find the words in his head. He came up on the house quietly.

Jamila looked up.

His mouth was dry. Sweat was dripping off his forehead. He tried to form a sentence.

She smiled.

"Jamila, will you come with me to the fair?"

Now they sat in the outrigger, and Jamila rested her head comfortable against his shoulder. Firecrackers were thrown in the air and bottle rockets were aimed from raft to raft. Kids tried to pace themselves, and vowed to last until dawn, but the excitement soon overwhelmed them.

By midnight, only the whisper of storytellers carried over the still bay. The palm fronds on shore rustled in the light breeze and sounded like rain. No lights could be seen on land, only faint embers from the bonfires on the beach when a sudden gust of wind licked off a layer of ash.

Figas looked out over the bay. Hundreds of paper lanterns highlighted the faint shadows of the flotilla. His right hand delighted in Beba's thick hair. It smelled like bittersweet tea. The smoke from the bonfires hung close over the water and curled around the cove.

Beba coughed and was about to question his choice of anchorage when he kissed her.

"Smoke always follows beauty." He tasted her caramel lips again, and studied the tiny mole on her left shoulder.

"Good recovery, sailor. I was about to mutiny." She pulled the blanket over them. Her curves fit comfortably in the bottom of the canoe.

"I don't know, should I rock the boat?"

"You-better-figa!" She leaned and almost tipped them. They laughed and kissed.

Anchara and Fioré watched the embers on the beach come alive with a gust of wind.

"So when are you going to make your movie?" She held his hand, studying the lines in his palm.

"I don't know, gypsy. What do you foretell?"

"Your heart line and your life line are crossed. Maybe you're about to take a trip?"

"I think I need to stick around here and do a little more research."

"Research?"

"Well, there's an area of research right below here," he said as he burrowed his nose in the curve of her neck.

Anchara shrieked as a stray bottle rocket almost annihilated them. After they had settled in again, she told him the story of her ancestors arriving on the island and how they had fought and argued with each other over the best land. Master P'O returned from his encounter with the Original and told the ancestors they were trespassing and had not asked to be invited before coming ashore. They returned to their ship humbled and ashamed at the way they'd behaved toward one another.

"So this festival is a kind of ritual reenactment?"

"Not a reenactment. In many ways, we're in the same vulnerable position our ancestors were in. We are all wondering if when we wake up tomorrow the Original will once again be welcoming. When the daughter of the island dives into the depths, will she return with a sign?"

"You're serious."

"Yes."

"What will happen if she comes up empty-handed?"

"I don't know. No one knows. In years past, it was all a bit of fun. This year's different. This year is real."

Fioré realized how absurd it would be to try to catch the event on film. He was reminded of Coleridge's idea of beauty as an infinite variety of experiences united and woven together. Even if he managed the longest single take in cinematic history, it would never come close to capturing the spirit of Viridis. After so many years behind a lens, giving up his artistic vision was a bittersweet surrender. He let out a relieved laugh that echoed over the water.

Anchara pressed her hips against his, changing the direction of his thoughts. He resumed his in-depth research. Unbuttoning, Anchara followed her own line of inquiry.

The first signs of morning found Rabbi Morten with a serious dilemma. His bladder was ready to burst, but he didn't want to wake Betty, who was curled around him. Plus, what was he going to do? Hang it over the side? He peeked over the sideboard at all the little boats crowded into the cove. He obviously hadn't thought the evening through to when it would be light. He decided an early morning swim in his skivvies was the most elegant solution. He got up slowly, trying not to wake his lover. He was turning to lower himself quietly into the water when she pushed him with her foot. The splash was heard across the calm bay, and the impact sent out a sizable wake.

The cause of the deep thunk was quickly understood and relayed over the water. When the rabbi tried to lift his girth back into the skiff, he became stuck. Half of his belly was successfully in the boat, while his short legs kicked. Catcalls were followed by howls of every description. "Look at those grape smugglers!" Ramona called out, referring to Schmuken's Speedo-style briefs.

Betty finally took pity and pulled him into the boat.

At the sight of her, a loud cheer went up over the bay. Unable to contain himself, Zeno hurled himself into the water and splashed about in a fit of hilarity. Those nearest in the cove stood up in their boats and applauded with deep appreciation. It didn't help matters for the rabbi that Betty was also in tears, though she was trying hard not to find it so funny.

"Don't worry, rabbi," Diya shouted. "What happens in Vegas stays in Vegas." Vaughn kept his head down.

Morten tried to draw some comfort from Diya's promise as he struggled to pull his pants over his wet briefs. The problem, of course, was that he lived in Vegas. And so did everyone else.

"There's nothing for it, Morty."

He knew she was right. They both stood up in the rowboat and held hands. They took a long bow and hammed it up, to everyone's delight.

Soon all the little boats of the bay paddled to the *Salamanca*. Figas and Beba tied their canoe to the nearest raft and made their way across the flotilla, stepping from boat to boat, until they were able to climb the rigging.

Mathanias Wood smiled from across the deck when he saw Figas come aboard. Zeno was clowning around with Rebus. The flames of the burning man had been scrubbed clean of grease. The morning light brought them to life.

"Which of those two is the devil?" Figas asked Beba. "Or can there be two?"

"Apparently."

Beba watched her mother climb the small temporary platform in the middle of the deck. Martin joined her. Es-sahra held up her arms to quiet the huge crowd on deck. She informed them that earlier a vote had been taken. It was decided that it would be too high for young Tsani, the current daughter of the island, to dive from the bow of the *Salamanca*. She would dive from the bow of a sailing canoe instead.

When Tsani heard this, she flew into a temper. She tried to explain how much deeper she could go with a higher dive. She had beaten all the other girls in the trials. It wasn't fair.

"I'm sorry, Tsani, it's been decided," Es-sahra told the young girl.

"Fine. Then I won't do it at all." The girl with the three pearls crossed her arms and stormed away. Neither her parents nor Es-sahra could calm her down. She had just turned ten years old, the youngest ever chosen as daughter of the island. It was decided another daughter must be chosen immediately. All those who were interested were told to line up on the leeward side of the deck, where they would draw straws. Martin held up a handful of freshly cut tea stems. The oldest was about to pick when Tsani climbed onto the railing at the bow.

Her mother rushed toward her, screaming, "Tsani! Come down! Now!"

But she was too late. A collective gasp went out as the young girl dove. Her slight figure hung briefly then disappeared in the morning glare. Those watching nearby looked for a splash.

Time became liquid. The whole of Viridis hung over the rail of the ship. The coral calcium of the bay turned the water crystalline. The crowd held their collective breath as time and the elements stood side by side. The broken surface of the water reflected the faces of the islanders, like facets of a cut stone.

A puff of morning breeze dulled the surface of the water. The excitement in the air began to curdle.

Martin, who was staring down at the water looked up at Hu and shook his head.

Uncle searched for a piece of calm on the surface to peer through. "Who was she really?" he wondered. "Lijuan, Green Tara, or Quan Yin?" She was a great bodhisattva pouring out her inexhaustible stream of compassion. Would she once again return to them to help those in need? Would she reemerge from the void with a sign? Or had their relentless cycle of renewal come to a close? He looked into the dark water and prayed that this wasn't the sacrifice Kuten had indicated. He looked over the bay to the uninhabited isle. High tide had erased the last footprints in the sand. Viridis. She was a tiny green pebble in the middle of the vastness of the great ocean, wrapped closely to the bulge of the earth. He felt as if he had never before set foot on her primordial shores. She shone like a leaf an hour old. A tiny wet pebble that remained after everyone and everything he knew had vanished.

Beba held onto Figas, who was shaking uncontrollably. He was unable to look over the rail any longer. His head pounded. There wasn't any part of him that could allow for a drowned girl. He sensed Beba's calm and crumpled to the deck. The pain between his eyes was unbearable. He could feel the grief passing through the crowd as one by one they realized that too much time had passed.

Doogan hugged Jamila tightly and held her face against his shoulder, away from the water. His eyes wandered across the bay to the shore. "With her coast so green," he mumbled to himself, holding back a sob.

Figas got up and scrambled around the deck. He needed something, anything heavy. He pulled at a length of chain, but it was secured to the windlass. Fletcher Kim heard him wrestling with the chain and ran over to help. "Figas, there!" She pointed to a red fire extinguisher, just like the one she had used to model her clay Buddha. It was hanging inside the open hatch.

Figas ran over and pulled it from its hook.

Beba turned just in time to see him jump over the rail, cradling the fire extinguisher. "Cedar!" The name spring involuntarily from her lips.

Figas's feet hit the water first. Beba was watching from above as he spun slowly around before disappearing into the dark water. Shadowy sinews wrapped his ankles in a cold grip and pulled him deep. The pressure in his ears was unbearable. His eyes were numb sockets. He was out of breath, but it didn't seem to matter at this point. He just needed to reach her. His eyes closed. And there suddenly she was. Cedar. She seemed to melt into him as he held her.

When the young boys realized what had just happened, they jumped in at once, splashing about like a handful of tossed stones.

Tsani's best friend, Na'ila, balanced on the rail and made a perfect dive. She plunged past the boys. She kicked her feet and reached with her arms. The salt burned and blurred her eyes. She blew bubbles out of her nose until her chest was empty.

Many fathoms down through the murkiness, she saw them. Figas was holding Tsani. A single beam of sunlight, shooting through the water, caught something in her hand.

CPSIA information can be obtained at www.ICGtesting.com
Printed in the USA
BVOW08*1826120116

432665BV00002B/5/P

9 781499 063622